GRANT OF KINGDOM

Grant of Kingdom

Harvey Fergusson

Introduction by William T. Pilkington

A Zia Book

UNIVERSITY OF NEW MEXICO PRESS
Albuquerque

Copyright 1950 by Harvey Fergusson. All rights reserved. University of New Mexico Press paperback edition reprinted 1975 by arrangement with William Morrow and Company. Introduction © 1975 by the University of New Mexico Press. Manufactured in the United States of America. Library of Congress Catalog Card Number 75-17378. International Standard Book Number 0-8263-0396-X.

INTRODUCTION

In the course of a writing career that spanned nearly six decades, Harvey Fergusson published ten novels, eight of which are set in New Mexico. Four of the eight—*The Blood of the Conquerors* (1921), *Hot Saturday* (1926), *Footloose McGarnigal* (1930), and *The Life of Riley* (1937) —are fictional studies of life in the twentieth-century Southwest. Overall they are the least successful of Fergusson's regional books. Far more entertaining and aesthetically satisfying are his novels laid in New Mexico's nineteenth-century past: *Wolf Song* (1927), *In Those Days* (1929), *Grant of Kingdom* (1950), and *The Conquest of Don Pedro* (1954). I do not claim that, from a purely technical standpoint, *Grant of Kingdom* is the writer's best work, but I believe that, if I had to recommend one of his books to an interested reader, *Grant of Kingdom* would be my choice. Set against the grandeur of the northern New Mexico landscape, the narrative sweeps us through half a century of regional history—sometimes violent, sometimes externally placid, but never static. A sense of movement pervades the novel and is one of the keys to its effectiveness. In narrative pace the story moves swiftly and compellingly, and as an artistic whole it has the power to move the reader both emotionally and intellectually.

Harvey Fergusson made his official residence in New Mexico for only twenty-two of his eighty-one years. But northern New Mexico is the locale that the writer knew most intimately; it is an area that he explored on horseback as a youth, and it is a country that inhabited his adult imagination with vivid urgency. Born in Albuquerque in 1890, Fergusson was descended from men prominent in his native state's commerce and politics. His maternal grandfather, Franz Huning, was a pioneering merchant in nineteenth-century Albuquerque, and his father, Harvey Butler Fergusson, was territorial representative and later the first congressman from New Mexico when the territory became a state. In 1912, at age twenty-two, Fergusson followed his father to Washington, D.C., where he lived and worked for over a decade. He put in a nine-year stint (1923–32) in New York City doing free-lance writing, and another decade (1932–42) in Hollywood, where he was employed by various movie studios as a screenwriter. The last thirty years of his life the author resided in Berkeley, California, occupying a small apartment in the lovely hills behind the University of California campus. He died there in 1971 of a massive stroke.

During the years he lived elsewhere, Fergusson often became homesick for New Mexico. He returned to his native state many times over the decades, sometimes for months at a stretch, usually in summer. He roamed the mountains, camped, hunted and fished, read—in books and on the face of the land— the well-preserved history of that arid country. It was on one of these forays, as Fergusson tells us in his prefatory note to the novel, that he first heard the story that eventually prompted him to write *Grant of Kingdom*. Though he does not give any specific details in his foreword, the writer obviously refers to the history of the Maxwell Land Grant, an enormous tract of nearly two million acres centering on the town of Cimarron. Ceded to Carlos Beaubien by the king of Spain, the land was held during the middle decades of the nineteenth century by Beaubien's son-in-law, Lucien Maxwell. (For those interested in learning more of the grant's history, incidentally, or possibly in making identifications between real-life personages and the cast of fictional characters, a good source is Lawrence R. Murphy's *Philmont: A History of New Mexico's Cimarron Country*, published in 1972 by the University of New Mexico Press.)

Grant of Kingdom is a book with many technical virtues—

realistic characters; complicated plot and point of view, both of which are smoothly and expertly handled; and, most impressive of all, a style as clear and sparkling as a mountain trout stream. Writing in the realistic mode popular in the early years of this century, Fergusson employed few figures of speech or other rhetorical devices in the novel, preferring instead an economical, unadorned prose style. A flowing succession of vivid images makes up the narrative. In his autobiography, *Home in the West* (1944), Fergusson says that for many years he struggled to simplify, to discard all flourishes and excess verbiage, to hone his style until it was razor-sharp in its precision and clarity. Style is one of the most attractive features in all Fergusson's books, but nowhere is that style more admirably displayed than in *Grant of Kingdom*.

But the most interesting and significant aspect of *Grant of Kingdom* is thematic rather than technical. The novel is, I think, Fergusson's fullest, most provocative treatment of New Mexico's history. *History* is the book's subject—not just historical facts (facts, to an imaginative writer like Fergusson, are merely the raw materials of art), but the meanings that are inherent in the facts. Fergusson makes clear in the foreword that his novel not only develops a specific fragment of regional history but also projects a much wider vision of man's collective experience. Indeed it seems to me that, like the South's William Faulkner, Fergusson in *Grant of Kingdom* effectively uses the history of a plot of land—"a postage stamp of soil," in Faulkner's phrase—as the microcosm of a region's past; as Faulkner is said to have fashioned a "legend of the South" from the history of Yoknapatawpha County, so from the story of the Maxwell Land Grant Fergusson creates his legend of the American West.

Fergusson apparently saw the history of the West as a great drama of endless change and the fortunes of westerners as the outgrowth of their ability, or inability, to adjust to change. When a person resists the current of change, Fergusson believed, the person and the institutions of which he is a part quickly wither and die. This principle explains the fate of many people and groups in *Grant of Kingdom*. The Spanish pioneers in New Mexico, for example, had been men who "built things and established order" (pp. 12-13). But by the 1850s, the decade in which the novel begins, the Taos *ricos* have grown fat and lazy; they despise the invading Anglos but can do nothing to repel them, an inflexible family and social structure having entrapped the *ricos* and assured their doom. Jean Ballard, on the other hand, perceives that his life as a mountain man has nearly run its course. The mountain men have outlived their usefulness and are now anachronisms; it is time for him to settle and build. He is duly rewarded for his farsighted decision to make a new life for himself on the Coronel Grant—until age and physical disability finally rob him of the capacity to adapt to change. This cyclical pattern—adjustment to change followed by failure to adjust—is repeated often in the novel. "Time and Change," Fergusson once said concerning the theme of one of his fictions, "are the mighty characters of this story." That comment might serve as the epigraph to the whole body of the writer's historical fiction —and most especially to *Grant of Kingdom*.

Fergusson's theory of history may be found fully outlined in two works of nonfiction: *Modern Man: His Belief and Behavior* (1936) and *People and Power: A Study of Political Behavior in America* (1947). Even a brief synopsis of that rather complex theory is impossible here. I suggest, however, that any reader seriously interested in Fergusson's fiction study those two volumes carefully. In them the writer defines such crucial terms as "medieval man," "modern man," and "the great leader." These are character types who appear, in one guise or another, time and again in *Grant of Kingdom*.

Jean Ballard, for instance, is a "great leader" in his day and his world. Ballard's hunger for power is tempered by belief in the ideal of order and community, a belief imbibed as a child along with his mother's milk. When he marries into the Coronel family, he is obliged to adopt a medieval life style. He is transformed into el patrón, "the absolute ruler of a minor kingdom, strictly feudal in its social structure" (p. 97). He establishes order by means of personal loyalty, rather than by smoothly functioning organization. Almost by force of personality alone, he brings peace, prosperity, and civilization to his grant, and his life's labors result in progress for an entire region. But by the time he dies, Ballard is no longer a leader; he is simply a human relic. He possesses no business sense, distrusting banks and risky investments. Inevitably he runs afoul of the go-for-broke economic system that settled over the West in the latter decades of the nineteenth century. For Ballard late in life, "work and physical danger are simple things to deal with. What makes life hard is the bewilderment of change and complication, the rush of people and money, the impact of unexpected things. . . ." (p. 153).

With the intrusion of railroads and money into what had been, even in Ballard's heyday, an unspoiled wilderness, an irrevocable change is worked: these instruments of modern society "destroyed one kind of man and created another" (p. 144). The man they create is the wheeler-dealer speculator and financier, Major Blore. Blore, for better or worse, is a "modern man" in every sense of the term. He understands the importance of proper organization, and he knows how to use money and technology. His lust for money and power springs from his childhood status as a poor white in the class-conscious South, and he discovers in the newly opened West a formative society in which he may freely indulge his ambitions. He delights in toppling so exalted an aristocrat as Jean Ballard; in this regard he is kin to Faulkner's rapacious Snopes clan, who gleefully and inexorably undermine the old ruling class of Yoknapatawpha County. But while Blore is ruthless in the acquisition of power, he is also, as James Lane Morgan affirms, "a man of great ability" (p. 301). Blore attempts (from selfish motives, to be sure) to usher the grant and its human inhabitants into the world of modern technology and finance, and thus to save them from what, in the twentieth century, is considered ruin and decay.

If Ballard represents "medieval man" and Blore "modern man," the character who bridges the gap is Daniel Laird. At first Laird sympathizes wholly with Ballard, wishing only to find his proper place in the feudal order and to serve his master as a faithful retainer. Fergusson calls Laird an "idealist," since he approaches life with many preconceptions; predictably, Laird's mistaken assumptions concerning man's behavior and capacities are finally demolished, smashed to bits by recalcitrant human nature. When he flees to the mountains, he gradually comes to realize that, by retreating into the beauty and tranquillity of nature, "he had tried to go back to his own childhood—to the remembered peace of long ago" (p. 275). He understands now that the individual must compromise and accept life as it is offered to him; he must change to meet changing conditions. His role in modern life is clarified by this revelation. He marries and enters the arena of power politics (but without wholly divesting himself of his former idealism), and he is amply rewarded in both economic and human terms.

Fergusson's spokesman in the novel seems to be James Lane Morgan. Morgan's connection with the grant is rather peripheral, but his comments set the story's people and events in historical perspective. His nostalgic epilogue, in particular, is a fitting recessional, a reminder (perhaps, for our age of ecological awareness, a warning) that the land, like man, has its life cycle: some of the human characters in the tale adjust to change and prosper, but after a half-century as the scene of furious conflict and exploitation, the land, at story's end, seems to have taken on the aspect of a tired old man, has aged and wishes only to be left alone. The tone of Morgan's memoir is mellow and warm, conveying sympathetic understanding for those who were caught up in the "great gust of passion and energy" that "struck this place," then blew itself out. Looking back across the years, Morgan can finally see some of the "meanings that are always obscured by the noise and dust of the present" (pp. 310–11).

Grant of Kingdom, I submit, deserves a high ranking in any qualitative listing of western American fiction. Of novels set in the nineteenth-century West, it is certainly one of the most suggestive and illuminating. It is chronologically inclusive, yet compact. It convincingly displays in microcosm the stages of social development, the cultural and technological forces, the procession of character types that have shaped the history of the West. Although readers today may see traces of racial or ethnic stereotyping in an occasional phrase or characterization, it must be remembered that such instances represent the feelings only of characters in the novel; in reprinting Grant of Kingdom the present publisher intends no endorsement of any such cultural prejudice, nor should prejudice be attributed to Harvey Fergusson, all of whose writings are marked by a deeply humanistic spirit.

In reviewing the book when it first appeared in 1950, the late J. Frank Dobie said that Grant of Kingdom, though perhaps defective in minor ways, would endure as a work of art because it somehow evoked the unique tempos of both "earth and metal." Dobie's focus on narrative rhythm is very much to the point. The story—and the style in which it is told—advances not only with the leisurely pace of a great pastoral kingdom, but also with the clangorous urgency of invading money and machinery. With grace and wisdom, Grant of Kingdom suggests both the tragic disruption and the hopeful promise of time and change—and that, after all, is the dramatic rhythm of all human history, not just western history.

William T. Pilkington
Tarleton State University
Stephenville, Texas

FOREWORD

More than twenty years ago I visited a beautiful valley at the foot of the Rocky Mountains and found there the crumbling ruin of a great house. Its walls were then still standing a few feet high, with great roof beams rotting in the rubble. I could count the rooms and there were thirty-eight of them, including a dining hall that might have seated a hundred guests.

When I learned that a man had ridden into a wilderness where no human habitation had ever stood before, had built that great house, founded a society and ruled it as long as he lived, my imagination was stirred. I began talking to old-timers and reading old books, slowly reconstructing an episode which began about 1850, shortly after the American occupation of New Mexico, and ended in the late seventies, just before the completion of the Santa Fe railroad brought the epoch of primary pioneering to an end.

The valley had been the heart of one of the old Spanish Royal Land Grants, and it had been truly a grant of kingdom, not merely to one man but to four, each of whom had achieved his moment of power in that dominion and by reason of that royal grant, as though the prerogative of empire had reached across space and time to quicken his life and test his qualities.

During the many years it has occupied my imagination, that

episode has been largely transformed, and so have all of the men and women who played their parts in it. This book is a fiction and neither its characters nor its incidents are to be identified with real ones. In fact each of its four principal figures is based upon a study of various men in the effort to make them true products of a period and a region and at the same time, as I see them, figures of a wider significance. For I am indebted to the actual episode for my theme. Here, it seemed to me, was a struggle for power in a small but complete society, isolated by distance and wilderness, which had much in common with the greater power struggles that periodically shake the world. Here were the benevolent autocrat creating order, the power-hungry egoist destroying it, the warrior tragically bound to his weapon, the idealist always in conflict with an irrational world, struggling to save his own integrity.

The chief purpose of the book is to portray these four men, each in his turn and in his moment of crisis—to trace him back to his origins and see him in the making, to show the form and meaning of his destiny. Two women stand beside the men as major characters because they shared in the same indomitable quality, the same spectacle of life sustained by courage. These six and all the others, men and women, who played a part in their destinies, have lived for me. If they live also for the reader I have accomplished all I hoped.

CONTENTS

INTRODUCTION	v
FOREWORD	xiii
PART ONE: THE CONQUEROR	
JEAN BALLARD	3
THE HOUSE OF CORONEL	31
VIRGIN EARTH	57
PART TWO: THE AUTOCRAT	
THE RECOLLECTIONS OF JAMES LANE MORGAN	91
CONSUELO	150
REQUIEM	157
PART THREE: THE USURPERS	
MAJOR ARNOLD NEWTON BLORE	161
BETTY WEISS	182
CLAY TIGHE	195
PART FOUR: THE PROPHET	
IN HIS OWN COUNTRY	239
IN THE WILDERNESS	263
IN EXILE	282
EPITHALAMIUM	294
EPILOGUE	
BY JAMES LANE MORGAN	299

PART ONE

The Conqueror

JEAN BALLARD

THE hot spring lay in a little glade at the head of a shallow canyon where the scattering piñon of the lower slopes gave way to the tall timber. In this month of May the glade was green with new grass and sprinkled with bright small flowers, white and red. East of it the forest was dark and tall but fringed with slim white aspens bearing pale new leaves. The Truchas peaks, still covered with snow, rose sharp and white above the trees. To the west the country tumbled steeply to purple depths where the Rio Grande crawled through lava gorges, then rose again to a pale blue horizon of distant ranges.

The spring had been dug out and walled with rock, no one knew when or by whom, so that it was wide enough to hold several men and chin-deep when they sat. It had been a place of resort for generations, perhaps for centuries, and for many kinds of men. Pueblos, Apaches, Utes and Arapahoe came this way, crossing the mountains, and always stopped to bathe. Mexicans came from Taos and Talpa and sometimes much farther south. Mountain men always camped there when they could and soaked their hard-used hides in hot water. To Indians the spring was sacred and the faint mist that wavered over its face was the breath of a living spirit. To all men the pale green water, with its tickling bottom of bubbling sand, was a healing caress in a rocky and dangerous world. In an informal way, the spring was a place of sanctuary. Men stopped here to relax and met to trade rather than to fight. So far as the record ran, no one had lost his hair here and sea shells had traveled through many hands from the Gulf to be swapped here for turquoise and buffalo robes. Every April a great grizzly bear came down from the peaks to scratch his mark as high as he could reach on a near-by tree and soak himself in the spring. More than one man had seen him heave his bulk out of the water, shake himself like a great wet dog and amble off into the timber, but no one had ever shot at him. In those days of muzzle loaders a grizzly was more dangerous than a man.

Jean Ballard and Ed Hicks had come to the spring to bathe and loaf for a week. They had made their camp in the edge of the timber under a great fir that would shed water like a tent. Each had spread for his bed a heavy prime buffalo robe and a Navajo blanket. They had built a rock fireplace for their cooking, driven sharp pegs into the trunk of the tree to hold their gear, and they had all the home they needed. Ballard had climbed up to the edge of the snow and killed a two-year-old mountain ram, the best meat in the mountains. They had brought bread and coffee and brown sugar from Taos, but to them meat was primary and they ate it three times a day, buttered with its own fat.

Now when the sun was high and warm they stripped to bathe. Ballard was a stocky, powerful man, round in chest and limb, with a ruddy face and black curly hair, as thick on his chest as on his head. He had dark blue eyes and was a handsome man in a massive fashion, but wholly unconscious of his appearance except that he was vain of the hair on his chest. When he was in town around women he liked to wear a scarlet shirt open at the throat to show his plumage.

Ed Hicks, ten years older, was by contrast a lean and stringy figure with a face as deeply riven as the mountains that had claimed his whole life. He was one of those restless, driven men, common on the frontier, who stayed in towns only as long as he was drunk, would leave his bones beside a trail, and knew it. This was not true of Ballard. At thirty-three he had been on the move for thirteen years, because he lived in a moving world, but he had always felt sure he had a destination, that his time would come to settle and build.

They eased themselves into the water a little at a time. They were not used to hot water and this was about as hot as the human skin could stand. When finally he was in it to his neck, Ballard settled back with a sigh of beatific relief, leaning his head against a rock and closing his eyes. For ten minutes he was conscious of nothing but the soothing warmth of the spring and the wind-whispering hush of the wilderness. Then he came suddenly upright and his eyes met those of his companion. Both of them had heard the same thing—the clink of shod hoofs striking rock far down the trail in the canyon. Both of them knew what it meant. Since the horses were shod it couldn't be Indians and it was not likely to be mountain men at this time of the year. It must be Mexicans from Taos. The sound grew louder.

"Five or six horses," Hicks said.

Ballard nodded and rose dripping from his bath.

"Come on, get out of there," he said.

"To hell with them greasers," Hicks protested.

"Get out, I tell you," Ballard repeated as he reached for his shirt. "There'll be women in that outfit, a whole family. They come up here the first warm days to cook the misery out of their bones."

"To hell with them," Hicks repeated. "It's getting so the whole country is full of people and a man can't have no peace." Nevertheless he climbed out of the spring and started dressing. He always did what Ballard said.

They were dressed but still squeezing the water out of their hair when the Mexican outfit came in sight, emerging from the steep canyon, and stopped politely a hundred yards away, all strung out in single file on the narrow trail. In the lead was an old man, lean and erect in his saddle, with white whiskers decorating a dark, weathered face. A younger man followed, then two women riding on great pillowy sidesaddles, two younger girls of twelve or thirteen, a heavily laden pack horse and at the rear another man, obviously a peon. These people never moved far without a servant. All of them rode good horses, even the peon, and the old man in front sat a splendid sorrel on a silver-mounted saddle.

Ballard walked slowly toward them, raising his right-hand palm forward in a slight and casual gesture, which it was customary always to make when approaching strangers in the mountains—a gesture which meant he bore no weapon and came as a friend. The two men dismounted to meet him. He knew the old man by sight as Don Tranquilino Coronel, one of the three or four richest Mexicans in Taos, who owned about fifty thousand little scrubby sheep, a great house and wide irrigated lands in the valley. The younger man was doubtless one of his sons. The Don stood with calm dignity, waiting to be approached, as befitted one born to power and command.

Ballard, long trained to quick and accurate notice, surveyed the whole group as he came near. His eyes came to rest on the younger woman, directly behind the two men and clearly revealed when they dismounted. She would have captured the eyes of almost any man. She was a large girl and a pretty one, with heavy dark hair about her shoulders. On horseback her figure was in part a mystery, but Ballard was sharply aware of the full round pressure of her breasts against her white linen bodice and the beauty of her half-bare arms and her hands, one of which now fluttered self-consciously about her hair. He was aware especially of her lovely coloring.

Many Mexican girls had sallow skins or swarthy ones, but hers was like the petal of a flower, all pink and white with a dusky underflush. Her eyes were a light, conspicuous hazel under long black lashes. As he drew near she smiled at him, slowly and deliberately, as Mexican women always smile at strangers, over the shoulders of her protecting menfolk.

"We intrude," the Don said quietly, as he gave the brief limp handshake of his kind. "We will wait. . . . There is much time."

Ballard knew his Spanish well. He was a polite man and Spanish is a polite language.

"A thousand times no," he protested. "It would be a great sorrow if we delayed you. We have a camp in the pines, we stay for a week. The spring is yours."

He bowed his head and made a sweeping gesture with his right hand, consigning the whole country irrevocably to the newcomers. The Don thanked him with dignity. Ballard smiled, bowed, withdrew, feeling triumphantly that he had mastered a delicate situation.

Back in camp he pulled down the meat from where it hung in the shade, unwrapped it and began slicing the back-strap, choicest part of the kill. He threaded round bits of meat on an iron ramrod, with bits of fat between. Skewered over the coals, this was the best eating he knew. Hicks regarded him with a sardonic and suspicious eye.

"You're cuttin' enough meat for a crowd," he observed.

"Maybe we'll have company," Ballard said.

Hicks snorted.

"Them rich greasers won't eat with you," he said. "They hate your guts and you ought to know it."

Ballard smiled and went on cutting meat. He never argued or quarreled. He knew Hicks was probably right. Mexicans were always polite but the rich Mexicans had hated the gringos ever since the wagons began crossing the plains.

They hated them more than ever since Kearney had taken over in Santa Fe a few years before. Moreover, Taos had always been the headquarters of that hatred. It was in Taos that rebellion had broken out the year after the conquest. The Taos rebellion had been a bloody fiasco with Indians and a few peons running amock and killing Americans until the army under Price drove them into Taos Pueblo and slaughtered them. Most of the rich Mexicans had taken no open part in that business, but everyone believed the all-powerful Padre Martinez of Taos had organized it and then disowned it when it failed. And everyone knew that what the Padre did had the backing of all the old families. He was their political boss as well as their spiritual adviser.

Down in Santa Fe, some of the ricos had begun to smile upon the Americans, and even in Taos, Kit Carson had married one of the Jaramillo girls, but most of the few rich Mexicans in Taos Valley expressed their quiet hatred by ignoring the existence of their conquerors, and none more completely than the Coronels. Probably no American had ever passed the heavy front door of their great adobe house, with its barred windows and hidden courtyards. They had all been polite, but only the girl had smiled at him. Mexican girls often smiled at Americans, and that was one more reason the men hated them.

After he had finished his work, Ballard went to the spring and washed his hands. Then he dug into his duffle for a bright red shirt he had bought in Santa Fe, put it on and combed his hair carefully with the aid of a bit of mirror—both the hair on his head and that on his chest. Like most of the mountain men he was smooth-shaven, and he was glad he had shaved that morning.

Hicks, sitting in the shade with a pipe in his mouth, rumbled a growing disgust.

"Puttin' on your wenchin' clothes, are you?" he queried.

"That shirt's enough to scare a horse but it won't do you no good with that gal. You got no more chance to lay a hand on her than you have to pat a deer on the rump."

Ballard grinned and went on with his toilet, wholly untroubled. He knew the girl was probably beyond his reach, but he had a hunch and a plan, and he always followed his hunches. When he was satisfied with his appearance, he sat down in the shade and watched the Mexicans, as he might have watched distant game he was planning to stalk. He knew Mexicans well and he knew what they would do because they always did everything the same way. He had seen Mexican women bathe outdoors before, both at hot springs and in rivers. Women of the upper class, such as these, would never bathe in a river, and only once or twice a year would they visit a hot spring, strictly for the purposes of health. The procedure was always the same. They came accompanied by their menfolk, who were always armed. The men sat down at a certain distance, about a hundred yards from the spring, as the Don and his son did now. The women brought great white robes, such as the Taos Indians wore in summer. Each of them tented herself under one of these, adroitly shed her few clothes and emerged in a long white cotton shift reaching to her ankles, so that she would be more completely dressed in the water than out.

Ballard knew all the etiquette of this occasion and he knew his hope of success lay in observing it exactly. He waited until the women were all in the water, showing only as a row of dark heads in a cloud of steam, bobbing to a medley of squeals and giggles. This was a rare and exciting occasion to them for they seldom got beyond the walls of their own house. When he saw they had made a bowl of amole-root suds and set it on the rim of the spring, he knew they were all going to wash their hair. That would keep them busy quite a while.

Now it was quite appropriate, he knew, since amenities had

been exchanged, to join the menfolk for a little platicando, which is the Mexican word for polite chat about everything that is not important or personal. Not only would this now be permissible, but it was the only possible approach. To pass or go near the spring from any other direction would be a breach of etiquette, and to go even one step closer to it than the men sat would be a cause of war.

He strolled casually toward the Coronels, followed by the half-reluctant Hicks, and was politely received, as he had known he would be. Don Tranquilino produced a tiny horn, just like a powder horn but much smaller, which was filled with native tobacco and a roll of cigarette papers made from corn husks. Each of the four rolled a cigarette, the Mexicans with great skill and the Americans awkwardly, because they were pipe smokers. The Don then clapped his hands. The peon had made a small fire near by and he now came running with a live coal skillfully caught between two splinters of fat pine. He waved it into flame, lit each of the cigarettes, bowed and withdrew.

Talk was slow at first, but developed a growing momentum. Hicks had nothing to say until the Don mentioned the trouble he had encountered in getting sheep herds across the Rio Grande north of Taos. Hicks knew all about that country. He presently smoothed a piece of bare ground with the palm of his hand and began drawing a map with a little stick, as country-wise men always did in those days. In just a little while all four of them had sticks and were making contributions to the problem of getting across the Rio Grande gorge. They were no longer conscious of difference and antagonism, they had found their common ground.

All of them were completely absorbed in their talk and their map except Ballard. He made a few marks, too, but his mind was not on the subject and he was soon watching the women again. The girl was already out of the water, statuesque and erect in her white robe, shaking and fluffing her heavy black hair in the sun. She was looking straight at him. Although she was too far away for him to read her face, he felt sure she was just as much aware of him as he was of her. He wished he had never taken his eyes off her. There must have been a revealing moment when she climbed out of the spring with her wet shift clinging to her body. . . . But presently there was another moment, an almost incredible moment. With a single swift gesture, like a great bird flapping its wings, she flung the robe wide for an instant, then gathered it tightly about her again, at the same time throwing her head back, as though in laughter. For just a fraction of a second he saw her naked—the perfect bowls of her breasts, the dark triangle between her thighs. . . . Maybe a gust of wind had caught the robe, maybe it had slipped in her wet hand. It could have been a wholly accidental gesture. But he refused to believe so. She had known he was watching her and no one else was. Improbable as it seemed, he felt sure she had flung him a challenge and a signal, offered herself in the only way she could. Whether she had planned it or not she had certainly jolted him. He had felt the impact of that glimpse as keenly as though she had reached out and touched him. He couldn't get his eyes or his mind off her. In months of hard work away from women he had almost forgotten them, as so often before. Now he found himself watching one with an eager helpless fascination he half resented.

A little later all of the women and girls were dressed and sitting on a great red blanket in the sun, drying their hair, over on the other side of the spring where the peon had unpacked their baggage. The Don and his son rose, turned to the others. This was the moment Ballard had been waiting for.

"We have much meat," he said, as the Don extended his

hand. "A two-year-old cimarron, very fat. It would be a great honor if you would eat with us."

As he spoke he was watching the Don's eyes. Ballard had faced a great many men when something was at stake—in trades, in fights, in poker games—and he had learned to watch a man's eyes and his mouth and to go by what he saw there. The Don's mouth was hidden behind his magnificent whiskers, but before this unexpected challenge his eyes wavered and fell. He was too polite to say no and he didn't want to say yes. He fumbled for words.

"It would be a great pleasure," he lied. "But it grows late. . . ." He looked over his shoulder at the sun. He jerked a thumb at the women. "The Señora . . . I will ask what she wishes. . . ." He turned to go.

Ballard stood watching him, feeling sure that now his fate depended on the women and probably on the Doña. It was customary in such a matter for a man to consult his wife, as a matter of form, but the male head of a Mexican household was supposed to be second only to God. His word was final. The decision was supposed to be the Don's. But Ballard shrewdly doubted that any man ruled his women as absolutely as he was supposed to do, and he doubted especially that Don Tranquilino truly dominated anything. That wavering look he had seen in the eyes of many Mexican men in recent years. They were being overwhelmed by a rush of energy from the East, which they could neither stop nor deal with, and they were losing confidence.

Ballard did not despise Mexicans as all Texans and most mountain men professed to do. These people had come into the country when it was wilder than now. They had built great houses and churches and good solid towns. They had learned how to irrigate the valleys and raise sheep on the open range. It was more than the gringos had done. Ballard had deep respect for men who built things and established order, and the Mexicans had done it—a long time ago. Years of easy authority, of leisure and fat living, had softened them, made them fearful of all invaders.

The Don was evidently not exercising any easy authority just then. He was in a close huddle with his wife and son and daughter and it was plain to see that everybody had something to say. In particular the girl seemed to be something less than the perfectly submissive creature she was supposed to be, for she was talking with both hands as well as her mouth, her silver bracelets flashing in the sun.

The Don finally left the others and returned slowly to where Ballard and Hicks waited. He bowed his head and spoke gravely.

"It will be a great pleasure," he said. "We will share your meat."

The Navajo blanket was spread in the shade. Ballard and Hicks were busy with their skewers, Hicks serving skillfully as chief cook, while Ballard solicitously served his guests. The peon brought forth round Mexican loaves, honey in the comb, cheese made of goat's milk, candy that had come north a thousand miles in trade and stone crocks of preserved fruits. He set a great jug of native wine on the blanket and a smaller one of brandy. Coffee was brewing on the fire. It was a feast.

Everyone ate with polite restraint, watching everyone else narrowly, eager to help, groping for words, as people always do when they are a little afraid of each other. Silver cups of heavy purple wine helped to loosen tongues, but it was Choppo, the tiny Chihuahua dog, who truly saved the occasion for he alone was wholly unembarrassed. A nimble little creature with a restless pink tongue, he had been taught to sit up and beg. The smell of all that good meat set him wild with eagerness, so that he ran from one to another, begging morsels from each, catching them when they were tossed in the air, barking his sharp demands when he was kept waiting.

Consuelo—now he had learned her name—threw her head back and laughed with delight, then brought her eyes down to meet Ballard's. The others laughed at Choppo, but these two laughed together, looking at each other with shining eyes, as though they had shared a secret of great joy.

When cigarettes had been smoked over coffee, the Don rose and all of the others rose too, with perfect decorum. This, Ballard knew, was the second decisive moment, but he had no doubt of what was coming. When a Mexican has accepted your hospitality, he always offers you his in return, and always in the same words. The Don spoke gravely again, as he extended his hand.

"When you are in Taos," he said, "my house is yours."

"I thank you," Ballard replied and he had never meant it more profoundly.

The Don's words, of course, did not mean what they said. Ballard knew he would not be likely ever to see Consuelo alone, that it might not be easy to see her at all. But at least, when he went to the formidable great front door and lifted the iron knocker, the portero would let him in. Nothing was sure, but a barrier had been crossed.

He stood watching as the Mexicans mounted and started away, both of the men saluting him as they turned their horses. Just before they disappeared down the canyon, Consuelo swung halfway round in her saddle, snatched the bright blue shawl off her shoulders and waved it high over her head in a splendid gesture of triumph and farewell.

Ballard started breaking camp right away, while Hicks, grumbling, went to catch the horses.

"I thought we was here for a week," he said.

"You can stay if you want to," Ballard told him. "I've got business in Taos right now."

They rode down the canyon, over a high shoulder of the foothills and descended toward the valley of Taos. It was a triangular splotch of bright cultivated green, spread like a shining robe across the dull gray and purple of sage and lava. Three bright clear streams, coming down from the mountains to meet and plunge into the Rio Grande, gave it the water of life, and it shimmered and quivered and sang with life in the May sunshine. The fields were all green with new-sprung crops and the cottonwoods along the ditches waved new leafage in the breeze. The bright abundant water of the spring thaw flashed like silver stitching in all the ditches, and their banks were heavy with the white fragrant blossom of the wild plum. The valley was filled with voices of birds as are all places where men have long lived and cultivated the ground. Few birds sing in a wilderness. Their abundant song is truly a voice of human being.

Ballard was little aware of birds, but he always noticed them when he first rode into Taos Valley, especially the meadow larks, bugling from the tops of walls and bushes, their voices seeming full of triumph, and the turtledoves, soft and urgent, crooning desire from every tree.

All of this Ballard had heard and seen many times before, and with pleasure, for almost every year of his trapping he had come back to Taos in the spring, and always he had been glad of the first glimpse of this green and singing valley. But never before had he ridden into it so joyfully as now, so filled with a hope that seemed foolish but would not down. He felt as though he rode to music and beauty was spread before his feet.

— 2 —

The Ballards were long settled in Rockbridge County, Virginia, where the great valley is narrow and fertile between the Blue Ridge and the Allegheny. They had lived there nearly a hundred years when Jean's father was born.

This part of Virginia had little in common with the tidewater region of great plantations and silk-stockinged aristocrats. It was settled by Scotch-Irish immigrants who moved south from Pennsylvania in colonial days and were all hardworking farmers. Three Ballard brothers bought land there and established families so that they became a powerful and numerous clan. They owned a few Negroes but worked hard in their own fields, raising wheat and apples, a few good cattle and many hogs which ran half-wild in their wooded uplands. They lived in good brick houses and set a table heavy with prime meats, fresh and cured, with home-grown vegetables and homemade preserves. Any man could ride up to their picket fences, rest his saddle and stay for dinner. On Sundays they drove behind fat teams to a Presbyterian church, uncomfortable in broadcloth coats and high stocks they never wore any other time except when they were married and buried. They went to Lexington about once a month to buy supplies and always attended court. In town they drank white corn liquor and talked politics. The young men went to dances and sometimes got into rough-and-tumble fights but held no grudges. They were confident men, secure and independent, who saw their abundant living come up out of their own land every spring—men who could not imagine either want or subservience.

William Ballard, Jean's grandfather, had three sons, of whom Samuel, his father, was the youngest, the best looking, and commonly called the "wildest." This meant that Samuel spent too much time hunting and chasing girls, that he had a restless foot and a quick temper. The other two sons stayed in Rockbridge County, living on the land they inherited, but Sam sold his share, bought a wagon and team and went through the Cumberland Gap to Kentucky. There he bought land near the headwaters of the Kentucky River, built a cabin and cleared enough ground to raise a crop of corn. But Sam, still unmarried, couldn't stay anywhere. He built a boat, floated down the Kentucky to the Ohio, a great brown waterway cleaving the massive and virginal forest which then covered all that part of America. He hunted and trapped all the way down the Ohio to the Wabash, then laboriously worked his way north to Vincennes and sold his furs for good money. Vincennes was the center of civilization for all that region, the capital of Indiana territory, already an old town where the French had been settled for three generations. With money in his pocket, Sam dressed up and did the town. He emerged from a month of social excitement standing in a Catholic church with a bride on his arm. She was Jeannette Bissot, of an old and well-educated French family—a small, pretty girl with large brown eyes and delicate hands. She knew of her husband only that he came of a good Virginia family, that he was very handsome and that she was happy and helpless in his arms.

Her ordeal began when they left Vincennes. Despite the fact that she had grown up in a wild country, she was a wholly civilized woman, for the French carried civilization wherever they went. She was afraid of the wilderness. She wept when she saw the Kentucky farm with its two-room cabin standing in a stump-studded clearing, the forest threatening it from every side. Nevertheless she went to work to make a home of it and had some success for about two years. Then Sam felt the urge to move again. He was in love with the wild country of the Ohio Valley, and soon he was building another boat. The Kentucky land was sold and they went down the great river again, to settle near its banks where it marked the line between Indiana and Kentucky. Jean then was a baby in his mother's arms. Sam built on his new holding what was called a "half-faced camp"—a shelter of poles and brush—and went to work again clearing forest. It was a year before he got a cabin built and made a crop of corn—a year when he lived by hunting and his wife struggled with cold and dirt and an open fire, also with malaria and dysentery.

Sam Ballard was undergoing a deterioration of a kind not uncommon in that day. Gradually he shed every trait and property that linked him with the society he had left. He sold his good coat to an Indian because he never wore it. His fine linen shirts were cut to bits to make patches for rifle bullets. He was now dressed always in buckskin, greased and polished by the constant wiping of his hunting knife. He was a man of the frontier and primarily of the forest, a man of rifle, ax and hoe, who loved the rifle better than the ax and the ax better than the hoe. Although he was a farmer after a fashion, most of his living came out of the forest, in wild meat and fur, in wild honey, ginseng and buckskin. To his wife the forest was a wall that cut her off from the world, through which her husband disappeared, sometimes to be gone for days at a time. To him it was a place of refuge and excitement, more and more the only place he felt at home.

Jeannette Ballard bore two daughters after Jean, both of them in a log cabin with a dirt floor and only a local midwife to help. It seemed only luck that she survived those first few years in the forest. Her lot became a little easier as her children grew. Both girls helped around the house from an early age, and Jean's life became a struggle to realize his mother's ideal of order and cleanliness. For although she never triumphed, she never surrendered. She had brought from Vincennes a few dishes of fine china and a little china clock of French make. The dishes were never used. They and the clock were set on a shelf, often washed and dusted, kept by her as a shrine to civilized living. Pioneer cabins of that day were nearly all dirty, with dirt floors, and often infested by vermin. Jeannette finally achieved a puncheon floor and she fought dirt without compromise as long as she lived. She was not an unsocial woman but she shrank from the pioneer society of log-rolling and husking-bee and camp meeting, full of hearty joy and stinking of corn liquor. All the few neighbors she knew spoke a dialect which became almost standard in the Mississippi Basin of that day, and she longed to save her children from it. Carefully she taught Jean to read and write and to speak correct English. Her only scoldings came when he said mought for might or fit for fought, or used a double negative.

From the age of eight or nine, Jean toiled in the fields with his father and helped his mother whenever he could. He became a hunter when he was so small he could not shoot the long Kentucky rifle without resting it in a forked stick, and when the old English double-barreled shotgun kicked him off his feet every time he pulled the trigger. He was a better shot than his father, and he too learned to love the forest. Often he would crawl out of his corn-shuck bed in the attic before daylight and tiptoe out of the house with a gun, to prowl through a dawn-gray forest where the oaks were ten feet thick, the hickories a hundred feet high and the great ropes of the wild grape laced the trees together. Soft-footed on the dew-wet leaf mold, he would surprise a deer on its way to water, or slip quietly beneath a tree where wild turkeys roosted and bring a great gobbler crashing down to earth.

He loved the forest, but his first allegiance was always to his mother and to the house. She had little time to give him but often at night she came and sat beside his bed. His hands in winter were always chapped and split to the red from working in the fields without gloves and setting traps in cold water for otter, mink and muskrat. She would bring a saucer of warm deer tallow and gently anoint his aching knuckles. It was a kind of lovemaking, the only tenderness she ever bestowed. With her hand gentle upon his, she talked always of great cities where men and women walked in silk and satin and rode in carriages and life moved to music. She had been to

New Orleans once in her girlhood and the greatness and beauty of Paris she knew from old people who had lived there. Her voice was soft with longing when she talked of these things. The world she talked about was only half real to her and to him it was a fairyland for he had never seen anything like it. But always she made him understand that life can be order and beauty, and always she kept for him a small refuge of tenderness in a world of toil and hardship and much brutality. She never succeeded in planting civilization in the forest but she planted the idea of it and the feeling for it in the consciousness of her son.

Jean was twenty when she died. In fact, she had been dying slowly for years for the malaria had never left her. Year by year he had seen her once-beautiful face shrivel and yellow until only her great brown eyes remained the same. Her small once-pretty hands had become clawlike—human pothooks worn by an endless struggle with heavy iron skillets and Dutch ovens. She had been sick so much of the time that her husband thought nothing of it, but Jean had a fateful intuition about this illness and stayed as close to her as he could, for both of his sisters had then married, the youngest at fifteen.

It was March, with snow on the ground and a cold wind keening around the eaves much of the time. All of the frontier people were deeply superstitious—about black cats across your path, and Friday, and walking under ladders and especially about a dog howling when someone was going to die. No dog howled that March, but almost every evening when he sat beside her bed, a timber wolf somewhere across the river lifted his muzzle to the sky and gave the deep-throated howl which is the most mournful far-carrying sound in the American wild. Jeannette had always despised superstition and she had taught Jean to despise it, but she heard the voice of the wolf with despair in her eyes. It was to her truly the voice of doom, the voice of the wilderness that had killed her.

JEAN BALLARD

Jean had to run and call his father when he saw that she was struggling for breath. Only when they sat on either side of her, holding her hands, did Sam become aware of crisis. In a few minutes she was dead. Begetter and begotten, the two now faced each other across the body of their victim, then bowed their heads and wept.

When spring broke after his mother's death, Jean would go down to the river almost every evening and sit there alone on the bank, listening to the soft deep voice of the flood-swollen current and watching the night slowly bury the forest on the other side. After a few weeks he began building a boat. His father watched him uneasily but said nothing. He knew Jean was going away. He did not want him to go but knew he could not stop him. Both he and Jeannette had known for several years that this quiet, thick-bodied boy was far more than a match for his father. Jean moved slowly and only after long thought but he was as hard to stop as a freshet or a landslide.

So when the time came for him to go, there were no arguments and no tears. His father gave him a rifle. His sisters came home and prepared much food for him, mostly jerked meat and corn meal and salt and a little sugar. He had a bale of furs of his own trapping and these were currency in the world of that day. He pushed his flat boat into the current and turned once to wave at the watching three before he disappeared around a bend. All of them knew it was probably a final parting but all over America young men were heading West with little chance of return. Jean was carried by the current of his time no less than by the great Ohio.

At first he felt a little lost but the farther he went the more he was sustained by a feeling that he went to meet his necessary destiny and by the excitement of penetrating the unknown. He rounded every bend with eager interest and poked into the forest where he camped every night, taking his meat where he found it. He saw a few other boats and passed landings where crude roads led inland but most of the time he floated through a wilderness, where deer came down to drink, wild turkeys sailed across the river on set wings and the sky was filled with thunderous clouds of pigeons and wild fowl night and morning.

When he reached the Mississippi he took passage on a steamboat from New Orleans and worked his way upstream to St. Louis. There for the first time he knew he had emerged from the world of his youth. St. Louis then was only a town of about fifteen thousand but it was one of the nerve centers of American life. White steamboats with great housed paddle wheels made a forest of their tall smokestacks on the water front, which was filled with the smash and rumble of moving freight and the shouts and singing of the Negroes who loaded and unloaded the boats. In bars and stores frock-coated gentlemen and gamblers off the river boats lined up with long-haired buckskinned men from farther west and traders and merchants, flush with silver money, draping heavy gold watch chains across their gaudy vests. Back from the river were old brick houses, some of which had already sheltered two generations, where Negro coachmen held horses while ladies in great ballooning silk skirts were helped into coaches. All of this Jean stared at with eager, hungry eyes. He was seeing something like the world his mother had described, but he had only half believed in its existence. Houses that were something more than shelter from the weather, houses built for beauty and comfort, were strange and a little incredible to him, and so were women with lovely arms and hands and flowerlike skins and great masses of soft hair—women who were not drudges but creatures of beauty and mystery for the delight of men. Houses and women and prancing sleek horses made him ache with envy and longing, with a feeling he had entered a world in which he had no share. None of these people seemed even aware of his existence. He had never been before where he could not hail any man he saw or knock on any door if he was hungry. He felt a quick resentment toward these people who walked apart and ignored him and would not share what they had. But the sight of the city stimulated him too. It made him aware of great energies and great appetites stirring within him. He felt denied but he also felt curiously confident.

Jean was moving west like a migrating animal, following his instinct and his nose, moved by a collective urge that was in the air of his time. He had heard only vaguely of the Santa Fe Trail, but now he talked to wagon men and trappers and learned all about Santa Fe and the big money in beaver. He asked many questions, listened carefully and remembered all he heard.

He did not consider and decide that he would cross the plains, but just became slowly sure that he would do so. He began making himself over in the image of the men he met, buying a rifle of heavy caliber, a wide felt hat and boots. Independence, where the wagons started, was only a few miles away, and hard jobs were to be had for the asking. He started as every greenhorn did, walking beside a team of oxen with a long prod, eating the dust of the prairie summer, burning his skin beneath the prairie sun. The forest he had fought all his life scattered and thinned and fell back like a beaten army and the earth seemed wide and empty as never before.

Jean reached Santa Fe at a time when the boom in beaver fur had begun to wane, although it was still to engage many men for years, while the wagon trade across the prairies was steadily growing. Beaver had been boomed by the fashionable vogue of the beaver hat. That oppressive ornament of male vanity now was going out of style and beaver fur was dropping in price, while many of the best streams had been nearly trapped out. Nevertheless Jean became a beaver trapper first because it was an easy thing for him to do. He had been a trapper from the age of eight as had almost every backwoods boy west of the Allegheny. He had grown up in a world where peltries were currency, where a coonskin bought a jug of whisky and a prime otter was good for a hundred pounds of meal, where men were dressed mostly in the skins of animals and only women wore fabrics they wove on hand looms. Jean had a lore and technique he could now turn into money. He knew all about land-sets and water-sets—how to anchor a beaver trap to a sliding pole so it would drown its victim, how to make scent that would bring quarry from afar, how to case and stretch and flesh a pelt, which was most important, for every man was known by the skill with which he prepared his furs for market. The men who rode the beaver trails were men of his own kind, nearly all of whom had come from Virginia, Pennsylvania, Kentucky and Tennessee, floating down rivers as he had done, changing from boat to horse when they passed the Mississippi. It was not hard for him to become one of them. For a while he worked for wages in one of the organized outfits that still went north to the Platte and Red River country, but in a few years he had become a free trapper, one of the mountain men. These traveled in small gangs, usually of five or six men, starting in early fall, trapping until heavy snow fell, or all winter on the southern streams, such as the Gila and the lower Rio Grande, emerging in the spring to sell furs in Taos or Santa Fe, at Bent's Fort on the Arkansas or at the great rendezvous on Green River, now past its best days. Each man had a saddle horse and a pack horse for his dunnage, a rifle and six traps. When they started they usually had some meal or flour, sometimes coffee and sugar, but before they saw a town or a trader again they became as carnivorous as wolves, eating straight meat three times a day, except for wild berries and fruits.

Most of them saw times in the dry south when they had to eat rattlesnake and prairie dog and were glad to get it.

These gangs appointed no leader, and no man was bound to obey another, or even to stay with the outfit if he wanted to leave. They had only one rule, which was never all to fire at once when they got into trouble with Indians. But almost always, on the long trails, one man became informally a leader, just as one horse always became the bell horse and led all the others when they were turned loose to graze. So one man always came to ride at the head of the gang as they traveled single file over the faint trails Indians had followed for years, but no white men before these. One man they all turned and looked at when it was a question of this way or that, of whether to go ahead in the face of a storm or hole up, of whether to trap a certain stream or look for better. Jean Ballard became one of those informal leaders even when most of the men he rode with were years his senior. He looked older than he was, he kept his mouth shut except when it was necessary to say something, and he was completely unflustered no matter what struck. Moreover, he was never lost. His sense of direction seemed never to fail him. This he had known for years, and the Rocky Mountains, with their heavily marked topography, were easy going for him after the flat forests of his youth, where many men had to blaze the trees in order to get back home, but he had always just followed his nose. This was a part of his native gift, his genius, and another part was that he had intuitions of a singular certainty. He was a man who noticed everything and he never knew how much he went by what he noticed and how much was pure hunch, but he believed in pure hunches. More than once he grew suddenly cautious when Indians were ahead, although neither he nor anyone else had seen a track or a wisp of smoke or heard a sound. One such time he remembered that his old yellow buckskin horse had suddenly pointed his ears against the wind. He always watched his horse's ears. A horse heard and smelled things a long way off and always pointed his ears toward whatever worried him. Anyway, he often knew trouble was ahead when no one else did, and this had been true so often that those who knew him would always listen to him.

So Jean became a greatly respected man in his own world, and he moved through it with more ease and certainty and less damage to himself than most. It was a violent world with a violent rhythm which men came to love if they could stand it at all. For five to eight months, and sometimes longer, they lived like wild animals, seeing neither house nor woman. Then for two months or three they were in a settlement with heavy bags of silver money to spend. When it was gone they were eager to take the trails again. Each phase had its own intense excitement and each was an escape and a relief from the other. Most of them were forever unfitted for any other way of life.

In the mountains they all lived and worked alike, disciplined by the hard necessities of food and fur and safety, but in Taos and Santa Fe especially, every man went to hell in his own way. Many of them stayed drunk, more or less, the whole time they were in town, ending in a sleep that might last for two or three days. There were men who had to have a fight after a certain number of drinks and went around challenging all comers until they got one. Most of these were rough-tumble fights, the aboriginal form of human combat, with men rolling over and over in fighting fury like tomcats, sometimes biting off ears and noses and gouging eyes. There were duels with hunting knives and a few with rifles which were usually fatal. Most men also gambled and games of poker and high-low-jack and the game kept going for days and nights, with men squatting around a blanket piled with silver Mexican dollars and gold slugs and all kinds of personal property.

A few held aloof from women, for some of them had lost all interest in the sex, but most men acquired a girl when they struck town and kept her until they left or got too drunk to do anything with her. In either Taos or Santa Fe a man could often buy a common Mexican girl for about twenty dollars, and Indian women were for sale for less than that. Many of them were Navajo women the Mexicans had captured and kept as slaves, but there were also men who made a business of catching Ute and Digger women and driving them into Santa Fe like sheep, letting them forage along the way, selling them for what they could get. Some became regular prostitutes, but most were to be bought like a horse.

Jean Ballard drank but he never got drunk, for he was a watchful man who had no desire to lose consciousness or fog his eyes. He spent long hours playing poker and almost always won, if only because he was sober and most of his opponents were drunk. He loved to bluff, watching a man's eyes, playing his hunches. The money he won never meant much because there was nothing to do with it. There were no banks or places of safekeeping and it was too heavy to carry on the trail. Often, when it came time to leave he gave away whatever dollars he had left. He had no conception of money as a form of power which can destroy both those who have it and others.

He had few fights because he was not one who loved fighting for its own sake. Most of the fighting was among men who made a sport of it and had a reputation to sustain. A man seldom had to fight if he minded his own business and Jean always did that.

Women interested him more than anything else in the towns, and he had many Mexican girls during his trapping years. All of them were girls of the common people. As a trapper among trappers he saw the aristocrats only at a distance. They truly lived apart from all others, looked and acted like a separate race. The common Mexicans were mostly the peons who worked the great estates and followed the sheep herds across the mesas, although some of them were small freeholders, owning a few acres of soil. They were the most oppressed and helpless people Jean had ever seen, living in tiny adobe houses, cooking their beans and chile over a corner fire, seldom seeing a whole dollar, completely at the mercy of their masters. Yet they were kind and friendly people. Many of them never married because they could not pay the fees of the church. They just set up housekeeping and lived together. So it was not hard for a Mexican mother to let her daughter go away with a gringo who had bags of silver money to spend. Any man could find him a Mexican girl. There were professional panderers who could arrange such matters for a price. But Jean never did business so crudely. He went about his wenching, as he did everything else, with patience, deliberation and adroitness. He wanted to perfect his Spanish and to learn about Mexican people. When he saw a girl who took his eyes he would call on the family, bringing always gifts, first of food and tobacco, later, at just the right moment, presents of money. He spent long hours platicando. He squatted with huge families about their bowls of chile con carne, learned to scoop up his food gracefully in a tortilla and to swallow the burning hot chile without gagging or wiping his eyes. He always addressed himself to the grandmother first, if there was one, and then to the mother, working his way down through the generations. By the time he got to the girl, he usually had the whole family eating out of his hand and that quite literally.

Some of these Mexican girls took a powerful hold upon his flesh. Many of them were pretty and they had a soft and voluptuous quality, a completeness of submission and response that made them wholly different from the shrill and nervous women, laborious and full of malaria, he had known in Indiana. But always Jean rode away in the fall. Always he promised to return and sometimes he did and sometimes not. His time had not yet come to stay anywhere or stick to anything.

For eight years he rode the beaver trail, with prices falling and fur becoming scarce. Then, just before the conquest, he turned to the growing wagon trade and traveled between Santa Fe and Independence for several years. Here, as anywhere, he became a man of responsibility. After three years he had charge of a wagon train for a wealthy Jew who owned a store and two saloons in Santa Fe, and he was making big money. But he grew weary of the dust and sweat of the great road. He had come to love the mountains. Knowing now much of Indians and Indian languages, he became a trader with Ed Hicks for his assistant. They traded with the Utes across the Rio Grande, and came to know that tribe as well as any white man could. Then they made a trip south into the Apache country, a precarious operation, for Apaches wanted to trade but could not be trusted. Nevertheless, they came back to Santa Fe with a herd of mules and horses the Apaches had stolen in Sonora and sold to the white men for beads, knives, powder and lead. It was a profitable operation.

In this fateful thirty-third year of his life, he and Hicks had come to Taos for the summer, planning another Apache trip in the fall. Taos was quiet now, with few trappers there, no big money, no fights, no three-day poker games. So the two mountain men had ridden to the hot spring, men of leisure, taking their ease, glad of peace and running water and tall timber.

After thirteen years in the mountains, Jean Ballard owned nothing but his outfit and as much cash as he could pack around on a horse, but he was a man of reputation, and also, in the lore and skill of his own world, a man of learning. He knew Spanish as well as he did English and he spoke them both with careful correctness, though slowly and with no great fluency. He knew enough of three Indian languages—Ute, Arapahoe and Apache—for purposes of trade. He knew the difficult sign language perfectly and could talk in nimble-fingered silence with any Indian. He was known also as a "good man with Indians" who could win their confidence and keep it. He lived in a world of incessant movement, and he was an expert on transportation. He was a master packer who not only could throw a diamond hitch, but could load a barebacked horse with a squaw hitch that would hold. He was a good judge of both horses and mules, who had only to look at teeth and feel shins and knees to know what an animal was worth. He had learned the wagon business and almost every mile of road that a wagon could travel west of the Mississippi. He knew an immense territory, from Sonora in the south to the Platte in the north, and from the Buffalo plains all the way across the mountains to the Great Salt Lake.

It was no common trapper Consuelo Coronel had flirted with at the hot spring. Whether by luck or by intuition she had picked a man of power, one who was born to command other men, and also one who felt deeply the need of woman, not merely as a complement to his flesh, but as an anchor to the earth and a center of his being. For man alone may be a conqueror but everything that lasts is built around a woman. And Jean Ballard was destined to be a builder.

THE HOUSE OF CORONEL

THE Coronel place stood on a low hill at the western edge of town, and was known therefore as La Loma. It looked almost as though it had been carved from the earth, or upthrust from it by some subterranean force—a great angular block of earthen wall, golden brown, plastered smooth, glinting in the sun with tiny bits of mica. Its windows were few, opaque with oiled paper and barred with wrought iron. A long narrow veranda ran across the front but no one ever sat there. The front entrance was a double door, iron-barred from within, which would have resisted a battering-ram. Behind the house was a square enclosed by adobe walls as high as the house itself, with cactus growing along its top. A solid double carriage gate, ten feet high, was the only way in from the rear. The house of Coronel was a very old house, a house of immense strength and stability, which kept its life secret and secluded, presented to the world a passive, impenetrable resistance.

For months Jean Ballard had felt that resistance as he had never felt resistance before in his life. He was a man with an appetite for difficulty, a love of struggle, but the house of Coronel offered him nothing to struggle with. It just let him sit. It also let him look at Consuelo, across a room, under the watchful eyes of at least one and sometimes two other women, and it let him say trivial things to her. Once in a long while he was left alone with her for a matter of minutes, and then they exchanged quick eager words. But there had been no word of hope. The correct procedure was for him to ask her father for her hand, but she had told him it was no use. She had been engaged since the age of six to a second cousin who lived in Santa Fe. This betrothal had been arranged by the parents of both, as was customary among the rich Mexicans. It meant a great deal to both families. It would unite two large estates, and had something of the necessity and importance of a marriage of royal persons. It had been endorsed by the great and autocratic Padre Martinez. It did not mean much either to Consuelo or to her affianced, for they had met only a few times, mostly at great Christmas gatherings, and their marriage had been unhappily delayed when he went south on a trading trip and was wounded by an Apache arrow. But for that she would have been married a year ago.

Consuelo had gone to her father, had tried to tell him of her love for the gringo. All Jean knew of that interview was conveyed to him in a shrug, a gesture of spreading both her beautiful hands, a single sentence.

"He won't listen to me," she said.

For many hours now these two had sat looking at each other, saying one thing in words and another with their eyes. They had talked a little in English. She had asked him to teach her English and this had given them a game to play and a little more private communication, though not much. For the most part they made only small talk. They chatted as though they were the most casual of acquaintances, and their chatter covered a tension of mutual need that had grown ever since the day they met. Jean had no doubt about his own feeling, nor yet of hers. She had given herself with her eyes and lips a dozen times, yet she was as much beyond his reach as if he had looked at her only through glass.

For the first time in his life he felt the massive, inert resistance of old established things, of a people fortified by wealth and custom and tradition, by a way of life stronger than they were, a social pattern which was a power in itself. They did not hate him as a person but they hated anything alien. Family was everything to them. Their whole society was a great family and it was organized to repel intrusion. They did not have to insult him or reject him or even close a door to him. They could freeze him out and wait him out. He might come and sit and sip chocolate for months and even for years and never pass any of the barriers of custom and manner that were set up against him.

He felt no hope—or almost none. There was something about Consuelo that slightly renewed his hope every time he saw her. She was a creature watched and guarded like a thousand-dollar horse, yet she never gave the impression of being helpless. She had a most unmistakable feeling of power about her—in the sweep of her walk, the tone of her voice, the toss of her head. He had noticed the same thing about a good many Mexican women. The men had gone to pot on too much easy living, but the women remained as lively and eager as ever. They had no rights but they had vitality.

Consuelo inspired confidence and she did not seem hopeless herself, but what could she do against the organized power of family and church, the trammels of custom that held her fast? Moreover, his time in Taos was growing short. Within the month he and Hicks must start for the south. They had bought all their supplies and trade goods and he had given his word. It was hard to go and still harder to tell her he was going. But he couldn't sit there all winter. Nor could he endure either the tension or the idleness much longer.

Always before he had forgotten women in the mountains. Something told him the image of this one was going to follow him down the trail, but even so, he knew he must go.

He tied his horse to one of the hitching posts in front of the house, as he had done so often before, and lifted the heavy knocker on the great front door. It was opened by the portero, a little old bearded man, one of the most trusted servants, whose whole use and destiny was to be guardian of that door and to know the exact right and status of everyone who knocked. The portero spoke a soft greeting, bowing with averted eye, and led him into the great sala. As always, no one was there but the little dog. Choppo was the only member of the household who felt free to show enthusiasm. He liked Jean, always barked a greeting and leaped to caress his hand with a soft pink tongue.

The sala was a long room, running all the way across the front of the house, with a low heavy-raftered ceiling and walls washed white with gypsum. There were two fireplaces in opposite corners, both banked in this hot season with fragrant boughs of juniper. Some of the wealthy families now were beginning to buy furniture from St. Louis, but not the conservative Coronels. Their house remained as it had been for three generations. Along the walls were couches made by folding mattresses and covering them with great Navajo blankets in large patterns of black and red. A light red cotton cloth was hung against the lower part of the walls to keep the whitewash from rubbing off. There was no other furniture except a few homemade chairs with rawhide seats and two low tables of excellent workmanship. Two windows covered with oiled paper admitted a dim light, shadowed by the iron bars without. The place was never warm, even on the hottest days, and it was almost soundproof. It created an atmosphere of its own, a block of cool sequestered silence. Coming in from the glare and heat of the August afternoon, Jean always felt as though he had entered a cave.

He sat down on one of the couches and relaxed. Almost always he had a long wait. In the past few months he had learned the habits of the family in great detail, and those habits never varied except that everyone seemed to have a vague sense of time. The same things always happened, but sooner or later and generally later. So chocolate was served in this room every afternoon some time between four and six. Anyone who had access to the house might come and be admitted and sit down. In due course the visitor would be given chocolate and would be greeted by some part of the family. The women always appeared first, the men later, or sometimes not at all if they had ridden out to supervise a shearing or the irrigation of their crops. Most of the visitors came on certain days of the week and Jean had learned to avoid these.

He was desperately hoping this day to see Consuelo alone for a few minutes. It was never for more than a few minutes, and whether he saw her alone at all depended upon who presided over their meeting. Any married woman of the family who was older than Consuelo might act as her chaperon, but so far only two other women had appeared. One of these was the Doña Anastasia, her mother, and the other was a widowed aunt, who lived with the family, known as Señora Catalina Romero y Salazar.

The Doña Anastasia was a woman of enormous weight, and to Jean an enigma of some importance. She was the most uncertain factor in the situation. He knew the men regarded him as an intruder who had to be tolerated for the sake of politeness until he went his way. He knew also that the aunt contemplated him with hostility and suspicion. She was a tall, lean, angular woman, somewhere in her forties he thought, who had lost her husband in the Navajo wars years ago and had never found another. Neither had she any children, a great sorrow to any Mexican. Perhaps she had been soured by her misfortunes. At any rate, toward the gringo suitor she had an uncompromising resentment. When it was her turn to guard the family virgin she always appeared first, gave him a perfunctory hand with a barely perceptible smile, sat down on one of the straight-backed chairs and remained there, silent, erect and watchful, until he departed. She always reminded him of a hungry hawk perched on a pine stub.

The Doña Anastasia was wholly different. She was slow and heavy on her feet and at this time of day she had but recently emerged from the profound slumbers of her siesta. Perhaps this was the only reason her daughter so often beat her to the reception room when Jean came to call. But he cherished a hopeful suspicion that the Doña, if not an ally, was at least not unfriendly. He had also an impression, dating back to that first encounter at the hot spring, that the women of this family were in league against the men.

He had studied the Doña's face for confirmation of his hopes but without achieving any assurance. Padded with fat, her wide, placid countenance was unrevealing as an egg. Her smile was habitual, and fell upon all, like the sunshine. Only the shrewd, kindly look in her small, half-buried eyes gave him the impression that he was in the presence of something cunning, subtle and perhaps not wholly averse to his desire—that and the fact that she always came in late and subsided into a corner, her hands folded across a great, smooth stomach, and seemed to pay no attention to the talk, whether it was in English or in Spanish. Often she nodded, and a few times she apparently dozed. One such time, sitting near Consuelo, longing to touch her willing flesh, he had started impulsively toward her. The girl had warned him with a quick lift of the hand and he had turned to see the mother's small, shrewd eyes suddenly wide open, watchful, enigmatic—the eyes of an old woman who had spent a long life watching people, prevailing by cunning and patience if she prevailed at all. He suspected the Doña had feigned sleep to see what he would do. He had learned long since that an old Mexican woman is often tricky as a pet coon. It was no wonder that among the common people so many of them were considered witches and suspected of working spells.

This day he knew Consuelo was coming first and alone, because he knew her step so well. He rose to meet her and she gave him both her hands. He resisted an impulse to seize her, to know the feel of her body and the taste of her lips at least once before he left her. There would be only a few minutes and he had to blurt his message.

"I must go," he told her. "You know that . . ."

The pain in her eyes stopped him.

"Two more weeks," she begged. "Wait two more weeks!"

"But of what use?" he asked.

"Two more weeks," she repeated, breathless with haste and eagerness. "It is all I ask of you. Promise me!"

"Very well," he said. "I would promise you anything. But why?"

Consuelo took a deep breath and smiled. She turned and seated herself with great composure.

"My cousin, Adelita Otero, is coming from Albuquerque for a long visit," she explained. Her voice now was chatty and easy as it had been tense before. "She will stay for the Fiesta of San Geronimo in September."

"Yes," he assented.

"I want you to meet her," Consuelo explained. "I am sure you will find her very sympathetic."

Muy sympatico. It was a polite and invariable formula. So he would tarry two more weeks to meet the very sympathetic cousin. It made no sense but he had promised. And the Doña Anastasia forestalled any further explanations by rolling heavily into the room, offering a limp, plump hand, murmuring a greeting so soft it seemed almost confidential.

The first meeting with Adelita left him even more bewildered. The two women came into the room together, Consuelo leading her cousin by the hand, while Adelita hung back, shy and giggling. She was a plump young matron, very dark, with a mass of coarse black hair and a small, round, pretty face. She gave Jean her hand with a faint pressure, averting her eyes, flushed and flustered. He felt at once that Adelita was friendly but timid and he worked to put her at her ease. When she found that he could speak Spanish as well as she could she visibly relaxed, conquered her childish giggle and began to prattle about her trip. Jean pretended a great interest in the road to Santa Fe. He was going south himself in a few weeks. He knew every foot of it, as a matter of fact, but he bombarded her with polite questions, and she responded with the profuse and irrelevant detail which encumbers simple minds.

Later the whole family came in, and several visitors, evidently come to meet Adelita. Each of them took him by the hand, greeted him and then ignored him almost completely. Now and then a word was tossed in his direction for the sake of politeness, but most of their talk was about their own friends and doings. He felt, as he always had felt in these gatherings, that he was an intruder and an alien.

Chocolate arrived in a tall pitcher of hand-hammered silver and was served in silver cups that were hot to the lips by an old woman who devoted her whole life to making thick chocolate, beating it into a perfect froth with a wooden beater she spun between her hands. It was heavy, cloying chocolate, almost a liquid candy, and he always found it hard to down. A little later he rose and bowed himself out to a chorus of faint farewells, eloquent of polite indifference.

He returned a few days later, because Consuelo had bade him return, but with a feeling of futility and defeat. Somewhat to his surprise, Adelita came in first, but Consuelo joined them almost immediately.

Because he had watched her so long and so intently he had become acutely aware of her moods, and he knew at once that she was filled with excitement, flushed and quick on her feet. He could see too that she had dressed as though for a special occasion. She always wore a bodice of white linen, which left her arms and shoulders bare and just revealed the cleft of her breasts, and a short red skirt, only a little below her knees. Her legs were bare, too, and she wore homemade slippers, so fragile that one night of dancing would ruin a pair. This bodice and skirt were the house dress of all Mexican girls and much alike in all classes. Consuelo was to be known as a person of quality by her fine linen but chiefly by her shawls and her jewelry. No Mexican woman was ever without a shawl, and her shawl revealed both her wealth and her taste. It was also the most expressive part of her costume. She could draw it about her in a way that expressed aversion or coquetry or dissent, and she could fling it off in a gesture of challenge or invitation. A Mexican girl was always doing something with her shawl and one of a wealthy family would have a shawl for every kind of occasion. He had seen at least a dozen different ones about Consuelo's shoulders. All of them were of silk, in bright colors; some had come all the way from Spain and some were worth a hundred dollars or more.

This day Consuelo wore a vivid shawl of bright yellow silk, worked with a design of scarlet flowers. She wore also a red flower in her hair and earrings which were disks of soft, pure gold, each set with a single pearl. She had never looked more beautiful, he thought, and her beauty made him acutely uncomfortable. He was a calm man, but for once his calm was failing him. Never had he looked so longingly at anything so completely beyond his reach.

Conversation limped and stalled. Consuelo played with her shawl, even twisted it in her hands, revealing a nervous tension he had never seen in her before. Adelita seemed to feel the tension too, watching Consuelo uneasily, giggling without reason. It was evident that she both feared and adored her gorgeous and strong-minded cousin.

Consuelo at last fixed her eye upon the uncomfortable girl.

"Adelita!" she said. Her voice was restrained but monitory, as though Adelita had been guilty of some nameless dereliction. Adelita giggled without mirth and squirmed in her seat. She looked pathetically young and helpless—a weak personality caught between two strong ones.

"Adelita!" Consuelo's voice now had an edge like a knife.

Adelita was plainly in misery, the victim of some painful inner conflict. She hesitated a moment longer, then rose. Her politeness did not fail her. She nodded to each of them.

"With your permission," she said. Then she turned and fairly fled from the room as though she had been pushed by an invisible hand.

Consuelo's eyes followed her to the door and watched it close. Then she dropped her shawl from her shoulders and leaned toward him.

"I want you to make me one more promise," she said. "That you will come back in three months, as surely as you live."

"I will always come back, as long as you are here," he told her. "You know that. But what then?"

"Do not ask me," she said. "And do not come to the house. But let it be known that you are in town."

All this mystified him.

"I am yours to command," he said. It was another form of politeness, but he was aware that he meant it exactly.

"If you do not come," she said, "I am lost."

"But I give you my word. . . ."

"You may be killed," she reminded him. He had noticed again and again that Mexicans always thought of death, often mentioned death. He never thought of it. He could not imagine his own extinction. He laughed.

"I never get killed," he assured her.

"Your life now is mine," she said, "for I am yours."

Even then, at first, he did not understand. For so long he had looked at her across impassable barriers. . . . It was her face that made her meaning clear. It seemed suddenly transformed. Her eyes were larger and deeper, they were all pupil. Her cheeks were flushed and her mouth, soft as a flower, was an open invitation.

He rose and went to her, aware of the tremor of his hands and the thunder of his blood. It seemed a rash, an almost incredible moment, but after he had found her lips, he knew there was no stopping. Their union was for him a fulfillment so intense it blotted out awareness of everything except the receiving warmth of her body, the clasp of her arms, her half-smothered cry of willing pain. . . . Afterward there was a brief moment of peace, of quiet triumph—then suddenly she pushed him away and the moment dissolved into comedy. She was sitting up again, both hands playing around her hair, while he was retreating to his chair in very bad order.

"Act as though nothing had happened!" she said breathlessly.

From where he sat he could see the red marks of his fingers on her bare shoulders.

"Your reboso!" he said, making a gesture of drawing a shawl about his shoulders.

"Your hair!" she said, as she obeyed him, while he smoothed his heavy mop with trembling fingers.

Then both of them began to laugh. They laughed together, looking into each other's eyes, as they had laughed that day at the hot spring. They were laughing when Adelita came back into the room. She resumed her seat and looked from one to the other of them.

"Tell me," she begged, "what is so funny?"

Consuelo shook her head, struggling to control her laughter, which was so much more than mirth and had filled her eyes with tears.

"Forgive me, dear cousin," she said at last, wiping her eyes. "There is no joke. We laugh because we are happy."

— 2 —

When Jean Ballard returned to Taos the mountains were faintly powdered with the first light snow, streams tinkled and gleamed with ice and a cold wind whispered across bare fields, tore the last dead paperly leaves from the cottonwoods, whipped blue wood smoke away from the chimneys of adobe houses.

He rode alone. He had left Hicks in Santa Fe to dispose of a herd of mules and a load of furs they had brought from the Gila country.

In Santa Fe he had made careful preparations. He had no idea what he faced or what he was going to do, but he wanted to look, feel and be strong and ready. He had thought first of a horse for a horse to him was a part of his personality. The pack and saddle stock he had used on his southern trip was gaunt and shaggy. This time he would not ride into Taos on a trail-worn cayuse, as he had done so often before. Instead he bought from an army officer for three hundred dollars a chestnut gelding, seventeen hands high—a single-footer that rocked him gently with a feeling of latent speed and power. He bought also a suit of buckskin, died black, well-cut by a Mexican tailor and trimmed with silver buttons—such clothing as the ricos had always worn before the wagons came, and such as many of them still wore. He paid forty dollars for a pair of boots that came from St. Louis and half as much for a wide black felt hat with a flat crown. He was no dandy but just now he was more acutely conscious of how he looked than ever before. He put on these clothes as a man might put on armor in preparation for battle. He bought also a small percussion-lock pistol he could wear inside the band of his trousers. It would never do to appear armed—or not to be so.

About a mile from Taos on the Questa road was a deserted one-room adobe house which had a good fireplace in one corner and a roof that would shed the weather. There was a spring near by and good winter-cured grass and piñon wood on the slope behind it. Water, grass and wood were the essentials of life to him. On the earthen floor he spread his robe and blanket. He had used the place before, and it was home enough for a trail-faring man. He never liked to be inside a town at night. Years in the mountains give a man an aversion to close human huddles.

The next day he dressed himself with care, saddled his new horse and rode into town. She had told him to let it be known he was there, and he made no mistake about that. He rode slowly about the streets, knowing his fine mount alone would draw many eyes, waving a greeting to friends, nearly all of whom were poor people he had known for years, buying supplies in a store and drinking native brandy in the small cantina where the mountain men had always gathered. None of them were there now. It was no time for a mountain man to be in Taos. He was probably the only gringo in town and therefore conspicuous. He did not even go near the house of Coronel.

Then his trial by patience began. He had nothing to do but go back to his camp and wait. It was the hardest of all things for him to do. He longed to take his rifle and go hunting. He knew there were good fat bucks in the piñon less than a mile away. But he did not dare to go that far from his camp. He might miss something. So he took an ax instead and cut firewood, much more than he needed, stacking it neatly in a corner, as though he were preparing to spend a month. At night he sat and stared at his fire, not lonely but restless and uneasy.

He was not a man to engage in useless speculations. He felt profoundly sure that something was going to happen but he could not guess what or when, and he did not try. He was painfully conscious he had lost his freedom for the first time since his mother's death. He knew he would wait all winter if necessary.

The second day a Mexican woodcutter came to his door. He knew the man, Enrique Lopez, as one who made a living peddling firewood in the town. He had two burros loaded high with split fat pine, as only a Mexican could load it. He invited Enrique into his house, gave him a drink of brandy, filled him up with hot meat and chile, chatted with him for an hour. The man might have been an emissary but apparently he was not. He had nothing to offer but a large appetite and a great many idle words. He might have questioned Enrique, too, might have found out at least whether Consuelo was at home. But he shrewdly refrained. If the man was not a messenger he might be a spy. He knew he was dealing with a cunning people and that he had probably created a situation big with trouble. So he asked nothing.

The next day a woman came by his door. He was on the sheltered side of the house in welcome autumn sunshine, squatting on his heels against the wall, smoking his pipe. He saw the woman in the distance, wrapped in the great black shawl all the common women wore. In the chilly morning wind it was hooded over her head and gathered tightly about her body. When she came near she spoke a soft, "Como le va," and when he responded she stopped and dropped her shawl about her shoulders so that he could see her broadly smiling face. He noticed too that she glanced quickly up and down the road to be sure that no one was in sight. He knew that she would have come into his house if he had asked her. She had heard of the gringo camped alone and she was interested. But he only exchanged a few words with her, and she commended him to God and went her way.

In the next few days several others passed his door. Each of them greeted him, stopped and chatted. Each of them raised his hopes a little, for any one of them might have been the bearer of a message. But he had been there nearly a week before the message came. It was brought by a boy of about twelve who accepted an invitation to eat, and ate in shy silence. Just before he left he took a letter out of the front of his shirt, handed it to Jean and departed.

The letter was from the abogado, Don Solomon Sandoval, a man he knew by reputation. It requested him, in terms of formal politeness, to call on the lawyer that afternoon at four and to drink a copita with him. In form it was only a social gesture, but Jean knew that now he was going to learn his fate.

Sandoval was a somewhat unusual figure in Taos in that he was not native-born but had come from Mexico City a good many years before. He was said to be not a Mexican but a Spaniard who had been brought by his father from Madrid and educated for the law. His legend was that he had been a brilliant practitioner, with a gift for intrigue, who had found it advisable to leave the capital for reasons not wholly to his credit. It was difficult otherwise to account for the presence of such a man in this country, which had been for two hundred years a remote and neglected outpost of the Spanish power. In Taos the abogado found little practice in the courts, but he nevertheless had become a man of power, chiefly because of his association with the great and all-powerful Padre Martinez. No one knew exactly what his relation was to the Padre. Padre Martinez had many agents and henchmen, not only in Taos but all over the territory. Although it was believed that he had conspired to drive the Americans out of

New Mexico after the conquest, he had not lost in prestige since then. The Padre was a man of truly great intelligence as well as one who loved power for its own sake. He had always hated gringos but he was too intelligent not to accept inevitable change. He was also too astute not to see that power can be won under one government as well as another. For thirty years he had held more power in New Mexico than any one man because he not only dominated the Church and all of the great land-owning families, but also commanded the allegiance of the poor, and especially of the Penitentes Hermanos, the bloody brotherhood, who crucified one of their own number every Good Friday. They were the only organized power among the poor. It was known that he preached in many of their Moradas. He also periodically protested the heavy tithes which the Church laid upon the poor. The tithes had never been lifted but the Padre had always stood forth as a defender of the poor, and as one to whom they could always come for help.

A man who commands the allegiance of both high and low is a man to fear and the Padre was feared. Moreover, a man who commands numbers as well as money has in his hands the making of a first-class political power in the best American model. The Padre had not overlooked that fact either. Of late he had betrayed a strange friendliness toward some Americans.

Jean Ballard, who had a natural gift for keeping his ear close to the ground and listening to the rumble of rumor, was aware of all this, but not at all sure how it bore upon his own destiny. He knew the abogado would very likely be speaking for the Padre as well as for the Coronels, that what happened now might well be a matter of policy as well as a family affair. He was aware that he, Jean Ballard, was now in some sense a part of a conquering power. But he could not imagine what weighty conferences might have taken place, what decisions might have been reached. Whether he faced a warning or a welcome was any man's guess. As he saddled his horse for the trip to town he was tense with the feeling that he went to meet one of the decisive moments of his life.

The abogado was formally known as Licenciado Don Solomon Sandoval, but to a great many who did not like him he was known behind his back as El Coyote. A coyote, in Mexican parlance, is a negotiator, one who arranges difficult matters and always for a price. All Mexican society abounds in coyotes and of many different kinds and degrees. For the Mexicans are not a direct people, they are deviously and elaborately indirect. They love both ceremony and intrigue for their own sakes, and they hate the blunt and the obvious. So the professional go-between has a large part in their lives. Jean Ballard had learned long since that almost anything may be arranged in a Mexican town if you can find the right coyote. If you see a girl in the plaza who gives you a meaning smile, it would be a rank breach of etiquette to approach her, but a perfectly correct procedure to make discreet inquiries about her. A long series of such inquiries might very well lead to someone who could arrange something very interesting. Jean Ballard had anointed the palms of a good many coyotes in the course of his social life and he had also had some business dealings with them. Before the American occupation it had been against the law for Americans to trap beaver in Mexican streams. All of the streams were trapped, of course, but this was always arranged by an elaborate system of briberies in which one never saw the final recipient of the bribe. Silver traveled from hand to hand, dwindling on its way, until it got to the right place. Because he spoke Spanish so well and was so patient and polite, Jean had arranged these matters for most of the trapping expeditions in which he had taken part. So he knew much about coyotes in general, but he had never dealt with such a mighty and subtle coyote as this Sandoval, who might indeed be a very high-class pimp on occasion, but on other occasions was nothing less than a minor ambassador. Only God and perhaps Padre Martinez knew what the abogado was about.

Jean knew that Consuelo Coronel was not the first girl of high family who had bestowed herself informally upon the man of her choice. In theory such a thing was impossible, but in practice it was known to happen. It was in fact the only mode of rebellion open to women in a society where they had no rights, where their destinies were arranged for them, sometimes when they were still in the cradle. The fact that the women were set to watch each other left a perceptible loophole in a wall of custom that was supposed to be impassable. When it was found that a girl of important family had improbably and shockingly violated the most important of all proprieties, there was a great disturbance within the afflicted family but never any open scandal. Those great earthen houses kept their secrets well. The matter was likely to come to the attention of the Padre but not of anyone else. For every marriage had to be sanctioned by the Church. If the union was suitable, marriage would usually be arranged. The bride would be likely to go away for a long visit and to return with her first-born in her arms. It was never good form to inquire about the age of a baby in any case. When the marriage was not deemed suitable the girl was even more sure to disappear for a while. It would be known that she had entered a convent, usually in Durango or Chihuahua. Sometimes a girl never came back. She became the bride of Christ. More often she did return, a more dutiful daughter, and there was one more child in a great household swarming with children, in a society where adoption was common custom. All of these things were well and discreetly managed. There was a method and precedent for almost everything.

In this instance the unprecedented thing, as he well understood, was that a gringo trapper had penetrated to the holiest of all holy places—that an alien seed had been planted in the sacred flesh of the right people, who had so long guarded their blood from such contamination that by this time almost all of them were blood relations. It was only by chance and daring that he had come among them, and his presence in the house of Coronel had doubtless been a subject of comment and suspicion for months. So it was not hard for him to imagine that he was about to receive bad news.

What he feared most was that Consuelo had already been sent away. In that case it might be impossible even to discover where she was. He might be politely informed that it would be useless for him ever to try to see her again, and that any inquiries about her would be rather more than indiscreet. For all of this to be conveyed to him in graceful hints, over a drink, with many good wishes—that would be typical of this people who loved good form and hated invaders, whether they came with guns or with exigent desires. . . . He could also imagine the abogado might be playing a game of his own, wholly unauthorized. He had no idea how corrupt the man might be, nor yet how much he knew. Without knowing more than he could infer from gossip he might be planning something like blackmail. When it came to creating a situation full of vague promise and polite delay, the Mexicans were artists. In this respect, as in others, there was something feminine about all of them.

So Jean went to face the abogado, alert, tense and suspicious, but determined to be polite and patient. He knew a rash word, a premature demand, a touch of irritation now could ruin everything. He knew also that he was about to hear a great many words. The abogado was famous for his eloquence. Like many cunning men he was fundamentally reticent and superficially verbose. Jean knew he would have to extract a fateful meaning from a cloud of vague and beautiful language.

At the abogado's house he was admitted as always by a portero, who led him across a courtyard and into a small square room which was plainly an office, a place of business. It was furnished only with a heavy homemade table of pine and two small chairs. Shelves against the wall held great heavy books, bound in leather and covered with a fine dust, which suggested that the labors of the abogado were not primarily intellectual.

As he expected he had a long interval in which to stretch his legs and listen to the buzz of a few flies. Then a woman entered and placed upon the table a fine glass decanter, filled with amber El Paso brandy, and two small silver cups without handles. There was another brief interval before the abogado made his entrance, beaming, hand outstretched. He was a short stout man in his fifties, very dark, bald on top of his head, with a fine rudder of a nose, faintly empurpled by the brandy he drank on all occasions, and small dark eyes under coarse heavy brows. He wore a coat of blue broadcloth with brass buttons and a high black stock—a formal and somewhat unusual attire for that country.

"You give me great pleasure," he announced. "Please to be seated."

After a few polite inquiries he poured two cups of brandy, offered one to Jean with a gesture across the table, and took the other himself. He gazed at it fixedly, as old topers often do, for a long thoughtful moment. It was customary seldom to lift a cup without a toast, especially when greeting a stranger, and the abogado was doubtless considering one.

"To health and money and the time to enjoy them," he proposed. It was a common toast, widely used. Jean nodded his thanks and they drank, the abogado taking his liquor with a single, swift gulp.

"By the way," he inquired, "how much money have you?"

Jean was a little surprised by the blunt directness of this attack. But he thought he understood. He was now wholly at the mercy of Sandoval. The abogado wanted to make this clear in the beginning, and also that his services were not to be had for nothing. Even if the news was all bad it was going to cost something. It would never do to resent this, to betray any suspicion, to bargain. Jean laughed with an affectation of great good humor, pulled out a small buckskin bag full of silver and tossed it on the table.

"I have only a few pesos here," he said, "but you know I can get more."

The abogado nodded solemnly several times.

"Yes," he agreed. "I know that. I know a great deal about you because I have made it my business to learn. I know that in Santa Fe you are highly regarded—by the merchants, by the freighters, by the army—by all who have dealt with you. I know that many men would give you money for the asking and take your word as bond. It is fortunate for you that I know these things."

Jean nodded his thanks.

"Your words give me the greatest of pleasure," he said. And this time he was not lying.

"For the service I am about to render you," the abogado spoke gravely, "money is no recompense. It is a mere token—the souvenir of a great occasion. What I count upon is your enduring friendship."

Again Jean nodded with the slow motion of solemn assent.

"My friendship is yours," he said, "and my purse is at your disposal."

"Let us say two hundred pesos in gold," the abogado proposed. "I ask no more than your word. I am a professional man and I live by the services I render my friends."

"You have my word," Jean assured him, "and you shall have the money as soon as I can get it. My compadre is even now selling mules and peltries in Santa Fe."

The abogado dismissed the crudities of financial consideration with a careless wave of the hand. He refilled the two cups with brandy and again, for a portentous interval, he gazed into the amber depths of his potion, as though searching for suitable words. Again he lifted his drink and this time his eyes were raised in reverence above the face of his guest, as though he addressed himself to the divine as well as the human.

"I drink to the welfare of your soul," he intoned, "to your repose in the bosom of God, to your eternal bliss in paradise."

This burst of pious eloquence made Jean blink at his brandy in sudden surprise, left him without a reply. But the next words of the abogado enlightened him and also warmed him with new hope.

"Are you a member of the Church?" he inquired.

Jean knew well that if he ever married Consuelo it would be in a Catholic church and as a member of it. The Church meant nothing to him, but he was perfectly willing to join anything if only he could also join Consuelo. He shook his head slowly as one who expresses a deep regret.

"I have lived far from churches," he said. "But my beloved mother was a French Catholic."

This last was evidently a fortunate word and a fortunate circumstance. For the first time he saw in the eyes of Sandoval something like a genuine response.

"Then you truly belong to the Holy Faith by birth and by right," he said. "The church of your mother is forever the home of your soul."

Jean bowed his head as one receiving a benediction, wholly

unable to match the abogado's words but completely alert to all of his meanings.

Sandoval now poured brandy for a third time, and Jean watched him with a feeling that fateful words impended as the abogado lifted his cup.

"I drink to the prosperity of your family, to the health of your children, to the beauty of your wife."

He delivered this one with a broad smile.

"But I am not a married man," Jean objected, giving grin for grin.

"No," the abogado agreed, looking thoughtfully at his empty cup. "But you are going to be, as surely as you live." His words, spoken slowly, contained the delicate implication of a double meaning. They were followed by a long pause. Jean felt that for the first time it was his lead.

"You speak the very words of my hope," he said, feeling his way with caution. "I have truly longed for a family, for a beautiful wife, for one whom you may know . . ."

The abogado nodded his approval, at the same time lifting a hand, as though to intimate that enough had been said.

"I am aware," he replied, "that during the summer you paid court to the Señorita Consuelo Coronel, but wholly without success."

"I waited upon the Señorita long and wholly in vain," Jean agreed.

"The Señorita herself perhaps was unable to make up her mind," the abogado suggested.

"She remained completely undecided." Jean spoke with the gravity of one who had borne a great disappointment.

"Her parents, perhaps, did not look with complete favor upon your suit," the abogado continued.

"The sentiments of her esteemed parents were not made known to me," Jean told him.

"You departed, no doubt, without hope, but with a great

longing in your heart," the abogado prompted, as though the case had to be completely stated in terms of the most perfect propriety.

"You read my heart like a book," Jean replied, his face rigid with a determination to play this comedy as long as necessary. "Have you any word of hope for me?" he ventured.

The abogado again executed his solemn nod.

"I am authorized to inform you that if you should renew your suit, it might be more favorably considered, both by the Señorita and by her parents, my very esteemed friends."

At this point Jean gave way to his one weakness as a man of manner—an irrepressible propensity to laugh in moments of relief and triumph. His laugh shocked and startled a good many people. It was a deep, explosive laugh that sprang from the bottom of his belly and went off like a clap of thunder, shaking him all over, turning his face red and bringing tears to his eyes. It revealed suddenly a latent power which was generally masked in caution and patience.

His whole relation to Consuelo had been a series of laughing triumphs and this, he knew, was the final triumph. Now he knew that she had won her battle. His laughter relieved a tension that had held him for months, and he was wholly unable to restrain it, although he could see that it shocked the abogado as though a gun had gone off in his face. It destroyed suddenly the perfect propriety, the solemn pretense of their interview. It seemed to make a mockery of the whole business. The abogado looked hurt and astounded, but even so it was seconds before Jean could control his voice.

"I ask your pardon," he said at last, and for the first time he spoke with honesty. "I have suffered long from doubt and anxiety. Your words give me great joy. I thank you and I ask your advice. How should I proceed?"

The abogado looked somewhat mollified. He rose and extended his hand, indicating that the interview was over.

"You are at liberty to call upon the Señorita whenever you wish," he said. "I can assure you of a welcome."

— 3 —

Jean Ballard dismounted before the house of Coronel and tied his horse, just as he had done so often before. The old portero greeted him without the faintest note of surprise in his voice and Choppo barked and leaped to lick his hand. Again he sat down alone in the great sala, which was just as it had been except that now a bright new fire of fat pine blazed red in each of the two corner fireplaces.

He heard her step and rose to meet her. For a moment they stood staring at each other as though neither could quite believe in the reality of this meeting. Then she rushed into his arms, laid her face upon his chest and burst into tears. He could feel the bulge of his unborn child pressing against his body.

"Oh, Juanito!" she cried when she had regained control of her voice. "It has not been easy! They tried to tell me you would not return. . . . I told them you would return if you lived. . . ."

He held her off, looking at her with admiration.

"What else did you tell them?" he asked.

"I told them I would marry you if I had to climb over walls to do it," she replied. "And I also told them that if they harmed you I would scratch their eyes out."

The lovers were left alone for only a few minutes. This was now a family occasion, a ceremonial one, with exact and invariable requirements. The Doña made her entrance next and there was no hesitation about her and no sign of either grief or embarrassment. She waddled right up to him, enfolded him in her great arms and received his kiss upon her brow.

"My son!" she said, and she said it with a possessive warmth and finality which made him sure he had had one friend at court.

The rest of the family then came trooping in, the younger girls first, the Don and his two sons bringing up the rear. The girls walked into his arms and received his kiss with untroubled grace and not the slightest reluctance, but the men looked as unhappy as though they had faced a firing squad. For the Don, especially, this was visibly a painful occasion. He swallowed hard, smiled rigidly, and his Adam's apple ran up and down his throat like a frightened squirrel. Nevertheless, he knew the requirements of the occasion and he was not a man to shirk his ceremonial duty. He embraced Jean, patted him on the back and kissed him twice, once on each cheek. Then each of the sons stepped forward and went through the same performance with the same stiff reluctance. Afterward there was a moment of embarrassed silence. All the necessary gestures had been made and no one knew what to do next.

Jean Ballard looked all around the room.

"What?" he demanded. "No one else to be kissed?"

His eyes fell upon the little dog standing at his feet, his eager tail seeming to wag his whole body. Jean stooped and picked him up in one hand.

"Choppo!" he exclaimed, "I almost forgot you!"

He lifted the dog to his face and Choppo caressed his nose with a quick pink tongue. Everyone laughed and the tension and uneasiness seemed to dissolve in their laughter. Then the Doña clapped her hands, a woman came in with steaming chocolate, and Jean Ballard sat down as a member of the house of Coronel.

VIRGIN EARTH

THE watershed of the Dark River lies on the eastern slope of the southern Rockies, where the mountains reach down from their bald rocky summits in long wooded ridges to the edge of the great plains. Rio Oscuro, the Mexicans named it, and so it was known when Ballard first saw it, but the Americans changed the name to Dark River. It could be called a river only in the Southwest, where any stream that carries water all the year around is a river. In fact, it is only a large trout stream which runs about twenty-five miles from its source to the foot of the mountains and then sinks back into the earth. It rises in a little lake at the foot of a peak above timber line, beginning as a bright thread of water creeping among the roots of the grass, then plunging suddenly into a long, dark, narrow canyon, alternately foaming through rocky gorges and disappearing into forests of spruce so dense that sunlight barely touches the water. This long dark cleft in the country is what gave the river its name. But below the box canyon, as the mountain men called such a gorge, the river emerges into a valley that widens as it falls toward the plain, the ridges dwindling and parting on either hand, the spruce giving way to tall forests of yellow pine, the stream running under a covert of wind-rippled willow, through open meadows, with here and there a tall perfect fir offering shade and shelter.

In this month of September, after the heavy rains of late summer, the country was at its best. On the upland meadows the short grass was so thick it felt like a heavy-piled carpet under the feet, and it was richly colored with the late blooming flowers of the high country. Down in the valley the wild oats would brush the belly of a deer and the river ran full and clear, with feeding trout marking perfect circles on the smooth green pools. The wild turkeys with their well-grown broods had come down into the canyons to hunt grasshoppers in the tall grass. Up on the ridges the black-tail bucks were thrashing the velvet off their new-grown antlers, getting ready for the season of lust and battle. Higher up in thick timber the bull elk were beginning to bugle. Black bears were feeding like pigs in the berry patches, turning over logs and rocks in search of ants and grubs, laying on fat against the winter sleep. The whole country was astir with the autumn business of feeding and breeding, in the last warm days of the year and under the full September moon.

This was a country that would look good to any man who loved country for its own sake, who wanted only to spread his blankets under a tree and take his meat where he found it. And it would also look good to any man who knew the value of things and wanted to own them and use them, for here was timber enough to build a city and a thousand acres of rich bottom land that could be plowed and irrigated, and range on the lower ridges and down on the flats for thousands of cattle and sheep and horses. Whether a man was looking for peace or for power, whether he loved the earth as it was or wanted to seize it and make it over in the image of his restless desire, this was a country that would stir his blood.

Jean Ballard rode over the divide from the other side of the mountains, crossing the summit twelve thousand feet above sea level, where wild sheep with great curling horns snorted and ran for the peaks, and a golden eagle, on rigid wings, wheeled around the sun. He rode alone, for this was a venture he would not ask anyone to share. He was mounted on his big chestnut and led a pack horse with a light load. His rifle was across the saddle before him and his long knife hung at his belt. For the first time in a year he was back on the trail, feeling alert and alive and glad of solitude and hazard. He rode across the alpine meadows, his horses sinking to their fetlocks in the lush, damp sod, and out upon a rocky spur from which he could overlook the whole of the watershed, spread at his feet like a great map in massive relief. There he pulled up and dismounted and sat down on a rock to look. A rare excitement pounded in his blood. He felt big and tense with hope and desire. For the momentous, the incredible thing was that all he saw, clear down to the wide valley and the vague spread of the plain, was his dominion if he could take it and use it.

— 2 —

For nearly a year he had lived in Taos, in a house his father-in-law had given him, with more servants than he needed and all the easy comfort of a way of life long established. During that period he had learned two things very surely. He had learned that he was profoundly married, for Consuelo held him, flesh and spirit. She had set limits to his life, made him a man who must spend his energy in the narrow circle of a binding attachment rather than scatter it all over the country.

He had also learned that he had married much besides a woman—an estate and a way of life and a social position. He could see that if he stayed in Taos he would become simply a part of the Coronel family and the Coronel domain. He could see also that in the course of years he might become the dominating figure in that great loose aggregation of people and lands and livestock which had grown slowly for generations. The Don was old and neither of his sons was a man of much ability. All three of them had begun by ignoring him with a politeness that covered a certain antagonism, but he had gradually won their confidence. He had made something of the slow conquest which the strong always make over the weak, which begins in resentment and ends in dependence.

In particular, they had begun to turn to him in time of emergency. The routine of their lives and their business they managed well enough. In fact, their great estate, as he had come to understand, almost managed itself. Everything was done according to habits and customs which had been established for nearly a hundred years. Every spring the great sheep herds were gathered and sheared and then driven to the mountains for summer range. Every fall they were brought back down to the flats for the winter, moving just ahead of the snow. Every spring also the irrigating ditches were dug out clean and the water gates were repaired and the fields were plowed and planted. Every fall there was a period of reaping with long rows of men swinging their scythes across the fields and others binding the grain and loading it into carts. Then came the ancient ritual of threshing, still done here as it had been done for a thousand years, with horses and mules driven round and round a circular threshing floor to beat the grain from the straw, and men and women tossing it into the wind to winnow it clean. It was a slow and laborious business which required a great many horses and mules and men and women and boys, and it might now have been somewhat improved, but there was no need to improve it, for these people had more peons and slaves than they knew what to do with. Moreover, tradition was sacred. This whole great aggregation, from top to bottom, was imbued with the love of the past and moved by the power of habit. No one wanted to suffer the pain of change, nor yet the sweat of hurry.

Not that the Coronels were idle people. All three of the men were much in the saddle, riding over their great domain, shouting orders to men who scampered like rabbits at the sound of their voices, knelt at their feet in supplication when they were displeased. On their splendid horses they were striking figures, erect and assured, exercising a godlike power over their henchmen and sometimes a godlike and condescending mercy. But Jean had come to understand that if they had stayed quietly at home everything would have gone on much the same, not only because everything was done at a certain time and in a certain way according to immutable custom, but also because the important men in the organization were a few trusted and able peons. All of these were organized like an army with definite rank, hard won and jealously guarded. So all of the sheep were under one man who was responsible only to the Don and needed few orders from him. He was the Mayodomo, the commander-in-chief. Under him was a certain number of caporals, each of whom had charge of three herds, and each herd was under an ayudante, who in turn had a couple of boys to assist him. It was an ancient hierarchy, in which men began as boys and worked their way up according to their seniority and their ability. The men of high rank were truly experts in their own way and they were supported by a great tradition. They had a loyalty to sheep which was second only to their loyalty to God. Many a caporal had laid down his life rather than desert his herds in a snowstorm, and many of them also had lost their lives to marauding Apaches.

It was the Mescalero Apaches who first gave Jean Ballard a chance to show his usefulness. Almost every fall, when the fat sheep came down from the mountains, the Mescaleros would make a raid, sometimes killing a man or two and always running off with a small herd of fat wethers. They openly boasted that they took what they needed. What could anyone do? You never knew when the Apaches would strike, and no one could catch an Apache in the mountains. Moreover, this sort of thing had been going on, like everything else, for about a hundred years. Every year a certain number of sheep were lost to the Apaches, just as a certain number were lost to wolves. It was in the nature of things. But Jean Ballard knew a great deal about Apaches, he was itching for action, and he regarded nothing as immutable. The sheep herders were armed only with bows and arrows and slingshots. Jean armed half a dozen carefully chosen men with good guns, which was in itself against all precedent, for the peons had always been kept unarmed. He did this on his own account and despite some feeble expostulation on the part of the Don. He knew about when the Apaches would strike. He learned that they had struck within a few weeks of the same time every year since the fall of the Spanish Empire. He then further violated custom by going out and camping with his carefully planted herd of sheep, sharing the beans and tortillas of his men, keeping all arms carefully concealed, setting a watch every night. When the Apaches struck at dawn, as they always did, they met a roar of rifle fire. Three of them fell and were scalped by the delighted peons, who had been thirsting for Apache blood all their lives.

This feat made a deep impression, not only on the Coronels but on the whole of Taos. "Killing Apaches" had long been a proverbial metaphor for telling boastful lies. Many men claimed to have killed an Apache but hardly anyone could produce an authentic Apache scalp to prove it. A man who truly killed Apaches, and brought home their hair, was a man of might. Jean found that he had suddenly grown in importance, and not only among the aristocrats. The peons began coming to him instead of to the Don when they needed help.

They had discovered that he had the peculiarity of doing what he said he would do, and immediately. They also began calling him Don Juan Ballárd, with the accent on the last syllable.

Don Juan Ballárd! The name would stick. He would lose his very identity. He would cease to be Jean Ballard and become a Mexican gentleman, riding the family acres, shouting commands to scampering men. His life had always been a thing of change and hazard, a continuous thrust against the unknown. Now he found himself staring down a long straight corridor of years without hope of struggle or surprise. The comfortable happiness of his marriage had been invaded by a growing boredom and restlessness.

— 3 —

The Don had moved rather slowly in the matter of a dowry. There would of course be a dowry. The daughter of a great family would always bring something to her husband, even if he too was a person of property. When she had married a man who did not own an acre, some sort of endowment was deemed a necessity. So the Don had given the young couple a house and a small amount of land in the valley.

Concerning the provisions he had made for his daughter and his son-in-law he was at once a little vague and a little apologetic, but Jean did not find it hard to understand the Don's intention and feeling. He wanted his daughter to be secure and there would never be any doubt about that. Jean would have his part in the management of the estate as a whole and his share in its abundant proceeds. It produced grain and mutton and wool enough for all and to spare. But the Don wanted above all for his great house and his valley lands and his sheep herds to descend to his sons, and most of it to his eldest son. Both Spanish and Mexican law would have made this compulsory under the rule of primogeniture. Since the American conquest, it was no longer so, but the Don had no intention of deviating from ancient custom or impairing the might and importance of his dynasty. He would bequeath his daughter nothing and give her little, so far as the Taos estate was concerned. But there was another part of the family heritage which had long lain unused. In fact neither the Don nor his sons had ever even seen it, and neither of the younger men was likely ever to make any use of it. This was a royal grant of lands on the other side of the mountains, which had been bestowed upon the family in the late eighteenth century, when the Don was a child. In a conference with Jean, he produced the deed to the grant, embossed on parchment, bearing the royal seal, with a certain pride and flourish. It was proof of the great and ancient importance of his family. He explained how the grant had been confirmed, after the revolution of 1821, by the Mexican government, and now, only a year before, by the American government. Governments come and go but property is sacred.

This grant was one of a series of similar grants which His Most Catholic Majesty, the king of Spain, had bestowed upon certain loyal subjects in New Mexico, only about thirty years before those loyal subjects had revolted against him and set up the Mexican Republic. At the time the grants were made the Spanish Empire was already a tottering power, both in Europe and in America. In America it was menaced from the east, both by the wild tribes and by the growing power of the United States on the eastern seaboard. It had been foreseen that sooner or later the enterprising Americans would cross the plains, first as traders and then, most probably, with an army. The plan was to establish on the eastern side of the mountains a long line of great haciendas which would act as a buffer against both wild Indians and even more dreaded whites.

Had the Spanish power survived and thriven, this plan might have been carried out. There would then have been garrisons of Spanish troops to protect the settlers. But the Spanish power had fallen and the government of the Mexican Republic had been nothing but a series of revolutions, so frequent and sudden that even a well-informed man seldom knew who was president at a given moment. New Mexico was a remote province and it had become almost a forgotten one. Who was going to cross the mountains and settle these lands, without military protection or escort, without in fact any kind of governmental backing whatsoever? Manifestly, no one. None of the owners of these grants had ever seen them. Their very existence was half-forgotten. Stretching all the way from the Cimarron in the north to the Capitan in the south, they remained just a part of the wilderness. To their owners each of them was only a beautiful sheet of parchment, enscrolled in three colors, signed by a monarch, worth in cash exactly nothing.

The Don was candid about all this. He made it perfectly clear that he did not expect his son-in-law to do anything with the grant or even to look at it. That whole country had long been a hunting ground for the most dangerous savages. A man could hardly hope to enter it and come back with his hair.

Just now the grant was without use, but the Don expatiated eloquently on its future possibilities. The Santa Fe Trail passed only a few miles east of the foot of the mountains. Settlers were coming to New Mexico in greater numbers every year. In ten years or in twenty these lands might acquire value. Even if Jean never saw them they would be a magnificent bequest for his children.

Jean listened and nodded his dignified thanks. He understood perfectly what the Don thought he was doing. He was keeping the farm for his sons and giving his gringo son-in-law the briar patch.

Jean betrayed no emotion then or later but he felt a sudden stirring conviction that his destiny had been revealed to him. Ever since his marriage he had felt as though he were waiting for something. Now he was suddenly sure it had come. For he knew the Dark River country where the grant was located. He had camped once, nearly ten years before, in the lower valley, and had seen those great rich meadows along the stream and the stands of virgin pine on either side. The limits of the grant were vague, for they were designated only by reference to peaks and watercourses, but it was clear at least that the lower valley and the pine forests and the rich grazing lands were included, and this was the vital heart of the region. Here was truly a royal gift if a man could use it. And Jean felt a calm confidence that if any man in the Southwest could go into the Dark River Valley and stay there, he was that man. For he not only knew the country but he knew as much as any white man did about the Ute Indians, who claimed the valley as their hunting ground.

When it came to making any use of the grant, the Indians were of course the problem. Whichever way you turned, in the New Mexico of that day, the Indians were the problem, and this had been true for more than two hundred years. When the Spaniards first came to the valley they had fought a great war with the Pueblos and had conquered them, but that had been the last as well as the first of their conquests over the Indians. The Pueblos had long since become a part of the valley civilization, owning their own lands, supplying the province with fruit and pottery. Within the valley, life had become fairly secure for the great landowners in their great houses. The wild tribes had no need or desire to assault these. But neither government nor conquest had ever been extended so much as five miles beyond the valley and a few other bits of arable land. New Mexico was, in fact, only a narrow green strip of civilization in a vast wilderness dominated by savages. The Apaches and Navajos to the south, the Utes and Arapahoe in the north, contained it in a kind of loose, informal siege. The northern Indians, for the most part, stayed away in the wilderness, making only an occasional raid, but also making the high mountains of the north an impassable barrier. The Apaches and Navajos, on the other hand, had become proud and powerful peoples, who levied tribute rather than made war, and went in for rape, murder and kidnaping as incident and sport. The Navajos had been stealing Mexican sheep for over a century and had founded large sheep herds of their own with stolen stock. They boasted that they took what they wanted and left the rest for seed. The Apaches made annual raids into Chichuahua, stealing herds of mules and horses, which they brought north and sold in New Mexico. Often the same stock was stolen again and sold in the south. The Apaches laughed at Mexicans, and some of them had grown rich in silver and blankets. Both they and the Navajos had captured many Mexican women and children. Some of these had become good Indians and some had been ransomed for heavy prices in silver and livestock. It was all a disgraceful situation and it had become worse since the fall of the Spanish power. Nor had the American army so far done anything to make it better. The American soldiers stayed in Santa Fe, playing Monte and courting Mexican girls.

What Jean Ballard proposed to himself, then, was a revolutionary move, a major feat in pioneering. He proposed to do what the Spanish government had intended, when it made those royal grants. He proposed to carry civilization across the mountains and plant it on the edge of the great plains, which must some day become a part of it.

He did not put the matter to himself in such terms. He was

not a man of words nor yet one with a conviction of personal importance. But he did feel that quickening of the whole being, that jump of blood and clutch of gut which every man feels when he faces a major challenge of his destiny. For this task, it seemed, had been presented to him by a most improbable fate. And for this task, it seemed, he had been training for years. Only a mountain man, such as he, could go into that country at all. The beaver trappers were the only men who had traversed the mountains, had learned how to travel and live in them, which was no small art in itself. But the mountain men had built nothing and conquered nothing. They had fought Indians when necessary but most of the time they had made friends with Indians, gone to bed with Indian women. Many of them had become more than half Indian themselves. They had penetrated the wilderness and the wilderness had made them its own. They had found the way but that was all.

Jean Ballard was one of those who had found the way. But more than that, he was one of the few men who knew the Ute language, who had lived and traded with the Utes. All of this did not make it easy for him to go into the Dark River country, much less to settle there. The Utes were as elusive as deer and as unpredictable as summer rain. Moreover, he knew that they had left their ancient range, devasted by American whisky and Mexican smallpox, in search of a place where they might be let alone. They were not going to welcome any intruder. But at least he could hope to parley with them if he could reach their camp, and he had great confidence in his ability to deal with Indians. He felt as though a job had been laid in his lap for which he was especially qualified, and at a time when all of his energies yearned for use.

This conspiracy of circumstance, with everything pointing one way, was what thrilled and moved him. It was the unformulated philosophy of his life to wait patiently for the ripe moment and then seize it. And the ripe moment he had always known, not so much by careful consideration, as by a slow and steady gathering of impulse and conviction—a growing, undeniable need of action. So he had felt when he launched his boat on the Ohio and again when he started across the plains. So he felt now. The springs of action were tightening within him. The finger of destiny again pointed the way.

It was characteristic of him that he moved slowly and said little. He waited until early fall because he knew then it would be easiest to find the Indians. He broached the subject to the Don in the most casual manner. He was going on a little trip into the mountains, he said. He might be gone a month. Where was he going? He might drop across the divide and have a look at the grant. Since it was his, he felt curious about it.

The Don was at once uneasy. By this time he was quite friendly to Jean, but always a little afraid of him. He instinctively knew his son-in-law for the kind of man who is apt to do new and startling things. The Don lived for the loving repetition of the familiar. He did not like new ideas of any kind. Moreover, like all Mexicans, he feared the mountains. He was a creature of the valley. Mountains were mystery and danger. He was in favor of leaving them alone. Of what use, he inquired, to make such a trip?

Jean did not want to alarm anyone or commit himself to anything. It would be useful at least to take a look at the country. No one knew even what was there.

"But you cannot go alone," the Don objected. "If you must go, take a dozen men with rifles, as you did when you met the Apaches."

Jean smiled and shook his head. He knew that if he went into the country with an armed band, he would never even see the Utes, unless they felt strong enough to drive him out. He reminded the Don he had been going about the mountains for thirteen years. He knew what he was doing. Mountain travel was his profession. This was just a casual jaunt to him.

The Don was far from satisfied but he did not know what to say or do. In this situation he inevitably confided in his wife and his sons. Inevitably the matter led to a family conference, for to the Coronels everything was a family matter. Jean found himself facing them all, alone against the field, painfully conscious that he would never be truly one of them— that he had married into an alien race. They did not sympathize at all with his restlessness, his curiosity, his need of action and conquest. But that was not all. He knew what worried them most. They were afraid he might take their darling daughter and go into that wild country to live—or try to live. That, of course, was exactly what he hoped to do, but he hated to disclose his whole intention to anyone until it became necessary to do so. If he went into the Dark River country and could not find the Utes, or if he found himself dodging arrows and riding for his life, then it was useless to go back—at least for the present. He had hoped to play carefully and keep his cards close to his chest. But he knew now they were going to force his hand. It was the Doña, a far more formidable person than her husband, who took the offensive.

"You know you cannot go to that country and live," she told him. "So what is the use of going at all?"

He could not quibble any longer.

"If I can find the Utes and make an agreement with them," he said, "I can go back and build a house—and I will."

"But that is impossible!" Her voice was tremulous with rising emotion. "For a man it is bad enough, but to take a woman with a young child in her arms. . . . No! It is too much!"

Jean sat silent and miserable but unyielding. Everyone

looked very grave. The Doña gulped her tears and resumed the attack.

"I called you my son!" she wailed. "I took you to my heart as a son! And now, and now. . . . No! I cannot bear it!" She buried her face in her hands, wept gently for a moment, then wiped her eyes and sat stubbornly shaking her head.

Everyone was looking at Consuelo. It became suddenly clear to all that the issue was hers to decide. No one knew it better than Jean. He had told her only that he planned a short trip across the mountains to look at the grant. She had said only, "But that would be dangerous." He had told her no, it would not be dangerous. She had not questioned him. She had learned that his reticence was often impenetrable. But now she knew what he intended. And now, once more, she held his destiny in her hands.

He could go into the Dark River Valley alone. She could not stop him. He could even compel her to go along if he decided to settle there. But to drag a reluctant woman into that country would be worse than fighting Utes every day. Moreover, he knew that he was not going to drag Consuelo anywhere, be his rights what they might. Like many another strong man, he felt equal to almost any kind of opposition except that of his wife. If the Dark River Valley was conquered, it would be as much her conquest as his. So he sat looking at her now, knowing his fate was for her to decide, just as he had sat looking at her in this same room, over a year ago, waiting for the moment that only she could create.

Consuelo knew her power and she loved it. That he had learned more than once. She also loved a dramatic situation. So now she was in no hurry. She let them all wait for a long moment. She wanted them all to know that she was the heroine of this occasion. Then she rose and went to stand by his side, facing her parents.

"The land is ours," she reminded them. "You gave it to

us." She laid her hand upon her husband's shoulder. "Where he goes, I go!"

Her few words knocked the argument dead in its tracks. No Mexican would deny the right and obligation of a woman to follow her husband, even if he were going toward certain death. They had hoped she would side with them, try to dissuade him. They had hoped she was more a Mexican than a wife. Now they knew they were beaten. The conference broke up in silence, and the two elders went away shaking their heads, as old people have always shaken their heads at the young, in futile dissent.

When they were gone Jean took his wife in his arms.

"You are truly my consolation," he said.

"And you?" she replied, her voice a curious mingling of tenderness and asperity. "You are my Juanito, my little boy who cannot sit still. . . . All the time you are gone I will worry. But this is the last time you go alone. If you return, I go with you!"

— 4 —

From where he sat, just below the top of the divide, Jean could see about a thousand square miles of steep and wooded country. Somewhere in it was a little band of Indians, which he had to find, and these, he knew, were the most elusive Indians in the Southwest. For the Utes were supremely the mountain Indians—the only ones who lived almost wholly in the mountains, ranging to the very summits in summer, descending to the sheltered canyons when the deep snows fell. The great tilted ranges west of the Rio Grande had been their home long before the Spaniards came. There they had lived as a secluded, almost an unknown people. Navajos and Apaches attacked them rarely and never followed them into the high country, for no one could catch a Ute in the mountains. It was like trying to catch a deer by the tail. Far from all routes of travel, they had come into contact with white men little, either in peace or in war, but they had been quick to resent any intrusion. They lived in small, scattered bands. Even a Ute of another band, it was said, did not dare to approach a Ute camp unannounced. The only way to find a Ute was to let him find you.

In the years before the conquest few traders had ever reached the Utes. Jean had been one of those few and that fact was all that made his present quest a hopeful one. Three years in succession he had ridden into the San Juan country with two horseloads of trade goods, had found the Moache band, camped with them for part of a summer, come out with profitable loads of Indian-tanned furs. Jean Ballard was known to the Utes as a good trader, and since his visits to them they had learned much about bad traders. Jean had taken them good iron pots and skillets, knives, cotton cloth, powder and lead—things they needed. He had taken no whisky. He had learned something of their language and had made some friends among them. In particular, he had made a friend of one somewhat unusual Indian, the young chief known as Kenyatch.

Making a friend of an Indian, he had long since learned, was a difficult and peculiar business. You never knew an Indian as you knew a white man. He neither confided in you nor asked you any questions. He did not reveal himself. He did not, in fact, seem to have a self as a white man has one. He existed only as part of a tribe. But an Indian who had not been ruined by contact with dishonest white men was always a good friend in two ways. He would never forget you, any more than a dog or a horse will forget you, and he would keep his word. Each year, when he had left the Moache Utes, Kenyatch had said: "Next year, when the moon is full in July, I will meet you there." And he would designate a certain camping place. Ten months later he would be waiting there, and business would be picked up where it had been dropped ten months before.

Kenyatch, he knew, would remember him—in fact, would remember every swap they had made, almost every word they had exchanged. Moreover, Kenyatch was a man of some power among his own people, and an Indian of unusual experience, for he had lived among the Mexicans. It was said that for a long time the Utes used to trade their own children to the Spaniards for horses. This was not because they did not love their children. All Indians are devoted to their children. But the Utes were poor and they were among the last Indians to acquire horses. They had nothing that was worth as much as a horse except a human being. So they had traded human flesh for horse flesh. Whether Kenyatch had truly been traded for a horse or captured in battle, it was certain that he had belonged for some years to a Mexican family living near Penasco, that he had served them as a sheep herder, and that when he was about sixteen he had stolen their best horse, run away and rejoined his people. As an Indian who knew Mexicans and could speak Spanish, he was a great man to his own people. Whether he was the leader of the Moache band or not, he was a man of influence among them. Jean strongly suspected it was the cunning Kenyatch who had led them into the Dark River country, after the great misfortunes which had befallen them.

Of these misfortunes he knew only by hearsay. He knew that a band of Indian traders of the worst kind had moved into the little Mexican settlement of Abiquiu, on the edge of the Ute country. These traders had sold whisky to the Utes. Whisky was deadly to all Indians, but especially so to these, who had never tasted alcohol. There had been terrible drunken orgies in which Ute had killed Ute. Their leaders had warned the traders away, but young men of the Moaches had sneaked into Abiquiu and bought whisky. Moreover, one of them, returning to his own people, had brought smallpox, probably caught from a Mexican woman. Mexicans had an epidemic of smallpox almost every year. Some of them died but most recovered. Most of the peon Mexicans were deeply pitted by the disease. But few Indians ever recovered from it. More than half of the Moache Utes had died, all in about a week. The survivors had made a great pile of their tepees and blankets and burned them in a huge bonfire. Then they had ridden away across the Rio Grande, in search of a new home, in flight not from battle but from smallpox and whisky—from a civilization which to them was more poisonous than a rattlesnake.

They had gone into the Dark River country because no Indians claimed it and no white man or Mexican ever went there. It had been only a summer hunting ground for various tribes and a place where small hunting parties fought each other when they met. There the Utes would live in constant dread of the Arapahoe. There they would find the winters hard and dangerous. A large band could not have hoped to survive, but this handful of mountain dwellers could do so.

Jean knew these Utes wanted no intruders of any kind. He knew any Mexican who crossed that summit would be a dead Mexican. He knew no trader would dare to cross it. But he also knew that if he could ride into the main Ute camp with his right hand lifted in sign of peace, Kenyatch would greet him as a friend.

He was sure he could find that camp if he were given a few days to look for it. Indians in summer made tiny fires, but a wisp of smoke would show. Also he could find Indian tracks. They would be the tracks of wandering hunters, but any track would lead finally to the camp. In a few days he could find them—but he was not going to have a few days to search. The Utes would find him long before he could find them.

It was amazing how a few Indians could guard a great country. They watched from the high points and nothing moved without their knowledge. They watched the trails for tracks—and there was only one way across the summit. You could no more enter their country undetected than you could walk into a white man's front yard without his knowledge.

Jean knew that hidden eyes would be watching him long before he could reach the lower valley. The Indians were like wild animals in that respect. A man rode through the wilderness, perhaps seeing little life, but the wilderness was always aware of him. A grizzly lifted his sensitive muzzle to sample the wind and moved quietly into the timber. A mountain lion crossed his trail and turned and followed on silent pads, just to watch this strange, noisy mammal on its way. Buzzards spotted him from a thousand feet in the air and came and circled above him to see if he would lie down and die or if something would kill him. Deer and elk knew he was coming long before he appeared. The beat of hoofs telegraphed his approach to exquisitely sensitive ears and the wind carried his identity to noses that were better than eyes.

The Utes would spot him as quickly and almost as far as a buzzard or an eagle. They would find his tracks and know as much as though he had sent them a message. Like other wild things, they would follow and watch, but being men, they would also consider. To a hunting party of young Utes, usually not more than three, he would be a tempting prize, with his two good horses and his rifle. And some of these young men had learned to hate white flesh, and to see it as poison. If they could get close enough, one arrow might do their work. This would probably be against the warnings of their leaders. A white man killed would likely mean more white men coming. But young men are eager and reckless.

More likely, the news of his presence would travel fast and would reach the main camp. He would be followed and watched while his fate was debated. If he only passed through on his way to the plains, perhaps they would let him pass, and he would no more see Indians than he would see ghosts. But if he stayed in the country they would reveal themselves, one way or another. And he was going to stay until they did. He had come on an errand of peace and diplomacy, and his pack horse was loaded with gifts, but he knew that he could not count on peace. He was taking a calculated risk.

This situation made him alert and tense. He was aware of suspense and he knew the suspense would intensify until something happened, but he also knew he could stand it because it was a familiar thing to him.

Most of his trapping years had been spent in Indian country, and often his situation had been just about what it was now. He would know that Indians were watching and would not know whether they were dangerous or not. So he knew exactly what he had to do. First of all, he had to stay in the open and as far from cover as possible. An Indian arrow was seldom effective beyond sixty yards. They might have a rifle or two, but these Moaches were very poor people, would have little powder or lead. Moreover, they were poor rifle shots, chiefly because they got no practice. . . . Stay in the open and keep moving. Ultimately they could come into the open too. And then? Well, it seemed a precarious enterprise but he felt curiously confident. He was a confident man, who always expected to have his way, and also a patient one. If not this time, then some other time. This was his dominion now and he meant to have it.

Before he started down the long drop to the valley he planned his route with care. He was above timber line at first and could see for miles in every direction. Then he reached the Dark River and followed it down a wide, shallow canyon which slowly narrowed and deepened. Presently there was a growth of short dense spruce on either side, but a hundred yards away, so that he still felt safe. As he lost altitude the canyon narrowed and deepened and the spruce crowded closer on either hand, as though it were preparing an ambush for him.

He had begun the descent about noon, and by three o'clock he felt sure he was spotted and watched. It was the old intuitive feeling of danger or presence he had known so often before, but as always he soon saw evidence to confirm his hunch. He saw where a frightened deer had run across the trail, hoofs spread wide and dew claws deep in the soft earth. Something had scared that deer out of the timber on the other side of the canyon. Then far below him, where the first tall timber appeared, he saw a small bunch of turkeys run to the top of a point, launch themselves one by one with a running start and sail beautifully across the open. Turkeys seldom took wing for any animal but a man.

By late afternoon, with the sun already touching the high summits, he was in the last wide open before the river plunged into its deep and wooded gorge. It was too late now to go farther and this was the last safe place to camp. He made his bed under a tree that stood alone in the middle of the open. His horses he hobbled and sat with his rifle in his lap watching them crop thick, ripe grass until dark. Then he tethered them under the tree. They had not fed long enough, but he knew it was "better to count their ribs than their tracks," as the Mexicans say. Even an Indian who wouldn't kill would steal a horse. He made no fire, but chewed dried beef and drank cold mountain water for supper. Afterward he sat with his back against the tree and smoked his pipe. The stream sang and chuckled and seemed to have human voices in it, as mountain water always does to a man who sits alone. A vesper sparrow tinkled his song in the aspen. Far away, down toward the plain, he heard the long, sad howl of a wolf, and briefly remembered back to the rolling Ohio and his mother dying, as he always did when he heard that sound.

Most men would have been crushed by the weight of this black, inhuman solitude, full of hidden eyes hostile or frightened, astir with life that cared nothing for his own. But he was used to it. As long as he could remember he had known moments like this. After months of talk and people and the warm clinging huddle of love, he was even quietly glad of it.

He sat there living in his ears as the light died. After a while he heard the hoot of a great horned owl on one side of the canyon and an answer from the other side. He knew he was probably not hearing owls. Indians used that call for a signal at night. They had been on either side of him all day long and they were with him still. . . . He knocked the ashes out of his pipe and went to bed. Indians never moved at night. They were truly afraid of the dark. But he must wake well before daylight, and he knew that he would, for he could set his mind to end his sleep at any hour.

It seemed only a moment later that he was wide awake, feeling the tingle of the cold hour before the dawn. The big dipper and the North Star told him the time. He was saddled and packed as soon as he could see the sharp tops of the spruce on the ridge above him, and he was climbing out of the canyon by the first full daylight, his horses humping and grunting up the steep grade. For he had to climb far above the canyon now, to get around the gorge, before he could drop into the comparative safety of the meadows below. This was the dangerous part of the journey, and he was almost painfully alert. He was not frightened but he could feel the growing tension in his muscles and his bowels. He began to wish something would happen soon—or at least soon after he got back into the open. Days of this riding with hidden eyes on either side, with the sense of something impending, would wear down any man. He had known men to go into a panic in Indian country, without having seen or heard a thing, and ride madly for the open, smashing through brush and timber like a frightened bear. So he held himself carefully in check. Now and again, when the terrain permitted, he made a wide swing to right or left and then came back to his line of travel, watching his back track at every turn, just as does a wary old buck who knows he is hunted.

By noon he was out of the timber, with a feeling of great relief, and riding through the open meadows at the head of the lower valley. But he was also worried. It began to look as though the Indians might watch him all the way through to the foot of the mountains without showing themselves. He rode swinging his gaze from right to left and all the way around the horizon, watching the ground for tracks, too. He might have to turn in and hunt them on foot. . . . Then, suddenly, he looked to his right where a low grassy ridge lay on the edge of the valley. There, just below the crest, three Indians sat their horses, watching, still as so many rocks. They were true wilderness Indians, such as he had seen long ago on trapping trips, naked to the waist, riding bareback, with full quivers sticking up over their shoulders. They were poised there, like wary wild animals, ready to disappear over the ridge if he made a hostile move.

A warm wave of elation and relief went through his body. He was not at all afraid now, for he understood the situation at a glance. They had been watching him for nearly twenty-four hours. Undoubtedly word of his presence had gone to the main camp, and these men had been sent to bring him in—if he was friendly. They would not make the first move. They were ready for anything.

He swung his horse about, facing them, lifting his right hand in sign of peace. One of the Indians lifted a hand in response, rode forward fifty yards alone, and stopped. Jean rode to meet him, greeted him in his own tongue, saw the quick flicker of surprise and pleasure in his eyes.

"Come and eat," Jean invited, making a gesture toward the level open beside the creek. The Indian grinned and nodded, beckoned to his fellows. Jean turned and rode to his chosen camping place, dismounted and unpacked, started his fire, all without so much as looking at the Indians, just as though this were a meeting long expected—which it was on his part. He was well prepared for this occasion. Shoot if you have to but feed them if you possibly can. That had been his method of dealing with Indians for years. Those who eat together truly become one. There might be white men who would share your food and knife you in the back, but not Indians.

He dug out bread and salt and brown sugar, dried beef and chile for a quick stew, above all coffee. Almost all Indians had learned to love coffee. He brewed a big pot, making it strong, and he cooked enough meat and chile for six white men. These bucks probably hadn't eaten since yesterday. Like all primitive men, they could go days without eating and eat enough at a sitting to last for days. They ate now swiftly and skillfully, licking their fingers clean. They did not talk. For the time being they lived in their bellies. Afterward Jean produced tobacco and corn-husk wrappers and they all smoked. Then the leader rose, pointing to the sun, and they helped him pack. Jean asked only: "Is Kenyatch there?" and the leader nodded. He led the way, Jean following, and the other two behind him. In single file they went up and up, by a route only an Indian could have followed, dropped into the upper canyon of a tributary to the Dark River, followed it clear above timber line. When they topped a low rise, Jean saw the camp in the distance. It was the prettiest Indian camp he had seen in years. There were only a dozen tepees, which meant not more than fifty or sixty Indians—all that was left of the Moaches. The camp was on the far side of a small lake at the foot of a rocky peak, the tepees mirrored in the still blue water, fat horses grazing on the rich upland pasture, brown children playing beside the lake, women working over hides pegged out on the grass. There was no sign of the dirt and rags, the general squalor, that invade an Indian camp so soon when it is near to white men.

The leader shouted and every Indian in sight lifted and turned his head but there was no evidence of surprise. When he dismounted, Kenyatch came forward, holding out his hand in grave welcome.

"You have come to trade?" he inquired.

"No," Jean replied, "I have come bringing gifts and I have come to talk. I have much to tell you."

Kenyatch nodded.

"Will you eat first?" he asked.

"I am not hungry," Jean replied.

Kenyatch led the way to a spot in front of one of the tepees, probably his own. He shouted an order and women came and spread tanned buckskins and a Navajo blanket on the ground. A dozen other men gathered, including three very old, toothless men. All of them greeted him and all sat down. Most of these, he knew, he had seen before. He knew also that these old men would have much to say, not to him, but in private council, for the Utes have great respect for the aged. But he felt more than ever sure that Kenyatch was the top man and this encouraged him. He knew too that he could speak to Kenyatch in Spanish, which most of the others would not understand. Afterward there would be a tribal council. If he could persuade Kenyatch, the young chief might have power enough to persuade the others.

He began quietly, feeling his way, by reminding Kenyatch of his visits to the Moache camp on the other side of the Rio Grande, of those good summers on the great pine-covered mesas, of an elk hunt they had taken together, and a great feast they prepared. Kenyatch nodded, his face curiously sad, like that of a wistful child.

"Those camps and that life are all gone now," he said. "Everything moves on and is lost. Nothing is left of those days now but my words and yours."

"Everything is change," Jean agreed. "And now change is quick. Down there, beyond the foot of the mountains, is the great road from the east. I have been working on it. A few years ago the wagons came in tens. Now they come in hundreds, bringing men who want to stay—farmers and miners and men driving cattle. Go where you will, men are coming, men by the thousand."

"That is why we have come here to the high mountains," Kenyatch said. "The mountains have always belonged to the Utes. We have always been able to live where others would starve or die in the snow. Here we hope to be left alone."

"You will not be left alone," Jean told him. "Men will come even to the high peaks looking for gold. They will drive cattle and sheep into the valleys and cut down the timber on the mesas. There will be fires and the game will be driven out. You have seen it happen before. Unless someone can stop them, it will happen again."

Kenyatch nodded, his face unmoving, except that his mouth set in a hard line.

"Perhaps we can stop them," he said. "We are not afraid to fight."

"You are brave men," Jean agreed. "But you cannot stop them. Where have the Indians ever stopped the Americans? They have stopped the Mexicans, yes, but never the men from the east. The great road down there is like a river. It cannot stop and nothing can stop it."

Kenyatch looked like a man listening to the word of doom.

"What you say is true," he admitted. "We are a lost people. We are not many, like the Navajos and the Apaches, and we do not live behind deserts where white men are afraid to go. The earth is good and it is large, and yet there seems to be no room for us. We are caught here between the valley on one side and the great road on the other. Where can we go? What can save us?"

Kenyatch was truly thinking aloud now, carried away by his own feelings. Jean was quick to seize his opportunity.

"I can save you," he said quietly. "I have come to save you. All this country of the Dark River, from the peaks down to the plains and on both sides of the water, belongs to my father-in-law, Don Tranquilino Coronel. It is a grant to him from the king of Spain. He has sent me to take possession."

Having lived among Mexicans, and being a smart Indian, Kenyatch knew about grants and even about the king of Spain and how he bestowed lands upon his subjects, but like all Indians he found this business of owning the earth a little hard to understand.

"How does your father-in-law own it?" he demanded. "He could not come here and stay alive as we can. No Mexican would dare to come here. The Mexicans all are women. It takes a man to live in the mountains."

Jean had known this would be the sticking point in the argument, and he was prepared for it.

"You are right," he said. "The mountains belong to the Utes because they have always lived in the mountains. I do not want to take the mountains away from you. I want only to build a home in the valley, to pasture cattle on the plains. Because I can claim all of this land I can keep other white men out. I can stand between you and them. I can say to you, here is your hunting ground and it shall be yours always. When the Arapahoe come up from the plains, we will fight them together. When the deep snows fall in the winter, my beef will be yours. I offer you my friendship and I ask for yours. This is my word and you know my word is good."

Kenyatch sat silent for a long moment. His face was more than grave, it was sad. Jean knew well enough what the Indian was thinking. He knew the Utes did not want any white man to enter their country. They wanted only to be left alone. But he knew also that his argument was unanswerable. They would not be left alone. And they knew he would keep his word. That was his whole strength. They distrusted and feared the world of white men, but they trusted him.

Kenyatch rose and held out his hand, indicating that the conference was over.

"We will talk tonight," he said, with a gesture toward the others. "We will give you our word in the morning."

He then led Jean to a small tepee which had been prepared for him, and left him with a grave good night. A little later a woman came bringing an earthen pot filled with a steaming stew of venison and wild turkey. Jean ate largely and stretched out on his blankets, pillowing his head on his pack, puffing his pipe, feeling completely at ease for the first time since he had crossed the crest of the mountains. Athough nothing was decided yet, he felt sure that he had won.

It was only half a personal triumph and he was aware of this. Kenyatch belonged to a dying world; he could hope for nothing but mercy. Jean Ballard belonged to a growing one, young, lusty and ruthless. He was strong because of what stood behind him, filled with the hope and power of those who ride on the wave of change. He was a man who belonged to the moment and the moment belonged to him.

In the morning the matter was quickly concluded, as Jean had felt sure it would be. Kenyatch assembled his little council again and once more Jean stood before it.

"We have talked," Kenyatch said, "and this is our word. If you build a house in the valley, we will be your friends. In return we ask only that you will let no one else settle on the lands you claim, that you will let no other traders come to us, and that you will sell no whisky to our young men. As for food, we will bring you gifts when we have plenty and you may give us what you will."

Jean held out his hand.

"You have spoken well," he said, "and you have my word for all you ask."

Then he turned to his pack and brought out a good rifle, powder and lead, which he presented to Kenyatch. For the others there were knives, beads and iron pots and skillets. Kenyatch gave him in return a beautifully tanned prime buffalo robe. Afterwards, young Indians brought his horses, helped him saddle and pack, and he rode away toward the rising sun.

He rode wholly relaxed now; suspense and struggle were over. It had been easy after all, once the Indians were found. Now he knew they were just a part of his responsibilities, as much so as the cattle he would bring into the valley. They would cost him a certain number of fat beefs every year, they would become more and more dependent upon him, but they would also be his watch dogs—against the Arapahoe, against all invaders.

In the wake of easy triumph came a moment of unwonted depression. For over a year now, everything had come his way, everything had yielded to his touch and his voice. Life had suddenly widened before him. Something in him distrusted all this bounty of fortune. He was a hard-bitten man and knew that life is hard. He felt safest when he saw danger and felt resistance. He knew they were always there.

Once more he rode down into the valley of the Dark River, past the place where he had met the Indians and on down into the wide meadows that lay below. Here his spirits rose again. It was the first time he had looked upon this country in five years and he saw now that it was even better than he had remembered. He had long been a wandering man without house or woman, but he came of a race of men who owned the earth, and he knew its value. He saw now a thousand acres that could be plowed and planted, more than he had thought. He saw how the straight, clean boles of the pine forest marched down a gentle slope to the edge of the valley, and how the flat lands farther down were tinged with the purple of ripe grama grass, the richest forage in the world. Where the stream reached the level prairie there were a few acres of high flat ground fifty feet or so above it. It was a place that might have been designed for the site of house—as great a house as man might wish to build.

He rode to the top of this little plateau, reined in his horse and feasted his eyes upon potential dominion. His eager imagination fenced and planted and builded. This bit of the earth would become whatever he could make it, and here would be no law except his word. He felt again the same thrill of wonder and desire he had known when first he looked over the valley from the crest of the mountains. For what had fallen into his hands was not merely a place to live and cultivate. It was the vital heart of a whole region, a place where men would gather as surely as he made it safe, a place to be ruled as well as owned, a means to power as surely as he had power in him. By chance almost beyond belief a king in Spain had granted him a kingdom.

PART TWO

The Autocrat

THE RECOLLECTIONS OF
JAMES LANE MORGAN

A TRAVELER by stagecoach over the Old Santa Fe Trail in the seventies first saw the Ballard establishment from the crest of a rolling ridge which bounded the Dark River Valley on the north. I think nearly everyone must have seen it, as I did, with a surprise that was almost incredulity. For seven days and nights I had been bumping across a prairie wilderness, jammed into a coach with six other tortured human beings, over a road which was not a road at all but only a terrible scar on the face of the earth, still hub-deep in mud this month of May, with wrecked vehicles rotting beside the wheel tracks and dead mules bloating in the mudholes, with stagecoaches, freight wagons, buckboards and carts fighting their way westward to a chorus of curses, shouts and whips cracking over the sweat-streaked backs of straining animals. Every twenty to fifty miles horses were changed at a station where passengers were given twenty minutes to gobble hardtack and salt pork drowned in its own grease, and to drink coffee black as tar and bitter as defeat. The land we crossed, especially the eastern part of it, looked rich and ripe for the plow, but no one stopped to claim it or cultivate it. In the whole prairie country no one had built anything that was meant to last. The stage stations were shacks or dugouts, just as the track-end towns were literally built in a week and deserted in a year. The impression, especially to one who had known the rather placid beauty of nineteenth century Europe, was that of enormous energy and vitality, but also of a kind of collective insanity. Everyone was rushing frantically somewhere—to Colorado or California or Santa Fe—in search of gold or a quick profit, cursing every delay, sparing neither man nor beast, fighting the very earth as a prostrate but unyielding enemy. No one seemed ever to relax or rest. Life roared, rattled and cursed by day and exploded into drunken laughter and the crash of gunfire at night. Only the prairie, where it rolled away from the road in green billows of waving grass, and the blue mountains that looked over the horizon, seemed to have anything of dignity or permanence.

Then suddenly half a mile away I saw a great house topping a low hill beside a stream—a house large enough to be called a castle, with heavy earthen walls, steep shingled roofs and dormer windows, giving it a resemblance, which many had remarked, to some of the chateaux of northern France. A grove of graceful mountain cottonwoods spread their shade around it and over its walls. Hollyhocks were pink and white behind the picket fence of its dooryard and a plume of blue wood smoke wavered away from its great kitchen chimney. At the foot of the hill many other buildings, mostly of adobe, were strung out along a road that paralleled the stream. The valley both above and below the village was green with well-sprung crops of oats and hay, and riven by the clear, quick stream, flashing among the willows. To the east the mountains lifted heavily wooded shoulders to sheer faces of rock and finally to peaks still tipped and streaked with snow. The place owed its beauty chiefly to the splendid roll and lift and color of the country, but what made it so surprising, gave it somewhat the quality of a dream or a vision at a first and distant look, was simply that someone here had stopped and built and planted, had imagined something and brought it into being, had peopled the wilderness without destroying it.

— 2 —

My own presence at the Ballard grant that day is soon explained.

A New Yorker by birth, I had been educated for the law at Harvard and had afterward spent more than a year in England and on the Continent, indulging a taste for history, which has always rivaled the law in my own interest. My father was a prosperous commission merchant, and when I returned to New York I entered his office as a legal adviser, expecting to spend the rest of my life there. A bad case of pneumonia developed into tuberculosis and brought my business career to a sudden end. I made a partial recovery but my physician assured me the dry air of the Southwest was my only hope of a complete cure. I was determined not to be idle, and my father's business connections in Kansas City enabled him to find me a place of a sort. It was learned that Jean Ballard, the owner of a large and heavily encumbered property in northern New Mexico, required the services of a resident lawyer. After some correspondence, it was agreed that I should visit the Ballard establishment as a guest with the hope that some lasting arrangement might be made.

In that spring of 1878, Ballard had been established in his great house beside the Santa Fe Trail for nearly twenty years. I knew a good deal about his business affairs from my own investigations in Kansas City, but nothing about those years of struggle and success and even less about the strange community they had created. The chief purpose of this memoir is to describe the Ballard kingdom—for it was no less than that— and to bring out its history much as I discovered it, so that the community and its making may be seen as one. Before I left the grant I felt that I understood both Ballard's triumph and his tragedy, and that understanding is what I hope to communicate here.

— 3 —

I was the only passenger who left the stage at the Ballard grant that day. No one appeared to meet me or took any notice of me, although I was aware of a hum and bustle of human activity, of talking and singing voices somewhere in the great house, of moving figures down among the minor buildings, of the distant thud of an ax, the beat of hoofs, the bleat and bellow of livestock. But I was much more aware at first of the painful state of my own anatomy. I stood there before the long front porch kicking the kinks out of my knees, stretching my arms, feeling my ribs, filling my lungs with air. A man released from the stocks or from a strait jacket would not have felt a greater or more needed relief. Then I heard a laugh and looked up and saw a man sitting alone on the porch, with his chair tilted back, his feet on the railing and a cigar between his fingers.

"It's a rough ride," he remarked as he rose and came to meet me, holding out his hand. "You must be Morgan. I'm Ballard."

I had been warned that Ballard was a sick man, afflicted with the stone, and that when his pains were upon him he was sometimes a bit explosive. But there was nothing about Ballard's appearance or manner to suggest that he was either sick or troubled. I saw a heavy, powerful-looking man of middle height, a little too thick in the middle but limber and well carried, wearing a red woolen shirt, blue trousers and fine cowboy half-boots. His face was ruddy, his eyes dark blue, his black hair thick, curly and tipped with silver. His shirt was open at the neck to show a hairy chest which was also brightly grizzled. The effect was one of striking color and vitality, of slow-moving, soft-spoken confidence and power. I have observed that some unusual men take on a protective look of insignificance, but not so Ballard. There was nothing pretentious about him but he looked like a ruler, stood out in any group and commanded attention without trying.

"Your room will be ready in an hour or so," he said as we sat down on the porch and he offered me a cigar. He was almost never seen without one, and they were the finest of Havanas. A Mexican boy of about sixteen appeared when he clapped his hands, took an order in Spanish and brought a bottle of imported cognac and glasses on a heavy hand-hammered silver tray. Ballard proposed my health with great courtesy and took his own liquor at a gulp instead of savoring it as a good brandy deserves.

The hour stretched into nearly two as we chatted casually while shadows mantled the mountains and lengthened under the trees. I was afterwards aware that Ballard had questioned me about a good many things—the condition of the road, the amount of traffic on it, business in the East—and I suspect that he was sizing me up in his own way, but at the time it all seemed easy, pleasant talk. He asked me nothing about myself, told me nothing about his own affairs and never mentioned the business that had brought me to his door. Nothing was accomplished, from my point of view, except that I became aware of a certain spontaneous sympathy between us. Ballard and I had nothing much in common, except that both of us had felt the stab of mortal illness, but I nevertheless felt sure that he and I would get along and that whether I could serve his purpose or not, he was glad of my presence. As I sat there looking at the mountains through the smoke of a good cigar, I felt curiously and unexpectedly at home.

When the boy came to lead me to my quarters, I asked Ballard rather bluntly what he wanted me to do.

"Look around," he said, waving his cigar in a wide inclusive gesture. "Take your time. Can you ride?"

I told him I could ride well enough to get over the ground.

"Go down to the corral in the morning and pick out a horse. There's a blue buckskin mare I think you'll like. She's a single-footer, easy as a rocking chair. But pick out any horse you like. Ride around. It'll take you a while to know this place. I told Joe Ankers down at the store to answer any questions you want to ask. Come and see me whenever you get ready."

For a man presumably threatened by death and bankruptcy, Ballard certainly showed a magnificent unconcern.

— 4 —

I had come west in the belief that I was rather well-informed about Ballard and his affairs. I had been told that he owned a large ranch, deriving its title from a royal Spanish grant, on which he raised both cattle and sheep. I knew he had made a great deal of money just before and during the Civil War and it was easy to understand how this had happened. The discovery of gold in California had created a huge market at high prices. Ballard had sent herds and flocks all the way across the desert, and had sold stock to others who made the long drive. Then the war had created a great government demand for beef, at Fort Union, at Fort Marcey in Santa Fe and for the newly created Indian agencies, where several thousand retired braves were eating government rations. For a decade money had poured in upon Ballard in fabulous sums, and he had evidently regarded it as a perennial flow, for he had spent it all and a great deal more. He had gone heavily in debt to wholesalers in St. Louis and

Dodge City, and had borrowed from several banks when cash began to be scarce. As a merchant he had extended an unlimited credit and as a host he offered the most complete and indiscriminate hospitality I ever saw. Anyone, Mexican, white or Indian, could eat at the Ballard table, or at one of the many Ballard tables, so long as he behaved himself.

Then had come the panic of seventy-three. Prices of everything fell, and especially the prices of beef and wool. Cattle were not worth what it cost to drive them to market. Ballard's potential assets were enormous, but all of his creditors were pressing him for cash, and cash was the only thing he lacked. The whole country was in much the same situation. It was rich in resource and running over with food, but nearly everyone was poor because money was scarce. And money was a terrible weapon in the hands of those who had it.

All of this information I had obtained from businessmen in St. Louis, and it was correct as far as it went, but it failed completely to take account of the actual character of the Ballard dominion. For Ballard had established not merely a property but a society, small but complete and organic. He was in fact the absolute ruler of a minor kingdom, strictly feudal in its social structure. For nearly twenty years it had grown slowly, as independent and self-sufficient as any principality in Europe. Ballard had not planned it, yet it was wholly a creation of his power and personality. When society is unorganized, personal allegiance always takes the place of law, and the force of individual personality is the only thing that can hold men together and create order. Ballard had established safety and a source of supply in a wilderness, and men had gathered about him. His dominion had grown out of the frontier chaos just as the walled towns of Europe grew out of the Dark Ages. As an example of the way social forms spring from conditions it was a fascinating study, but as a business problem I think it would have given any lawyer a headache. The farther I pursued my investigations, the more bewildered I became. Here I am trying to describe the Ballard dominion as I see it in retrospect, rather than to tell the long story of my own inquiries.

— 5 —

As nearly as I could estimate, about fifteen hundred human beings, Mexican, white and Indian, lived on and about the Ballard grant. At any one time about a third of them were Ballard's employees, but all of these and all of the others were permanently in debt to him. They were at once completely dependent upon him and completely at his mercy. Certainly it had been a mercy liberal to a fault. No one had ever gone hungry in the Ballard dominion, whether he worked or not. Ballard had been completely tolerant of almost everything except violence and theft. The penalty for these crimes was simple and primitive: it was expulsion from the kingdom. If a man misbehaved once he might get a warning. If he repeated the offense, he disappeared between dark and daylight. There was no legal apparatus whatsoever and none had ever been needed. So far as felonies and misdemeanors were concerned, Ballard had established something like Utopia. No doors were locked and nothing was guarded, but neither was anything ever stolen, except that children of three races were always pilfering food from the kitchen.

The most famous symbol of Ballard's achievement as a ruler was the cash drawer in his combined office and council chamber. It was the bottom drawer in a huge chest of drawers and was known to every traveler who passed that way, for many of them had seen Ballard dip into it for a handful of cash whenever he needed it. This unlocked drawer was said to contain seldom less than ten or fifteen thousand dollars in bills and silver, but it was just as safe as any vault.

Much more impressive, in my own opinion, was Ballard's way of handling dangerous characters, for it must be remembered that almost every man then wore some kind of weapon, and that the frontier produced a class of professional fighting men, jealous of their reputations. All the mining camps and track-end towns were plagued by them. Some six-shooter artist would periodically ride into town, announce that he was the boss and issue a challenge to all comers, including the officers of the law. He seldom lasted long, but he always burned gunpowder and shed blood. A good many of these difficult gentlemen had passed through the Ballard grant and some of them had tried to stay. They were of course easily identified, and each of them presently met Ballard in a seemingly casual way. Ballard never wore a weapon and there were never any witnesses to these meetings who were near enough to hear what was said. It was known only that Ballard stood very close to his man and talked to him in a low voice. Most of these trouble-makers were gone next day, but a few stayed and became good cowboys.

Despite the fact that his manner was easy and genial most of the time, Ballard's voice and presence carried an irresistible authority. Men were afraid of him and of his power, as they had reason to be, but no one could say that he ruled by fear. His power rested firmly upon the fact that he had established peace and security in a world where both were rare.

The farther I pursued my inquiries the more I was impressed by Ballard's instinctive gift and power as a leader and organizer and by the way his personal influence permeated the whole of his dominion, making it truly something created in his own image, but I was also appalled by his shortcomings as a businessman. In this respect he certainly belonged to the past and not to the future. From the standpoint of a lawyer the most disconcerting fact was that Ballard did not know what he owned. I had studied the ancient Spanish document from which his title derived, and it was incredibly vague, bounding his lands by peaks and canyons which were often hard to identify. All of these royal grants had been confirmed by the treaty of Guadalupe Hidalgo between the United States and Mexico. A surveyor-general had been appointed by the president, and the owners of any grant could procure a survey and a clear title by demanding it. Ballard as sole owner might have had his lands surveyed at any time, and it seemed to me at first almost incredible that he had not done so. No lawyer would have overlooked the fact there were dangerous possibilities of corruption in such a survey, especially since the surveyors were paid by the mile for running the lines. It seemed to me that Ballard might have claimed almost anything, up to a couple of thousand square miles, but the worst of the situation was the obvious temptations it presented to anyone who might see an opportunity to force him out.

It was clear enough from his papers that Ballard owned the arable part of the Dark River Valley and the watersheds on either side, but what the grant included beyond that was somewhat a question of opinion and still more an opportunity for fraud. For there was only one other bit of land in the whole region to which any other man had clear title. This was a small "community grant" a few miles north of the Dark River. Community grants had been made by the Spanish Crown to groups of poor Mexicans who farmed small individual allotments and held in common fifteen or twenty square miles of grazing land. This one was evidently designed to give the owners of the great estate an assured labor supply, and so it had worked for Ballard. After he had made life safe from the Indians on that side of the mountains, a typical Mexican village had been built on the community lands with its tiny plaza, its flat adobe houses clustered about a church which saw a circuit-riding priest perhaps twice a year, and its Morada on a near-by hilltop—a sinister, windowless adobe block, with a great cross planted before it, where the Penitentes Hermanos, the flagellant religious sect of the common people, held its bloody rites. Every Good Friday a procession of half-naked men marched out of the Morada, their backs ripped with flint, bloody to the heels, whipping each other across the snowy mountains in bleak spring weather to the scream of a primitive flute and the rumble of their own chanting.

Most of the few hundred inhabitants of this primitive village with its goat herds and chile patches belonged to a single great family named Royball, and it was ruled by an old man, Anastasio Royball, who held the office of village Alcalde and was also Hermano Mayor or chief of the Penitentes. Anastasio was an absolute ruler in his own little kingdom, no less so than Ballard, and a good deal more deadly, for the Penitentes had a way of disposing of all rebels and dissidents, quietly and finally.

The family and state of Royball supplied Ballard with all of his sheep herders and they were experts, with Anastasio as Mayodomo. In return the whole village got its supplies at his store and all of its inhabitants were always in debt to him— a type of relationship to which their kind had been accustomed for centuries. Plaza Royball contained a good many Mexicans who were handy with a knife and some who lived there because their reputations on the other side of the mountains were not good, but Ballard's sheep were a sacred trust to them. On the morning after Good Friday, when Royball-town was full of sore backs, Ballard always sent Anastasio a gallon of horse liniment and a gallon of whisky, which went far both to ease the pains of the mortified flesh and to sustain the feudal spirit. Moreover, all of these people had an almost religious devotion to Ballard's wife, who was a powerful but inconspicuous influence in his kingdom. She, more than Ballard, was to the Mexicans the symbol and representative of the ancient aristocracy which had always ruled them. It was to her their women went when children were sick and every baby born in the village got a present from La Patrona. When she went among them, they stood with heads uncovered, just as they did when the priest came to town.

This was the traditional part of the Ballard kingdom, which he had taken over from the Spanish background, with all of its conventions and relationships resting upon ancient use and wont. But it was only half of his dominion and his problem. The Mexicans handled his fifty thousand sheep, but his cattle herds, numbering at least ten thousand head, and his thousand or more of horses were in charge of hard-riding, guntoting Americans, mostly from Texas. It was an impressive part of Ballard's achievement that he had kept peace between these men of two races who then had a traditional enmity, going clear back to the fall of the Alamo. A Texas cattleman was of a human species as definite and true to type as an English bulldog or a thoroughbred horse. All of them talked with the same twang, wore their guns low on their hips and customarily referred to Mexicans as greasers or yellow bellies. But this prejudice they had to lay aside when they entered the Ballard dominion. His Mexican village and the handful of Ute Indians who lived up the canyon were his special pets. He stood between them and the whole world.

The Texans constituted no such definite and established society as the Mexicans did. Just as the Mexicans instinctively huddled together and built a town, so the cattlemen seemed to want to get as far apart as they could. Fiercely self-sufficient men, they wanted room and isolation and no intruders. They had drifted into the country, one by one, somewhat mysteriously, after Ballard had made it safe. Wherever permanent water sprang and good grass grew within twenty or thirty miles of the Ballard store, some lank horseman had built a little house of adobe, or of logs if he was near enough to timber, and a circular pole corral with a snubbing post in its center. Usually he came driving a small herd of cattle and it would have been the worst of bad manners to inquire where he got them. Maybe he had picked up cripples and strays in the wake of the great drives from Texas to the railheads at Dodge City and Abilene. Maybe he had roped and branded wild longhorns in the brush country along the lower Rio Grande. Maybe he was just lucky at finding Mavericks wherever he went. A man who was good with a rope and a running iron could always get a start in life in those days. Some of these men bunked alone but usually if you rode to the door of one of the ranch houses a slim blonde woman would appear, with two or three tow-headed kids peering from behind her skirts, and tell you her man would be home about sundown.

All of these ranchers, in their own opinion, were squatters or homesteaders on the public domain, although I think few of them had filed any papers. None of them was located in the Dark River watershed and that was all Ballard apparently claimed as his own. Moreover, he had welcomed these men, for he wanted to people the country. He had given all of them credit at his store and taken their fat steers in trade. They almost all worked for him more or less, on his roundups, with his trail drives to market, as broncobusters and horse wranglers. He knew them for what they were—rustlers and gunmen, more than one of whom had killed a man in the cowtown brawls. He did not trust them, but he knew he could depend upon them because they had to depend upon him. His cattle herds were among the safest in the West, not only because these men respected his brand but because they would have made short work of anyone who did not. The only thing a good rustler feared was another good rustler.

Ballard was not exactly a cynic. He was too good-humored and tolerant to fit the word. But he certainly did not rely upon the higher nature of man. He would hire a known horse thief if one came to his door. A good horse thief often had a special gift for handling horses, and if he needed a little watching, how many men did not? Ballard never asked a man any questions, never intruded on his private life and never offered any charity. He practiced only one form of benevolence and that was toward children. If a man brought his wife and kids to town, the kids were always fed while their mothers shopped. Ballard would not tolerate a bawling brat. He would always send someone to put something in its mouth, usually a long red and white stick of candy. I think Ballard truly liked children but he also knew that the hardest man on earth is apt to be soft about his offspring.

— 6 —

All my investigations of the Ballard dominion led me to the heart of it, the place where everyone else came, the thing which held it together—and that was the store. Although he now seldom entered his store himself, Ballard was a major merchant, and trade was the lifeblood of his dominion. For many years he had freighted all his own goods over the Santa Fe Trail in his own wagons. Now most of it came by established freight lines, but his store was still the only considerable point of supply between Santa Fe and the Raton Pass. To me it was the most fascinating part of his establishment. I was something of a merchant myself, my father was a trader, my grandfather had run a country store in upstate New York. Merchandise was in my blood. I loved the smell of a store, the palaver of sales talk, the clink of money, the mingling of men brought together by their shared necessities. The give and take of trade has been the making of nations, and here I saw it in a patriarchal and elemental form.

The store building was a long low adobe with iron-barred windows, a high-walled wagon yard at one side, a hitch rack in front where ponies dozed on three legs, a front porch with benches where cowboys rested their spurs on the railing, Mexicans puffed tiny brown cigarettes, Indians sat wrapped in blankets and in the long immobility of primitive men to whom time is nothing. Within, the store smelled richly of coffee, tobacco and whisky, of hides, pelts, leather and dry goods, and of the mixed human throng that poured through its door. On Saturday afternoons and nights it was crowded and kept eight or ten clerks hopping. All of these were Mexicans who spoke fair English, a little Ute and enough sign language for business purposes. They made much better clerks than Americans, who generally lacked patience, politeness and the gift of tongues.

At the far end of the store was a small office where, for twelve hours a day, Joseph Ankers, the genius of the place, bent over his great ledgers and conferred with his clerks, seldom appearing in the store himself except when some large deal was in the making. Ankers was a tall, lean, pink old man, with thin white hair and thick white whiskers, with fine ascetic features and a great dignity. He was in his early sixties but looked older. A man of small education who spoke a strictly American English, he was nevertheless a good businessman and a good bookkeeper. He had been in Ballard's employ for fifteen years and was one of perhaps three men Ballard undoubtedly trusted.

The store was as much Ankers' creation as Ballard's, and its stock was truly a creation—a thing perfected through years by trial and error, a major feat in memory and judgment. Its items were numbered in thousands, for Ankers had to supply all the needs of a whole community, anything a man might want from a dose of quinine to a shotgun or a plow, and he had to buy in a market eight hundred miles away. Moreover, only a small part of his business was done for cash. He had to receive everything the region produced and credit it against his sales. Only deals for livestock on the hoof were made by Ballard. Everything else was appraised and credited by Ankers. He was a man of high professional pride and almost painful conscience. He could make a rather large profit without compunction, but it gave him genuine pain to be unable to supply any human need or to refuse any article in trade that might conceivably be negotiable. Mostly he took in hides and furs, beans and chile, but many exotic items claimed his attention first and last. He had to weigh gold nuggets and estimate the value of turquoise. He once turned a handsome profit on three Apache scalps, which finally reached a museum in Europe. One of his most embarrassing deals was for two live bear cubs, which grew to weigh a hundred pounds each and occupied a pen in the wagon yard for more than a year before they went east in a crate and fulfilled their commercial destiny under a circus tent.

Ankers welcomed me as a fellow merchant and one who knew something of accounts, which few did in the West of that day. From his books and his talk I finally gained a clear picture of the Ballard dilemma, even though I never quite reduced it to a balance sheet. Ballard in effect had a mortgage on everything in his dominion. By simply demanding payment of the debts on his books he could have taken every ranch and waterhole and every head of stock within fifty miles. It was easy to understand that he would be reluctant to do so, but such a drastic measure would not have solved his problem in any case. There was not enough cash market for anything. He was not fairly a bankrupt but any concerted action on the part of his creditors could force him to sell his holdings, drive him out of his kingdom.

How could Ballard and his dominion be saved? That was my problem and it was a bewildering one. It seemed hopeless to raise a loan, both because Ballard's credit was already strained and because a mortgage on his holdings would be a danger. I could see only one way to keep him solvent and in power. That was to procure a survey of his holdings, incorporate the grant, cut up the rich lands of the valley into small allotments and put them on the market. With settlers pouring west and a railroad building, I believed the lands could be sold fast enough to carry the debt and would ultimately pay it.

At first the scheme made no great appeal to me, nor did I feel sure that Ballard would accept it, but when I began to explore its possibilities, it grew upon me strongly. I remember well that one morning I climbed a high hill south of the river, from which I could survey the whole of the valley and its surrounding lands, spread before me like a great map. I may truly say that on a hilltop I saw a vision and came down an inspired man. For it struck me suddenly that the potentialities of the Dark River itself had never been exploited or even considered. At the head of the valley was a perfect natural site, where a dam would create a deep lake of several square miles, impounding flood waters that now were lost in the sands. A great area east of the valley could then be irrigated, one much larger than the valley itself. Moreover, the dam would furnish water power, more than enough for a flour mill and for a sawmill with several hundred square miles of virgin pine timber at its door.

It must be remembered that I was young and that this was a day of dreams and schemes, when the unused and unconquered earth challenged the imagination. I found it easy to picture a city in the valley and the plains plowed and planted all the way to the eastern horizon. The railroad would reach the settlement in three or four years. No one knew its exact route but it could not possibly ignore a growing town. Land values would rise steadily as it approached. There would be a boom in town lots as well as in farm lands. The place would rival Denver, might well replace it as the metropolis of the Rocky Mountains.

Briefly I tasted the ecstasy of vision, the lust to create and transform. I could imagine how Ballard must have felt when first he looked upon the Dark River country as a savage wilderness and resolved that he would claim it for civilization. He had seen a vision and had made it real. He had been a great pioneer. In this new development he would become, of course, something of a figurehead. His authority over his people would be of the greatest value, but the actual administration would require one who was both a lawyer and a businessman.

The longing for power is strong in us all. I truly wanted to serve Ballard, to keep his dominion intact, but I could not escape the conviction that my own destiny had suddenly been revealed to me. I knew that Ballard trusted me and that he trusted few. I knew that his day was nearly over. How right and inevitable it all seemed! Ballard had taken the first step. He had created a walled town—walled by the wilderness, depending upon its isolation for its integrity. The wall had been breached, the turbulent vanguard of civilization was pouring in. Someone must meet it and deal with it. Someone must preserve the order he had created, extend his conquest, master the new forces of money and machinery which were transforming the whole world. . . . I felt suddenly full of energy, as though new life had been poured into me. As I went down from the hill, my heart was pounding, partly from exertion but mostly from excitement.

I felt bound to lay my plan before Joseph Ankers first, since he was my only appointed consultant. I expounded it to him at length, and I believe with some eloquence. In fact, I was surprised at my own flow of words. I built an imaginary city for the old man, who sat patiently puffing and tamping his pipe until I had done. Then he spoke shortly.

"I don't believe he'll do it," he said.

"But why not?" I demanded. "It's the only way."

"The Utes, for one thing," Ankers said. "When Ballard moved in here he made an agreement with them that he wouldn't let anyone else settle in the valley. Of course, if he lives long enough, he'll finally have to sell the grant as a whole, and then the crowd will come. But he's never sold a separate acre and I don't believe he ever will—not while the Utes are here."

"But the Utes!" I expostulated. "They're just a handful of beggars, good for nothing. They'll end up on a reservation somewhere anyway...."

"Yep," Ankers agreed with his invariable sweetness. "You can't save the Indians and they ain't worth a damn now. But they was good men once and he ain't forgot it. When he first come here, before he built the big house, the Arapahoe from down on the plains took a crack at him. They wanted to wipe him out before he got any stronger. About fifty warriors charged down out of the timber one morning just after dawn. Ballard had only his wife and about six Mexicans on the place. The Indians killed a couple of his men and drove the rest into the little adobe house where he lived, all but one Mexican boy that took to the brush and sneaked up the canyon to where Kenyatch and his Utes was camped. The Arapahoe thought they had Ballard dead to rights. He and his men had three rifles and they killed a few Indians, shooting through the windows. They say the Doña loaded guns for the men and knocked an Indian off his horse with a shotgun. But they couldn't get out and they couldn't get water. It looked like just a matter of time. Then, along about sunset, Kenyatch and his braves came tearing down the canyon, yipping like a pack of coyotes, all riding bareback, in a dead run, stripped to their breech-clouts with their faces painted black. They had rifles Ballard had given them and a few old horse pistols. They went through the Arapahoes like a dose of salts through a mule, shooting under their horses' necks. Then they split into two bunches, tore up onto the high ground, on both sides of the river, piled off their horses and poured in the lead. The Arapahoe had Utes all around them and Ballard and his men in the middle. It didn't last long. Only about half the Araphoe got out of there alive and they never tried it again."

Ankers paused to light his pipe.

"An army officer told me the Utes was the best light cavalry he ever seen," he went on. "They maneuvered like a flock of ducks on the wing and they could shoot off the back of a running horse the way only buffalo hunters can. . . . Like you say, they ain't worth a damn now. They got nothing to do but eat government beef and beg whisky. A man with nothing to do ain't no man at all."

Ankers' little story left me silent for minutes. It seemed to recreate a lost world, doubtless the one where Ballard's memories lived, where his obligations were rooted. I understood a little better about the Utes, but I still did not see how they could stand in the way of necessary change.

"Anyhow," I said, a little weakly, "I've got to put it up to him. There's no other way."

"Yep," Ankers agreed. "I reckon you've got to put it up to him."

My enthusiasm had been temporarily depressed but it rapidly recovered. A man loves nothing so much as his own idea and I became more and more infatuated with mine. I even worked out a scheme for giving the Utes an allotment of the farmland I proposed to create, teaching them to plow and plant, making them over into good hustling Americans. I began to see myself as a benefactor of all concerned. I could hardly wait to lay my plan before Ballard. I knew I faced difficulties, but I felt the logic of the situation was irresistible. The historical process was on my side. "Manifest destiny" had been a political catchword of the years since the war with Mexico. It seemed to me the manifest destiny of the Dark River Valley to become an expanding center of civilization, and I felt that I had a fateful part to play in the sweep of change.

— 7 —

It was easy enough to see Ballard but not at all easy to talk business with him. I knew that by common report. A good many men had found a business interview with Ballard almost as hard to arrange as an audience with the Pope. Controlling vast resources as he did, and sitting on the main line of travel, Ballard had long been the object of a great many plans and solicitations. Men came to the Ballard grant with all sorts of projects to lay before him. All of them were welcomed, fed and housed, some of them hung around for weeks, but few of them ever saw Ballard alone.

During the period of his great expansion Ballard had traveled widely and spent much time in the saddle, but at this stage of his life he lived by a simple routine. His mornings were spent in his office, transacting such business as he considered necessary. He took his midday meal alone and always followed it with a siesta. In this as in other respects, he lived like a Mexican gentleman of the old regime. About four in the afternoon, in warm weather, he almost always appeared on the front porch and sat there, with his cigar in his mouth and his feet on the railing for a couple of hours. If he did not appear it meant he was ill. No one ever saw Ballard when he was ill unless his pains struck him suddenly. He had never been known even to admit that he was an ailing man, and I think few knew he was.

Anyone could join Ballard on the front porch and he received all comers with the same good-humored courtesy. On quiet days sometimes Kenyatch, the old Ute chief, would come and sit with him for an hour. Kenyatch was a ridiculous figure, addicted to begging drinks and afflicted with a passion for wearing white men's clothes. Sometimes he would appear in an old army coat with gilt epaulets, and again in a seedy frock coat and a beaver top hat, which he adorned with an eagle feather. Ballard permitted no one to sell liquor to the Indians, but he would always give Kenyatch a drink and they would hold pow-wows in a mixture of Ute and Spanish, mostly about the days of danger and excitement they had shared. Daniel Laird, the builder, was another who often came when Ballard sat alone, but never stayed when a crowd formed, as it often did. For when Ballard had many guests, his afternoon on the porch became an informal reception, with two or three boys serving drinks, and army officers, scouts and traders making a picturesque and noisy company. Ballard seemed to enjoy a throng, and he could tell a good story, although he was more a listener than a talker. But it was a strict convention of these social gatherings that business could not be discussed. Anyone then might ask Ballard for an interview. If he was willing to give it, he would always say: "Come to my office in the morning." Otherwise he simply said no. No one ever pleaded or argued with him. He had the great gift of calm and absolute refusal.

Ballard had told me to let him know when I was ready to talk, so that I felt entirely justified in asking him for an interview. He smiled and nodded. "I'm busy these days," he said. "I'll send you word when I have time." I contained my bulging ideas for three weeks, and then ventured to approach him again. He didn't resent my insistence in the least and neither was he moved by it. "Take it easy, Morgan," he said. "There's plenty of time."

I didn't believe there was plenty of time, and this stalling was not at all in keeping with the Ballard tradition. He was famous for his quick and final decisions, but I could not escape the impression that now he was evading.

At first I felt a good deal of youthful pique. It seemed to me I was not being taken seriously. I even thought of serving Ballard with an ultimatum, of demanding that my plans be considered, and of going away if he refused. Fortunately this mood evaporated, partly because Ballard made obvious effort to show that he appreciated my presence. When he had important guests he always introduced me as his lawyer, his right-hand man. I was present at most of his afternoon gatherings, and as I sat watching him, I began to consider the situation a little more from his point of view and less from my own.

Ballard always remained an enigma to me. He never revealed or explained himself and there was nothing obvious about him, but during these last months I came to believe that his apparent serenity was that of a man who knew his day was nearly over and had the courage to face the fact. He had lived through a period of spectacular change. He knew the destroying power of change and he knew he sat in its path. It promised him nothing he wanted. I think what he loved was the past, as do most men over fifty. Moreover, he must have known the future for him was short in any case. Perhaps he had a good deal of the fatalism which often belongs to men of action. A man who has faced gunfire, heard the whisper of a bullet in his ear, has none of the comfortable illusion of security and permanence that most men cultivate all their lives, never acknowledging death even on their deathbeds....

I think Ballard had also an enormous egotism, too assured to need any assertion. He didn't in the least believe anyone else could take over his kingdom and rule it. It was the body of his being and with him it would go.

All this was largely speculation on my part, but it had at least the value of relieving my impatience, of letting my own dream of conquest quietly subside. I was never an ambitious man, but only one with an inflammable imagination. Did I truly want to destroy this place and this moment, let in the rabble of the track-end towns, imprison the river and turn loose a screaming buzz saw on the ancient forest? In the idle and reflective mood that now possessed me, I knew that I did not.

— 8 —

Early autumn now had touched the mountains, splashing the ridges with the brilliant yellow of the aspen, filling the heads of the canyons with the rusty red of scrub oak. Days were cool and bright and made for riding. Nights were chilly enough so that fire glowed red on the hearth at the great house and in the big-bellied stove down at the store.

This last Indian summer I spent in the Dark River Valley lives in my memory as one of those enchanted periods we all know, when some brief and accidental harmony falls upon our lives, when we are at peace with ourselves and the world seems to come smiling with gifts in its hands.

I had not done much for the Ballard dominion, but I began to understand that it had done much for me. I had stopped coughing and gained ten pounds. I had ridden until I was more at home on a horse than on my own feet. The sun had burned me to the color of a Mexican, and I had learned enough Spanish so that I could often sound like one. I wore cowboy half-boots and blue jeans, a faded shirt and a wide hat. I rolled little brown cigarettes and blew smoke through my nose. I had taken on the color of the country so completely that I was no longer a stranger in it anywhere. I went to all the Saturday night dances and mastered the choppy Mexican waltz to the complete satisfaction of the nimble brown girls who were my partners. I had sat by the stove in the store until I had become accepted as a part of the coterie that gathered around it almost every night to swap gossip and tall tales. I seemed everywhere welcome and everywhere at home. I experienced the rare delight, possible only in youth, of becoming part of a new environment, living a new life, seeming to myself another person.

Part of the charm of this life, to me, lay in its rare combination of society and solitude, of easy human contact and easy escape. Almost every day I would ride into the mountains with a rifle across my saddle, alert for a shot at a buck or a turkey but bent primarily on losing myself in that beautiful wilderness where a forest a thousand years old talked softly to the wind, and the waters ran clear, and the wild things turned to stare as though I had been the first human intruder. Almost always I could find a new canyon to explore or reach a summit from which I could see new country. I saw the elk herds break and run, their great antlers laid back along their necks, their hoofs clicking like castanets. I watched a grizzly at his laborious business of turning over stones and logs in search of grubs and ants, I jumped blacktail bucks out of their high windy beds and saw them go bouncing down the slopes in twenty-foot leaps. In that unspoiled country one could still see big game by hundreds of head in a day. Often I did not fire a shot, and when I did, the roar of my rifle seemed to violate the ancient peace of a prehuman world. More than once I got well lost and trusted my horse to bring me home, as he always would if I gave him his head. Sometimes darkness would fall before I saw the great house far below me, alive with light and fire, dwarfed by the heights I rode. Then I would spur forward, eager for a drink and dinner, for the warm human huddle of the great dining room, the clasp and laughter of dancing girls.

The evening meal at the house of Ballard was always a social event. Seldom did less than twenty men sit down to the great table. Sometimes there were nearly a hundred, and those of minor importance had to wait for a second serving. A truly astonishing variety of human beings passed through that great dining room, for almost everyone who crossed the plains stopped at the Ballard grant. There I met Kit Carson, the most famous scout of his day, a stocky, bowlegged little man with a high small voice and a modest manner, who nevertheless gave a most unmistakable impression of strength. Lord Dunraven, the famous British sportsman, who had faced charging lions in Africa, spent a week at the grant and killed a grizzly bear. A young German ethnologist, named Bandelier, was another visitor. He pumped Ballard by the hour with systematic questions about the Indians, and Ballard, to my surprise, endured this cross-examination with the most perfect patience. He always seemed to know a good man when he saw one. Bandelier was wholly unknown then, but he became famous before he died.

All such distinguished visitors sat down at the same long table with cowboys and trappers and casual travelers, but important guests were seated near the head of the table and were always served first. The fare was of a patriarchal abundance, with game and beef in great haunches and sides, with trout from the creek and vegetables from the garden. Powerful corn whisky from Turley's still at Taos and good red El Paso wine were free for all. Everyone was served on hand-hammered silver plates, which had long been the standard service of the Mexican ricos. There was no china and little glass. Mexican boys did all the work of serving and clearing. In fact, most of the visitors to the Ballard dominion seldom saw a woman, unless at a distance.

This regime was somewhat surprising until you understood that the Ballard household was a Mexican household, designed in a tradition that went clear back to the Moorish regime in Spain. Ballard ruled his grant, or at least the masculine half of it, but his wife ruled the house, and it was a house divided strictly into masculine and feminine parts. There were, in fact, two separate structures, connected by high adobe walls and a small courtyard. The front structure contained the great dining and receiving rooms, and the quarters for all male guests. The rear structure was a feminine world where, I am sure, Ballard himself never intruded without his wife's permission. She also ruled the kitchen and all the women who worked in it, but her influence did not stop at the door. All the Mexican women on the grant came to her when they were in trouble, especially when children were sick. She had a long line of petitioners before her door every day. She dispensed simple remedies, gave away enormous quantities of food, and often let her visitors kneel and pray in her private chapel, which was said to be a room of great beauty. All of her part of the house was reputed to be as luxuriously furnished as the masculine part of it was bare and simple, but a male person could know of this only by hearsay.

This strict separation of the masculine and feminine spheres was common to all of the aristocratic Mexican houses, but in most of them the whole family dined together except when there were many male guests. Only intimate friends and relatives would sit at the family table. Ballard, during all of his later years, had enjoyed no privacy except in the solitude of his own rooms, so that the traditional division of the household had become almost complete. Only three or four times in a year did the Doña Consuelo appear in public, generally at formal receptions in the great front hall. These usually took place when distinguished visitors, especially army officers, were accompanied by their wives. The ladies always were housed in the feminine half of the establishment and had their meals with the Doña, but after dinner a reception was held at which they appeared in the most formal costumes they possessed and the officers were in full military dress. Even Ballard then donned a coat and necktie, which had almost the effect of a disguise.

To these gatherings the Doña Consuelo always came late and she always made a most effective entrance. Once I saw her flanked by both of her daughters, but usually they were away and had been most of the time for years. The elder had married an army officer and her sister then was in a convent in St. Louis. The two girls, I learned, had been tutored by their mother until it had become necessary to send them away to school. Obviously, the grant was no place for them after a certain age and their absence must have been a trial for both their parents. The younger sister was a beautiful girl and must have been almost an image of her mother's youth, for she had the same hazel eyes and rose-petal skin. She bore her mother's name and was said to be a great favorite with her father, but he treated her always with an almost formal courtesy, as though he did not quite trust his own emotions—a trait which marked all of his personal relations. I remember that when little Consuelo came for a brief visit that first summer, she brought him for a present an immense beaver hat, then considered the very summit of male elegance. Ballard accepted the two-pound headpiece with grave courtesy, but I think he never put it on. After his daughter had left he presented it to Kenyatch, who wore it on important occasions as long as he lived.

When his wife appeared, Ballard would always go to meet her, bend over her hand with formal courtesy, lead her into the room and present her to all of his guests. She was a large woman and somewhat stout, but it was easy to see that in her youth she must have been a spectacular beauty. In fact, she still had beauty—the beauty of perfect carriage and bearing, of gracious self-assurance without any trace of pretension or hauteur. I am no believer in the value of the aristocratic tradition, but generations of security and assured social status do give some men, and even more, some women, an almost perfect manner, and the Doña was a striking example of the fact.

I wondered, as many others must have done, what sort of relation existed between these two proud people. Except at these gatherings, they were never seen together. Some said that the Doña had withdrawn from her husband as completely as she had withdrawn from the world, that her whole life was bound up in her religious devotions and her charities, but this may have been merely a part of the legend that gossip creates.

The romance of their marriage was a famous one, touched with scandal. It was said that her family had permitted her to cross the mountains with her husband partly because her first child was born a little too early for the strict conventions of her class. Even better attested was the mutual devotion of their early days in the wilderness when they built their first small house in the Dark River Valley and lived there at peril from the Indians in a long isolation before the great highway came to their door. It was said the Doña, defying the custom of her kind, rode astride like a man and followed Ballard on the trail and the roundup. It was told of her too that she went out and found him once when he was lost in a blizzard, taking food and blankets, resolved to bring back her husband or die with him. There may have been much romantic invention about all this, but Mexican women are famous for a kind of fiercely possessive devotion which seems peculiar to their blood. . . . It was not hard to imagine that his sudden success had come between them. It had certainly taken him away from her, for he was a great traveler in those days, managing his own wagon trains and trail herds, covering thousands of miles in the saddle, riding relays of blooded horses. At this period of his life he was reputed to have been a man of many affairs, who had girls wherever he went, from Santa Fe to St. Louis. No one seemed to be able to name any of these mistresses but that did not disprove their existence. Ballard had a singular gift for keeping his private life private.

It was obvious that the Doña had played a most unusual part in his career. The grant had come to him through his marriage. All that he possessed and all that he had done was based upon it, and his kingdom was as much her creation as his. Watching them at one of the great receptions, I noticed that his eyes followed her as long as she remained in the room— that he seemed to be completely absorbed by the consciousness of her presence. Whatever their relations may have become, I somehow felt sure that she remained the dominating influence of his life.

— 9 —

The great house was a spectacular thing and a unique one, but it was more a hotel than a home and singularly apart from the life of the community. That was centered elsewhere, chiefly in the store and in the community hall where dances and all other public gatherings were held, and it came to interest me far more than the picturesque processions of strangers I saw at the great house. In fact, I discovered in myself a strong and surprising tendency to go native. Nothing pleased me more than to be taken for a cowpuncher or to be invited to dinner at one of the houses in Royball-town. I went to the dance hall almost every Saturday night, and also again on Sunday, if it happened to be one of those Sundays when its presiding genius, Daniel Laird, was present to lead the singing and turn loose his magnificent voice in a recitation from the Bible.

Next to Ballard himself, Laird was the most prominent man in the community and this despite the fact that he certainly did not court prominence. He was a shy and solitary fellow who lived alone in a log house of his own building a mile or more from the valley. He had no intimates and was almost always seen alone except when he performed a public function. He was generally called "the preacher" behind his back, but never to his face, because he did not care to be known as a preacher, and in fact he was a preacher only incidentally and almost accidentally. His peculiar position in the community had been imposed upon him by public need and demand and by his own qualities and powers. I never saw a man who made fewer claims for himself or took his leadership in a more modest and casual spirit.

A tall, lean man in his middle thirties, with long arms and powerful shoulders, he was a Tennessee mountaineer by origin and a builder by profession—a hard-working man who had built almost everything on the Ballard property except the great house itself and the one who kept all the corrals and outbuildings in repair. Like all men of his type, he was an axman primarily, who could build a house with no other tools than an ax and a drawknife and without an ounce of iron, using wooden dowels and pins in place of nails. But he could also make good planks with a pitsaw and had provided the Ballard establishment with its first wooden floors. Later he had built a small sawmill, powered by a water wheel and capable of producing a thousand board feet a day. More than that, he had mastered adobe construction and bossed half a dozen Mexicans when adobe walls had to be built or plastered. He was also foreman of the gang that supplied the establishment with all its firewood, swinging a six-pound, double-bitted ax himself, chiefly because he loved the tool.

I had once spent several months in the southern highlands in search of health and I could see that in all of his aptitudes and talents Laird was a typical product of the region. He came of the pioneering strain that produced Daniel Boone and carried civilization across the Allegheny barrier. His amateur preaching, his singing of hymns and folk songs, his scratchy fiddling of "Turkey in the Straw" and "Old Dan Tucker," his mastery of the primitive arts of healing were all common accomplishments of hillbilly tradition. The southern mountains abounded in unordained preachers, most of whom were also singers and often herb doctors as well. I learned that Laird's father had been such a primitive master of the Word, a minor backwoods revivalist, and doubtless Daniel had learned all of his tricks at home. He was essentially a hillbilly preacher gone west, but he was by no means to be explained wholly in terms of his origins. He was a remarkable man, as I think his subsequent career abundantly proved, and he bore a somewhat unusual relation to his fellows, standing apart from them and yet dominating them without effort whenever they gathered around him. There was a kind of power in him which was hard to explain, but certainly his voice, more than anything else, had determined his destiny. Without his great vocal powers, I feel sure, he would have been a contented recluse. As it was, he had only to open his mouth to command attention. He sang at his work and he sang as he walked the hills. Men could hear him coming a quarter of a mile away, and almost always they would stop to listen. His singing voice was powerful and true, if limited in range, but his speaking voice was almost perfect. It filled a room without effort and people always turned to look when they heard it.

It was his voice which had made him the moving spirit of all the gatherings that took place in the town meeting hall—a long, low adobe structure which had been built as a warehouse for wool, and later converted to public purposes, chiefly because it had a good wooden floor. Laird first had been called upon to preside at funerals and weddings, chiefly by the wives of the ranchmen—lonely women, starved for any kind of social life. Later he had been persuaded to hold meetings on Sunday mornings, and these were strictly in the tradition of his background. He simply recited passages from the Bible, interspersed occasionally with original remarks, and then led his congregation in the singing of hymns.

I attended these gatherings without fail and they were much like typical backwoods meeting-house performances, but of an unusual quality. Laird had discovered several good voices among his feminine followers, and the singing at its best was superb. But his own recitation of the Holy Word was the most impressive thing. Whether he loved God I do not know, but he most assuredly loved the Bible. Although his speech had the inflection of the mountain dialect, so that he said "cheer" for chair, and "hyar" for here, he yet spoke the language of the Bible, simply because he had soaked himself in it. He was a natural lover of words, and to him, I think, the Bible was the whole of literature, the only book he truly knew. But more than that, it was also a perfect vehicle for his voice and there is no doubt that Laird loved to hear his own voice. I noticed repeatedly that as he recited the great Biblical poetry he always threw back his head, looked up and over his auditors, seeming wholly unaware of their presence, making word-music for its own sake, fairly hypnotizing himself. All of his favorite passages he recited with peculiar emphasis, seeming always to give them a new meaning and value. So in the Twenty-third Psalm, he always emphasized the personal pronouns, announcing with eloquent conviction, "The Lord is *my* shepherd, *I* shall not want. He maketh *me* to lie down in green pastures. He leadeth *me* beside the still waters." And when he intoned Ecclesiastes, proclaiming "Vanity, vanity, *all* is vanity," that resounding *all* seemed to reduce all human effort and pretension to eternal futility. It was an impressive demonstration of the power which sound can add to sense.

Sometimes Laird would half scandalize his audience by reciting a passage from the Song of Songs, and in this rich poetry his great voice seemed to be at its best. It did not bear so heavily upon certain words, although I noticed a tendency for his voice to linger with caressing eloquence upon anatomical details, giving his recitation a sensuous quality of which he was probably unaware.

> *Thy* lips *are like a thread of scarlet,*
>   *And thy speech is comely;*
> *Thy* temples *are like a piece of pomegranate*
>   *Within thy locks.*
> *Thy* neck *is like the tower of David builded*
>   *For an armory,*
> *Whereon they hang a thousand bucklers,*
>   *All shields of mighty men.*
> *Thy two* breasts *are like two young roes that are twins,*
>   *Which feed among the lilies.*

While Laird softly boomed his chant of desire, lean ranchwomen in gingham dresses and sunbonnets, with hands reddened by dish water, watched him with adoring eyes, sometimes visibly swaying to the music of his voice, while the few menfolk who came to his meetings stared uncomfortably at the floor. I wondered whether he knew what he was doing, and I doubted it. But he kept his distance from women with the utmost care. He was never seen alone with one, and no woman was ever known to go to his house. He visited the ranch houses and the homes of the Mexicans only when he was sent for in case of sickness, and then he seldom ministered to women. There were several midwives in the settlement who also practiced a limited art of healing, but no doctor nearer than Fort Union. Laird had added to his traditional lore of herbs a limited knowledge of materia medica, but he relied mainly on heat and pressure. He was an expert of mustard plasters and hot compresses, and like all such frontier healers, he was supposed to have a gift of touch. He could "rub the misery out of your back." He was at his best with children and was credited with curing several cases of pneumonia.

After hearing him intone the sacred word on Sunday mornings, it was a little surprising to find Laird always at the dances on Saturday night and presiding over these most profane gatherings with the same easy authority he brought to his Sabbath congregations. But here, it appeared, his presence was official, in that Ballard had asked him to take charge of these explosive gatherings after several of them had ended in rather damaging fights.

The Mexican baile was then even more than now an institution all over the Southwest, and those in the Ballard dominion were typical. A Mexican orchestra of three pieces, led by an aged and blind fiddler, announced the dance by touring the settlement in the afternoon, the leader mounted on a white mule, fiddling as he went. Everyone, Mexican and gringo, was welcome, and all male persons paid a small price, which was usually tossed into a hat. No introductions were required. Any man could ask any girl to dance. This did not mean that he could talk to her or sit beside her, or claim her acquaintance off the dance floor, but he could dance with her in becoming silence and then return her to the side of her duenna. The girls and their chaperons sat in a long row all around the room and the men crowded about the doorway. Just as in Santa Fe and all of the other larger towns, these were always biracial gatherings. The girls from Royball-town in their white bodices and red petticoats, the young Mexicans from the sheep camps with their black hair heavily oiled, ranchmen bringing wives and daughters, cowboys from the

Ballard bunkhouse, all crowded into the hall, made the sanded floor rasp in time to the fast and wheezy music. Guns were checked at the door and knives were supposed to be. No liquor was allowed inside the house. But in spite of these precautions, any baile was an explosive mixture of sex, corn whisky and racial antagonism. In fact, many young men felt that a baile which did not break up in a fight was a failure. In Taos the mountain men used to start a riot whenever they thought the party was getting dull. Ballard himself had been through many a dance-hall brawl, but he would not tolerate any of this traditional bellicosity on his own premises. With his sure instinct for all the means of power, he knew that mobs and factions are the enemies of authority, and that trouble between the two races would split the country. He was also quick to see the value of Laird's towering presence and commanding voice. So dances took place only when Laird was there. He was what they called in the cowtowns the official bouncer, but he seldom had to bounce anyone and he brought a good deal to the dances besides his long reach and resounding voice. He never waltzed, but he led and called all the square dances and sometimes joined the orchestra with his fiddle. I watched him with much interest, and I am sure he was quick to spot trouble in the making. Often he brought it to an end by calling for a square dance, dissolving the hot couples, the dangerous triangles, in a dancing, laughing crowd. The most impressive evidence of his power was the way he adjourned the dances, which he always did at midnight. He would pick up his wide black hat off the floor and stand with it in his hand until the music had come to an end. Then he would put it on his head and walk out, followed by the whole crowd. Of course, he had the power of Ballard behind him, but his person seemed to contain a certain authority by natural endowment.

Only once did I see Laird intervene to stop trouble. That

time he saved young Bob Clarey from a knife, with the help and support of practically the whole crowd, white and Mexican. For young Bob was a favorite figure in the settlement and his romance with Adelita Royball had become something like a public institution—the leading subject of local gossip. Young Bob was the only son of a widower ranchman, known simply as Old Bob, who had the usual waterhole and corral and log house about twenty miles from the store, and the usual herd of about a hundred half-bred longhorns. Old Bob belonged to a type all too common in the frontier—a man driven by some obscure impulse of social avoidance, who had pursued solitude halfway across a continent—a lean, thin-lipped man with small eyes peering suspiciously from under thick brows. He was a good and honest cowman, but one who could not trust the world or his fellows. He came to town only about once a month for a wagonload of supplies and a mild spree. Young Bob, on the other hand, was around the place most of the time. His whole life and character seemed to be a reaction against the old man's taciturn seclusion. He had great social gifts and he used them. His self-assurance and good feeling were supported by his remarkably good looks, for he was handsome as an actor and wholly aware of the fact, with dark curly hair and blue eyes, a perfect build, an easy carriage, and a smile that never seemed to wear out. He rode a white pony which he washed carefully in the creek every few days, white goatskin chaps on Sunday, and a great white hat which must have cost him a month's savings. He carried a big Colt six-shooter low on his hip, but had never been known to shoot at anything but a mark or a coyote. He was a star of the local rodeos, a crack roper and broncobuster—a congenital showoff, but one with real courage. Everybody liked him and women adored him. As Waverly Buncombe remarked, when he rode down the street, you could hear the girls sigh like a rising wind. But he had only one girl, so far as anyone could learn, and that was the eighteen-year-old daughter of Old Man Royball himself—the tyrannical ruler of sheep and sheep herders. It seemed as though Bob's dramatic instinct had dictated his choice of a love as it did almost everything else in his life, for this affair was inevitably conspicuous and potentially dangerous. Old Bob was said to have threatened to disown his son if he married that coffee-colored wench, and old man Royball had retaliated by muttering that he would run young Bob out of the plaza if he ever came there to see her. What success these two had in meeting alone I do not know, although there was reason to believe they did not fail completely. But on the dance floor they got together with impressive grace and velocity, and there no one could deny them. For the dance floor in Mexican tradition is the sanctuary of lovers, and Bob and Adelita were a pair of gifted dancers. The swift choppy waltz, which was the product of rough and sanded floors, they could make into a thing of speed and grace, but the cuna or cradle waltz was their specialty. In this the two dancers seized each other by the shoulders, leaned far back and whirled round and round, making a cradle which was never bottomless. Bob and Adelita would waltz in a close embrace for a while, then go into their ecstatic spin, belly to belly, her long hair flying loose, while other couples circled the passionate whirlpool of their delight. Adelita was a slim, pretty girl, brown as an Indian, with an immense mane of black hair that seemed always to escape whatever discipline she tried to impose upon it, so that after an hour of dancing she looked like a happy young witch, peering through her own tresses, tossing them with a splendid gesture of abandon. It was a delight to watch them and they were both quite conscious of giving a good show.

Inevitably, Bob had a Mexican rival, and inevitably he came to the dance full of alcohol and with a hidden knife. The trouble started in the usual way, with both men claiming the same dance. Adelita lifted her pretty nose and glided into the arms of her beloved Bob. The Mexican snatched him by the shoulder, spun him free. Bob swung his right in good Anglo-Saxon fashion, the Mexican staggered and came back with a flashing blade drawn from his sock. Laird, watching from the platform, landed between them in one long bound, got them both by their collars and held them apart, dangling helpless at the ends of his mighty reach. It was an amazing show of strength—the strength of a man who has swung an ax all his life, building muscle all the way from wrist to shoulder. The whole crowd closed in on them, the Mexican was ejected by common consent, and in two minutes the dance was going on as though nothing had happened. There was a kind of quick crowd justice in the incident. The aggressor was known to all, and a sheep herder helped a cowboy boost him through the door.

I had observed Laird for months before I ever saw him alone, and it would never have happened then except for the fact that both of us were fishermen. Almost everyone collected a few grasshoppers and snatched a meal from the creek once in a while, but only Laird and I cared for trout fishing as a sport, following the creek with our long, limber willow poles, using horsehair leaders, angling for the big ones that lived in the deep holes. It was characteristic of Laird that he met me several times before he began to recognize me as the same fellow he had seen before. He was always smiling and pleasant, an evident lover of the human race, but he seemed to focus on individuals with a certain difficulty if not with reluctance. When we finally got into conversation one day he seemed suddenly to accept me as a friend and invited me to have dinner with him—a distinction he conferred upon few.

He lived in a one-room cabin of squared timbers, standing alone in a tall grove of yellow pine, with a deep brown carpet of needles covering the ground. I was told that he had declined to live there as a squatter and since Ballard sold no land he had laughingly deeded Laird half an acre. Within, the cabin was bare and neat, furnished only with a long built-in bunk, two homemade chairs and a table, shelves for his supplies and pegs on the wall to hold his collection of axes, of all weights from two pounds to six and all sharp and shining. A heavy rifle hung on a rack of elkhorn. Laird was a hunter when he needed meat but never fired a shot near his own place because he liked to see the wild things about.

He was shy yet self-possessed and fed me amazingly well on fried trout and boiled potatoes, excellent biscuits, wild raspberries and cream, and a big tin pot of strong coffee. He also poured me a generous slug of El Paso brandy, but took none himself.

"I've drunk enough of that stuff to last me a lifetime," he explained with an apologetic grin. The remark struck me as revealing, but it was the only revealing one he made. He did not talk about himself at all, but he questioned me at length about my travels—about New York and Europe and ships and the ocean, which he had never seen. He sat listening with an intent, abstracted look, as though trying to imagine a world wholly beyond his experience, making me feel that I was in the presence of a starved intellectual curiosity, a mind of power and appetite which had never even discovered its own need. Yet the man seemed at peace with himself. He had a long, angular ruddy face, deeply lined for one of his age, with thick sandy hair and bright gray eyes under heavy brows—eyes as keen and steely as a blade. But his wide, slow-spreading grin was full of peace and good feeling.

It was a warm evening and after supper we sat a little while on a bench in front of his cabin smoking our pipes. From his doorway you could see nothing but the great pines, now spreading their long wavering shadows on the carpet of needles that covered the earth, and there was no sound but a breath of evening breeze and the tinkling song of a vesper sparrow. Any man, I thought, might find peace in a place such as this, if he was a man who could live with his own mind—and if the world would leave him in peace.

— 10 —

I never heard but one man say anything against Laird and that man was his chief, if not his only, rival as a public character—a peculiar individual bearing the musical name of Waverly Buncombe. According to the legend he had bestowed upon himself, Buncombe was the errant scion of a wealthy and prominent family in South Carolina, who preferred the wild, free life of the frontier to the aristocratic ease and luxury he might have claimed as his own. It was true, at least, that a county in South Carolina was named for the Buncombe family, and that Waverly had been born there, but the stories he told about himself, like those he told about others, seemed to contain a large element of romantic invention. For Waverly was a storyteller and a gossip by avocation, one who had dedicated his life to spreading the news, whether it was any credit to anyone or not, and to lending it the embellishment of his imagination, which was lively, and also of his wit, which was irreverent, sometimes malicious and often obscene. Nobody professed much respect for Waverly, but everyone listened to him and many feared him. Moreover, as I came to understand, he performed a genuine and necessary social function, for he took the place of a newspaper. He made it his business to know everything about everybody and to tell everybody else. I believe that every primitive community harbors such a semi-professional carrier of the word, and Waverly was a talented example. To give him his due, he was a shrewd man and a gifted observer, but even these talents did not fully account for his unfailing knowledge of what was going on. He seemed to sense events in the making, to know what men were going to do before they did it. In a word, like all gifted gossips, he had a touch of genius. And where news travels only by word of mouth, gossip has an enormous importance. In such a community everyone has his legend and Waverly was the keeper if not the creator of legend. Everyone's reputation was to some extent at his mercy, and he was not always merciful, but he was always entertaining. Moreover, he had a philosophy of a kind—a profoundly skeptical philosophy. He did not believe at all in anyone's pretensions and very little in anyone's virtues. If he did some men, and also some women, a grave injustice, he also punctured a great many false fronts. I cannot say that I admired Waverly, but I enjoyed him, and I listened to him with the mingled feeling of guilt and delight which we all bring to the tongue of gossip. Moreover, I did not find it hard to justify myself. If I heard a good many dubious stories from Waverly, I also learned some useful things about the little world I had set myself to understand.

Waverly's favorite hangout and listening post, at this time of year, was the big iron stove in the front of the store. It was also mine, and by this time I had become an accepted member of the group which gathered there in the evening to swap news and tell stories, with Waverly supplying the greater part of both. In personal appearance, he did not quite fulfill the ideal of southern aristocracy from which he claimed descent. He was a man of moderate stature, with a long hatchet face, a long nose, notably sloping shoulders and long arms. As I heard a cowpuncher remark, he looked as though he had been built to crawl through a knothole. The only thing that marred his tapering symmetry was the huge wad of chewing tobacco he almost always wore in the left side of his cheek. It seemed to interfere not at all with his gifted utterance, and like all veteran lovers of the plug, he could hold his juice for an incredible length of time. When he did spit, he had impressive accuracy. Not only could he hit a cuspidor infallibly at four feet, but he could drown a fly perched on the edge of it.

By profession, Waverly was a cow-camp cook, and to all accounts a good one. In those days of the open range and the long drives, his calling was an important and a well-paid one. A camp cook not only cooked but bought supplies, drove the chuck wagon, was the practical and moral equivalent of the quartermaster in an army. He had to feed crowds of hungry men on short notice, in all kinds of weather, often getting breakfast for twenty cowpunchers long before daylight in a pouring rain. Waverly discharged this difficult function on all the local roundups and whenever Ballard sent a trail herd to Fort Union or Santa Fe, but his work was sporadic in the nature of the case. Most of the time he was a gentleman of leisure and of language.

I do not believe that Daniel Laird was much aware of Waverly, but Waverly was acutely aware of the preacher. Laird could not be called a pretentious man but he was one who stood apart from his fellows, had no share in their quarrels and scandals, kept his own life to himself. He was the shining mark gossip is supposed to love and Waverly certainly loved to shoot at him. Nothing about the preacher had his approval. As a singer he considered Laird "just a good hog caller where there ain't no hogs," and he put no faith in the man's ministrations to the sick. "Sure, he'll cure you if he can do it with a dose of salts or a bucket of hot water, and if he can't he'll bury you right nice." But what annoyed him most was the apparent austerity and purity of Laird's life. Waverly believed not at all in the value of chastity and very little in its existence. Moreover, it had small place in the customs of a country which abounded in willing brown women and had a long tradition of erotic license. Perhaps if he had been able to discover the preacher in some weakness of the flesh, he would have been more tolerant of him, but Laird was one man whom scandal had never touched.

The subject came up one evening when Seth Larrick, foreman of Ballard's cowpunchers, remarked upon the fact that Laird seemed "downright skeered of a skirt." When called upon to attend the sick, he declined ever to be left alone with a woman.

"There ain't no mystery about it," Waverly remarked. "You can't chase women and play Jesus at the same time. He's afraid some gal will tumble him off his high horse."

I thought the remark showed insight as well as malice, and this was true of much that Waverly said. On this and other occasions I had the uncomfortable feeling that my friends and neighbors were being stripped naked for my inspection, but sometimes Waverly dispensed information that was truly useful. So it was Waverly who called my attention to Major Arnold Newton Blore, a man destined to play a rather large part in the subsequent history of the Dark River Valley. I had met Blore at the dinner table, but to me he was just one of the many guests who accepted Ballard's hospitality for a few days or a few weeks. I did not in the least suspect his fateful importance, but Waverly did.

"I don't know what he's up to yet," he told me. "But he ain't here for fun. I can tell that by the way he noses around."

Major Blore was a Confederate veteran who had risen from the ranks in Lee's command to become an artillery officer of exceptional skill. Of his present occupation nothing was known except that he made his headquarters in Denver, and like nearly everyone else in the Denver of that day had "mining interests," which probably meant that he was a promoter and dealer in mining stocks. He had very markedly the soft speech and elaborate countesy of a Virginian, and contrived to invest himself with an air of importance, slightly touched by the kind of pomposity which is so often the weakness of men deficient in stature. For Blore was a very short man and obviously conscious of the fact. I doubt that he would have been more than three inches over five feet in his socks, but no one ever saw him that way. He wore upon all occasions riding boots of the most expensive make with very high heels, and he further extended himself at the other end by means of a large felt hat with a high crown. His carriage also had something lofty about it. The appearance of a man, and especially the first impression you get of it, has always seemed highly revealing to me. Major Blore seemed to be always engaged in lifting himself, and doing it with a certain aggressive confidence, which was expressed in the bulge of his barrel chest and confident carriage of his rather large head. Seated behind a desk or at a table, he might have been taken for a large man. His features were handsome, dominated by a Roman nose and decorated with a silky blond mustache which effectively concealed his mouth. His eyes were bright blue, prominent, and curiously unrevealing. I did not like him, but he gave an unmistakable impression of personal power, nourished on a habit of command.

My next news of him came also from Waverly. It appeared that Blore had promoted a horse race in which a nag of his own was to be matched with Ballard's favorite three-mile horse, the celebrated Fly. Waverly mentioned this matter only to Seth Larrick and myself, and he did so in a portentously confidential tone.

"If you want to make some easy money," he told us, "bet on Blore's horse. He's putting something over on the old man, sure as hell."

Blore had arrived at the Ballard place alone in a buckboard—a light two-horse rig which was then the favorite means of rapid transit when any baggage had to be carried. The buckboard was drawn by a pair of chestnut geldings which were gaunt from hard driving when he arrived, streaked with sweat and caked with dust. No one paid much attention to them and no one had seen anything of them since Blore's arrival. Blore had used one of Ballard's saddle horses for his rides about the grant. Only Waverly had noticed that Blore tended his team himself, grooming them daily, taking them out of the stable only briefly in the evening for a little exercise, measuring the oats he fed them with the utmost care.

"He takes care of 'em like a couple of babies," Waverly reported. "And they're worth it. They're Kentucky thoroughbreds, sure as I'm a foot high. Hardly anybody out here knows a thoroughbred when he sees one but I seen a lot of 'em back home."

Waverly was right about that. Horse racing was the commonest of all sports in the West of that day, but it was not a sport of professionals and thoroughbreds. Cowboys raced their ponies, almost always for a stake. Every ranchman had at least one horse in his remuda that he would bet a few dollars on. Ballard loved a horse race and had a small stable of running horses he used for nothing else, but even these were native stock, mostly mustangs of exceptional speed and power, or crosses between a native mare and a blooded stallion. Thoroughbreds were too delicate for a frontier world and endurance was valued more than speed. A good horse was one that could outrun pursuing Indians or overtake a herd of buffalo and keep his rider in their midst long enough for a kill. Races were always over long distances, at least two miles and often three. There were no circular tracks. Any long straight stretch of road would serve the purpose, such as the one that paralleled the river near Ballard's house. When a race was to be run the course was carefully inspected for gopher holes and loose rocks, starters and judges took their positions at either end and all was ready.

As became evident later, Major Blore was not merely interested in winning a horse race. Like many others who had come to the grant with a plan and a purpose, he had found Ballard cordial but also supremely elusive and he had used his horses with notable cunning as a means of approach to the royal presence. Evidently he had heard of Fly and of Ballard's pride in the black stallion, and he had asked to see the animal, explaining that he was a bit of a horseman himself. Pedro Gonzales, a skinny little Mexican about forty years old who was Ballard's jockey and chief hostler, reported the result to Waverly, who gave it wide currency.

Pedro brought the stallion out of his stall, mounted him bareback, and rode him up and down for Blore's inspection. Fly was a horse of magnificent appearance—a mustang which had been caught wild on the prairies east of the grant. All of this wild stock was of course descended from horses the Spaniards had imported in the sixteenth century. Much of it was of the finest Barb and Arabian blood, the same strains from which our own thoroughbreds are descended. Most of it had deteriorated as a result of interbreeding and crossing with all kinds of range stock, but an occasional mustang was found which seemed a perfect specimen of the original Arabian type, and such was Fly. He had the small pointed head, the tiny ears, the powerful arched neck and deep barrel of the Arabian, and also the perfect grace of movement—a horse far more beautiful than any of a more specialized type.

Major Blore watched the horse for some minutes, had the boy bring him to a stop, inspected his forelegs with a practiced hand, viewed the wide spread of his chest from in front, opened his mouth with the easy touch of an expert, and carefully considered his teeth.

"That's a fine horse, Ballard," he said finally. "But he's not a running horse. I'm surprised you should think he is. He's too short-coupled and too heavy in the rear."

Ballard laughed with delight.

"Major Blore," he said, "if you can find anything that can

beat that horse for two miles I'll make it worth a thousand dollars to you."

"Why, for the matter of that, Ballard," Blore replied, "I'll take one of those nags of mine right out of harness, ride him myself, and make your mustang look through a cloud of dust. That boy of yours is twenty pounds lighter than I am, but I think that much of a handicap is no more than fair."

"You've got yourself a race right now," Ballard told him. "I never looked at your horses, but I've been backing Fly against all comers, sight unseen, for four years. He's never lost but one race and that time he threw shoe."

Ballard was no innocent where horses were concerned. He knew Fly was not fast by eastern track standards, but he had complete confidence in the courage and bottom of his horse. Another horse often led the stallion for more than half the distance and sometimes took a long lead, but on the home stretch Fly would run his opponent down like a hound, seeming stronger at the finish than when he started.

A crowd of several hundred gathered to watch the race. Most of those who had money tried to bet it on Fly. Only Waverly bet all he had and all he could borrow on Blore's horse.

When I saw Blore mounted I knew at once I was looking at a man to whom horses must have been a profession, one who had in all probability been a jockey. At this time he was in his late thirties, and had doubtless put on some weight. It was easy to imagine that ten or fifteen years earlier he had looked like a typical track professional. It was significant that he had his own racing saddle and his seat was the one that only jockeys use, with his knees up around the mount's withers. Most of those present had never seen such a rider and some of them laughed at him. Pedro Gonzales was a picturesque contrast. Like most of his breed he was more than half Navajo and he rode stripped to a breech-clout, as all Indians do, with only a blanket and surcingle on the horse's back.

I took my stand with the judges and saw the two horses come down the course with Fly slightly in the lead and Blore hanging on his flank. It was easy to see Blore had chosen that position and was saving his mount with perfect control. When they were not more than a hundred yards from the finish, Blore rose in his stirrups, laid on the quirt and gave the rebel yell. He shot ahead two full lengths and finished with Pedro dodging clods from the flying hoofs of the thoroughbred. The little Mexican was a bewildered and heartbroken man. He turned the stallion and rode back toward the stables without meeting an eye or saying a word.

Ballard was a perfect loser. He extended his hand to Blore with a broad grin.

"You've got a good horse," he said, "and you know how to ride him. It was worth a thousand dollars to see you. Come to my office in the morning and we'll settle up."

That final word, I have no doubt, was what Blore had been working for.

— 11 —

I had a premonition, based partly on Waverly's delicate hints, that this first private meeting between Ballard and the Major might be an important one, but I was a little surprised when Ballard sent for me the next day about noon. As I crossed the porch on my way to Ballard's office, I met Blore leaving the house. The little man was flushed, his bulging blue eyes were bright with excitement and he walked with a kind of strut, like a victorious gamecock leaving the pit. He gave me a smile, a nod and a quick appraising look.

I found Ballard seated behind the long heavy table at which he transacted all his business. It was a bare table except for a big inkpot, a few pens and a wide Pueblo bowl which Ballard used for an ash tray. During the past twenty years, hundreds of thousands of dollars had flowed across that table, both ways, most of it in silver, for everyone liked heavy money in those days. Ballard was famous for the way he would go to his cash drawer, take out a huge canvas bag of silver dollars and count out what he owed, tossing the coins onto the table in handfuls. He had always dealt lightly with money. If he was buying a herd of sheep from a poor Mexican, he would always toss a few extra dollars and say: "That's for the dog." First and last he had tossed a lot of money to the dogs. I don't think he had much respect for money. He had a sharp eye for land and livestock, for water, fur and timber, but the importance of money had always eluded him.

Ballard was leaning back in his big homemade chair with its rawhide seat and wide arms. He looked tired and a little grim, but he was perfectly composed. He greeted me with a smile, and waved me to the chair Blore had just left. There was no sign of disturbance about him except that the cigar he took out of his mouth was almost chewed to pieces, and the bowl before him was piled high with ashes and with badly chewed cigars. When he was serene Ballard smoked a cigar slowly and carefully, without getting his teeth into it. If he chewed the weed to pieces, you could be sure he was disturbed.

He was silent for several minutes after I sat down, and when he spoke it was very quietly.

"Morgan," he said, "Major Blore has made me an offer for the grant. He represents a syndicate of mining men in Denver. . . . The offer is pretty good."

He sat looking at the end of his cigar for a long time.

"You don't want to sell," I ventured finally.

Ballard shifted in his seat, plowed his hand through his hair.

"No," he said, and his voice took on a certain intensity, while he continued to stare at his dying cigar. I felt that he was talking as much to himself as to me. "I never wanted to sell anything. I always wanted to hang on, to hold things together, to make things work. When I came in here I promised the Utes I would never let in any settlers as long as I controlled the valley. That agreement doesn't bar me from selling the place as a whole. I have a right to sell." He paused a long time. "And I've got to sell," he said finally.

I asked him only if he was sure there was no alternative. He nodded slowly.

"I've got to be frank with you now, Morgan," he said. "I've kept you waiting for months, but the time hasn't been wasted. You've been learning about the grant and I've been learning about you. I've seen this moment coming for years. I knew I would need a lawyer and that he would need to know all about this place. I knew I would need a man I could trust and I can't trust a man until I've watched him a long time."

He paused again, and I knew this confession was costing him an effort. It was no part of his habit to confide.

"About three years ago, when the market for beef went flat, I went back to St. Louis. I talked to bankers and I talked to doctors—two kinds of men I don't like. All the news they gave me was bad." He said it calmly, as though he were talking about someone else, but when he spoke again there was a stir of power, a note of belligerent pride in his voice.

"If I had another ten years," he said, "I would give myself the pleasure of telling Major Blore to go to hell. No man could come in here and take this place over unless I would let him—I don't care how much money he might have." He looked a long time at the end of his cigar. "But I haven't got ten years, nor anywhere near it. A man is a fool to start what he can't finish. And I've got to think of my family. This way they'll be safe."

I knew I was listening to a man who had heard a sentence of death and accepted it. Ballard's affliction now is often cured by surgery, but then it was considered incurable. I could understand well enough the temptation he had resisted—the temptation to fight and to go down fighting, to use his power to the last ounce and the last moment, be the result what it might. He knew that peace and order in the Dark River Valley were his creation. He knew his power over his own people. A great deal of Eastern and some British capital was invested in the Western cattle business in those first decades after the war, and a great deal of it was lost. The herds of the strangers melted away. They fell prey to the lean riders with the quick ropes and the running irons. Ballard commanded all such men in a region nearly a hundred miles wide, and none of them had anything to gain by a change of masters. It was simple truth that he could have defied any usurper and also that his defiance would have meant something like war in the long run, both in the courts and on the ranges. . . . Ballard had decided against a fight he couldn't finish. He had decided a long time ago. He had fought out his battle with himself. It would have been impertinence to argue or advise, nor did his attitude invite any expression of sympathy.

"What do you want me to do?" I asked.

"I want you to dicker with Blore," he said. "This is a job for a lawyer. When you see his papers, you'll understand. He's a cunning little bastard and no mistake." He smiled, and there was a shrewd look in his eye.

"I didn't commit myself to a thing," he added. "I just told him that I would talk to my lawyer. You've got a clear field and you have my permission to say what you please. Boost the price if you can. But there's only one thing I've got to have. I've got to have a year—I think it's all I'll need."

— 12 —

When I faced Blore across a table two days later and examined his papers, I knew at once that the situation was hopeless, so far as saving the grant for Ballard was concerned, and the fact is even more evident in the long retrospect than it was then. While I had been dreaming of myself as an agent of the future in the Dark River Valley, Blore had been cleverly at work for more than a year. He had begun by forming a syndicate of capitalists in Denver. Six men of money were represented in it, but the chief of these was one Colonel Alonzo Tweedale, like Blore a Confederate veteran, and one who had made a great deal of money in the Pike's Peak mining boom. Tweedale was president of the organization and he was a millionaire or somewhere near it. It was called the Rocky Mountain Land and Cattle Company, but its stated purposes were inclusive—to buy and sell both lands and cattle, to erect sawmills and build dams and irrigation works, to lay out town sites, to develop mining claims. No specific lands were mentioned in the charter, but it was aimed primarily at the Spanish land grants of the Southwest, with the Ballard grant as its first victim. Blore had other papers covering this phase of the plan. In short, he had gone secretly to all of Ballard's creditors and had promised each of them payment in full, provided a sale was consummated. He had asked each of them in return to agree to file suit against Ballard in the event that Ballard refused to sell. Not all of them had agreed, but enough had done so to make Ballard's resistance futile in the long run.

What, I asked myself, could Ballard have done if he had been granted that ten years of life and health he longed for? He could have made a great deal of trouble, but he would have been like a man standing in the path of a flood that grows slowly from a rill to a torrent. For I knew then and I see even more clearly now that I was looking at a blueprint for empire—the empire of property, of ownership, of money. Settlers were pouring west in a picturesque throng. That was the obvious, the spectacular thing. But behind the settlers was coming a stream of money, of organized capital. It was invisible, but it was the potent, the irresistible thing. Money was the new conqueror, the power destined to triumph and rule for generations.

The West for fifty years had been truly a world of free wealth. It is hard for anyone who did not see it to understand that world. Men drove their wagons across hundreds of miles of rich black soil without ever a thought of settlement or ownership. The cattle range was one vast communal pasture where any man might graze his herd. The forests stood waiting the ax and no one thought them worth seizing. Gold and silver and fur were there for the taking. The problem was not to find wealth but to hold it and defend it and find a market for it. It seemed as though there was more of everything than men could ever use.

With the thrust of rails across the continent, free wealth was doomed, although only a few were shrewd enough to know it. The world of money and monopoly then was in the making—the world of fences and titles and mortgages, the world of the few who have and the many who want. Money worked a vast and inevitable transformation in the West—I do not belittle it—but it destroyed one kind of man and created another. The men such as Ballard, who conquered the West, were reckless men with a touch of the heroic about them. Some of them were good men and some were deadly men, with blood upon their hands. But money is never reckless and never heroic. Money is cunning and it finds and uses and creates cunning men. Money has a long arm. It may kill but it seldom faces its victim.

Blore was the agent of money. His strength was not in his right arm, nor in his personal power, but in his complete and devious scheme, and in the money that lay behind him. If Blore had died or vanished another would have come to take his place. I know now that Ballard's day was over, and I think he knew it too. Ballard was a shrewd man, but not a man of money or of financial schemes. Money had been only a plaything to him—a counter he tossed across a table with a lavish hand. Money was his nemesis as surely as rifles and whisky had been the nemesis to the Indians.

As I sat looking at Blore, I knew I faced a cunning man, and I proposed to practice a little cunning myself. I came of a race of traders, of men who win their victories on the pages of a ledger, who fear nothing but the figures in red. I knew that business is business and that making a bargain is an imaginative art. In a word, I proposed to bluff. I had no doubt that Blore was a gifted liar, and I did not propose to be outdone in the arts of invention.

Our meeting was cordial in the extreme. It had an atmosphere of mutual esteem which was somewhat bogus and of mutual confidence which was wholly so. We trusted each other as do a couple of tomcats maneuvering for position before a fight but nothing of this showed in our manners. We drank our brandies and lit our cigars as though this were the friendliest occasion anyone could imagine. I complimented Blore on his horsemanship. He in turn, it appeared, had heard of me and of my father and was delighted to find himself dealing with a man who knew the necessities of business and also its amenities. We were delighted with each other and each of us was busily engaged in trying to spot the weakness in the other.

I began by saying that I personally favored the sale, regarded it as a good and necessary thing. In effect, I was working for Blore, trying to expedite his business. But my principal, I indicated, was a bit difficult. He did not understand finance. For him possession had always been rather more than nine-tenths of the law. What he believed in was personal power, and of this, I felt bound to make it clear, he had a great deal.

I knew well that what Blore and his backers most feared was the lawless men and the lawless spirit which then infested the West. The fact is that the notion of private property, as something sacred and inviolable, had never been established west of the Mississippi. A man who built his house and corral beside a waterhole felt that he owned it because he used it, but he would not deny the right of anyone else to share the surrounding range. Livestock on the range had a way of changing hands in a most informal fashion. The feeling was general that a calf belonged to whoever put his brand upon it, and few thought it a crime to shoot a calf when they needed beef, without any regard to the brand under which it was born. Only a horse thief was truly a social outcast because to steal a man's saddle horse was often to leave him helpless. For twenty years the cattle barons fought a war with rustlers who were not truly criminals but only men who had never learned a proper respect for vested interest. In the Rocky Mountain country that war was just beginning, but I knew men such as Blore and Tweedale were aware they proposed to invade a lawless world, and they were afraid of it— for money is always timid. So I placed a gentle and diplomatic emphasis upon the fact that the men who surrounded the Ballard grant and dealt at the Ballard store were all lawless men, rustlers by origin if not by profession, men who wore their guns whenever they wore their clothes. I made it clear that Ballard controlled them and that it was not going to be easy for anyone else to do so without his good will.

All this, of course, was true enough. But I contrived a delicate implication that Ballard's mood was a defiant one, that his good will was worth a great deal, that it might be won with my expert assistance, but it was going to cost something.

While I held forth, Blore sat watching me with those bright, bulging eyes of his. They were as unrevealing as a couple of polished doorknobs. I have never trusted men with eyes of that kind. Feeling betrays itself in the muscles around the eyes, in a twitching corner or a mobile lid, but a pop-eyed man has little of this expressive play. He has the steady stare of an owl or a lynx. . . . Blore's face did not give him away, but I noticed that as he listened he kept crossing and uncrossing his legs, as I could tell by the shift of his body, and this, I knew, is always a sign of nervousness. I had him worried and I had him guessing. I paused to relight my cigar and sat waiting for him to lead. He shifted his pins twice before he spoke.

"All right, Morgan," he said. "What do you want?"

I knew then that I had the advantage. After all, I had had it from the first, so far as bargaining was concerned. I knew a great deal more about Ballard and the grant than he did. No doubt he and his backers were irresistible in the long run, but they could have a great deal of trouble and I was in a position to make trouble. So now I made my major bluff. I told him that I thought the sale might be arranged provided Ballard was left in charge as manager. I knew, of course, that Ballard would accept no such arrangement, but I felt almost equally sure that Blore would not. The shake of his head was emphatic—a quick, nervous reaction.

"I'm afraid my principals wouldn't agree to that," he said shortly.

I nodded gravely. I pointed out that the administration of such a property would be an exacting job. I thought the identity of the manager was a legitimate consideration in the making of the deal. Whom, I inquired, did he have in mind for the position?

Blore did not hesitate for an instant.

"I expect to take it myself," he said. He spoke with a finality, a confidence, an intensity, which revealed the man at last. I knew now, what I had suspected all along, that Blore was a power-hungry man. I have no doubt that the first article of his own private agreement with Tweedale was that he should rule. He wanted to move into the great house, sit in the place of absolute authority. The power that Ballard had built was the thing he had bargained for, dreamed of, coveted. Doubtless he had also imagined a great expansion, as I had done. I faced a man with a vision, backed by a passionate desire. I knew he would not renounce it, and I also knew he would pay for it. I felt sure that now I was in a position to dictate. I boosted the price about fifty thousand dollars and specified that Ballard must have a year to put his affairs in order. On these terms, I told Blore, I would do my best to persuade Ballard that he must sell.

Blore sat silent for a moment, which contained a good deal of suspense for me, although I knew well enough what he was thinking. He was wondering how much of my talk was bluff, how much power I had with Ballard. He could refuse my terms and still force Ballard out—in the long run. But it might be a very long run and a very hard one and that was just what he didn't want. It had taken him many months to perfect his scheme and to get Ballard's ear. He couldn't afford to let the moment pass without a decision. He nodded slowly, smiled. Like all cunning men he was infallibly smooth.

"Agreed," he said lightly, as though we had been bargaining for apples. "Fifty thousand dollars more or less is not important in a deal of this size. The year is more than I had expected, but I'll agree to that too, provided Ballard will sign within a week."

The signing was a brief occasion but an impressive one to me, for I knew that I was watching a ruler abdicate and a man resign his life. I had gone over all the papers with Ballard before we called Blore in. There was nothing more to say. Ballard took a pen and signed his name slowly and carefully in his large upright hand with its powerful downstrokes. He pushed the paper across the table to Blore.

"All right, Major," he said quietly, "it's all yours. . . . And God help you!"

CONSUELO

During his last summer in the Dark River Valley Jean Ballard seldom appeared on his porch in the afternoon, as he had done for so many years, but he often went there late in the evening and sometimes sat alone far into the night. Because he had been alone so much in his youth it was easy for him to go back to solitude now. In his early years of mountain wandering he had sat alone beside a thousand campfires, and like all solitary outdoor men he had learned to live upon his own mind, without benefit of printed page, simply ruminating upon his own experience, licking the wounds it had given him, savoring the flavor of its good. After he had come to the valley, for many years his life had been driven and crowded and his thought had all looked ahead, facing exigent necessity. . . . All that was over now. Now he sat alone again as the night deepened and the life about him disappeared and went to sleep. For a while he saw lights scattered all up and down the valley road and heard talk and laughter and the tinkle of music. One by one the lights died, the voices fell silent, the night seemed to swallow the human world. It seemed to blot out all he had built and done in so many years, leaving him alone once more with stars and mountains, with the voices of wind and water—and with all his former selves. Now that his life was leaving him he seemed to possess it more completely than ever before, to see it whole and clear for the first time. He remembered now all the blunders of his younger years, all the times he had seemed blind to the value of things, but he also remembered much of peace and much of passionate delight. There were many things to regret, but even so, the night was crowded with the ghosts of good moments, as though all of them were coming back to say good-by. He was one who had loved life and to such men memory is kind.

— 2 —

There in the dark Consuelo came back to him. It was the first time in years she had come to him, but he was not wholly surprised and she came quietly and confidently, as though this had been a tryst long appointed, as though both of them had known that in the end she would return, and he laid his hand upon hers to let her know she was welcome. Evening after evening they sat silent for the most part. Even in the years when they had been so close they had not talked much except of trivial things and necessary things. They had never tried to explain themselves to each other. Their relation had rested upon wordless understanding and especially upon her intuitive understanding of the fact that he could not communicate much of himself, even to those he loved, that he was a man shut up in a reticence deeply rooted in his past. Ever since boyhood, life had called upon him for cunning and caution, for alertness. He had grown up in a wilderness and had kept all his life something of the silent watchfulness of the wild. For many years he had been an armed man watching his back track. Then for many years he had been a man of power who had learned over and over that safety lies not in trusting men but in seeing them for exactly what they are. He had learned how to live and triumph, he had grown strong enough to be merciful, but he had never opened his mind to anyone.

It was Consuelo who began to speak of the past as though she knew instinctively his mind was ranging back among the years. She spoke quietly and casually of little things, of moments and details, and he listened and nodded and sometimes chuckled. Her voice was truly the voice of the past for it had never changed. There in the dark she was the past come alive and speaking. She spoke mostly of the first years, the hardest years, before they built the big house and before the great road came to their door. Then it had been three days on a good horse to Taos when the weather was open, and no human habitation was nearer. When the deep snows fell it might as well have been a thousand miles to anywhere. They were locked away from the whole world.

It was not pioneering as he had known it in his youth. They had come to the valley with cattle and sheep and fifty good horses and six peons. They built a house of squared timbers there where the great one stood now and quarters down along the river for their followers and corrals and a barn. They were ricos and Consuelo created at once a bit of the world that had produced her, with servants that came when she clapped her hands and a good cook and chocolate, wine and sugar, the luxuries of her kind. But the wilderness did not know they were important people. The wolves almost wiped out their first band of sheep, mountain lions killed their colts and calves. Even before the Arapahoe tried to destroy them, little war parties of young Indians were always sneaking in, stealing a beef or trying to stampede a herd of sheep. For a long time it looked as though this had been a crazy adventure, just as everyone had said it would be. After three years they had less stock than when they started across the mountains. That fall the Apaches were known to be raiding all over the territory from the Gila in the south to the Brazos in the north, and it was followed by a winter when the snow almost buried their house. A rumor spread in Taos that they had both been killed, that an Apache had tried to sell Ballard's scalp, and another rumor had it that Consuelo had been taken captive and was to be held for a ransom. In the spring, the Don, old and sick as he was, led an armed party across the mountains to look for their bones. Followed by fifteen young men armed with bell-mouthed buffalo guns and horse pistols, he came riding down the valley and found Jean Ballard planting oats and shearing his few remaining sheep and Consuelo bossing her kitchen and singing to her child. They gave a great feast for the visitors, killed a beef and barbecued it, poured out the last drop of their wine and said no, they were not going back, they were never going back. They stood together in their doorway and waved long farewells to the departing riders, watched them out of sight, then turned and embraced each other and laughed.

Those were the best years, the hard years, when they lived in a little world of their own creation, bounded by mountains, admitting no intruders, living wholly for each other. But were they really hard years? That was a simple life with a simple discipline. Wolves and mountain lions and thieving Indians were nothing to what came later. Work and physical danger are simple things to deal with. What makes life hard is the bewilderment of change and complication, the rush of people and money, the impact of unexpected things, the swelling current of destiny that sweeps a man along even though he rides it successfully, that sweeps people apart, that wipes out whole patterns of living and creates new ones. This he had come to understand, though he could not say it, and he hoped she understood it too. Now in the long retrospect he understood what had happened to him and he wished he could explain it to her. He remembered so well the barren poverty of his boyhood, the great hungers of his youth, the avid longing with which he looked upon the wealth of St. Louis and of the ricos in Santa Fe and Taos. For so long he had been a landless man, a homeless man, a wandering man always in danger, one who lived on the meat he killed like a wild animal and went for months without seeing a woman or sleeping in a bed. Much of that life had been good to live and much of it was good to remember, but it had been a life of danger and denial, outside the warm circle of love and safety and secure possession. Marriage had been his first taste of tenderness since his mother died, his first taste of security in the possession of anything. He had been happy in the early years in the valley, would have asked nothing better, had expected nothing very different. But then had come the sudden burst of fortune, the flood of money. He had discovered in himself great powers and great appetites that might otherwise have slept all his life. He had long been a leader in a small way, one who had ridden at the head of a band and told others what to do, but he had never dreamed that he could command so much, that so many would bow to his will and jump at his word. Now that it was over he could see that for years he had been drunk on power and money, never quite losing his head, always quick and cunning, but driven by a lust of command and possession and by a great restlessness that sent him back and forth between the mountains and the railroad towns. The women he had taken had been nothing more than fruits of triumph, like the splendid horses he rode in relays. He had learned how desire sprouts in the moment of triumph and how women long to yield to any form of power they can feel. He had never meant to turn away from Consuelo and none had ever taken her place, but he had lived for years in a fever of success that grew on its own triumphs, and when it began to subside he had learned, as everyone learns, that he could not go back to the past, that he had been destroying one thing while he was building another. He saw all this, like a picture on a wall, but he had not the words to tell it. He could only repeat a phrase over and over.

"I was a fool, Carita," he said. "I never meant to go away from you. . . . I was a fool."

She wanted only to comfort him now as she might have comforted a child.

"I do not blame you, Juanito," she told him. "It was my fault too."

"I had been so poor," he said. "I had wanted so much. You cannot understand that. You always had everything. . . ."

"Yes, I can understand," she said. "And you finally had so much more than I. You had the whole world to deal with and I had nothing but you, especially after the girls had gone away to school. As long as they were little and I could teach them, it was different, but the world seems to claim everything, to take everything away. . . ."

"I never meant to leave you," he repeated.

"It was my fault as much as yours," she told him. "If I could have remained beautiful it might have been different. Oh, my beloved, I could never admit this before, but I was a vain woman! I could not bear to grow old. I turned away from you because I could not bear to be less beautiful in your eyes. . . . I must confess, Juanito! I was jealous even of my own daughter that she had my beauty and I had it no longer, that your eyes were all for her. . . . It was then I turned to God. . . . For the love of God! For the love of God I turned away from you because I could no longer be to you what I had been before. I spent long hours on my knees, staring at my lighted candles, my little ivory Jesus with his painted wounds, my Virgin of Guadalupe in her niche with her folded hands and her eyes rolling at Heaven. I wanted to love something that would never change, I wanted to lose myself. For long hours I lost myself. Time fell away from me and a day died in a moment. But I did not see God. I saw only pictures of the beloved past. I did not yearn for Heaven. I wanted only my own lost beauty and the moment of our love. . . ."

"I never knew . . ." He fumbled for the words that came so easily to her. "If I had only known!"

"I understand that, Juanito," she said. "I did not blame you then. I do not blame you now. I am sorry only for my own vanity. . . . May God forgive me!"

Her voice was a music moving to the high pitch of her feeling—a music that carried him all the way back to the first moment of their love. Her voice was the music of the unforgotten past, the perfect and finished past, of all the vivid moments that can never be again. He remembered them just as vividly as she did but he had not her gift of words. He too was filled with a great, troubled warmth of feeling but he could not utter it.

"I have come back to you now, Carita," he said gravely. "Nothing else now seems to be worth anything. . . . If God will not forgive us, we can forgive each other."

REQUIEM

AT HIS own request Jean Ballard was buried in a grove of yellow pine on the crest of a knoll overlooking the Dark River Valley and at his own request the only service was there beside the grave. Nearly a thousand people, the largest gathering ever held in the valley, followed his body to the hilltop and banked the slopes. Nearly all of the Mexicans from Royball-town were there, most of the cattlemen who had traded at the Ballard store and ridden the Ballard range, a group of officers from Santa Fe and Fort Union, and the wives of all these kinds of men, nearly all of them in black, the Mexican women hooding their faces under their great black shawls, looking like figures of death in a frieze. Only the Utes did not come to the grave side. Down at the foot of the hill they had set up a great lodge, made of buffalo hides, a relic of the days of their power, and there they gathered to mourn Ballard in their own way.

It was also Ballard's wish that his friend Daniel Laird should preside at his funeral. The big mountaineer stood up with his hat in his hand and recited the prayer for the dead. Afterward he was silent for a long moment, as though embarrassed or tongue-tied, and a faint rustle of uneasiness ran through the crowd. Then Laird delivered one of his rare speeches.

"The man we have come here to bury was a friend to all of

us, and one we will long miss," he said slowly, and his great voice at once commanded the crowd. "Here in the Dark River Valley there has been peace among men for many years and that peace was made and kept by him. In all the years I have lived here no man has ever gone hungry. His table was set for all humanity. In all of those years there has never been a thief or a beggar among us, because no man felt his need denied. We have all sheltered under the strength of our friend, far more than most of us know. Now that he is gone we will learn that he was great, and some of us will learn in pain and trouble."

He paused for a long moment and then began again, even more slowly.

"We mourn that our friend is dead," he said, "but let us not have sorrow only, for death is kind. Let us rejoice that his long pain is over, that all suffering has an end, that he now can lie down and sleep in the earth he loved, the earth that gave him being—that he shall have rebirth in new forms of life, that tree and grass and flower shall take up his fallen clay and lift it once more to the sun."

When he had finished a sound of chanting came up from the valley and the whole crowd turned to look. The Utes had emerged from their tepee and formed a long column, all of them stripped to their breech-clouts, with their faces painted black. They moved in a slow dance to a deep booming chant, their feet and their voices both in perfect time. It was their ancient dance of mourning for a fallen chief, and in it they seemed to regain some long lost power and dignity, so that all stood and watched them in reverent silence until they disappeared into the forest and their chanting grew faint and was lost in the wind. Then the clods fell, the tall woman in black gave one great sobbing cry, the people turned away and began to talk again.

PART THREE

The Usurpers

MAJOR ARNOLD NEWTON BLORE

ARNOLD BLORE did not feel the war as a personal defeat until he rode home after Lee's surrender. Not until he saw his house and his father did he understand that the only world he knew had been destroyed and that he had to seek a new one.

For him the war had been a triumph so absorbing that he had thought little of anything except his own fortunes. He had gone through it all unwounded. He had tasted power for the first time. He had commanded hundreds and destroyed thousands. For most men war was misery and horror but for some it was a great fulfillment, releasing energies and desires they had never known they possessed, and Blore was one of these. His swift rise from the ranks was almost incredible to himself. His knowledge of horses and his rare gift for managing them was his first asset, and it gained him quick promotion to the rank of sergeant, but he soon discovered that he had also a gift for command and a talent for maneuver and for artillery fire. His opportunity came in the long wilderness battle, when both the commissioned officers of his battery were killed and command fell upon him by right of rank. In a swift and daring maneuver he brought his guns to a hilltop, flanked an enemy column, saw men stumble and fall in the sweep of his fire, saw a regiment break and scatter and turn into a futile mob. He got his commission promptly. In war nothing counted but ability.

Arnold Blore loved artillery, although he had never thought of himself as a fighting man. In all his life he had never wanted to fight with his own hands. But he loved the roar of the great guns, the flame and smoke of destruction. He loved a power that struck like a thunderbolt when he spoke the word. Battle filled him with a great elation, almost an ecstasy, and this feeling was always associated with the thunder of a battery, which was the very voice of battle to him. He was never confused or frightened. The only thing that gave him pain was the sight and sound of wounded horses. He did not mind seeing men fall. This surprised him at first but he accepted it rather easily because it was a great advantage in battle not to feel any personal shock.

He never understood how much the war had meant to him until it was over. When the guns fell silent, life seemed suddenly tame and flat. He felt small again, riding home alone, with no command behind him, no battle before.

— 2 —

He did not have far to ride. The Blores lived on the Virginia side of the Potomac, north of Washington, in a region that had been horse country since colonial days—a country of rolling hills and good grass. His grandfather, Edward Blore, had bought the place and established a stud farm there when he was an old man, and his father, William, had built the red brick house with the white-pillared porch—a house which expressed a social aspiration long denied.

Arnold rode down a rutted lane bordered by massive junipers and very old cherry trees which had been planted by birds that perched on the rotting rail fences on either side. In this month of May the cherry trees were in bloom, bobwhites whistled from the fence posts and wind rippled the grass in wide pastures. The house stood in a grove of forest trees with thick woodland climbing the hill behind it and pastures sloping down to the river in front.

As soon as he saw the place he had an impression of neglect and decay. The lawn had grown into long grass with broom sedge and even a few briars creeping in. The rose bushes on either side of the driveway had spread into an unkempt bramble, and a startled grouse went whirring out of their cover, making him feel as though he rode into a wilderness—as though the woodland and the wild were creeping up on the old house, now that the power had gone out of it. He could see white paint peeling off the pillars and green paint peeling off the shutters and the heavy-odored honeysuckle had almost buried the porch.

Arnold's mother had died before the war and his sister had married and gone to live in Maryland. The old man was living there alone now, except for a few Negroes who had stayed because they didn't know what else to do. At the height of their fortunes the Blores had owned about a dozen slaves— house servants and stable hands and a couple of men who tended a garden and a small orchard. The Blores raised nothing but horses and truck for their own table.

Arnold knew that his father had not been well, that the war had destroyed the market for horses, that the Negroes were a net loss. He had been prepared for hard times but not for the air of desolation and decay that possessed the place. He felt as though he had come back to something dead. The house was silent as a deserted house and it remained silent for a long moment after he knocked. Then he heard faint movement within, the door swung open and there stood old Cora, the great, fat, chocolate-colored woman who had been the family cook for about eighteen years, had fed him and wiped his nose when he was a child. She stood staring at him for a moment with her mouth open, as though she couldn't quite believe in his existence. Then she came forward and put her arms around him and said over and over, "You is home again! You is home again!"

Cora was one human he had always counted on and he felt something of the warmth and security of childhood in the pressure of her great soft body. He had always liked Negroes, as he liked horses, because they were submissive. He could guess that Cora now was doing more than anyone else to keep the household going. But he was staring over her shoulder at a large, shapely, full-bosomed yellow girl of about sixteen who had followed Cora into the hall and now stood giggling self-consciously. Cora released him, looked from one to the other of them, seemed to unite them in her broad smile.

"Don't you know little Milly?" she demanded. Then he knew this was Cora's daughter, who had been just a dirty child around the kitchen when he rode away. She was clean now in blue calico and a red headcloth and she came forward and gave him a soft, slavish hand and giggled at him again and purred something inarticulate in her musical Negro voice. He felt a sudden unwilling stir of desire toward her as he took her hand—a certainty that her soft yellow flesh was waiting for him, that he could sink into it and be mired there, in a way of life that had lost its hope and promise but still had a powerful hold upon him because all the roots of his being were in it. In the presence of these two women with their clean Negro smell, their caressing voices, he sensed what had happened. They had moved in on the old man, moved in on the house and taken it over, just as the woodland had moved into the grounds. He could feel them reaching out for him, wanting to capture him, suck him down into this easy half-rotten world.

"Yoah Pappy ain't right well today," Cora murmured as she led him toward the sitting room and opened the door.

The light was dim in there but it was enough to show a disorder of scattered papers and tobacco pipes, bottles and glasses. William Blore was seated behind a heavy table and when he rose Arnold could see that he was quite drunk. He lifted himself with both hands on the table and tottered forward—a short bowlegged man of sixty with powerful shoulders like all the Blores. Although they loved and married big women, they all bred true to the same type in the male line, as though an inexorable providence had designed them all to be jockeys.

"By God, my boy, I'm glad to see you! Have a drink. Pour him a drink, Cora. By God, everything will be all right now!"

He retreated to his chair and slumped back into it with heavy relief. Cora poured whisky and water, and turned to Arnold.

"Now I's gonna get you the best dinner you's et since you went away," she told him. "Chicken an' yams an' snaps and biscuits. . . ." She swept out of the room, laughing happily, possessive and assured. She had food and woman to offer and she could conceive of no other need or desire.

When they were alone, William Blore pushed his glass away from him with sudden resolution, shook his head, seemed to lift himself out of his stupor by conscious effort.

"Arnold, my boy," he said, "I lied to you just now. Nothing is all right. Nothing is worth a damn. This country is ruined. Racing is all over and money is all gone and you can't sell a two-year-old for what it costs to raise him. What am I now? Just a goddam nigger-loving poor white! . . . Arnold, my boy, I hate to see you go, but you've got to go. I've been making up my mind to that ever since I heard it was all over. There's nothing I can do for you here, and nothing you can do for me. There's two good colts in the pasture. That's all I've got to give you but they'll take you anywhere a horse can travel. . . ."

— 3 —

The house of Blore was founded on a horse and it had been associated with almost the entire history of thoroughbred racing stock in the South. The Virginians especially had always loved racing, but the quarter horse, short coupled and fast for a few hundred yards, had been the race horse of colonial days and racing had been only an informal sport. Not many thoroughbreds were imported until early in the nineteenth century. The famous stallion Fenwick, whose blood was to run through American racing lines for many generations, was one of the first of them. He was imported by Wade Hampton who went to London to make the purchase. At the same time he employed Edward Blore, the British jockey, who had trained the great stallion and ridden him to all his victories on the British turf. Blore proved to be an even better investment than Fenwick. He served the Hampton family as head trainer and jockey for twenty years and won much money for his master. He saved his wages, married a big girl from the mountain country of western Virginia, and established a stud farm of his own about 1830. His son William came into the property in 1845 when racing in Virginia was at the highest point of its development. Almost every great estate had its private track and there were public courses at Fairfield, Broad Rock, New Market and Tree Hill, where the ruling families of three states came together every year for a racing season. The racing balls of those days were the most exclusive and elaborate gatherings in the South.

It was William Blore who bred the famous stallion Timoleon, and Timoleon founded the family fortune. No stallion in American racing history had ever sired so many winning colts. Mares were sent to him from all over Virginia and South Carolina and as far south as New Orleans. He had a prodigious fertility. In one year he covered nearly two hundred mares at a hundred dollars a leap. His loins were a gold mine. They enlarged the Blore acres, built the red brick house with the white columns, bought the slaves which gave William Blore all the trapping and service of a Virginia gentleman. Moreover, Timoleon brought many of the most famous gentlemen of Virginia to his house. They treated him with distinguished courtesy but they did not invite him to their houses. They came to see Timoleon, who had breeding in every sense of the word. William Blore welcomed them and took their good money and began quietly hating them.

In the course of three generations the Blores underwent a peculiar social evolution. Edward Blore was the happiest of the three because he had the training of an English servant. All his life he dropped his H's and took off his cap or pulled his forelock when he approached his betters. He had the indestructible, inborn cockney feeling for caste. Moreover, he was too completely absorbed in horses to care much for human society. He raised a famous mare called Creeping Kate who won him much money on the Virginia track, and she became the love of his later years. It was said he never bred her because he was jealous of the stud.

William Blore looked almost exactly like his father, but he had a different speech and manner. He never quite mastered the soft southern inflection but neither did he speak like a cockney Englishman. He had a deferent manner in all his dealings with his proud customers but it was an uneasy deference that covered a resentment. He resented his own uneasiness as much as he resented the perfect manners of his patrons who were fortified by a snobbery so complete that they were not conscious of it as such. William Blore was a shrewd little man with a keen mind. He knew he was more intelligent than many of these gentlemen. During his best years he was also more secure and prosperous than most of them. In these last two decades before the war the Virginian aristocracy had renounced none of its pretensions but it lived upon a dying economy. Tobacco lands were worn out and Virginia planters lived more and more by selling Negroes to be sent to Alabama and Georgia where cotton was booming. William Blore knew that many of them were selling their own blood. He thought it more dignified to breed horses for the market than men. In his later years he drank a good deal. When he was mildly drunk and among his family he became a man his patrons would hardly have recognized, with a mouth full of earthy epithet and profanity whenever he talked about them.

In Arnold Blore the transformation of speech and manner became complete. He spoke exactly like a Virginia gentleman and he had southern courtesy in a form that was slightly exaggerated but good enough so that strangers always took him for a gentleman. But of course he was not a gentleman. He was a horse trader, a trainer, sometimes a jockey. And he was the grandson of a cockney servant in a society which worshiped ancestry and status. Arnold Blore learned from childhood how to be faultlessly polite to the men he dealt with and also how to despise them. Although he did not know it, he had toward these people the same attitude the Negroes had toward the whites—an attitude subtly compounded of hypocrisy, cunning, envy and contempt.

— 4 —

The Shadwells lived only a few miles from the Blores, but they lived in another world. They were related to the Washingtons on one side and the Pendletons on the other and their lands had been in the family for five generations. The estate contained about a thousand acres of which more than half was woodland, but the rest of it had once been good tobacco land and highly profitable. Most of this now was worn out and grown up to oldfield pine and broom sedge. A few hundred acres of corn and some garden truck were all their fields produced. They raised hogs which ran half wild in their woodlands and they made famous hams and bacons, or at least the old Negro who had charge of their smokehouse did. They still had about thirty-five Negroes, although once the estate had supported more than a hundred. Almost every year they sold a few, generally black field hands, but sometimes it became necessary to sell one of the yellow Negroes who worked around the house, and belonged to families the Shadwells had owned for generations. This always brought tears to the eyes of both slave and master, but Mark Shadwell was heavily in debt and Negroes were his most negotiable assets. He was a dignified gentleman in his late fifties, took his debts lightly and never let them curb his hospitality. The Shadwells could still entertain twenty at dinner and more than that at hunt breakfasts. Of course the place produced abundant food, including game from their own forests and hams from their own smokehouse. And there were only four of the Shadwells now—the old man, his fat and ailing wife, his son, Mark junior, who was charming and devoted his life to hunting, and his seventeen-year-old daughter, Gracie, who was already one of the best horsewomen in the country and could take a four-rail fence in her sidesaddle in perfect form. Gracie was a spontaneous, undisciplined creature, large and mature-looking for her years, who spent much of her time riding around the country alone, often taking a few fences just for the fun of it. She scandalized older women by her horsy talk and the freedom of her manners, but she went her way gaily and unconcerned. Gossip could not really damage a Shadwell, and everyone knew that Gracie was a fine girl but too much for her parents.

The Shadwells had several blooded mares which they bred to important stallions and once in a while they produced a colt that sold for large money. One of these colts brought Arnold Blore into somewhat intimate contact with the Shadwells, for the colt inevitably came to him for training. The Shadwells knew horses and could breed horses, but none of them could train a colt. The old man was past the age for such an undertaking and Mark junior had an unstable temper. He made horses nervous. Only Gracie had the real feeling for horses, the mysterious gift of hand and voice which horses seem to recognize almost instantly. Gracie might have been a trainer if she had been a man and not a Shadwell.

This colt, who was named Diomed after a famous stallion of colonial days, came to the Blore stables less than a year before the war, when Arnold was twenty-four. Arnold was already taking over much of his father's work, had trained several winners and had a reputation of his own. Diomed came to him wholly untaught. He put the colt through his first paces at the end of a long rope and in the sand pen, nailed his first shoes and saddled him for the first time. By that time he felt sure the colt was going to be a winner, and told his father so. They made the Shadwells a good offer for Diomed, but old Mark wouldn't sell. He said the colt belonged to Gracie, had been given her for a birthday present. This, of course, was mostly pretense. The colt was a family asset and would be sold at the right time, but Mark Shadwell was smart enough to know that if the Blores wanted to buy Diomed he was probably worth keeping until he was a two-year-old.

When the colt began to show his class, the old man and his son and Gracie all stopped at the Blore track, singly or together in a casual way, to watch Arnold work with him. The men soon lost interest, but not Gracie. She was a true horse lover and Diomed was her current love. He was a beautiful sorrel gelding with a coat that shone in the sun like new gold and the large full soft eye of the horse that is naturally gentle and never shows his whites to his masters. Gracie continued to stop at the Blore track every time she went for a ride and that was several times a week. At first she only stopped outside the fence, waved a greeting to Arnold and sat her horse to watch the colt go through his paces. But she could no more keep her hands off Diomed than she could keep her eyes off him. Soon she was riding into the paddock to examine his carefully wrapped ankles, to pat his neck, to feed him a carrot, and she and Arnold had several good talks, all about horses. This sort of visiting was an unusual thing for a woman to do in that time and place, but somehow not unusual for Gracie, who always went where she felt like going. When she was ready to leave, Arnold always cupped his two hands to hold her foot and boosted her onto her horse, for no woman could mount a sidesaddle unassisted.

After that first talk Gracie's visits became more frequent and Arnold began to anticipate her coming with eagerness. He spent more and more time with the colt, just in the hope that Gracie would come along. He was always watching for her, always saw her in the distance and waved to her and she waved back. She always dismounted now, and after the workout was over they would sit side by side on a bench near the track and talk, sometimes for half an hour. They never talked about anything except horses in general and the colt in particular, as though it had been tacitly understood that this was their only common ground and that their relation must be strictly confined to it. But it was amazing how much they found to say, and how much they laughed together. Arnold felt sure that Gracie was happy with him and he was happy with her but she also gave him a growing feeling of insecurity.

All his life he had lived inside the shell of his carefully cultivated manner, so far as almost everyone except the family was concerned. It was a manner he had inherited and perfected and he felt safe behind it. He had learned never to express his feelings. But he knew that with Gracie his defenses were in danger, especially when she sat beside him.

Gracie was not a beautiful girl but she was an attractive one. She was just a shade taller than Arnold and a little heavier. Her face was broad and good-humored, with large gray eyes, and a sprinkle of freckles across her nose. Her thick yellow hair was a little unkempt so that she was always tucking it up and brushing it back. She wore the long, voluminous riding skirt all horsewomen wore in those days, but in warm weather she never wore the jacket that went with it. Her blouse left her forearms bare and she had beautiful arms and hands—large, strong hands trained from childhood in a struggle with tugging bridle reins. To Arnold she looked perfect, as ripe fruit and newly blown flowers are perfect. He had never fallen in love before and he did not understand exactly what was happening to him. He talked horse and laughed and everything seemed to be all right, but all the time he was looking into her eyes and she was looking right back at him, never evading his steady, eager stare. His manner was holding up all right, but he was filled with a disturbing mixture of reverence and lust. He longed to serve Gracie, to do something heroic and astonishing for her, and he also longed to possess her large, soft, virginal body. The thrust and swell of his desire seemed a hidden, guilty threat to his careful manners, and when he cupped his hands to lift her into the saddle he was aware that they trembled a little. Once her horse swerved, throwing her leg hard against his body. She did not apologize but laughed happily and rode away, throwing him a smile over her shoulder, blushing but not at all confused. He knew then that a moment was coming, that there would have to be a climax.

It came one day when she had hoisted herself precariously to the top bar of a gate beside the track and perched there watching him work with the colt. When he had finished and turned Diomed over to the stable boy he came toward her and she held out both hands for him to help her down. She descended into his arms gracefully and easily, almost inevitably. He did not feel as though he had committed any aggression. She seemed to fall into his arms as a ripe peach falls into the hand that touches it. But when he had her there he could not let her go. He held her tightly and he could feel the beat of her heart against his ribs and the full, firm pressure of her breasts. He pushed her head back and kissed her hard on the lips. For a moment she was limp in his arms. He had a moment of triumph for her mouth was open and his tongue touched hers and he knew something in Gracie was answering to his desire. Then she pushed him away and stood staring at him with tears in her eyes and her lips trembling. She seemed suddenly transformed. In a moment a challenging, willing woman became a frightened, bewildered child. Then she covered her face with her hands and began to cry.

"Don't cry, Miss Gracie," he said, "I'm sorry."

He was more than sorry, he was sick. He stood before her, weak and helpless, until she dried her tears and walked over to her horse without looking at him. He cupped his hands and boosted her into the saddle, and she whirled her horse and rode away in a dead run, as though she had been overcome by an impulse of panic flight.

He never saw her again except a few times at a distance, and every time he did, he felt that same sickness in the pit of his stomach.

Mark Shadwell came over a few days later and took Diomed away. He was exceedingly polite and a little apologetic about it.

He said they simply couldn't afford to go on with the training, at least not this year, with war threatening and the bottom dropping out of everything.

Even then, a few months before Sumter, many people in Virginia didn't believe there would be any war, and others thought it would not amount to anything. When it broke out, Arnold Blore enlisted at once, despite the protests of his father. William Blore didn't believe in secession or feel that he had any stake in the conflict. He felt that the war was an unnecessary disaster which had been brought on by these proud sons-of-bitches with their peculiar institution and their highfalutin talk. Arnold did not argue with his father. He was not interested in the issues of war either but he had a sure, intuitive conviction that war had meaning and value for him. He was full of war, and only half aware that Gracie Shadwell had sent him into battle.

— 5 —

When Arnold Blore left home again after Lee's surrender, he went first to St. Louis, driving the two young thoroughbreds his father had given him, hitched to a light wagon called a democrat. Almost everyone in the South who started west after the war went first to St. Louis, unless he was bound for Santa Fe by way of Independence. St. Louis was the boom city of the Mississippi Valley. It doubled its population ten years after the war and had almost two hundred thousand people when Arnold first saw it—a great overgrown town sprawling along the river where docks were multiplying to meet the greatest fleet of steamboats the river was ever to carry, and climbing the low hills from its turbulent roaring waterfront to the red brick dignity of its best residential streets. Because timber was scarce almost everything was built of brick, even the sidewalks, and for the same reason everyone burned soft coal, which darkly smudged the great red city and buried it under a black cloud when the wind was down. Americans were pouring into St. Louis from all over the South, but German immigrants of the first wave were coming even faster, creating the first large foreign colony of the West.

It was easy to make money in St. Louis and Arnold Blore made good money from the first. Inevitably he became a horse trader because horses were the only commodity he knew. He gained a capital by selling his two thoroughbreds for high prices, rented a small stable and began buying and selling horses. He had a sure eye for a colt that could be given style and sold at a fat profit, and he was also good at matching pairs and selling them to the carriage trade. Soon he was renting horses and equipage of all kinds, as well as selling them. His livery stable became one of the best in the city. But Arnold Blore was not content to stay there, and knew from the first he was not going to stay. In St. Louis he had become what his father had been—a purveyor of horse flesh to gentlemen. He did not know exactly what he wanted but he knew this was not it. He also knew that sooner or later he was going farther west. He was one of thousands of men who felt the same way. In those years men were drifting west in a vast unorganized migration. Many of them, like Arnold Blore, were unattached men with a tingle of excitement in their blood, carried over from the war. They were too restless to be easily captured by women and tied to a place. They tended to go from one boom town to another, and the country was full of talk about booms and big money. All through the years he spent in St. Louis, Arnold Blore was hearing more and more about Denver, which had grown in a few years from a mining camp to a city of more than fifty thousand with some of the finest bars and hotels in the West. When he got a good offer for his livery stable, he sold and set out for Denver, once more driving his own fine team, but this time with a substantial account behind him in a St. Louis bank. He was no longer a drifting veteran of the war. Now he was a capitalist.

On his way west he stopped briefly in Dodge City, which was then at the beginning of its brief career as a cattle-shipping point on the westward-crawling railroad. He struck the town in the spring and saw the bawling herds of longhorns pour into the shipping pens, saw the Texans take over the town and shoot it up, saw the bars and gambling joints rake in money by the bucketful, saw men fight like wolves over the too few women who were shipped in by the carload from Kansas City and St. Louis. Blore loved the sound and smell of a boom town as he had loved the sound and smell of war, and he moved through it as he had moved through war, with quiet, efficient self-confidence. He never wore a gun and never got into trouble. He avoided women and drunks and looked for horses and bargains. The place abounded in both, and Blore left it richer than he had come, but he felt sure it was not a place to stay. It was doomed to dwindle as the rails reached westward.

In Denver he knew almost at once that he had found a home. Here was a town with a solid center of banks and hotels and wholesale houses, a town where money was piling up, a town that was going to last. He bought a livery stable and became a horse trader again, but soon his stable was only one of his interests and the one he talked least about. He invested discreetly in mining shares and also in real estate. Here too he had the curious experience of becoming a southern gentleman for the first time in his life. Here he was Major Blore, a Confederate veteran with a distinguished record. There were other men in Denver who had been Confederate officers and they constituted an informal club which met in the best bars, talked about the war over their whiskies and addressed each other with the utmost courtesy and always by their military titles. Some of them talked also about their families and the good old days before the war, but in the West it was bad manners to question a man about his past, and Major Blore did not talk about anything except the war.

The West was a belligerently democratic place, and at the same time it was busily founding a new aristocracy of money. In the West one man was just as good as another and ancestry counted for nothing, but already there was beginning to be a distinction between the few who accumulated money and the many who did not. For the West had a spendthrift tradition. Money was easy to make. A man might make a stake in a month or a year and throw it across the bars and the gambling tables in a few days. There was always more where that came from. It was customary for a lucky man to buy drinks for the house when the house might contain a hundred. Men lived in a world of waste and abundance and most of them could not imagine the end of it.

Arnold Blore could appear lavish when he thought it was necessary, but he held onto money instinctively. Money in the bank made him feel larger and stronger. It gave him the feeling of safety and power other men got from a weapon on the hip or in the pocket. Money, like the great guns of the war, was a weapon that reached a long way and worked without the sweat and strain of personal violence. Arnold Blore avoided men who went broke and wanted to borrow money, and he had an affinity for those who had money to lend, at good interest. In this way he became part of a little group which was beginning to gain control of Denver—those who owned most of the land it stood on, and most of the buildings and many of the mines. Town lots and mining claims were so far the chief forms of vested wealth.

When he had been there about five years, Major Blore was a well-known figure in Denver. He had no intimates but he had a great many acquaintances, all carefully chosen. He was infallibly smooth and polite, with a slight touch of pomposity which sometimes caused men to laugh at him behind his back, but never before his face. He had an especially charming and gallant manner with women, and women often liked him, despite his short stature, but the women he met socially found him elusive. No man ever had a more perfect and formal manner with the wives of his acquaintances. He knew that women set men against each other and that this is the most unprofitable and damaging kind of hostility. He had also learned that a woman can disarm a man and take him captive, and Major Blore did not propose to be taken captive. He did not feel safe with any woman he could not buy and pay for. Denver abounded in women who could be had for a price, and he was a discreet and secretive connoisseur of such, judging woman-flesh with the same delicate feeling for form and action that he brought to horse flesh. Major Blore was not an ascetic but he was a dedicated man, as saints and poets are dedicated men. He wanted power and he sacrificed everything else to that end, not by a mighty effort of abnegation, but instinctively and shrewdly, with a quiet contempt for the emotional booby traps in which most men flounder.

— 6 —

The Spanish land grants of the Southwest came to his attention by accident, when he read in a newspaper about the Federal law which provided for a government survey whenever a majority of the owners requested it. His alert and hungry intelligence smelled opportunity in that brief item. He knew that those who own the earth rule it. He had always wanted to own land but so far he had seen no opportunity to acquire more than a few town lots, and these did not at all satisfy his desire.

Major Blore had imagination and he could imagine a man gaining control of something like an empire in the West. There it lay unused, by the millions of acres, but it was peculiarly difficult to gain title to any large part of it. East of the Mississippi land had been owned by the ruling families since colonial days in great tracts granted by the British crown, but the public domain of the West was now subject to the new Homestead Law, which provided that any man might have a quarter section, provided he lived on it and used it. The law was designed to create a world of small freeholders and the means of preventing this had not yet been perfected. Already there was beginning to be a business in "relinquishments," so that shrewd men might pick up homesteads here and there without effort, and some men hired others to homestead for them. But this was too slow and picayune a process to appeal to Major Blore. It was an exciting revelation to him that the Royal will had created ready-made empires in the Southwest, as well as in the East. Moreover, most of them were still in the hands of the Mexicans, a people who were rapidly losing power and property. He felt an intuitive conviction that he had discovered a great opportunity.

It was at this point that Major Blore became a true pioneer. So far he had been only a shrewd man following booms and picking up some of the easy money they put into circulation. Now he had an idea of his own and one that was eventually to be used by many others. He said nothing to anyone about what he was doing but he became a student of the Spanish Land Grants of the Southwest and one of the first. He had never been a student before, but he worked at this task with the concentrated intensity of a scientist bent on discovery. He learned enough Spanish so that he could read it with facility. He made two trips to Santa Fe and spent months pouring over the records. For a long time his researches were wholly discouraging and a man with less confidence in his own ideas would have relinquished the project as hopeless. All of these grants had been held by Mexican families for generations and the families had been incredibly prolific. Most of them had so many heirs that to hunt them all out and procure a survey and a valid title seemed impossible. Then he came across the Coronel family and traced the history of its holdings on the eastern slope of the Rockies. Here was one great estate which had been captured and held by a single man. Like a hound on a hot trail he followed the story of Jean Ballard from Santa Fe to Taos, from Taos to the Dark River Valley, from there to St. Louis. He traced the man's rise and he saw the inevitability of his fall. Before he went to his friend, Colonel Tweedale, his scheme was complete to the last detail. There was no question he could not answer, no contingency he had not foreseen. He saw only one danger—that Ballard might not live to see a deal completed. For he had learned all about Ballard's health and knew the man might die any time, leaving his great estate in weak and scattered hands. He therefore urged upon Tweedale the need for haste and Tweedale did not hesitate. He set about organizing the syndicate in Denver while Blore was engaged in his delicate mission to the Dark River Valley.

— 7 —

During the year before he took charge of the grant, Major Blore was a busy man. He went first to Denver and reported to his principals, then to St. Louis where final arrangements had to be made with all Ballard's creditors. After that he went to work upon his bold plans for the exploitation of his prize. The necessary survey entailed a trip to Washington, and it also entailed a highly private and very delicate arrangement with the surveyor who was to make it. This, in fact, was the largest single outlay the syndicate had to make besides the purchase price. After receiving a rough estimate of his probable holdings, which would total nearly two thousand square miles, the Major prepared advertisements to be published in St. Louis, in Kansas City and even in eastern cities. These made it clear that a city was to be founded on the Dark River and that an auction sale of town lots was to be held on a certain stated date. The river was to be dammed, creating a vast area of irrigable land, and the advertisement contrived to imply that this was already an accomplished fact without quite saying so. A sawmill would make lumber for construction available on the spot in unlimited quantities. Investors were urged to waste no time if they wished to share in the first great boom of the empire which the United States had taken away from Mexico in 1849.

The Major's last stop was in Dodge City, Kansas, then at the height of its importance as a cattle-shipping point and track-end town. He knew that Dodge City was full of land-hungry men with guns on their hips. He knew also that it was a town whose boom days were nearly over. He proposed to acquire there certain employees, who would have to be carefully chosen, and also settlers who would be given special consideration in order to attach them to the interests of the syndicate. The Major knew what he faced and he knew it probably included some trouble.

BETTY WEISS

AT THE time of her murder in Dodge City, Dora Hand was perhaps the most famous woman between Kansas City and Santa Fe. Dora was a prostitute who belonged to a brief moment in American history that gave her profession something of the power and importance it had in the Renaissance and in the seventeenth century when Ninon de Lenclos ruled her court of lovers and courtesans seduced kings and prelates. Dora seduced mayors and town marshals and Texas cattle kings, who were the great men of her world, but she also became a valued and powerful member of her community and she seems truly to have charmed it. Men who had known her described her fifty years later as graciously beautiful and remembered her singing voice as the most lovely thing in a discordant world. Perhaps these old-timers were a little in love with their own memories but there can be no doubt of the powerful impression that Dora made on her contemporaries. Neither can there be any doubt that, as one of them remarked, she elevated her profession considerably.

In general it had not been an elevated profession in the early West, nor in the early days of Dodge City. Dodge began as a shipping point for the buffalo hunters who destroyed the southern buffalo herd and shipped hides east in bales. Most of these men were of the toughest breed that ever forked a horse or pulled a trigger. They lived by wholesale slaughter and by way of relaxation they got drunk, fought rough-and-tumble and went to bed with almost anything that looked like a woman. They seldom washed and never bathed and when they lined up at a bar the last man to catch a louse on his own person had to pay for the drinks. The women who entertained them were brawny wenches, short-haired and painted like Indians—predatory bats who knew how to roll a drunk and seldom let a man get away with a dollar in his pocket.

When the cattle herds came streaming up the Chisholm Trail and three thousand cowboys hit the town, all this was changed. The Texans were violent but chivalrous men with cultivated tastes in women, horses and whisky. Often the outfit that brought a Texas herd over the trail was about half a family party of wild young men with pockets full of money. They wanted high-class women and they got them. Girls came from St. Louis and Kansas City in response to advertisements for waitresses and entertainers, and the whole town would be down at the station to look them over. They had to be pretty to make good and some of them were beautiful. Some of them were also smart and piled up money in banks and more than half of them eventually married. For these women were something more than whores. East of the river people had migrated in family parties, but west of it men went alone and the women who followed were the female pioneers, always a small minority, practicing an heroic polyandry. Often a pretty girl would become for a season the exclusive property of one Texas outfit and would be known to all as the sweetheart of the Turkey Track or the Bar-L-K. Nearly always one or more of the cowboys would offer to marry her, but these belles seldom married until their popularity began to wane with their looks. Nearly all of them preferred six or seven devoted lovers and much money to one husband and a job keeping house on a ranch.

These women always took charge of the town's charities and the sick and the down-and-out were their children. The celebrity of Dora Hand was due as much to her philanthropy as it was to her voice or her figure, which was a perfect specimen of the big-breasted, swivel-hipped blonde type men then admired. At night Dora wore gowns that just barely covered her nipples and the way she could switch her caboose was something men rode miles to see. But by day she wore calico and even a sunbonnet and was a hard and humorous Samaritan who gave what was needed and couldn't be fooled. Her singing had the same dual character. It was said she had sung in Grand Opera, which may be doubted, but she had a contralto of great power and some range. At night she could make cowboys weep into their chasers with her sentimental ballads, and on Sunday morning she always attended the one little Methodist chapel on North Side Hill and led the singing of hymns. The Reverend Dwight was her best friend and her chief assistant in her charitable work. Moreover, she packed his church, which might otherwise have been neglected. Sometimes she brought two or three of her girls with her and almost always, in the last year of her life, at least one, a slim girl named Betty Weiss, who also had a voice, though not one of such volume and authority as Dora's. The two of them standing up there in the choir loft, always dressed in black, lifting up their voices to God, were a sight men long remembered.

Dora's death was an accident, a simple case of mistaken identity, but it threw the town into a dither as no killing had done since its founding. Dora presided over the feminine adjunct of a large and lucrative establishment owned by Mayor Kelly, known as "Dog" Kelly because he was the first man to import greyhounds and cultivate the sport of chasing antelopes and coyotes with them. The Kelly joint, like many of its day and kind, included a bar, a restaurant, a long gambling room, a dance hall and bedrooms upstairs. It also included a two-room cottage at the rear where Mayor Kelly had lived until he rented it to Dora Hand. The mayor had a long-standing feud with the Texans, and especially with the great King and Kennedy outfit. The Kennedy cowboy who killed Dora Hand emptied his six-shooter late one night through the flimsy wall of the Kelly shack at the exact spot where the bed was known to stand, and then departed southward on a fast horse, confident he would be proclaimed a hero by his fellow Texans for killing the mayor. He had the honor of being trailed and captured by three of the greatest man hunters in the West—Bat Masterson, Bill Tilghman and Wyatt Earp—and he didn't learn that he had killed Dora Hand by mistake until Bat Masterson knocked him off his horse with a shot that shattered his right arm. When told what had happened he expressed his gentlemanly regret that his own wound had not been fatal.

The whole town mourned Dora Hand but the person most affected by her death was Betty Weiss. When someone came to the dance hall the day Dora was killed and wanted to know who was in charge, Betty stepped forward and said, "I am," in a tone that left no doubt in anyone's mind. She was, from then on. She had what it took to run things and she ran them, although she was only twenty-six and looked younger.

Betty was a contrast to the smooth and undulating Dora, being slim, nervous, quick and sharp, with dark brown hair and gray-green eyes, but she took over completely the dual role of her predecessor, managing the town charities in a very businesslike fashion and lending the church her moral and vocal support. She was also both more luxurious and more exclusive than Dora had been. She furnished her own quarters in a style such as Dodge had never seen before, with thick carpets, lace curtains and a beveled mirror in which she could contemplate her elegant person full length. She employed a Negro maid who announced all visitors, not all of whom were admitted. In fact, it was a mystery and a subject of speculation as to who achieved the ineffable favors of Betty Weiss and on what terms. Her public appearances as a singer were fewer than Dora's had been and more spectacular. She was much the best-dressed woman in Dodge, specializing in furs, always entering a room enveloped in mink or beaver, disclosing her slim white shoulders and pointed bosom with a certain grace and dramatic effect. In a few years she was almost as famous as Dora had been.

— 2 —

Betty Weiss was born in St. Louis of German Lutheran parents who came to the United States in the first wave of German immigration. Both of them died in one of the early outbreaks of cholera when the dead were hauled away in wagonloads and the city for a while was almost deserted. Betty was only a few years old at the time, and she spent most of her childhood in a Lutheran orphanage, where she wore a uniform and marched to meals and classes and to church on Sunday at the stroke of a bell. In the orphanage Betty learned to read and write and sing hymns and she also learned that she was an incorrigible rebel with an innate hatred of routine and authority. She ran away three times and was brought back by the police. Her mentors were as much relieved as Betty when she was adopted at the age of sixteen by a German family that ran a restaurant. They treated her strictly as an economic asset and put her to work as a waitress, but Betty was not slow to achieve her independence. Before she was eighteen she got a job at wages and defied her foster parents to bring her home. She also quickly made a place for herself in the kind of German society to which her parents had belonged—a society of small shopkeepers and of carpenters and bricklayers who prospered on the swift growth of the city. They were a thrifty, laborious, well-fed and prolific people, who spoke more German than English and had a social life of their own. Betty went to many balls and also to beer gardens where people came in family groups and the young folk danced and flirted while the elders drank beer and talked. On Sundays she went to the Lutheran church because she saw all her friends and acquaintances there and she sang in the choir because she liked to sing. She had many suitors and might have married almost any time, but she didn't. She was outrageously fickle and elusive. Whenever a nice German boy began to talk about marriage she would turn him down and shift her favor to another. Older women began to speak of her with disapproval.

Betty was a reticent girl. She did not confide in anyone nor argue with anyone but before she was nineteen she had a set of strong and definite convictions, acquired mostly by way of her senses which were exceptionally acute. She knew that she hated drudgery and especially the smell and the greasy feel of dish water which became for her the chief symbol of domesticity. She resented the complacent, domineering German male, reeking of beer and sauerkraut, who regarded it as his duty to keep his wife both pregnant and busy. She knew she would never submit herself to one of them. She knew also that she lusted after luxuries and especially after furs and fabrics. She spent a great deal of time staring at things in shop windows and well-dressed women, especially in silk and fur, were the only humans she envied. Her body longed for the caress of silk far more than it had ever longed for the weight and pressure of an amorous male. Betty knew that she was a greedy and undutiful girl, and she had some moments of guilt and doubt, but she had also the self-knowledge of the born adventurer, the instinctive certainty that she did not belong where she was, that her destiny was still undiscovered.

— 3 —

The man Betty married promised her everything she wanted and looked to her like the fulfillment of a dream. He was no part of the social world to which she belonged but a stranger, named Ronald Nelson, who came to the restaurant one day for a cup of coffee and returned almost every day for a long time because Betty worked there. He was tall and dark and superbly dressed with a pearl in his ascot tie and a diamond on his finger. He reminded her of an actor she had seen in *East Lynne* and in fact he was something of an actor, among other things. By profession he was a gambler who had been working the river boats between St. Louis and New Orleans, and who had decided upon a journey to California. But he did not tell Betty any of this. He told her a long and highly circumstantial story about a plantation in Louisiana which he had inherited. He did not begin by proposing marriage. He took her out to dinner and to shows and tried every time to persuade her to visit him in rooms he had rented over a store down on the water front. But Betty demurely refused. She thought she was being too smart for him, and when he put a diamond on her finger and told her he could wait no longer, they must be married that night, she felt sure of triumph. They were married all right by a justice of the peace and with a perfectly authentic license, and they went for their honeymoon to Kansas City, where urgent business required his attention before they could go south.

The honeymoon lasted a week and was a great success. It came to an end when Ronald Nelson simply walked out one morning and never returned. It took Betty a long time to understand and accept the fact that she had been deserted. For the first and for the last time she had been the victim of her own vanity. Even before the marriage she had been convinced that this man was her secure possession and afterward she had felt even more sure that his body belonged to her. When he failed to appear after twenty-four hours, she went to the Kansas City police in the firm belief that he must have met with foul play—a thing which could easily happen in Kansas City to a man who wore several hundred dollars' worth of jewelry. For that matter, there was never any proof that Ronald Nelson had not been murdered and thrown into the river, but the police quickly ascertained that he was not alive anywhere in town and their concern with him there ended. In those days men disappeared into the West as a wild animal disappears in a forest. But the police also knew a good deal about Ronald Nelson which they felt bound to tell his pale and shaken bride. They were able to ascertain that he had a very bad reputation as a gambler, that he had operated on the river under at least four different names and that he had been married under at least three of them.

During her days of uncertainty Betty had felt weak and crushed, for Ronald was an accomplished lover and he had revealed to Betty the fact that she was a passionate woman. But when she understood what had happened to her, her mood suddenly and significantly changed. She was filled with a great rage not only against Ronald Nelson but against the entire male half of the human race and against a world which could deal such a blow to her enormous pride. Rage seemed to run through her body like a hot liquid, filling her with furious power, with a longing for action and destruction. If she had been able to find his track she could have hunted Ronald Nelson with a gun. Briefly she enjoyed her rage almost as much as she had enjoyed some of her orgiastic moments in her lover's arms. When a detective tried to put his arm around her she slapped him with such emphasis that she knocked his cigar out of his mouth. Despite her bad manners, or perhaps partly because of them, the Kansas City police offered to pay her fare back to where she had come from. But Betty knew that whatever happened she was not going back. Nobody she knew was ever going to learn the story of her humiliation. Nor was it difficult to discover somewhere else to go. The great new wooden railroad station in Kansas City was crowded with people who were bound for the end of the rails, and it was also plastered with advertisements for waitresses to work in Dodge City at wages that seemed fabulous to Betty, and they included transportation. She landed in Dodge City two days later, badly shaken and rumpled, with a cinder in her eye, but nevertheless one of the best looking girls on the train. Men booted and spurred, with guns on their hips, were lined up four deep to watch her get off the train. For a moment she stood open-mouthed and bewildered. Then Dora Hand, almost motherly looking in her diurnal costume, came forward and put her arm around the girl and said, "Come with me, dearie."

— 4 —

Both Betty Weiss and Dodge City were at the highest point of their respective importance when Major Blore called upon her. Deborah, her Negro maid, brought Betty a card one evening which informed her that Major Blore would like to see her and that he represented the Rocky Mountain Land and Cattle Company. Betty sent back word that she saw gentlemen only by appointment. The Major in turn communicated the intelligence by way of Deborah that his call was of a purely business character, that his time in Dodge City was limited and that he would greatly appreciate a brief interview. Betty let him wait twenty minutes while she put on her most elegant gown and had Deborah do her hair. She felt nothing more than a mild curiosity about the Major but it was one of her two primary business principles always to make the best possible impression on a man. The other was never to trust him.

The Major wore the black frock coat, high-heeled riding boots and great white hat which then represented the height of frontier elegance. He could not have been more formal, more courteous or more respectful if he had been interviewing a queen. He accepted a chair, laid his great hat upon the floor bottom up, removed a map from a portfolio which he carried and proceeded to give Betty an illustrated lecture upon the properties, organization and intentions of the Rocky Mountain Land and Cattle Company. He was careful to explain that the syndicate commanded a capital of several million dollars and that he was prepared to offer bank references to prove it. Betty listened carefully, her green eyes narrow with amused suspicion.

"If you're trying to sell me real estate," she explained when the Major paused for breath, "it's no use. I never buy anything but clothes and liquor."

"I have nothing to sell you," the Major explained gravely. "I am soliciting your assistance in a great undertaking."

Betty received this announcement in silence. The Major uncrossed his legs, crossed them again and cleared his throat. It was evident that he was approaching the serious business of the interview and that it was also a somewhat delicate business.

"One of the company's enterprises," he explained, "will be a first-class hotel. It will include, of course, a bar and the usual games. I feel sure it will be the best establishment of its kind west of Kansas City. We would like to have you take charge of it. I am prepared to offer you a contract for a year and I feel sure the terms can be made satisfactory."

Betty considered this for a long moment.

"Why don't you get a man to run it?" she inquired. "I never heard of a joint that was really run by a woman."

The Major permitted himself to smile for the first time.

"We want to attract people to our town," he said. "I am sure you will be more of an attraction than any man we might employ. Of course, you will have whatever assistance you need."

"You mean you want me to be the two-story front," Betty suggested.

The Major raised a deprecatory hand.

"As you may imagine," he said, "I have made the fullest possible inquiries about you. I have no doubt at all of your business competence. Needless to say, your gifts as an entertainer are also a consideration."

Betty again paused before she spoke.

"I'll have to think it over," she said at last.

"Thank you," the Major replied. "May I suggest that you have nothing to lose? As a track-end town, Dodge City is near the end of its boom. I flatter myself that we have something more substantial to offer."

Betty nodded.

"I know this town can't last," she agreed. "I'll see you again before you go."

— 5 —

The next day Betty sent word to her friend Clay Tighe that she would like to consult him on important business. Tighe was at that time one of the half dozen most famous peace officers in the Southwest. He had been marshal of Hayes City and of Abilene, and was known as the man who tamed that refractory town. He had also been a deputy marshal in Dodge City. At the moment he was out of a job, due to a change in the city administration, but the services of Clay Tighe never went begging and they were worth anywhere from five hundred to a thousand dollars a month.

Betty Weiss trusted no man wholly, but she had more confidence in Tighe than in any other man she knew. For one thing, he had never shown the slightest interest in her as a woman. This piqued her vanity, but it gave her confidence that his advice was truly disinterested. For another thing, he never needed money. Finally, he had a reputation for honesty of a kind that was rare in the world they both inhabited. And she knew Clay Tighe would know something about Major Blore. It was part of his business to know about everybody in town.

"I don't trust that little shorthorn," she told him, after she had described the Major's visit. "He's too smooth. I'm afraid he's got something up his cuff."

"I don't trust him either," Clay said. "But there's no doubt that he's got the money and a clear title to about a million acres. I looked into that very carefully."

"Why so?" Betty inquired.

"Because he made me a proposition too," Clay explained. "He's here shopping for help and settlers. He'll take about half of Dodge City out there if he has his way."

"I suppose you'll be his trouble-shooter," Betty said.

Clay nodded.

"He's got a lot of squatters to deal with," he explained. "I don't like the proposition much, but there's big money in it and a chance to get hold of good range with water on it. . . . And somebody's got to do the job," he added.

"You took him up, then," Betty guessed.

"I told him I'd go out there and look it over," Clay said.

"Will you let me know what you think?" Betty asked.

"I'll write you a letter," Clay promised. "But I probably won't know any more about the Major then than I do now. He's as hard to figure out as a Chinaman in a poker game."

CLAY TIGHE

CLAY TIGHE put on his gun every morning as regularly as he put on his shirt and a great deal more carefully. After he had shaved and dressed he took his heavy gun belt off the post of his bed where he always hung it last thing at night, and buckled it around his waist, always exactly the same way, so that it rode aslant his body from just above his hip bone on the left side to just below it on the right, and slightly behind. He then drew his heavy frontier-model six-shooter, with its seven-inch barrel, from under his pillow—for he had slept upon it every night for fifteen years. He first unloaded it and then inserted it carefully in the holster, which had been molded to its form by soaking the leather in water and letting it dry on the well-greased gun. The holster had to hang so that his long slender fingers just reached the tip, and it was tied to his leg by a thong so that it could never flop or slide. When he felt sure the gun was perfectly placed he always practiced his draw several times. If there was a mirror in the room he practiced before the mirror so that he could study his own performance with the critical care which is the mark of the virtuoso. He would first execute his draw very slowly and perfectly. His hand traveled up the length of the holster in a long, smooth caress, his lower three fingers closed on the grip, his index finger curled around the emergent trigger, and the ball of his thumb at the same time drew back the hammer. In one long, smooth movement the gun swept upward to an exact horizontal and the hammer fell at that exact moment. After he had made his draw slowly and deliberately, he repeated it several times until he felt sure he had reached his maximum speed. He always knew whether his draw was working perfectly or not. If he had taken more than one drink the night before, and sometimes if he had been with a woman, he might be a fraction of a second slow at first. Then he would practice it until he felt sure it was perfect. This movement of hand and arm was as vital to him as his breathing or his digestion and for the same reason: his life depended on it. Clay Tighe's gun was the creator of his destiny, the instrument and symbol of his power. He was wedded to his gun and only death could part them.

His morning rehearsal was a small part of the time he devoted to his art. Unless urgent business interfered, he emptied his six-shooter at a mark every day, then carefully cleaned and reloaded it. He also fired a few shots with his short Winchester of the 1873 model, then the world's deadliest repeating arm. Tighe could shoot his rifle not only from the shoulder but also from the hip, holding the gun hard against his side and swinging his whole body.

Tighe was a man-killer, an expert in homicide. His life, his reputation and his earning capacity all depended upon the fact that he could kill more quickly and more surely than any but perhaps half a dozen men in the Southwest, and it is doubtful whether any of these was his superior. Yet he had killed but two men since the end of the Civil War, and both of those had shot at him and missed before he pulled a trigger. For Tighe had early reached that high degree of gunmanship which made his reputation his chief asset. He seldom shot because he seldom had to shoot. At least fifty times he had gotten the drop on his man before the other gun cleared its holster. Even more often he had arrested a man without even drawing a gun. It was said of him, as it had been said of many other supreme experts with the six-shooter, that he bore a charmed life. Tighe knew exactly what the charm was. It lay in the fact that the other fellow was always frightened. Sometimes he was too frightened to draw a gun and sometimes he was too frightened to hit anything. For fifteen years Clay Tighe had walked unscathed because men were afraid of him.

He walked unscathed but he did not walk at ease, for he was a marked man and a shining mark. A great many men would have liked to kill him. Some of these bore him a grudge because he had disarmed and arrested them—and to have your gun taken away from you was then supreme disgrace. More of them would have liked to kill him in fair fight simply for the glory of it. To kill Clay Tighe in fair fight would be not only high achievement but also the way to a reputation worth money. He knew a few men who would have shot him in the back if one had seen a safe chance. Few men were shot in the back in the West of that day because it was not a gesture that won social approval, but as Tighe was wont to remark in this and other connections: "There's always some son-of-bitch . . ."

Tighe was a striking figure of a man, a little over six feet tall, perfectly carried, wide in the shoulders and narrow in the hips, with a handsome aquiline face and deep-set gray eyes which carried a curious warning glint even when he smiled. He belonged to that order of athletes who combine great strength with a certain quick sensitivity, expressed in his long tapering fingers and the easy grace of his movement. He had nothing in common with the thick-skinned bull-like strength of the typical rough-and-tumble fighter or the man who loves a knife—the gouging, biting human brute who longs to destroy with his hands. Tighe had something of the artist about him and a little of the actor. He was a perfectionist who exercised a supreme skill for its own sake.

Walking down the street he looked to be relaxed and unconcerned but he was not. He was alert as a wild animal almost every minute of his waking life, except when he had wide space between himself and his fellow beings. He looked at every man he met and his glance was peculiarly keen and perceptive. He had been called cat-eyed. He had ears like a deer or a rabbit and he was habitually aware of the footfalls of a man behind him, and of any pause or change in his gait. One evening he met a cowboy who might have borne a grudge against him, nodded a smiling greeting and passed on, heard some slight, indefinable movement behind him and whirled with his hand on his gun. In the twilight he saw a bright flash from a hip pocket and his quick gun leaped to its deadly level, hammer raised. . . . He stayed his trigger finger just in time. The man had whipped out a white handkerchief to blow his nose and he never knew he had been within an instant of death.

When Tighe sat down in a room he always sat with his back to the wall and as close to it as he could get. If he went to the bar for a drink, which he seldom did, he always knew who was behind him.

Clay Tighe was a mighty man, one of the rulers of his world, and he walked with the knowledge of death and carried death in his hand.

— 2 —

Tighe grew up in Illinois in the forties and fifties—the green and placid Illinois where Abraham Lincoln rode the circuit and told his stories. Clay was a fighter from the age of six but he was never a bully or an undisciplined fighter. His father, Judge Tighe, saw to that. The judge was a moderately prosperous farmer and a country justice of the peace who achieved a local celebrity by reason of his strict and incorruptible sense of justice. He had jurisdiction only over minor civil cases and misdemeanors but this made him the judge and arbiter of many personal encounters. When a man was brought before him for disturbing the peace or charged with assault and battery, Judge Tighe worked long and hard and summoned all possible witnesses to ascertain who had started the trouble and how. His self-appointed mission in life was to suppress and punish transgressors and he had the courage to put prominent citizens in jail and to earn the enmity of men who were considered dangerous. He applied exactly the same principles to the education and upbringing of his son that he used in court. If Clay got into a fight and showed any signs of it, he had to prove that he had fought in self-defense. Otherwise the judge would always administer a rather severe thrashing with a doubled trunk strap, accompanied by a lecture on the principles of human justice and social order. "The old man gave me hell at both ends," was the way Clay Tighe described his early training.

Clay Tighe rebelled against his father's teachings and left home early but he lived to understand that the old man had provided him with a mission and an ethic he could not escape. A feeling for justice and order had been impressed upon his young mind and pounded into his young bottom. He became a deadly man but never a ruthless one. He spent his life stopping trouble, sometimes dead in its tracks.

Judge Tighe was a stout man with a great reverence for intellectual achievement and for Abraham Lincoln. He wanted his son to study law and to fulfill his own thwarted ambitions, but this lean and restless sprout of his loins was a creature of another kind. Clay longed for action, clean, deadly and precise. He was a hunter from the age of eight and could topple a squirrel out of a high hickory with a bullet through its head. By the time he was twelve he was one of the best shots in the county and won turkeys and beefs at shooting matches, competing with grown men. When he was only eighteen he left home against his father's wishes and headed west. The Tighe farm on the Illinois River was only about two hundred miles from the Kansas-Missouri border, where the prologue to the Civil War was being fought by pro-slavery settlers from the South and free-soil men from the North—a hard-riding, bushwhacking struggle in which men committed murder and larceny for the glory of God and in the name of freedom.

Clay Tighe said he was looking for land and work, and the Immigrant Society was offering both in an effort to build up the population of free-soil men against the southern raiders. But half consciously Tighe was hunting trouble—a young warrior with an itching trigger finger, moving instinctively toward the smell of powder and the thrill of battle. Inevitably he joined the Jayhawkers, riding with the famous Jim Montgomery who became a terror to the men from the South. Clay was a hot young partisan fighting for free soil and the ideals of Abraham Lincoln, but the Jayhawkers were only one degree removed from banditry. They burned fences and cabins, destroyed growing crops, stole horses and cattle, were not above lifting poultry off a roost or raiding fields for green corn and watermelons when provender was scarce. It was a warfare of ambuscade and running skirmish with a fine rattle and bang about it and little execution. This was the least creditable part of Tighe's career and the one he said least about in later years. It was chiefly significant as the time he first encountered the instrument of which he was to become one of the greatest masters. The border wars were fought largely with the old cap-and-ball six-shooter. Some of the Jayhawkers carried three and even four of these primitive revolvers in their belts and were famous for the way they could fill the landscape with smoke and lead. With the instinct of a master young Clay strove for speed and precision and had perfected a deadly draw before Colt became famous.

When the Civil War broke out Clay did not enlist. He was a shrewd young man with an aversion to military discipline and a sharp awareness of his own value in good hard dollars. He went to work for the Union army as a civilian teamster at several times a soldier's pay. Within two years he was a brigade wagon-master, commanding many men older than himself. His job was not merely to move supplies but to find routes that were safe from bushwhackers. He was so good at this that he became a master scout and sometimes a spy—one of those highly paid and expert men who were the eyes of the army. It was characteristic of Tighe that he came to the end of the war with money and a whole skin as well as a reputation.

Again he moved west only a few hundred miles from where his fighting career had begun. He was in Dodge City shortly after the railroad arrived and became one of the first of the hide hunters. Wherever he went work was waiting for his deadly hand and eye. Government is said to have secretly backed the buffalo hunters because the Indians could not be conquered until the wild meat was destroyed. Clay Tighe was a master buffalo hunter who owned his own team and outfit and hired three skinners. He shot a great Sharp's buffalo gun which was accurate at five hundred yards and weighed fourteen pounds. The trick of his trade was to kill buffalo dead in their tracks, so that the others wouldn't scare and run. Sometimes he killed thirty or forty from one position, shooting until his shoulder was pounded black and blue and his great rifle was too hot to handle. It was a mighty feat in wholesale slaughter and it paid big money while the herds lasted.

Then suddenly the buffalo were gone from the Kansas

ranges. Almost at once, like the next act in a planned pageant, the first bawling longhorned herds of Texas cattle came pouring up from the South. The bales of buffalo hides vanished from the station platform, whitewashed cattle chutes were built beside the railroad track and a stream of beef on the hoof went rattling east to Kansas City and Chicago, while Texas cowboys, full of money and hard liquor, took over the town and almost tore it to pieces. It had neither law nor men to cope with this sudden invasion. Clay Tighe stood and watched them—a young man out of a job, but not for long.

The Civil War was over but almost every man in the West was still a touchy partisan and every town was split into two factions. The Texans all were Confederates, hating Yankees and niggers with a proud, self-righteous and trigger-happy hatred. Since the war, killing niggers had been almost as much a legitimate sport in southeast Texas as killing Mexicans had been in the years after the fall of the Alamo.

There were always a few saloons run by Texas partisans but most of the men who owned Dodge City and tried to rule it were Northerners and many of them were Union veterans. In the face of this gun-toting, spur-jingling mob they were helpless. They had a town marshal and several deputies, but when the Texans decided to shoot up the town, these officers could only close the doors and lie low.

Shooting up the town was a sport that enjoyed a measure of social tolerance, but murder was not. Clay Tighe was standing on a street corner smoking a cigarette when he witnessed murder, ruthless and inexcusable. Across the street a Negro named Jeff Chandler was painting a sign on the two-story front of a new store. Jeff was a huge man, weighing over two hundred and fifty pounds, and one of three or four Negroes in the town. He was a good carpenter and painter, a respected and busy citizen, who wore no weapon and always sang at his work. Four Texas cowboys, all drunk, came tearing down the street at a fast gallop, reeling in their saddles as only a drunk can reel without falling, brandishing their six-shooters, firing a few shots into the air. Two of them suddenly swung their guns on the giant Negro, riddled him from behind, and dashed on down the street. All four of them brought their horses to a squatting stop in a cloud of dust before the Happy Hour saloon—a Texas stronghold—while Jeff Chandler fell from his scaffold like a shot bird and lay bleeding in the street.

Within three minutes the street was full of men—men of two factions, all wearing guns. Texans poured out of the Happy Hour, sized up the situation, hustled the guilty men inside, formed a solid rank before the door. Ben Gilroy, owner of the Happy Hour, came shouldering through the crowd with a cocked shotgun in his hands, took his stand in front of them. Across the street Jim Sellers, mayor of Dodge, assembed his marshal and two deputies. He ordered them to disarm Gilroy and arrest the two guilty men. The officers took one look at the assembled Texans and the Gilroy shotgun and declined the assignment. Ed Brown, chief marshal, suggested that just now was not a propitious time to make arrests. The attempt might touch off mob action, cost much human life.

The argument had merit. Gilroy was a famous killer, and especially handy with his high-grade, handmade shotgun. The street had suddenly become a no-man's land. Any armed men who tried to cross it might become a target at the first step. But Sellers, unarmed and fat, with glasses on his nose, was a man of nerve.

"If we let the bastards get away with this, we might as well give them the town," he said, addressing his police force. "You boys are fired!"

He spoke doubtless in the spirit of sincere disgust and without considering his next move, but his champion was at hand. Clay Tighe spoke quietly.

"I could take that gang," he remarked, studying the Texas

tableau with a thoughtful eye. Mayor Sellers turned and looked at him. Sellers ran the largest store in town, owned about half of it, knew Clay Tighe as a customer and a buffalo hunter. He contemplated the young man for a long moment. Then he turned to his chief marshal, took the badge of office off his vest and pinned it on the man from Illinois.

"All right, Clay," he said. "You asked for it. Go to it."

Clay Tighe now started a short walk that carried him to fame and decided his destiny. He started it in a hush so complete that he could hear the hard breathing of excited men and his own soft footfalls in the dusty street as he stepped off the high board sidewalk.

Clay did not know why he had spoken, then or ever. He had heard his own quiet words with a kind of surprise. But he was not a man who thought much about his motives. He was one who always had his eye and his mind on the objects of his action. His eye just now was on the right hand of Ben Gilroy, where it grasped the stock of his shotgun. Gilroy held the gun diagonally across his body, like a hunter expecting a bird to flush. He could bring it into play with one swift movement. But Clay Tighe knew he could draw and fire before the long barrel of a shotgun could describe its arc. He knew also that he could see the beginning of that movement in the hand and wrist of the man who held the gun. He knew the cowboys crowded behind Gilroy were mostly drunk and too close together for effective action. So he walked slowly and confidently across the street with his hands at his sides, not touching his own weapon. Gilroy broke the silence.

"What do you want, Tighe?" he asked.

Clay stopped.

"I want you to throw that gun into the street and send those two boys out with their hands up and without their guns," he said quietly.

There was a long pause before the shotgun hit the dust, but after that everything was easy. The guilty cowboys were delivered to the law by their own partisans and Clay Tighe had become chief marshal of the hottest town in the West. His reign there was the beginning of law and order in the track-end cattle towns. They did not become quiet and peaceful places, but neither did the men from Texas ever again flout the government with impunity.

— 3 —

At thirty-nine, when he met Major Blore, Clay Tighe was a famous man, and like many another famous man he was beginning to feel the burden of his reputation. For a good many years he had truly enjoyed it. To be in danger, alert and unfrightened, is to be supremely alive. Clay Tighe had known the intensity of life as men who live in the mild boredom of perfect safety can never know it. But he had come a long way since he first rode west, tingling with the hope of battle, almost aching to use the skill and power he knew he had. He had grown from the wild boy who rode with the Jayhawkers to the man who could rule a town and do it without bloodshed. He was quick as ever, but the eagerness of his youth was gone. The long tension of incessant alertness had begun to tell. Something in him now longed for peace and safety—but battle and danger were his only trade. He could no more lay aside his gun than he could take off his skin.

Tighe was still erect and powerful but he looked old for his years. His black hair was brightly streaked with gray and the lines around his mouth had a hard and permanent set. His face in repose looked grim and a little sad, as do often the faces of men who have looked upon much violence. His deadly skill was still at its height and he knew it would decline. Few experts of the trigger finger were at their best much after forty. He had watched the careers of a good many such on both sides of the law. Some of them developed a ruthless hatred for their kind, began to kill for the love of killing. These never lasted long. Others he had known began to drink at a certain age, and these had even shorter lives.

During the past few years Tighe had spent more and more of his time alone, in a solitude that he enjoyed because it was safe. He felt best now when he rode across wide prairies where he could see a rider a mile away. Tighe was a man armed against his fellows and he liked a lot of space between himself and them.

He had never longed for possession. Money had come to him easily and he had never thought much about it. He had the adventurer's instinctive wish to remain unfettered. He had taken women lightly and he had never longed to own the earth. But out of his later mood had grown a dream of a wide, wild land he could call his own. It was not a home he longed for so much as a private wilderness to stand between him and a hostile world.

That longing, more than anything else, was what sent Clay Tighe to the Dark River Valley. He could have taken up a homestead anywhere, gathered a few cattle and a woman, become a settled man. But he wanted more than that. He wanted miles around him, not acres. He wanted a safe and private world.

Clay Tighe had seen the Dark River Valley once years before, when Ballard was at the height of his power. He had ridden from Abilene to Santa Fe, had stopped at the great house, talked to the great man, been invited to linger as long as he liked. He had stayed at the house only two nights but he had gone on a lone antelope hunt north of the valley and had camped at a spring near the foot of the mountains, called the Berenda Spring. It was a beautiful spring of clear, cold water, bubbling up out of white sand, flowing a steady stream, bowered by willows and lined with watercress, shaded by a few great mountain cottonwoods. He remembered the flat, wide mesa spreading westward, tinged purple by the ripe forage of early fall, where the white-rumped antelope skimmed the mirages like flying birds. Then the Berenda had been to him only a good place to camp. Now he thought of it as a refuge. And he also thought he was strong enough to take it. But that was not all that moved him toward the Dark River Valley. Tighe was a proud man and always aware of himself as a man with a mission. He felt sure trouble was making in the Dark River Valley and he thought if any man could keep the peace there he could do it.

Over and over, all his life, Clay Tighe had found himself riding toward trouble. Every man's life has a recurrent motif which is the beat and rhythm of his destiny, the thing he can never escape. Time and again he finds himself facing the same challenge, moving the same way.

Clay Tighe had ridden toward trouble a hundred times but this was the first time he had ever hoped it was the last.

— 4 —

Tighe was known by reputation all over the Southwest but few men in the Dark River Valley would be likely to know him by sight. So it was part of his canny plan to reach the valley after dark, to spend a day and a night asking questions, looking and listening. He wanted to know as much as he could before he faced the little Major.

Long before he reached the valley he saw a red glow in the sky, and when he was still a mile away he heard a wild, mechanical scream, which he knew for the voice of a buzz saw tearing its way through pitchy pine. When he topped the rise north of the valley he understood. They had been cutting down the forest on the mountainside beyond, the litter of tops and limbs had caught fire as they generally did in the wake of careless cutting, and the sawmill was working all night in the red glow of destruction. It shone on the faces of busy, sweating men and on the bare yellow lumber of new buildings going up on both sides of the road that paralleled the creek. The little Major wasn't wasting any time. The drive of his nervous energy was already tearing down a forest and putting up a town.

Tighe remembered a summer night years before when all he could hear from the porch of the great house were a few low voices and the music of wind and water. Now he rode down a noisy, muddy street with two saloons and a store already running, all three of them one-story buildings with two-story fronts. It was all familiar to Clay Tighe—the cow ponies and buckboards at the hitch racks, the gun-belted men coming and going through the swinging doors of saloons, the rattle of bad piano music, the tattoo of boot heels on the new board walk, the rumble and guffaw of male voices. In effect he had spent about fifteen years patrolling this same street, for every frontier town took the same form, drew the same kinds of men, made the same noises. This was the seed and sprout of American civilization overleaping its own frontiers. This was the way it grew and spread, biting into the wilderness, setting up a town without law, a community of men each for himself and most of them armed to take what they wanted. Tighe knew this street for his business and his destiny. The little Major had built him a town. It was Clay Tighe's job to make it behave.

Down at the far end of the street he saw a sign he knew would be there. It too was painted on a high board front and it said "Livery Stable" in letters he could read a hundred yards away. He could have found it in the dark by its horsy odor and the steady munch and grind of feeding stock. He rode through a wide door into a space between stalls where the light of a great lantern hanging from a roof beam shone on the polished rumps of stabled horses. A short, stocky, bowlegged man came to meet him, offered his hand as Tighe dismounted.

"I'm Ed Kelly," he said. "What can I do for you?"

"My name is Tighe," Clay replied, watching the man's eye for sign of recognition. He could see nothing there but a lively curiosity. "I'd like to leave my horse for a day or two, maybe longer."

"Aim to settle here?" Kelly inquired as he took the bridle rein. Curiosity about strangers was not good form but this was a polite and casual question.

"Hope to," Tighe replied. He pulled his rifle out of the saddle scabbard and started to loosen his cinches.

Kelly meditated a full minute before he asked another question. It was an impertinent and also a significant one.

"Pro-grant or anti-grant?" he asked.

"Neither," Tighe told him softly. "I'm just a poor cowboy looking for a waterhole."

Kelly surveyed Tighe's outfit thoughtfully—his three-hundred-dollar horse and his hundred-dollar saddle, his forty-dollar boots and the new Colt tied to his leg.

"Have it your own way," he said.

"Hope to," Tighe replied, as he turned away.

— 5 —

Outside the door of Blore's office, which had once been Ballard's, sat a huge black man who answered to the name of Shad. He was now a famous figure in the Dark River Valley, simply because he was the first Negro who had ever appeared there. When he arrived the Mexicans, most of whom had never seen a Negro before, had come miles to look at him and follow him about the streets.

Shad was primarily a groom Blore had imported to care for the team of blooded trotters that drew his buckboard and the five-gaited Kentucky saddle horse he rode. But Shad seemed to be also a valet, a cook and a bodyguard. No one had ever seen him more than about fifty yards from the Major. When Blore rode abroad Shad rode behind him, exactly as an orderly rode behind a cavalry officer. All the Major's arrangements had something of the military about them.

Shad greeted Clay Tighe with a wide grin, a soft voice and a perfectly obsequious manner. He opened the door for him and bowed him through it. Tighe was expected and welcome.

The little Major sat behind a wide flat-topped desk at the far side of the great room, which had been transformed with heavy red curtains at the windows, red and black Navajo blankets on the floor, and shiny new furniture. He rose and greeted Tighe with a handshake, waved him to a chair, offered him a cigar. Tighe refused it, rolled a small brown cigarette with quick dexterity, blew a cloud of smoke, and waited calmly for the Major to open the proceedings.

"I think you'll agree that we have a fine development here, Mr. Tighe," he said, "and I'm delighted to have you join us."

"Thank you," Tighe replied with the perfect self-assurance of a man who knows his own value. "You have a very fine development and you also have the making of a fine little war."

The Major's eyes showed his surprise, but he was not at a loss.

"You seem to be well posted," he remarked. "Perhaps you know more about the situation here than I do."

"Maybe I do," Tighe replied. "I got here day before yesterday and I've been circulating around and picking up the news."

"I'll be very glad to have your impressions," the Major said.

"Well," Tighe spoke with slow deliberation, "my impression is that your survey takes in about four times as much territory as Ballard ever claimed. I don't know how you did it, but it's a government survey, on file in Washington. It's the law now and the law has got to be enforced."

"I'm glad you feel that way about it," the Major said.

"If I didn't I wouldn't be here," Tighe told him. "But a lot of these little ranchers that moved in and settled on what they thought was the public domain don't agree with me. They think they've been robbed."

The Major nodded easily.

"We have a little problem in law enforcement," he said. "I feel sure we can solve it."

"You haven't had much luck so far," Tighe informed him. "You made Happy Jack Marcos a deputy sheriff, and about two weeks ago you sent him out to the Bostwick ranch to serve a dispossess notice on Bill Bostwick. Is that right?"

The Major nodded.

"Your deputy found about twenty of the neighbors sitting in a row on the corral fence, each of them with a Winchester in his lap. Happy Jack just took one look and came back home with the papers in his pocket. Is that right?"

"Marcos isn't man enough for the job," the Major said. "That's why I sent for you."

"You didn't send any too soon," Tighe remarked. "A week ago you drove out to see Jack Shane at his ranch on the Rayado. Shane is your own man and you spent the night out there. When you got up in the morning your buckboard had been taken to pieces and one wheel was in the top of a tree and another was down in the creek and it took half a day to put it together again."

The Major laughed.

"I took it as a joke," he said.

"It was no joke," Tighe told him. "It was a hint and a warning. I suppose you know three or four of the boys have told around how much they'd like to get a shot at you."

"I'm used to being on a firing line," the Major remarked. He was obviously unfrightened and Tighe felt a half-reluctant respect for him.

"If you get yourself killed," he said, "it's going to be downright embarrassing."

"I'll try to be discreet," the Major told him. He scrutinized Tighe for a long moment. "May I assume, then, that you will join us here?" he inquired.

Tighe laughed.

"It's a fair question," he said. "I'll take the job if I can have it on my own terms."

"I don't think we'll have any trouble about the money," the Major replied.

"I'm not as much interested in money as I am in land," Tighe explained.

"We'll be glad to have you settle here, of course," the Major was quick to agree. Tighe nodded.

"I've got my eye on the Berenda Spring," he explained.

"That's one of the best locations on the grant," the Major remarked.

"I know it is," Tighe said. "That's why I want it. I want about ten sections on both sides of it. I'll pay your regular acre price and you can take it out of my wages."

The Major was thoughtful for a moment.

"We hadn't planned to sell holdings of that size," he said. "I'll have to consult my principals, but I believe it can be arranged. Meanwhile, I trust you'll accept a commission as deputy sheriff and take over. There's an office for you adjoining the new hotel."

"All right," Tighe said, and started to rise.

"Just a minute." The Major raised a delaying hand. "There are a few other things . . ."

"Shoot," Tighe said, relaxing in his chair and starting another cigarette.

"There's a character around here named Laird who seems to be making most of our trouble for us," the Major explained. "He did all of Ballard's building for him and he's some kind of a preacher, out of the Tennessee mountains."

"I heard him when I was here a few years ago," Tighe said. "He's got a voice like a range bull on the prod."

"Yes," the Major agreed, "and he can't keep it quiet. When the government survey was completed here about a month ago he got all the ranchers together and made them a speech. He gave them to understand the survey was—well, that the lines had been stretched. He claimed to know all about the original grant."

Tighe blew smoke and nodded.

"What did he tell them to do?" he inquired.

The Major hesitated a moment.

"I don't know that he gave them any specific advice," he said, a little uneasily. "But he worked up a lot of bad feeling against the company."

"Does he pack a gun?" Tighe inquired.

"No," the Major said, "I believe not."

"Well, he's got a right to shoot off his mouth." Tighe spoke with the finality of one who has no doubt about his principles. "If he tries anything else, I'll take care of him."

"Don't misunderstand me," the Major said smoothly. "I wouldn't want anything to happen to him. That might only make things worse. But I wish he would go somewhere else."

"I'm not going to start running people out of town," Tighe said. "That's not my way. It'll have to be understood I handle everything my own way here."

"Of course," the Major agreed. "I just wanted you to know about him."

"I know plenty about him," Tighe said. He started to rise again and again the Major raised a detaining hand.

"One other thing," he said. "We're having a little community celebration next Sunday. There will be an auction of town lots, and we've imported an auctioneer from Kansas City to hold it. After that we're going to have a barbecue and a rodeo, and probably a dance at night. . . ."

"That's about the worst thing you could do," Tighe interrupted quietly. "You've got two factions here now. All the old settlers are on one side, and all the men who have come to buy land from the company are on the other. They hope to see the old-timers dispossessed and then grab the good locations for themselves. It's a nice little mess and you ought to know it. If you bring them all together and let them get full of liquor, something can pop any minute."

The Major nodded imperturbably.

"I'm not suffering from any illusions," he remarked. "But this gathering can't be avoided." He paused a moment. "I thought you might open the exercises with a little exhibition of your trick shooting. I'm told you're one of the best performers in the West."

Tighe blew smoke and looked at the end of his cigarette. He knew the Major was proposing to put him to the test, and he knew that couldn't be avoided either.

"All right," he said at last. "If you're bound to have a show, I'll police it for you, and I'll show the boys how to handle a gun. But I want it understood that from now on you won't hold any celebrations without asking me. What we need is a spell of peace."

The Major laughed as he rose and held out his hand.

"I agree with you completely about that," he said.

Tighe walked slowly to his new office, shaking his head

from time to time. "A smart little bastard," he said to himself, "if I ever saw one."

— 6 —

The auction day celebration drew a crowd of nearly three hundred, not counting Mexicans and Indians. They did not count, of course, either as potential customers or potential trouble-makers because they had no money, wore no guns and had nothing to fight about. Everyone ignored them.

Two men were conspicuously absent. The Major refrained from attending, thereby establishing a policy which governed him throughout his administration. He was seldom seen outside his own office and only a select few ever saw him there. When he traveled, he moved rapidly, sitting his big sorrel fox-trotter like the soldier he was, with the faithful Shad covering his rear.

Daniel Laird who had presided over almost all public gatherings before Ballard's death also stayed away, and Tighe was glad of that. He knew the preacher had a following and a man with a following was just what he didn't want around. Waverly Buncombe was the master of ceremonies on this occasion and Tighe had difficulty in recognizing him at first. He remembered Buncombe as a good chuck-wagon cook wearing jeans and a hickory shirt. Now he wore a long frock coat, a wide black hat, a high collar and a thick black tie—a costume which had become standard for gamblers, saloon keepers, mayors and other citizens of the first importance and dignity. It was generally understood that Waverly now worked for the company, although in exactly what capacity no one seemed to know. He was said to be one of the few who had regular access to the Major's office and it was easy for Tighe to guess that he supplied Blore with an extra pair of ears and eyes.

Waverly made a dignified and impressive master of ceremonies, superintending the four Mexicans who were roasting a whole beef over an open pit, discarding his enormous chew of tobacco to introduce Tighe as "the most famous peace officer west of Kansas City, who will now entertain you with a little exhibition of his skill in the use of that instrument of his profession and symbol of his authority—the Colt pacifier."

Tighe usually wore only a single gun, but he was one of the few men in the West who could shoot with both hands. For this occasion he wore a fancy two-gun belt of hand-carved leather, with the holsters built into the strap. He began by tossing a tin can thirty feet away and blasting it, first with one gun, then with the other, making it hop into the air like a live thing, hitting it again before it fell to the ground. He then gave a demonstration of the rare art of fanning, holding a gun in his left hand and beating the hammer spur with his right, delivering five shots in two seconds with enough accuracy to put them all in a tin bucket at ten yards. After that, he held out both guns butt first, as though he were surrendering them to an opponent, then reversed them with lightning speed by rolling the trigger guards around his fingers, delivering two accurate and simultaneous shots. But the final demonstration of his speed was the most impressive. He stood with his hands at his sides while a boy tossed a can into the air, then drew and hit it just as it reached the top of its arc. This final number got a round of applause from the assembled company, most of whom wore six-shooters themselves and all of whom knew they had seen the work of a master. Tighe bowed and withdrew, admitting to himself that the Major's idea might not have been such a bad one after all.

Throughout the rest of the afternoon he moved about among the crowd, receiving congratulations and making acquaintances. One of these was young Bob Clarey, who offered his hand and his wholly convincing tribute.

"Gosh!" he said. "I wish I could shoot like that!"

Tighe saw a chance to make a friend and he knew he was going to need friends.

"You can, son, if you'll practice," he said. "Look me up some day and I'll teach you what I know."

After the auction and the shooting match there were roping and bronco-riding contests. Bob Clarey won the latter by staying his time on top of a white outlaw called Twister, by reason of the terrific sidewise wrench he put into his bucking. Tighe was able to return the boy's congratulations with the utmost sincerity. Bob was a born rider with an infallible sense of balance—one of those who seem to dance with the frantic horse, anticipating his every plunge and turn.

When the crowd swarmed around the barbecue pit Tighe kept moving around among the guests, watching for signs of trouble, but he heard no arguments and saw no fights, although he could spot men of both factions and most of them wore guns. He was not greatly surprised at this. He knew tensions had not risen to the point of violence yet, and he knew his presence made a difference.

The only test of his authority came that night at the dance, when he stood at the door and held out his hand for every man's gun as he entered. A few hesitated briefly, as though about to question this procedure, but none of them refused and the dance was peaceful except for the usual fight between a cowboy and a Mexican over a Mexican girl. When the Mexican flashed a knife, Tighe neatly put him to sleep with a skillful tap of the gun barrel. It was an essential part of the practice of frontier police work, and the art of it lay in rolling the barrel as it struck, so that the man was stunned without breaking the skin or risking a fracture.

Young Clarey again was a star performer at the dance, doing the cradle waltz with his beautiful Adelita, practically monopolizing the floor for one number by the sheer speed and grace of their performance. This Bob Clarey, Tighe saw, was a young man with a gift for being in the middle of things.

Tighe got back to his combined office and living quarters about midnight, after he was sure the crowd had scattered and both saloons were closed, with the feeling that he had done a good and exhausting day's work. He pulled off his boots, sat down and poured himself a stiff drink. Just before going to bed was the only time he could take a drink with perfect safety. He was rolling a cigarette when he heard a light knock. He rose, stuck his gun in the band of his trousers and opened the door, standing far enough back to have room for action. The yellow bar of lamplight fell upon a short, plump Mexican with a smooth round face—a man of perhaps forty years. "Mr. Tighe," he said, "I am Ernesto Royball. I work in the store. May I talk with you?" He spoke softly, in excellent English with a slight Mexican accent. Tighe saw that he wore no gun. He extended his hand.

"Come in, Ernesto," he said. "Sit down and pour yourself a drink. What can I do for you?"

"Nothing, Mr. Tighe," the little man replied, as he helped himself to whisky. "I saw you shoot this afternoon. I have heard much about you. I think I can help you here."

Tighe was not at all surprised by this proposition. He had known that someone such as Ernesto would appear before long. In each of the towns he had tamed, men had come to him secretly, offering to serve him as spies and informers. He had long since learned that a man in a place of power always has such followers, as surely as a dog has fleas.

Tighe knew well enough that he was now part of a situation in which no one trusted anyone else. He had no doubt at all that Blore had his spies, that every move he made himself would be reported to the little Major and would also be known to the leaders of both factions among the cowmen. He knew he too needed someone to look and listen for him.

He was essentially a policeman and no policeman can do without informers. Treachery begets treachery and espionage is a contagious disease. . . . The only question was whether he could trust the little Mexican.

"Tell me about yourself, Ernesto," he said. "I need friends here. Maybe we can work together."

"I went to the Brothers' School in Santa Fe," Ernesto told him. "Anastasio Royball—you know him?—he is my uncle. I worked in the store for Ballard and now I work in the company store. I know everybody. I hear a lot of talk."

Tighe reflected quickly that a Mexican might be his safest ally. A Mexican was on neither side in this struggle. He understood too the feeling of feudal loyalty a Mexican has for anyone whom he accepts as his patron. In this situation, he thought, he would rather trust a Mexican than one of his own breed.

Tighe judged men by their eyes. He knew the fighting eye and the veiled eye of treachery and the eye of the man who never reveals himself. He did not think about men or consciously classify them, but he trusted the impressions he got when he looked into their eyes. Ernesto had soft brown eyes—the eyes of devotion, the eyes of the born follower, of the eternal child in search of a father.

"All right, Ernesto," he said. "We'll make a deal. You know of course that you'll have to be careful how you come here."

Ernesto nodded and smiled faintly.

"You can trust me, Mr. Tighe," he said. "I know my way around." He paused a moment. "We had good times here in the old days," he spoke wistfully. "Ballard was a great patron. He knew how to keep the peace. Now the place is full of trouble. The old-timers meet almost every night in Ed Kelly's saloon. They all say they'll shoot before they'll move. They scared that Marcos right out of town. They say you won't last either."

Tighe nodded.

"There's been a plan to get rid of me most of the time for the last fifteen years," he remarked. "Who does most of the talking down there at Kelly's?"

"Old man Clarey, for one," Ernesto said. "He sounds pretty bad when he gets a few drinks in him."

"I think I can reach him through his kid," Clay said confidently. "The kid is all right."

"Yes," Ernesto agreed. "But if you try to serve papers on any of them, I think you'll have trouble right away."

"I'm not going to serve any papers—at least not for a long time," Clay said. "I'm not taking any orders from Blore. I'm going to try a lot of persuasion first. If I can get a few of the boys to sign up with the company the rest of them will probably come along."

After Ernesto had left, Tighe got out a map of the grant and tacked it up on the wall of his office. It showed the locations of all the ranches the survey had taken in. There were thirty-two of them, and he knew that each one was a potential trouble spot, and that most of them he would have to visit alone. It would be a long job but he faced it with some confidence. He knew all about the kind of men he had to deal with.

He began by giving himself a week to get acquainted with the town. Its heart and center was still the store—the one that Ballard had founded before the war, and that the company had taken over. But the company had built also a huge frame structure which was a combined hotel, restaurant and bar. This, apparently, was the place Betty Weiss was supposed to manage, when and if she arrived. Tighe had written her, saying simply there was a town all right and a lot of money going around. For the time being, Waverly Buncombe seemed to be functioning as a general manager at the hotel, although he circulated so widely, talked so much and told so little about his own business that he was a somewhat enigmatic figure. So far, Tighe observed, there were no public games in the company saloon and no girls except authentic waitresses. Evidently the Major wanted an orderly town if possible. But the hotel was crowded with strangers, some of whom Tighe could identify as professional gamblers and gunmen, the kind who had followed the tracks west and here had taken one jump ahead of them. They were waiting to see how big the town would boom. Like all such towns it was full of exciting rumors. Blore was said to be planning a dam across the narrow part of the Dark River Canyon which would irrigate the plains and bring in settlers by the thousands. The railroad was expected to reach the town within two years and it would probably become a division point. The company was said to have a huge contract for ties and bridge timbers. Prospectors were combing the near-by mountains and every few days there was a rumor of a rich gold or silver strike. The town now had an assay office and it was always busy. It also had a combined barber shop and undertaking parlor, a blacksmith shop, a butcher shop which often had a bear or a buck hung before its door. A lawyer had opened an office in a tent, and a small tent city was growing up across the creek like mushrooms after a rain.

Everyone agreed the town had a future, but so far it looked like a boom town only on Saturday nights when all the ranchers came to the store, as they had been doing for so many years, and joined the strangers in a buying and drinking spree. The newcomers all gathered at the company bar, but Tighe was quick to see that the old-timers shunned it completely and went to the little saloon that Ed Kelly ran as an adjunct to his livery stable. Already each faction had its headquarters and its leaders. Tighe knew his job was to keep them apart and slowly dissolve them. He circulated between the two bars, watching the eyes of men, making an acquaintance when he saw a chance, spotting those who went out of their way to avoid him. He found three ranchers he had known in the old days in Dodge City. Bill Bostwick was one of them and Tighe shook hands with him and said, "I'll be out to see you one of these days." "Glad to see you," Bostwick said, but he spoke uneasily.

Tighe found time also to give young Bob Clarey the shooting lesson he had promised, and quickly found that the boy had natural speed and dexterity. Thereafter young Bob wore his gun tied to his leg, exactly like Tighe's, even canted his hat at the same angle and gave his friends to understand that he too would become a peace officer, a ruler of towns and a tamer of bad men. Tighe could see that the boy had the makings of a crack shot, but not of an officer of the law in a lawless country. There was not enough iron in him or enough guile. He was still friends with everybody, too much absorbed in his girl and his horse to be aware of the growing tension.

— 7 —

Tighe timed his ride to the Bostwick ranch so that he could take a roundabout way and get there about sunset. He traveled roundabout, starting in the wrong direction, because he didn't want anyone to know where he was going, and he planned to arrive at sunset because he knew Bill would get home about that time. He saw the ranch from the top of a low hill, half a mile away—a pole corral, a long low house under cottonwoods with a blue plume of smoke going up from its rock chimney and not another sign of human life clear to the wide horizons.

Bill was unsaddling his horse when Tighe rode up and they walked together to the house where his Mary was frying venison in an iron skillet and opening the oven door to look at a pan of browning biscuits, while fragrant stream poured out of a tin coffeepot and the table was all set with a pat of homemade butter and a jar of wild plum preserves. An invitation to dinner was inevitable and Tighe had counted on that. He never talked seriously to a man with an empty stomach if he could help it. All through the meal he chatted about the early days in Dodge and Abilene, the trail drives, the weather, an elk hunt they might take together when the first snow fell—everything but business. Not until both of them had rolled and lighted their cigarettes did he mention what had brought him there.

"Bill," he said, "you've got a nice little ranch here. I want to help you hold it."

Bill was a tall lean man of about thirty with a permanently red face and neck, a large Adam's apple and deep-set blue eyes—a kind of man you nearly always found on a ranch twenty miles from a neighbor. It seemed as though fat men always stayed in towns and these lean and quiet ones were often stubborn and suspicious.

"I aim to hold it," Bill said bluntly. "I think that survey is a fraud."

"I don't know anything about the survey," Tighe told him. "That was before my time. But what can you do about it? You can hire a lawyer and it'll cost you more than to buy your quarter section from the company."

Bill sat silent, looking at the Winchester in the corner, and Tighe knew he was thinking he didn't need a lawyer. He knew how fiercely these men resented anything like invasion, how strong was their feeling that possession and use were the whole of the law. . . . He went on quickly to outline the company's terms. They were fair terms, assuming that the company had honest title to the land. They had doubtless come straight from headquarters in Denver. The company was offering to sell any squatter the quarter-section he lived on, with its water rights, at a very moderate price per acre, or else to buy his improvements at a fair valuation. Tighe argued now like a lawyer. It would be the easiest way in the long run, he said, to get a clear title to the ranch. Otherwise there was a long process of filing and waiting and proving up, even if the company was ousted. He knew he was talking sense, and so did Bostwick.

"I'll think it over," the rancher said. That was all Tighe had hoped for. He dropped the subject at once, talking a little while about trifles, smoked a last cigarette and rose to go. Both the Bostwicks pressed him to stay the night, but he knew when to make an exit. He rode away into starlit wilderness, feeling mildly triumphant and also more secure than he ever did in the light of day.

Most of his days now were devoted to such diplomatic missions. He visited first the men he had known farther east and those with whom he had established an acquaintanceship in the town. No doors were slammed in his face, no one refused to listen, most of the ranchers invited him to dinner. He knew well enough these were his easiest cases. There would be some die-hards who would bluster and threaten but he hoped to reduce them slowly to an isolated minority. He knew that most men will always follow the crowd.

Saturdays and Sundays he patrolled the town and visited both of the saloons every night before he went to bed. The company saloon was always crowded, with new faces present almost every night, and with a couple of private card games flourishing in the back room. But Ed Kelly's little joint seemed to have an ever-dwindling patronage, until finally one night he found the bowlegged proprietor all alone. He took a short beer for the sake of sociability.

"Where's your congregation tonight, Ed?" he inquired.

"Home, I reckon," Ed replied. "Most of 'em live quite a ways out."

This was true enough but it was also true that for weeks there had been a small gathering at Kelly's almost every night. Often he had noticed that conversation seemed to lag when he entered, but as long as the boys were all together there, he could watch them. Now he didn't know where they were. He went home slightly troubled.

Ernesto Royball confirmed the worst of his fears a few nights later. The little Mexican looked painfully worried. Tighe had learned long since that Ernesto was a true friend of peace—that he saw violence in the making and longed to prevent it—and this had greatly increased his faith in the man.

"The boys are riding every night," he told Tighe breathlessly. "Two of my cousins—they camp with their sheep on the Rayado—they saw them!"

Tighe nodded gravely. Night riders! He knew all about them. He had been a night rider himself in Kansas. When men banded together and rode in the dark, they were almost always a minority trying to beat other men into line by threat or violence.

"How many did they see?" he asked.

"At least ten," Ernesto reported. "Carlos said he thought they were headed for the Bostwick place."

"That's bad," Tighe said. "Did he recognize any of them?"

"No," Ernesto said. "Old man Clarey is probably one, and all that bunch that meet in Kelly's place. . . ."

"Do you think Laird is putting them up to this?" he asked.

"I don't think so," Ernesto said. "He is a good man. He cured my little boy when we thought he would die. Up at the plaza we all like him. Some of the women think he is a Cristo and has healing in his hands. He was always a peacemaker in the old days. He stopped lots of fights."

"But he did make a speech about the survey, so I heard," Tighe said.

"Yes, I heard him," Ernesto said. "He told them about the Royal Grant. He said Ballard had showed him the paper. He said it was hard to tell where the lines ran, but they couldn't possibly take in what the company claims. He told them they had a right to know."

"Was that all?" Tighe asked.

"Well, no." Ernesto spoke a little reluctantly. "He made quite a speech. You know how he can talk. He quoted from the Bible. I remember he said the earth belongs to those who plow it. Of course, we don't plow much around here, but he made the boys feel they had a right to their ranches."

"The hell of it is, he's probably right," Tighe said gravely. "Blore must have bought that surveyor. But what can you do? These poor suckers have got to buy or move and they ought to know it."

"The trouble is, some of them want to fight," Ernesto said. "There is always somebody who wants to fight. . . ."

"Yes," Tighe agreed, "and if they want a fight, they'll have to have one."

After Ernesto had gone Tighe sat long pondering a situation he didn't like. He had great confidence in his ability to deal with men one at a time. If a man had sense and courage he would almost always listen to reason, and if he was a fool and a coward you could almost always scare him. Like all frontier officers, what he dreaded was the mass movement—the mob and the gang. Every lawless town tended to produce them. Tighe knew the natural history of mobs. He knew it was possible to break one up in its early stages, but once it got moving it could not be scattered. You could only face it with a gun, then, pit your life against it. It was much the same with a night-riding gang. It started as a mob, gained leadership and organization as it went along. He knew the time to stop this one was early. He knew this gang was probably going to every rancher he had visited, trying to undo his work, whether by threat or persuasion. He knew if that continued he would have to start serving papers—and that might mean open war. Tighe had lost his taste for war. First he would face alone every man he could find. It would take time, but all of them came to town sooner or later.

He managed first to meet Bill Bostwick in the store.

"Bill," he said, "if anyone bothers you out there, I hope you'll let me know. I'm here to keep the peace."

Bostwick didn't meet his eye.

"I reckon I won't need any help," he said quietly, and then walked away.

Tighe knew that was bad, and he knew even better that things were going against him when another man he had visited crossed the street to avoid meeting him. For the first time in a good many years Clay Tighe could sense that his prestige was falling, that his authority and power were being defied. He was not the celebrity here that he had been in Dodge and Hays City and Abilene. Most of these men had heard of him but they had not seen him perform, except on a tin can. He had believed he could manage this situation without ever drawing a gun. With a slight tightening of the gut and tautening of the nerves he understood now that he was going to have to prove himself—how or when he still couldn't see.

Old man Clarey was the only member of the night-riding gang of whom he felt sure. He doubted that Clarey was the leader but he had been the chief talker for a long time. He had told several men that no goddam sheriff was ever going to run him off his own ranch. Tighe had encountered this loud-talking kind of man many times before. Almost always he proved to be more a bluff than a menace. The truly dangerous man seldom made much noise. Tighe had counted on

Clarey to subside as others accepted the company offer. But now he knew he had to tackle Clarey, as being the only one of the enemy he could identify. He knew also that he had to meet him on the street, in the most casual way, and this took time. All of the ranchers necessarily came to the store, soon or late, but the old-timers seemed to be staying away from town as much as possible. Tighe could guess that they were meeting at some ranch house, laying their plans, making their midnight visits. . . . It was a week before he saw Clarey coming down the new board sidewalk past the company hotel, and he went to meet him.

He confronted the man squarely, brought him to a stop.

"Clarey," he said quietly, "I'm coming out to see you one of these days. I've got a little business to talk about."

"You've got no business with *me!*" Clarey said, his voice rising shrilly on the last word. "You've got no business on *my* ranch. I warn you now! If you don't want trouble, stay off *my* land!"

He glared at Tighe a moment, then pushed past him and went his way. Tighe stood staring after him a moment. "There would be one son-of-a-bitch . . ." he said to himself.

He carried back to his office a disturbing impression of small, bright, humorless eyes, with a spark of rage in them, under shaggy brows. They reminded him of the eyes of a wounded bear he had faced once, reared upon its hind legs, ready to charge. He remembered, too, the rising, strained inflection of the voice. He knew the type—the man who has violence bottled up inside him, who contrives crises half consciously because something in him always craves a crisis.

For once in his life Tighe spent days of indecision. He knew now that he had to make a move, but he didn't feel sure yet what he had to do. It was the indispensable Ernesto, making a cautious midnight call, who brought his doubts to an end.

"They are saying that Clarey has you bluffed," he reported. "They say you are afraid to go out there and take him."

"Just exactly who is saying that?" Tighe inquired.

"Buncombe, for one," Ernesto said. "When he starts talking about anything, it goes all over town. He's just a big mouth—that's all he is. He says Clarey has a buffalo gun right by his door. He's going to nail you when he sees you coming. . . . Of course you can't believe a word Waverly says."

"No," Tighe agreed, "but you can believe he has reason for saying it. Blore owns him, tooth and toenail."

After Ernesto had gone, Tighe sat thoughtful for a long time. Ruefully he faced the fact that the little Major had been too smart for him. Given time and no interference Tighe believed he could have reduced the rebels to a helpless minority who would sell out and move. He felt sure he could have settled the problem without ever serving a paper or drawing a gun. But the Major wanted quick action. He probably also wanted a show of force. Tighe spoke aloud to himself, as he always did when troubled.

"The hell of it is, he's going to get it. Now I've got to do something or else quit—and I can't quit."

He waited two more days. He spent them chiefly looking for young Bob Clarey, hoping he might yet reach the father through the son. But Bob was nowhere to be found and hadn't been seen in town for weeks. He was evidently sticking close to the home ranch, and doubtless that meant he was loyal to the old man.

— 8 —

On his decisive day, Tighe rose long before daylight. He inspected his six-shooter and tested his draw with care. He loaded his rifle and ran half a dozen shells through the action to be sure it was working smoothly. Then he mounted and rode out of town in the dark and solitude of the small hours.

Tighe's professional pride was deeply involved in this situation. He knew there was only one alternative to what he intended doing now—to admit he could not do the job alone and raise a posse to help him. That would be easy. Any of the newcomers who hung around the company bar would be glad to follow him. In effect, he would then be putting himself at the head of the other faction. He could ride to each of the disputed properties and serve a notice of dispossession by force of arms. Unless the night riders all were rank cowards they would then gather at one of the ranches and wait for him. There would be a pitched battle at short range with Winchesters.

Any fool could bring a tense situation to a climax, make a bloody mess of it. Most of the men Blore might have hired would have done just that, and done it in the first place. Clay Tighe was famous for the fact that he could dominate men, and even whole towns, without raising his voice, much less drawing his gun. He took pride in being a keeper of the peace. He still believed he could have kept the peace in the Dark River Valley if no one else had meddled. He still hoped he might regain his dominance without firing a shot. If he could serve papers on Clarey, or disarm him and bring him to town, he would at least have gained time.

Dawn was breaking when he got off his horse a quarter of a mile from the Clarey ranch, walked to the top of a low hill and studied the house from a screen of juniper and piñon, like a hunter stalking dangerous game. As the light widened in the east, he could see four saddle horses in the Clarey corral, feeding at a hayrack. Four men were more than he had expected but there was nothing for it. One of the horses was white and he knew that probably meant young Bob was at home. This also was bad news. A third horse, he knew, probably belonged to Bill McComas, a young cowboy who worked for Clarey from time to time. Bill was a harmless and simple young fellow, who wore a gun because it was customary, and he probably wouldn't fight. Tighe couldn't guess who the fourth man was.

He would have liked to catch the old man there alone, but he knew that would be pure luck, and he could not afford to wait and try again. He had to take the situation as he found it.

It was cold in the summer dawn. He stamped his feet and threshed his arms while he waited. He couldn't afford to be stiff or slow when he went to the door. . . . It was nearly an hour before he saw the signal he was waiting for—a thin blue wisp of smoke from the chimney. The men were awake and starting to cook breakfast. This was the traditional, the only right time to make an arrest. He mounted and rode slowly down toward the house, picking soft ground so there would be no sound of shod hoofs striking rock.

The Clarey house was a long low block of a structure, built of squared timbers, solid as a fort. The door was in the middle with a window on either side of it. Both windows still were closed by solid wooden shutters, and Tighe knew this was luck for him. Otherwise he might have had trouble approaching the house unseen. As it was he rode up within ten yards of the door and dismounted, turning his horse parallel to the house and dropping his bridle rein on the ground. The well-trained sorrel would stay right there until he got a signal to move. As he walked quietly to the door Tighe could just hear low voices within, a man whistling softly and the spat and sizzle of breakfast in a frying pan. He knocked loudly on the door. Instantly there was silence. He waited a minute that seemed very long and then knocked again. This time he heard a quick step and the door opened a few inches. For about three seconds he looked into the small, glaring, fanatical eyes of old man Clarey. Then the door closed with a bang, and without a word.

Tighe knew that meant war. He whipped out his six-shooter, covering the door with it, backed away swiftly and got behind his horse. There he holstered the revolver and drew his short Winchester from the saddle scabbard. Then he slapped the sorrel on the rump and the horse moved away, turning its head slightly so as not to step on the trailing bridle rein. Tighe stood rigid, the cocked rifle hard against his hip. Its muzzle was trained on the door. But he was watching both windows as well.

This was a feat of arms he had practiced often, but had used only once before when he had taken three Mexican horse thieves out of an adobe house. He knew that now, as then, it was his only chance. He could deliver a shot to the door or to either window, swinging the gun with his whole body, and do it far faster than he could level and shoot a revolver. Tense and ready he stood, a fair target. Clarey could have war now if he wanted it. The choice was his.

For three long minutes nothing happened except that Tighe could hear voices again. Then there was a terrific pounding on the inside of the door.

"Tighe, Tighe!" He knew the voice must be that of Bill McComas. "Don't shoot! I'm coming out. . . . I don't want no part of this!"

"All right!" Tighe called. "Come out with your hands up."

The door popped open, McComas popped out and the door slammed behind him. McComas stood visibly trembling, his mouth open, his hands high.

"Unbuckle your gun and let it drop," Tighe told him quietly. And then as the gun hit the ground, "Now go back in there and tell the rest of them to come out the same way."

"They won't do it!" McComas spoke in the strangulated voice of terror. "I argued with the old man. The damn fool won't move."

"All right, get going," Tighe said.

McComas jumped over his own gun and sprinted for the cover of the corral fence. Tighe's eyes never left the door. The strain of waiting lasted minutes longer, then the door jerked open a crack and he could see the muzzle of a gun in it. His rifle roared and spat flame. Blue smoke briefly obscured his vision but he knew he had hit his man. He could always call his shots.

He worked the lever of his rifle like lightning, and none too fast. He swung on a crack between the shutters of the left-hand window. A rifle barrel had poked them open, and this time the two shots were simultaneous, but Tighe still stood. Within he heard a thud and a groan. He stood fast, ready again, knowing two men were down but there must be a third to deal with.

For an intolerably long time nothing happened and he could hear no sound. There might be no third man after all, or one bullet might have struck two. . . . He had to do something. He strode up to the door and began kicking at it with all his strength, chancing a shot through the wood. The door crashed open and he jumped through it, rifle ready, almost falling over the body of old man Clarey, who lay on his back with arms outspread, a round, dark bullet hole between his eyes and a dark pool of blood widening beneath his head. Over by the window a second man knelt beside a fallen one, supporting his head. The kneeling man turned his head and Tighe recognized Daniel Laird.

"He's dying," Laird spoke in a tired, flat voice.

It was all over. Tighe suddenly felt all the tension drain out of him. He leaned his rifle against the wall and went and knelt on the other side of young Bob. The boy was shot through the lungs. Tighe knew that by the pinkish foam about his mouth and the sound of his breathing. Bob looked at Tighe with eyes wide in an expression of pained surprise.

"I wish, I wish, I wish . . ." he said. But no one ever knew what he wished for a great gout of blood welled up out of his mouth and he fell back and died. Laird covered his face and the two men rose and faced each other. There was no strain between them. They moved slowly, like old men, with the weariness of profound reaction.

"They're both dead," Laird said.

"Yes," Tighe agreed. "I had to do it. . . . They both had a shot at me."

Laird nodded.

"I've been out here with them three days," he said. "I tried to persuade them not to fight. I knew you would come."

They went out, closing the smashed door as best they could, and Tighe waited while Laird saddled his horse. They rode back toward town slowly, slumping a little in their saddles, and for a long time they rode in silence.

"I'm sure sorry I had to kill that boy," Tighe said at last, speaking as though to himself, looking at nothing.

"Yes," Laird said.

"The old man asked for it," Tighe said. "But I'm sure sorry about that boy."

Again they rode in silence for slow miles, and again Tighe spoke, as though from the depth of his own reflections.

"I guess I had to kill somebody," he said. "This will settle it. Nobody else will try anything now. If Clarey had killed me all hell would have broken loose."

Laird said nothing and they rode all the rest of the way in silence. As they neared the town Tighe could see a crowd gathered and growing on the sidewalk in front of the company saloon. He knew Bill McComas would have watched the fight, would have known the Clareys were both down when he saw Tighe enter the house. The news was there ahead of him and that was bad.

"You better cut for home," he told Laird. "I'll take this bunch alone."

Laird nodded and turned off across the creek toward his own cabin.

The crowd in front of the saloon was almost all company men and curious strangers, with a few Mexicans who had heard the news, and a few women. There was nothing hostile about it. As Tighe dismounted a few men came forward holding out their hands, but Tighe waved them away, shaking his head.

"I don't want any congratulations, boys," he said. "And I don't want a crowd. Break it up!"

Most of them were turning away when he saw Adelita coming. Her long hair was down around her shoulders, her face was a mask of agony and her great dark eyes were fixed upon his. They held him in his tracks and she came right up to him, her face within two feet of his.

"Is he dead?" she demanded. "Did you kill him?"

Tighe nodded grimly, dumb with distress.

"You killed him!" Her voice rose to a screaming pitch of grief. "Why did you kill him? What had he done to you?"

She covered her face with her hands for a moment, then looked up at him again, and this time he saw fury in her eyes.

"Murderer, murderer, murderer!" She hurled the words into his face like missiles. "You murdered him!"

She turned and walked slowly away, her face buried in her hands again, her heavy disheveled hair draping her shaken shoulders like a mourning veil.

Tighe went into the saloon and found it empty except for the bartender.

"Give me a double brandy," he said.

He lifted his drink and stared at it for a long moment, noticing that his hand trembled slightly for the first time in many years. He downed the brandy at a gulp and set down the glass.

"It takes a woman to make you feel things," he remarked.

PART FOUR

The Prophet

IN HIS OWN COUNTRY

AFTER the killing of the Clareys, Daniel Laird was seldom seen on the streets of the town. He spent much of his time in the mountains with a rifle or a fishing rod. It was only in the mountains that he now had any feeling of peace, especially when he lay on the ground under the pines and listened to the long, deep breathing of the wind. This was a thing he had done ever since he could remember for he had always been a man of the forest. The great trees had often given him a feeling of peace and sometimes a kind of ecstasy. Sometimes he felt as though the wind was one with his breath and his body with the earth beneath him. Even now, when so much bitterness stirred inside him, he could walk himself tired and rest upon the earth and recover a moment of peace.

It was only a moment, for the whole way of his life in the Dark River Valley had been destroyed. There was much building in the valley but no work for him. He could not ask Blore for work and Blore was an absolute ruler. He never went near the meeting house now, for he knew no one would come to hear him. Dances still were held there every Saturday night and he saw the lights and heard the music and felt the cold weight of his exclusion. When he went to the store to buy supplies, men he had known for years refused to meet his eye or crossed the street to avoid him. He felt the eyes of strangers upon him, sometimes saw them pointing at him, always knew they were talking about him.

Only fragments of gossip had come to him, mostly through a few Mexicans who remained his friends because he had helped them when they were sick, but he knew what people were saying about him, as well as though he had heard their words. He knew they all blamed him for the killing of the Clareys, said he had persuaded the old man to fight, said there would have been open war if he had had his way. No one blamed Tighe for the killing. Everyone said Tighe had done only what he had to do. Tighe now was the great man of the Dark River Valley, the man who had brought peace with a gun. Everyone now had either signed up with the company or sold out and moved. Peace had come for everyone except Daniel Laird, the man who had wanted only to tell the truth and see justice done, the man who had longed to serve his fellows. . . . In his own mind he defended himself hotly, sometimes talking to himself as he strode along. This added a new phase to his legend, for many, especially among the newcomers, now said he was crazy.

He defended himself, he composed long soliloquies of self-justification, but it was all in vain. He was learning the painful fact that blame begets guilt, that no man can stand alone against the disapproval of his fellows. When he walked down the street he felt guilty in spite of himself, he peered suspiciously over his shoulder, he all but slunk through the town, hoping no one would notice his presence. Guilt hounded him, it drove him into the wilderness where the great trees spoke in soothing voices and the ancient earth received him into her bosom and let him rest. But only for a moment. . . . Worse than guilt was the longing for violence that had grown upon him. He could feel it in his breast as though it were a living, separate demon that had crept into his body. It poured a poison into his blood, changed the whole quality of his being, so that his great hands clenched as he walked. His muscles yearned for violence as a thirsty mouth for water. More than once he took an ax, just to relieve his feelings, felled a dead pine and reduced it to kindling, fighting it furiously until he was drenched with sweat and knew the passing relief of complete exhaustion. Such angers he had not tasted for years, not since the wild period of his youth when he had fought a few times in drunken fury and had known what it was to feel the warm blood of a man on his hands.

He did not blame most men now, those who turned away from him, but he despised them. What cowards they were! The ones who had listened to his words and agreed with him and offered to follow him now were afraid to be seen with him, afraid to meet his eye. The same men who had said they would chase Tighe out of the valley at the point of a gun now saluted Tighe when he walked down the street, paid him the craven homage of the yellow soul. Laird had persuaded himself once that he loved his fellow beings. Now suddenly he saw them as a pack of wolves who bit from behind and hunted in the dark and turned upon the fallen fellow. . . . But his rage, the rage that blinded his eyes and made his fingers writhe, was all against two men, Waverly Buncombe and Major Blore. He knew Blore was the man who had killed the Clareys, without ever lifting his hand, the one who had destroyed the peace. And he knew that Buncombe had played jackal to Blore's lion, had spread all the lies, had created the situation that made it necessary for Tighe to use a rifle. When he saw either of these men on the street he felt a rage that made him literally sick, so that he turned his eyes away. And both of them too had invaded his dreams. Not since his childhood had he known such vivid and terrible dreams. In one of them he was looking at Blore over the sights of a rifle. The Major was riding toward him from a great distance, growing slowly larger, while the bead of the front sight settled over his heart. Daniel awoke just before he pressed the trigger, with the feeling that he had been within an instant of murder. . . . The dream about Buncombe was even worse and it woke him repeatedly. He had Buncombe down on the ground and his fingers were around the man's throat, but he did not choke him. He pulled his head off, as he had seen a farmer pull the head off a chicken. Buncombe's neck stretched to an incredible length and then broke with a pop and a great spurt of blood. Daniel felt the warm blood all over him and woke to know that he was bathed in his own sweat.

He knew he was in a bad way, knew he ought to leave the valley, but a stubborn something in him would not let him leave. He had heard a rumor they were going to run him out—that Buncombe had boasted he would leave town on a rail if he didn't go pretty soon on his own horse. . . . Daniel Laird was not going to be run out of anywhere! He loved this country. It had been home to him for ten years. But maybe he would have gone if he hadn't heard that rumor. . . . Let them come! His hands clenched and his blood pounded when he thought about it. Let them come! He didn't care how many. . . .

— 2 —

As he went back to the mountains in search of peace, so he also went back to the past, reviewing his life as he had never done before, feeling the mystery of it, wondering how he had become what he was. And this too brought him a measure of peace, detached him from his own misery, gave him escape from the present, sent him all the way back to the Cumberland country where the little far-scattered farms lay in the coves beside bright leaping waters, and the mountains were clothed to their summits in virgin hardwood forest, the finest forest in the world, rich in timber, nuts and berries, fat with game. There men lived in log houses, raised corn with a hoe and ground it at watermills, made white liquor in their own stills, hunted for most of their meat and used buckskin for most of their clothing. It was the simplest, the most primitive and unchanging life that white men lived anywhere in America, and it was a hard life, but when he remembered it now, especially his childhood, he saw it all bathed in sunlight and moving to the music of singing voices—the singing of hymns in little mountain churches, the singing of folk songs that told long stories, his mother singing to the beat of a wooden churn.

Daniel Laird was raised on an ax and a rifle, a spelling book and a Bible. He knew many bits of the Bible by heart before he was fourteen because it was all he had to read, because he loved the sound and flavor of its words and also because it had been read to him, quoted to him, shouted at him, ever since he could remember. For the southern mountain country was truly vocal and vibrant with religion. It rocked and shouted and sang in the name of God. Religion was even more a social activity than a faith. Most public gatherings were religious gatherings. Every community had its little log church, and camp meetings brought people together from as far as you could ride a horse in a day. At the best and biggest camp meetings people went wild and rolled on the ground, men and women together, and sin and salvation were sometimes part of the same occasion. Besides the main denominations, there were innumerable little sects, and almost any gifted preacher might found a sect of his own. Also, any man with a good voice might become a preacher, for most mountain preachers were unordained, farmed six days a week and preached on Sundays. Daniel's father was such a preacher and he was rated one of the best, chiefly because of the great and stirring power of his voice. The best preacher was the one who could get people to rocking and shouting the quickest, for to these mountain folk religion was a great communal excitement. They sobbed and bellowed and rolled and crawled but they truly achieved an escape from the limitations of self, a feeling of unity with Jesus and with each other.

In his boyhood Daniel knew much happiness of a simple, laborious kind, so that when he remembered it now it had almost the quality of an idyll. He worked hard with an ax and a hoe but he always had great strength and did his work easily. He was known as a "loner" who did not run much with other boys but liked to roam in the woods by himself when he was free. Every community had its loners and they were recognized and tolerated as such. Daniel was a good hunter and a first-class woodsman, who knew how to find wild honey and ginseng, and also all of the herbs the mountain people used in their doctoring. His mother had some reputation as a healer and he kept her supplied with herbs and learned something of her art. Like most solitary boys he stood somewhat apart from his family, escaping the tyranny of his two older brothers and of his father by taking to the timber like a woods-born shoat whenever the family atmosphere began to cramp him. He did not easily yield to the crowd feelings of church and camp meeting. He felt more at peace in the woods and more at one with the earth than with his fellows.

When he was seventeen he shot up suddenly to his full height and strength and the white stream of desire poured through his body, destroying the peace he had known in his best boyhood years. Then he began to join the gang of wild young men who gathered at the crossroads store. At first they would have none of him but he won his way by pinning each of them to the ground in a wrestling match. A few of these matches became fights when someone lost his temper and struck a blow. Daniel did not like to fight but he was terrible when he got started and he felt sick, win or lose, when it was over.

The gang Daniel went with attended every camp meeting they could reach, sometimes walking twenty miles, for these were the great excitements of their lives. They always had a jug of white corn liquor and they would lurk in the edge of the woods, a little way from the crowd, and prime their spirits with long burning swigs while they listened to the preaching and singing and shouting. They could tell by the noise the meeting made when it was reaching its highest point of excitement and then they would edge into the crowd, bellowing their hallelujahs as loud as the next fellow. All of them had the same idea, which was to get hold of some woman in a high state of excitement and edge her out of the crowd and get her down in the dark. There were always widow women who knew what was coming, and some married women who got away from their husbands, but it was dangerous business and sometimes there were terrible fights back in the shadows.

Some of the young fellows who came to camp meetings just to get drunk and chase women would be carried away by the preaching and singing and end up crawling toward the mourner's bench. Daniel never had that experience. By the time he was twenty-one he had been to many camp meetings, but he had never been saved, he had never come to Jesus. There was something in him that resisted the pull of the crowd, just as something in his body fought off the ague that shook most of his fellows. The better the camp meeting, the less he felt a part of it. If it was a good camp meeting the people always first began jigging and shouting, then fell on their faces and began to roll or crawl. Daniel's father remembered the great wave of revivals that swept over five states in the year 1802, when people gathered in thousands and sometimes fifteen preachers were working at once—all of them sweating to beat hell, some irreverent soul had said. In that great day hundreds fell all at once, like wheat before a scythe, his father had told him.

Daniel had never seen anything like that, but he had seen a good deal of jigging and crawling and he had never wanted to jig or crawl. At the best camp meeting he ever saw there were thirty or forty on the ground at once and some repentant sinners mounted the platform beside the preacher and shouted their confessions at the crowd. Daniel was full of corn liquor but still wholly unmoved when he climbed up on the platform and began bellowing in his great voice. He did not know or care what he was saying and neither did anyone else. They shouted hallelujah and praise God no matter what he said. "You can all go to hell!" he shouted at last, and they all answered him with a chorus of amen. Standing there above them, looking down on them, he felt more than ever detached from his fellows, but yet he longed for union with something. Presently he noticed a woman on the edge of the crowd who was going round and round with her eyes closed, dancing herself dizzy. She was a slim, blonde woman and a stranger to him—one who might have come from as much as twenty miles away, which was a long distance in the mountains. He went down to her and danced with her and caught her when she fell. Picking her up in his arms he carried her quickly into the shadows, and no one saw him or tried to stop him.

"Oh, for Christ's sake!" she murmured when he laid her on the ground, but she did not struggle, and afterwards he went heavily to sleep.

When he woke it was sunrise of a perfect June morning, with the slanting light silvering the leaves and a chorus of birdsong ringing softly through the forest. The woman was gone, everyone was gone. Daniel had a great thirst. He went down to the branch and took a deep drink and bathed his head in the cool water. Then he lay down under the trees and a feeling of great serenity and clarity came over him. It seemed as though the woman had purified him of all desire, the alcohol in his blood had set him free from his own body, and the peace of God had truly descended upon this spot, now that all the people were gone. He felt like a disembodied mind contemplating his own destiny with a new detachment. For a long time he had been dissatisfied with his life and had thought of taking the long trail west. Some young men from the mountain settlements went west every year, but not nearly so many as from other regions, for these mountain people were passionately attached to their home country. So Daniel had never made up his mind to go, but this morning he suddenly felt sure he was going. He felt as though he were called to go, and also as though the ties that bound him to a region had been all at once dissolved. He felt now that he could be at home anywhere on earth.

— 3 —

Daniel walked to Independence, Missouri, equipped with an ax and one silver dollar. He got there with the same dollar and a few more. Almost any farm would put him up for the night. Sometimes he chopped wood to pay for his supper, but he was seldom asked to do so. When he came to a sawmill he would stop for a few days and work at felling timber, and sometimes he helped to raise a house or roof a barn. Everywhere populations were growing, men were building things, the country was filled with the thud of axes, the whine of saws, the crash of falling timber.

He had no difficulty in getting a job as a teamster over the Santa Fe Trail, for he moved westward with the first great wave of migration after the war, but when he reached the high prairies in Kansas he almost wished he could turn back. For the first time he saw a flat and treeless world, and it made him acutely uncomfortable. He felt better when he reached the Rocky Mountains, saw tall timber and clear running water again. He stopped at Ballard's great house chiefly because of the fine forest and the great mountains that rose behind it. He asked for a job and got one splitting firewood at the kitchen door. In a few months he had learned enough Spanish to boss the gang of Mexicans who supplied the great house with firewood, and within a year he had charge of all the building operations on the grant. Ballard was quick to spot a useful man and one he could trust. Daniel knew he owed his success almost wholly to Ballard's friendship. They were never intimates because neither of them had any intimates, but he was one of the few men who went to Ballard's office whenever he chose, and once in a while they sat and smoked together on the porch. Everyone knew that Ballard stood behind him and Daniel knew this made him a secure and privileged man, but he never understood how he came to occupy the peculiar position he did in the Dark River Valley. He had never intended to preach there, but he often sang at his work and his public career began when the women asked him to lead them in singing hymns. Neither had he wished to become an amateur doctor, but he began by patching up sick and injured Mexicans who worked for him, and this led to other calls for his services. Then Ballard asked him to take charge of the dance hall and keep order, and he became famous for his fiddling and his calling of square dances, which he had known all his life. So he became an important man—one who was listened to, obeyed and sent for in emergencies—and he enjoyed his importance.

He had acquired a role in the community and a legend, and he became more and more the creature and the prisoner of the part he had to play. It gave him authority over his fellows and it also set him apart from them, and especially from women. He went alone into houses where children were sick and it was known he could be trusted there. Had he begun to lay hands upon women he would have been quickly tangled in the briary bush of jealousy and desire. For the same reason he knew he could not afford ever to lose his temper. He never carried a weapon and no one wanted to fight him barehanded. He was known for the way he could boss his Mexicans without ever raising either his voice or his hand. He used his great strength only when he had to stop others from fighting. So he became a keeper of the peace in the community—but above all he kept the peace of his own separate being, and the need of his isolation grew upon him. In the best of his years in the valley he achieved a serenity he had never known before. He lived insulated from most of the shocks of human contact, from the muddle of lust and anger in which most men live, and this was nothing he had sought or chosen but a destiny which had befallen him.

When Ballard died after the grant was sold he knew a great grief for the first time in his life, and he had a sure premonition of trouble, but he had never imagined his own function and way of life would be destroyed as they had been. At first he had risen to a new importance. Men had flocked to hear him when he spoke in the meeting house about the grant and the fraudulent survey. They all felt a need of leadership and it seemed at first as though Daniel Laird had succeeded to some part of the power Ballard had held. He had planned to organize the ranchers, raise money and employ a lawyer, and for a while his plan had prospered. Then Blore had moved into the great house, and within a month everything was changed. Blore brought new settlers with him. Suddenly there were two factions and both sides were talking war. No one would listen to him after Tighe took over, and he became aware that Buncombe was working to destroy him. It was amazing how quickly the whole character and quality of life in the valley had changed, how men who long had lived at peace with each other suddenly began to quarrel, how tensions grew that made violence inevitable. It amazed Daniel

Laird still more how the tension and the violence had invaded his own being. The man of peace had become a man of righteous anger.

— 4 —

Except for a few of the Mexicans there was not a man in the valley he could surely call his friend, but this was not true of the women. Now and then he met on the street the wives of some of the ranchers, the old-timers he had known for years, and these nearly always nodded and smiled. He had never had more than a nodding and smiling acquaintance with most of them, but they were grateful to him for the Sunday meetings he had held. Now he was grateful for their smiles as never before. One day Mother Fenton stopped him on the street, planting her bulk in his path so that he could not have avoided her if he wished. She was a great fat woman of sixty, who had raised a family of five boys, all of whom had scattered over the country in search of land and cattle. She and her husband, Bill Fenton, lived alone on a little ranch where they raised a few blooded cattle and horses. Fenton was a man of peace who would go to almost any length to avoid trouble. He had refused to get his dander up when the grant was sold. He had shrugged his shoulders and signed up with the company. Ma Fenton also declined to let anything disturb her serenity and good humor. The Fentons had stayed out on their ranch and tended to their stock while others fought and argued. Mother Fenton was one of the few who had called Daniel by his first name, and she addressed him now with the complete confidence of her all-embracing kindliness.

"Daniel," she demanded, "why don't you hold meeting any more? A little singing would do people a sight of good right now."

Daniel stood before her, feeling the blood mount into his ears, aware that he was blushing with pleasure and confusion.

"I'm afraid nobody would come, Missis Fenton," he said humbly, blurting the truth out of the depth of his despair. "I'm afraid nobody wants to hear me any more."

"Nonsense!" She spoke to him with good-humored severity, like a mother to her child. "You come down here next Sunday and open the doors and I'll have people here to listen. I promise you that!"

Daniel thanked her and hurried away, feeling pleased and shaken and not at all sure of himself. But he knew he would do it. The dance hall stood there empty every Sunday, and who was going to stop him? He would like to see anyone try to stop him! His anger began to rise again. But he went to the hall the following Sunday full of doubt.

Mother Fenton had assembled exactly eight women, five of whom were strangers to Daniel. But he recited to them from the Bible, led them in singing and discovered that two of the stranger women had good voices. Before the singing was over the crowd had more than doubled, and it included several men who were also strangers to him. All these people, he knew, had come simply because they heard the singing and were curious to know what was going on, but he felt better after the meeting than he had in weeks. He saw that he still had power to draw people together and make them listen to his voice. Maybe, after all, he still had a place here and something to do. He knew he would go to the hall now every Sunday as long as anyone would come to listen.

His second meeting was larger than his first and the third was still larger. Most of it was feminine but more men came each time. Few of the old-timers appeared but new people were coming to the valley every day and most of these cared nothing about the troubles of a few months ago. Daniel began to see that he might gather a wholly new following, and he longed for a following as never before.

He did not speak to these people in his own words at all. His method as a preacher was simply what he had learned from his father and all the other mountain preachers he had heard. All of them shouted passages of Holy writ at their hearers, then led them in song and then shouted again, working always toward a climax of crowd excitement. Daniel did not depart from this primitive pattern but neither did he try for any fervid response. He had never truly cared much about his hearers. Always he had chosen passages from the Bible which expressed his own mood of the moment—and every conceivable mood and notion seemed to be expressed somewhere in that great book. He combined passages to suit himself, even changed them a little, chanting their eloquent music in his great voice for the love of its sound and the release it gave to his feelings. So at his second meeting he recited only fragments from Ecclesiastes between the hymns.

"The words of the wise are heard more than the cry of him that ruleth among fools," he told them solemnly. "Wisdom is better than weapons of war; but one sinner destroyeth much good."

And at the end of the meeting he chanted lines that had been running through his head for weeks:

> *Remember, the evil days come,*
> *And the years draw nigh,*
> *When thou shalt say, I have no pleasure in them.*
> *Because Man goeth to his long home,*
> *And the mourners go about the streets,*
> *And the dust returneth to the earth, as it was,*
> *And the spirit returneth unto God, who gave it.*

Then he took his hat and walked out, looking at no one, but several women stopped him and thanked him, and he got back to his cabin glowing with a sense of power, feeling sure he had moved these people.

It was at his third meeting that he first noticed Betty Weiss, and he felt sure it was the first time she had come, for she stood out from the crowd like a huckleberry in a bowl of milk. She was nothing like the other women, the wives of ranchmen. She was slim and elegant in a black dress which was open at the throat and tight about her small pointed breasts. She sat always near the middle of the hall and well up front. She looked at him steadily all through the meeting, and he could not keep his eyes away from her. He was acutely aware of her pale face, delicately rouged, of the dark mass of her hair, the curious green of her eyes, her shapely well-tended hands. He had never seen anything like her. She looked as exotic here as a cockatoo in a flock of barnyard hens. And she was a gifted singer. When he started a hymn he would nod to her and the two of them led and dominated the singing with great success. He felt as though she had come to help him, was trying to help him. . . . He knew little about her except that she ran the hotel and was a figure of mystery and a subject of gossip in the town. He knew some said she was Blore's woman—that he had imported her for his own amusement and made a job for her. He didn't care who or what she was. He knew only that she had moved into his imagination as soon as she entered the hall. He knew she was none of his business, he didn't want to think about her—but her image seemed to follow him home and stay with him, like an importunate and persistent ghost.

— 5 —

A few days after his third meeting Ernesto Royball came to his cabin, knocking timidly on the door, asking permission to enter. Ernesto was the first visitor who had come to him in months and he welcomed the man and gave him a drink. He had known Ernesto for years and once had treated him for a sprained back.

Ernesto was all friendliness and he talked for a long time about small and unimportant matters—about how late the rains were this year, and how many wild turkeys there were along Ute Creek, and that trade at the company store had nearly doubled. Daniel knew Mexicans well enough to be sure Ernesto was leading up to something. A Mexican always approached serious business indirectly, by way of a long preamble. Finally Ernesto got to it, obviously diffident and embarrassed.

"Those meetings you are holding, Mr. Laird," he said. "I'm afraid they may make trouble for you. I am your friend, Mr. Laird, that is why I tell you."

Daniel felt his anger rising again and he held it down with a conscious effort; he did not speak until he felt sure he could speak softly.

"Did Major Blore send you to tell me this, Ernesto?" he inquired.

"No, Mr. Laird!" Ernesto was emphatic. "Nobody sent me! I come because I am your friend and I don't want you to have trouble. I don't want anyone to have trouble. We have had too much trouble already. But I know the boss—he doesn't want meetings. He doesn't like to see people get together—I know that!"

Ernesto was fairly sweating with sincerity and embarrassment. Daniel felt sorry for him.

"Thank you, Ernesto," he said. "I know you are my friend."

He would not say any more than that. They chatted for a little longer and Ernesto refused an invitation to supper and went away. Daniel sat thoughtful for a long time after his visitor had gone, but he was not truly considering what he would do. He knew he would go on holding meetings, and if for no other reason, because he wanted to see Betty Weiss again, and hear her voice and feel her strange green eyes upon his own.

He had been hoping she might speak to him after a meeting or smile at him. She never did either, but the feeling that they were moving toward each other, that an intercourse had sprung up between them, grew stronger each time he saw her. It was easy for him to watch her, sitting there in front of him, without appearing to do so, and he became aware of every detail of her person—of the sprinkle of freckles across her nose, the slant of her eyebrows, especially of a faint pink birthmark upon her throat. It was an irregular splotch about the size of a dollar and looked like a pink map of Australia he remembered in an old schoolbook of geography. He noticed that when she sang with him this spot grew darker, becoming more vivid and visible with the play of her blood. Her expression told him nothing but it seemed as though this mark upon her throat betrayed the rise and fall of her feeling.

The longing to speak to her grew upon him, and then suddenly he found himself speaking to her in words he had known for years. He had spoken them many times before but never before had they meant anything to him. Now he found them the very music of his feeling.

> *Thou art beautiful, O my love, as Tirzah,*
> *Comely as Jerusalem,*
>   *Terrible as an army with banners.*
> *Turn away thine eyes from me,*
>   *For they have overcome me.*

It was easy for him to utter this fragment, to speak it to her as directly as though they had been all alone in the hall, to build his whole recital about the Song of Songs, as he had often done before. Immediately afterward he started the singing again, drowning his own emotion in sound, covering up quickly his confession of love. He knew it had been that and he felt sure she knew it. For the little banner upon her throat flamed scarlet at his voice.

In spite of himself he spoke to her again, for it seemed as though the sacred words had been made for his speaking.

> *Thou hast ravished my heart, my sister,*
>   *my bride; thou hast ravished my heart*
> *With one look of thine eyes,*
> *With one chain of thy neck.*
> *How fair is thy love, my sister, my bride!*
> *How much better is thy love than wine!*

Again he sang, feeling as though he sang to her alone, and seeing again the flaming answer of her blood. He closed the meeting quickly and hurried home, feeling curiously weak and undone. He sat down in his great homemade chair and mopped sweat from his brow. It seemed as though all the disciplines and armors of his being had suddenly melted, so that he sat there helpless, obsessed, with her image dancing in his brain. No woman had ever disturbed him this way before. He knew that she had caught him in a vulnerable moment, that another time he might have dismissed her from his mind in a little while. But the fact remained that she had invaded his imagination—that he could not escape her any more than if she had stood before him.

Finally he rose and poured himself a large jolt of Taos whisky, the first he had tasted in years. He cooked and ate his supper mechanically, then went and sat before his door as he had done so many other evenings. It was near the end of summer with the aspens just beginning to show a little yellow and the long, lush grass strident with the chirp of crickets, intoning their final chorus before the white death of winter fell upon them.

He had sat there many another summer evening, puffing his

pipe, with a feeling of profound peace. Nearly always he had sat alone but he had never felt lonely. He had felt companioned by everything that grew and lived about him—by the music of crickets and of the wind in the trees and the evening song of vesper sparrows. He had sat apart from people, from the settlement, but he had been at peace with it, he had borne a good and necessary relation to it. He had never known how necessary that relation was until it had been destroyed. Now there were men in the town over the hill who hated him, who wished him ill, and their hatred flowed into him, filling him with their own malevolence, destroying his peace of mind as completely as though they had marched upon him in an armed band.

He was a shaken and troubled man now, full of conflicts he could not resolve. Something in him wanted to get away from this place, as far and as fast as he could. At moments he felt like rounding up his horse and striking out for the mountains. He didn't care where he went if only away from people. Something in him wanted to get away from the woman too—from the helpless and vulnerable feeling she caused him. But another part of him felt like going down to the town, hunting her up and offering himself to her. . . . He knew what rank folly that would be, but he was full of foolish notions. And he didn't truly want to run, either. He wanted to stay and fight—to defy and denounce and destroy. . . .

It was dark now and getting chilly, as late summer nights always did. He went inside and busied himself building a fire, using fat pine that threw a red bright light, against a log that would burn a long time. The red flame eagerly eating the pitch, purring softly into the log, was a companionable thing. He sat there for a long time, soothed a little by warmth and light, but with a disturbing conviction of approaching climax. All his life he had been a man of premonitions and now he knew he was waiting, with hope and yet with dread.

When her knock came at the door he didn't move for a full minute. Although he had not expected her so soon he felt almost sure it was she and he waited to get a better hold upon himself. Why, in the name of God, should he be so disturbed? He was not afraid of her, not afraid of anyone, yet if he had known a mortal enemy stood on his threshold he would not have been more shaken.

When he opened the door he saw a slim dark woman-figure, wrapped and hooded in a great black shawl such as all the Mexican women wore winter and summer. She dropped it about her shoulders and smiled at him.

"May I come in?" she asked. Her voice was casual and friendly as she entered, surveyed his quarters with evident curiosity, then seated herself in his only other chair. He sat down opposite her, tongue-tied for the moment, aware of his pounding blood. She looked him up and down with a quizzical smile. He felt as though she were looking clear through his clothes—felt sure she knew just how much she disturbed him and was enjoying her power.

"Nice little place you've got here," she remarked. "Nothing fancy, but nice and clean and quiet. I bet you like it."

"Yes," he said, "I used to like it."

"Before all these Texas billies turned against you," she said, as though perfectly confident she was speaking his mind.

"Well, yes," he admitted.

"They tell me you never have any women visitors," she said.

"That's right," he admitted. He got up and went and put another log on the fire, not because it needed wood but because he needed something to do.

"It's getting cold," he remarked.

"I thought it was about time you had one," she told him, declining to discuss the weather.

"It was kind of you to come," he said.

"But I didn't come just to keep you company." She spoke gravely now. "I came to warn you. That little shorthorn up in the big house—he's bound and determined to get rid of you one way or another. You ought to get out of here, and the sooner the better. I think you ought to know. . . ."

"Thank you," he said. "I know they've got it in for me."

"He wanted me to help." She blurted her confession in quick words, a little disturbed for the first time. "But I don't want to talk about that. . . . That bloody little shorthorn! I never did trust him. If I didn't have my own money tied up in that joint, I'd get out of here myself."

She paused, and he sat looking at her, making no reply. She went on hurriedly, moved by some confessional impulse, as though she wanted to strip her mind naked before him.

"I went down to that hall the first time just to look you over," she said. "I wasn't going to do what they wanted—honest I wasn't. But I wanted to look at you. I thought you must be some kind of a damn fool, and in some ways maybe you are, but you're a good man, too. I can tell that."

"Thank you," he said. He grinned for the first time. Her explosive candor made him feel easier.

"I know a lot about men," she said. "Men are my business. And you're the only good man I ever saw, except maybe that preacher in Dodge City, and he wasn't really a man. . . . I can tell about men, and mostly they're all alike. Some of them are worse than others, but when they get their shirts off they're all alike and you can't trust them from here to the door." She paused for breath. "But you're different!" she finished decisively. "I never saw anything like you before, but I know you're different."

He plowed a restless hand through his hair, bewildered by this flow of words.

"It was kind of you to come and tell me," he said.

She leaned toward him to emphasize her words.

"I'm telling you to get out of here," she said. "It ain't healthy for you around here. And I'd sure hate to see anything happen to you, honest I would."

Daniel sat looking at her, shaking his head. He didn't want to argue with her. He wished now she would go. He wanted to lay hands upon her and he knew he couldn't do that. Time had been when he had laid hands upon women easily but his long isolation from them had built up a wall he couldn't pass. She sat there almost within reach of his hand and yet wholly beyond his reach. He didn't want to argue with her. He wished she would leave.

"You won't go!" she said, reading his face.

"No!" He shook his head again. "Nobody can run me out."

She made a gesture and a mouth of mild exasperation.

"Just stubborn," she remarked.

He rose and held out his hand, hoping to be rid of her. He wanted her, but he wanted none of the soft and vulnerable feeling she gave him. He wanted to be hard, free and ready.

"I thank you for coming," he said, "and for giving me warning."

She rose too but she didn't take his hand. Instead she walked right up to him, with a slight swagger about her hips, smiling with perfect self-confidence.

"You want me to go, don't you?" she inquired. "But I'm not going. I can't go now, honest I can't."

She paused for a moment, spread her hands in a gesture that might have been invitation.

"I came to warn you," she said, "but that ain't all I came for, honest it ain't. Not after all those beautiful words you said. Nobody ever said such beautiful words to me before."

She stood a moment more, smiling up at him, wholly unabashed—then flung her arms around his neck and glued her mouth upon his in the full, wet, clinging kiss of the woman claiming her own.

He seized her by both shoulders, his fingers biting into her flesh, moved by a first impulse to fling her away, to free himself. Then he swept her up in his arms and laid her on his bunk, fumbling at her dress with clumsy, eager hands. Nothing existed for him now but her body.

She squirmed in his grasp, giggling with delight. She did not share his mood of enraptured confusion at all, nor yet his inner conflict. Something in him wanted to be free, but she wanted only union.

"Go easy," she advised him quietly. "You've got all night to do this. I'll undress if you'll let me."

With the red glow of the fire upon their bodies they faced each other in the final candor of nakedness. She was silent and easy in his arms when he picked her up again, and he was gentle now, in complete surrender to her and to his own desire. Into her willing body he poured the burden of his loneliness, the tension of his hatred, the pressure of his need for union with his kind, all the forces of his destiny uniting to drive him into her—aching, urgent flesh swelling to fill the void, limpid juice of life pouring into the void, eternal stream of life turning back to its source—lost fragment of life going back to its home, limp in the peace of its inevitable return.

— 6 —

It was near dawn when she prepared to leave him, dressing herself slowly, fussing with her hair before his fragment of a mirror, making a long business of it, while he sat watching her. Finally she turned to him, spreading her hands in a quick, questioning gesture.

"You know I can't come here any more," she said.

He made no reply.

"They would follow me and find out," she told him. "They wanted me to put you in a spot like that."

She stood looking at him for a long moment, and then she made her plea.

"Go away with me!" she begged. "Or meet me some place else—I don't care where. I don't care what we do. You're my man now—don't you see? I thought so before and now I know it. I can't let you go!"

He rose, shaking his head, knowing he was denying himself as surely as he was denying her, hating the hard thing within him that dictated this denial.

"I can't leave here," he said. "They would say I had run. They would think they had run me out. I can't do it!"

She stood looking at his rocklike face for a moment. Then she made another quick gesture with her eloquent hands—a gesture of angry assent—and turned and picked up her shawl and threw it around her shoulders. She stood before him again and her eyes softened. She kissed him lightly on the lips and gave him a pat on the cheek that was half a slap.

"You're just a damn fool after all, ain't you?" she said tenderly. Then she turned and went, closing the door firmly behind her.

Daniel sat down in his great chair and lit a pipe. He sat there for a long time, thinking nothing, staring at the familiar walls of his house, knowing now it would always be empty without her.

IN THE WILDERNESS

A CROWD was forming in the company saloon and Ernesto Royball, who always had his nose in the wind, was there to watch it. He had known for days that Waverly Buncombe was at work on this project. He knew some men had been told that Daniel Laird was going to be run out of town—some said tarred and feathered—but most of them had been told only to be on hand, with a mysterious hint that there would be free drinks and excitement. Waverly was clever. There were nearly forty men in the room now and most of them didn't know what to expect, but all of them had been chosen carefully. Waverly knew the kind of a man who could be depended upon to join a mob. About half a dozen of those present Ernesto recognized as company henchmen. They were running the show, setting up the drinks, priming the crowd to exactly the right point, welding it into an instrument that would follow a leader. Waverly was behind the bar but he was not serving drinks. He was standing where he could watch the faces lined up on the other side. When he thought the moment was ripe he went around the end of the bar and shoved a table all the way across the room, to the far end of it, making a great rumpus about it, so that everyone turned and looked. Then, with an air of mock solemnity, he mounted a chair and from the chair he climbed to the top of the table, the whole crowd watching him. With a solemn face he lifted his right hand for silence, and all the voices died. Then he made a slow gesture with both hands as though he were opening a book and laying it on a table before him.

"Brethren and sistern," he intoned, in a portentous burlesque of Daniel's mighty voice. "The subject of our little discourse this evening is—Me and Jesus and how we can be told apart."

He raised his hand again to still a burst of laughter, then spoke in a wholly different tone.

"Boys," he began, "this town has got one citizen it doesn't need. . . ."

Ernesto Royball did not wait to hear more. He felt sure now it was going to happen. He slipped out the door and ran all the way to Tighe's office, a hundred feet down the street. Tighe came to the door in his carpet slippers, with a cigar between his fingers. He had been taking life easy for weeks. He took one look at Ernesto, wide-eyed and breathing hard, and shook his head.

"Come in," he said, "and sit down. I know you're full of bad news."

Ernesto nodded his head rapidly three times.

"Yes!" he gasped, "they're going after Mr. Laird. They're all down at the saloon, about forty of them. . . ."

Tighe showed neither surprise nor excitement. He asked a few questions, then sat thoughtful for a moment. He looked at his watch.

"Ten-thirty," he remarked. "They probably figure to find him in bed. That's about their speed!" He spoke with profound contempt. "Forty to one, and they hope to catch him asleep." He pulled on his boots now and took his gun belt off the head of his bed.

"I can't stop them down at the saloon," he said. "They've got a right to gang up. But I sure can stop them up at Laird's place."

He buckled on his gun, settling it carefully into place.

"That goddam little squirt of tobacco juice!" he remarked. "There's always some son-of-a-bitch. . . ."

— 2 —

Laird's cabin was dark, as he had expected, and he pounded long and hard before he saw the light of a lamp and heard the thud of bare feet. The door opened and the big man in his cotton nightshirt stood staring at him in amazement. Tighe did not waste any time in apologies.

"Get your clothes on," he said shortly. "I think you're going to have company."

Laird blinked and shook his head, still only half awake.

"What do you mean?" he demanded.

"I mean Waverly Buncombe is working up a mob down at the saloon," Tighe explained. "From what Ernesto told me I judge they plan to call on you."

Laird was wide awake instantly, as Tighe could tell by the quick change in his eyes, the tightening of the muscles about his jaws. Somewhat to Tighe's surprise, he looked almost eager. It took him no more than three minutes to splash cold water on his face, pull on his clothes and boots.

"Are they on their way?" he asked quietly.

"Not yet, I reckon," Tighe advised, "but it probably won't be long."

Laird had turned away and was standing before the row of six axes that hung between pegs against the wall at the far end of the room. They were the tools of a master axman, all of the blades shining clean from the expert touch of the whetstone. Laird stood looking at them a moment, then chose a five-pound, double-bitted tool with a straight handle—a veritable battle-ax. He turned back to Tighe with the ax in his right hand and the trace of a grim smile about his mouth. Tighe, a specialist in fighting men, eyed him with interest and a growing respect. He sat down and stretched out his legs.

"You and I will be the reception committee," he suggested.

Laird shook his head firmly several times.

"I thank you for coming," he said, "but I don't want any help." He spoke with great finality.

Tighe rolled a cigarette and lit it before he spoke.

"I'm an officer of the law," he explained. "It's my job to keep order."

"I know," Laird said, "but this is my business. I don't want any help."

Tighe took a deep puff of smoke and sat looking at the end of his cigarette a moment before he spoke.

"Well." His tone was judicious. "I've always said a man has a right to make his own fight if he wants to. I never accepted any help myself."

He rose and held out his hand.

"Good luck," he said.

— 3 —

When Tighe had gone Daniel went out in front of his house and kindled a small fire. The ground was open there, with tall pines a hundred feet away, making a black wall of shadow beyond the red light of the blaze. He kept a pile of logs for firewood at the side of the cabin, and he now went to work furiously, cutting and splitting, piling wood on the blaze, then building a pyramid of longer pieces until he had a bonfire that roared like an angry beast. Its quivering tongue of flame leaped ten feet in the air and sparks went dancing and dying as high as the treetops. Daniel went back to his cabin, put out the lamp and stood in the doorway, well back from the light of the fire, waiting. It was a dark night and the glare of the fire made it seem darker. Nothing was visible beyond the dance of shadows at the edge of the red stage he had set. He stood waiting, gripping his ax, aware of his quickened breathing, thinking nothing, knowing only that he was tense as the spring of a cocked rifle.

It seemed a long time but it was not more than ten minutes before he heard them coming—the shuffle of many feet in the trail, a few low voices and a cough. Then he glimpsed the wavering, small light of a single lantern, the only thing that broke the solid black of the night beyond the fire. The shuffle of feet came nearer and there were more voices for a moment—and then silence. He peered half blindly across his lighted arena. He could discern a few faces, but they seemed to recede rather than come nearer, and the light of the lantern went out. His muscles relaxed and he blew out his breath in a snort of disgust. The goddam yellow bellies! They were afraid to come into the light. . . . He waited a moment longer, then strode out into the open and stood beside the fire, holding his ax aloft, its blade red in the glow.

"Here I am!" he shouted. "I heard you were coming for me. . . . Here I am!"

He paused and peered again into the wall of darkness. He could see dimly a huddle of figures and light fell upon a few faces but not a sound came out of the darkness. . . . They were afraid! Suddenly he threw back his head and laughed, a great bellowing laugh that was a shout of defiance. He took three strides forward, holding the ax before him, shaking it in a vibrant tension of rage.

"Come on, you yellow bellies!" he shouted. "You came to get me, didn't you? I dare you to show your faces."

But there were no faces visible now and he was aware of the shuffle of feet again, far down the trail. He went forward cautiously, peering into the darkness, his eyes getting used to it. At first he thought all of them had gone, but then he saw a single figure, leaning against a tree with his feet crossed and his arms folded, in an attitude of negligent repose. He heard a low chuckle, went closer, recognized Tighe.

"I trailed along behind them," Tighe explained, "just to see the fun. They didn't know I was here."

Daniel suddenly felt limp in reaction. He stood shaking his head slowly.

"The goddam yellow bellies!" he said.

Tighe laughed again.

"You didn't have to kill any of 'em," he remarked, "but you damn near scared 'em to death. They didn't want any part of that ax. Their feet began to get cold as soon as they saw you."

He straightened up and made a gesture of respectful salute—the tribute of one unfrightened man to another.

"Good night, preacher," he said. "You put on a fine show."

— 4 —

Daniel went back into his cabin, filled and lit a pipe with hands that trembled a little. He sat down, suddenly weak in the knees. As always after a fight or a burst of rage, he felt a little sick—sick with guilt and fear, not fear of anyone else but of the violence inside him. For an awful moment he had hoped they would rush him, he had longed for battle, even for carnage. . . . He sat appalled before the image of what might have happened—if they had not been such cowards.

They had failed him as enemies even more completely than they had failed him as friends. But he knew they had succeeded in their purpose. They had run him out. He had sworn no one should run him out, but he knew now that he was going. He couldn't stay here now. He had to get away from this place in order to get away from his own feelings—from the anger and hatred that were eating him up.

He rose and began making his preparations, feeling a little better as soon as he was at work. He had no plan except to get away from this place, to be gone before morning, to bury himself in the mountains. He was vaguely aware that he was in flight, not only from this place but from human society. He wanted to get as far from people as he could.

He went through a familiar routine now, for he had made many trips of a few days or week. He pulled out from under his bunk the heavy canvas tarpaulin he used for camping, threw his blankets upon it and a few clothes and other possessions. Two rawhide paniers he filled with supplies—bacon and flour, coffee, sugar and salt, dried fruit, an iron skillet and a cup, cartridges for his rifle. He knew exactly what he needed. When he had finished packing he went out in the dark to find his horse, listening for the tinkle of the bell around its neck. He had only one horse, a big gray fourteen years old, slow but sure-footed on a trail. When he went into the mountains he always packed his horse and walked, after the fashion of a prospector. He was a footman by origin and habit, one who could walk thirty miles a day. Both he and the gray knew the trail up the canyon so well their feet could find it in the dark.

By the time the sun rose he was ten miles from town, near the summit of a high, bare ridge. Down the other side of it was a little branch canyon where he planned to make his first camp, and that was just as far as his knowledge of his destiny went. He stopped to rest, letting his horse crop the heavy grass, sat down and filled his pipe. From this spot for the last time he could see the town, miles away and three thousand feet below him. From where he sat it looked incredibly small and insignificant, a minor blemish on the face of the earth. The roads were scratches, the fields were angular scars, and a few faint blue wisps of smoke above the houses told that men and their fires were at work down there. Already he felt freed of the place and freed of the madness he had known the night before. He picked up the halter rope and set his face toward the mountains.

Late in the afternoon he saw the spot he had in mind a few hundred feet below him. The little stream there ran through an open level place two hundred yards long—what the mountain men called a park. Now in early September it bore heavy grass, sprinkled with the pink blossoms of wild cosmos. The stream was mostly hidden by a cover of willow and alder, but here and there flashed free in the sun. A few great fir trees were widely scattered over the open, each of them marking it with a long shadow. Below and above the open the canyon pinched narrow and impassable and the mountains rose steep and wooded on either side. The little park seemed made for a haven, a peaceful and sunny spot shut away from the rest of the world.

Daniel had been here before and knew exactly where he was going. He unpacked his horse under a big fir tree with a spread of twenty feet. The ground beneath it was bone dry for no rain could penetrate its lofty cone of evergreen foliage. It was safe to camp beneath a tree now that the lightning storms of summer were over. When storm came again it would be the first soft-footed invasion of the snow, creeping down from alpine summits. But first there would be days and maybe weeks of Indian summer, the best of all seasons in the high country.

He worked slowly, soothing his spirit by familiar tasks, by the exercise of easy skills which had always been associated with the peace of faraway quiet places. He hobbled and belled the gray and sat a moment watching him crop the rich forage. Then he made his bed under the tree, partly rolling it and propping it against the trunk so that it made a couch where he could lie and smoke his pipe. Like all men of long wayfaring in the mountains he knew how to be comfortable in camp. He built a rock fireplace with a good draft, drove pegs of hard, dry wood into the trunk of the tree to hold his gear, hung his paniers from convenient limbs, and his home was in order. He cooked his supper just before dark. An hour later a sudden, great weariness dragged at his eyelids and he went heavily to sleep.

— 5 —

For a week he enjoyed a feeling of peace such as he had not known for months before. It was the peace of life suddenly simplified, relieved of all the jolt and turmoil of human contact, of all the inner conflict that tears a man apart, makes his life a struggle for sanity. He felt as though he had gone back briefly to the uncomplicated happiness of childhood, and also as though he had returned to a familiar and beloved thing. The wilderness was one of his oldest friends and the wilderness is everywhere the same, with the same vast hush about it, the same feeling of an indestructible repose, of a soothing indifference to the nervous sputter of human being—of life become conscious and frightened, aware of time and death.

There were many men in the West who spent most of their lives alone in the mountains—prospectors and trappers who went away for months, sometimes for a year or more. A good many such men had come to the valley in Ballard's time to buy supplies at his store and hang around for a few days. Daniel had always looked at them with interest, talked to them if he had a chance. Some of them were surly men with a glint of suspicion in their eyes but others had a look of childlike sweetness and peace upon their faces. These often were eager to talk—for a little while. Then they would pack their burros and disappear again.

Daniel now played with the idea that he might become such a man. He knew he could find a living in the mountains and do it better than most. He did not plan, he merely let his imagination explore a possible destiny, for he felt sure he had left one life behind him and was on the way to another—what kind of a life he did not know. He did not want to plan or decide. He wanted to sleep and eat and live in his senses. He wanted to live as though tomorrow was none of his business.

It was not at all hard for him to spend his days. He explored his little region and became acquainted with all of its life. He knew the band of elk that came down to the creek at the upper end of the park to drink every morning, led by a bull with antlers like a picket fence. Morning and evening he heard the great bull bugle far up on the ridge. He knew the brood of blue grouse, nearly full grown now, which lived only a hundred yards from his camp. When he came near them they all fluttered into a tall spruce and sat there, craning their necks at him, curious but unafraid. "Fool hens" the gringos called them. Any creature that trusted a man was a fool. . . . A small black bear appeared every morning on the ridge where an old burn was red with ripe raspberries, and Daniel spent hours watching him gather the fruit, standing on his hind legs like a fat, awkward child, pulling the loaded bushes down into his mouth. Daniel did not kill any of these creatures. He did not want to shatter the peace with the roar of a gun. Most of his living he took from the creek which was alive with trout. Like most men in the mountains he carried a hook and line twisted around his hatband. He had only to cut a willow switch and catch as many grasshoppers as he needed fish. He could pick out the ones he wanted in the glass-clear pools, letting his bait drift over their waiting mouths.

Every day near noon, when the sun was warm, he stripped and bathed in the largest pool he could find, the icy water turning his body red with its tonic shock. Afterward he lay flat on the grass in the bright sun until he was dry. This reunion with earth and water was the high point of his day, the moment when peace seemed perfect. More than once he found his lips framing the words of the Twenty-third Psalm. "The Lord is my shepherd, I shall not want." For the moment he had transcended all want, had achieved the quiet ecstasy of merely being.

— 6 —

He became aware of the first rift in his contentment, after ten days of perfect solitude, when he found it hard to sleep and began lying awake listening to the voices of the running water. Ever since he reached the valley he had slept long, dreamless hours but now he woke before dawn and lay there listening. That he should hear voices in the running water was neither a new experience for him nor one peculiar to himself. All men who have slept much beside swift mountain streams know that running water in a rocky bed is full of voices. It makes an incredible variety of sounds, from indistinct murmurs and low chuckles, as of people talking apart, to loud laughter, and sometimes, when its volume is swollen by a storm, it shouts and roars. Often before Daniel had lain awake at night in the mountains listening to the talk and laughter of a stream, untroubled by it, but now the sound began to harass him and keep him awake. For the voice that emerged more and more distinctly was the voice of the woman, Betty Weiss, and with the sound of her voice came her image. His vivid imagination had been his curse more than once and now it was haunted by a single figure. He had hardly thought of her since leaving town and yet now the night seemed suddenly filled with her presence. First she would be away off there, somewhere in the dark, laughing at him in a mocking tone, and then she was beside him, naked and white, so vividly that he flung out his arm to grasp her. There in the dark in the wilderness he embraced a phantom that stirred all the longing of living flesh. He knew again the fragrance of her hair, the clasp of her thighs, the spastic roll and surge of her responsive body. And then she was gone again, she was away in the darkness, laughing at him, while he lay alone and tormented. More than once he rose before dawn and built a fire and made coffee, solely to escape this image that haunted and mocked him. His feeling toward her now was one of anger, of resentment. Everything else he had left behind— all the hatred and fury the town had stirred in him. Only this image of a naked woman had followed him into the wilderness, had caught up with him, as though it had been a living creature on his trail. A strange thing about it was that in imagination, in retrospect, she seemed more desirable, more perfect and necessary than she had seemed in the flesh. And always she was laughing at him, taunting him, that he had been fool enough to leave her. And he could see that he had been a fool. If he had gone away with her, if he had taken his fill of her, then he might have been free of this pursuing wraith, of the clinging memory of her flesh. As it was she had destroyed his peace completely.

After several tormented and sleepless nights he found himself one morning climbing the ridge, going back to the summit above the town. He sat there for a long time staring down at it but not truly seeing it. It was himself and his own destiny that he surveyed. It seemed to him that he was confronting himself and his own necessities now for the first time.

He faced the fact that he wanted to go back down into the valley, hunt up the woman, offer himself to her, surrender completely to her and to his own desire. But it was not only the woman he had fled in vain. He knew that he needed to get back to people, any kind of people, that his dream of solitary escape had been pure illusion. It was as though the image of the woman had followed him to mock him, to make him aware of his own folly. He could understand too that he had tried to go back to his own childhood—to the remembered peace of long ago. He knew that because briefly he had succeeded. For days he had felt like a child again, alone in the beautiful forest, but that interlude was over.

He knew he was not going back to the valley. That was impossible. He knew in this moment of clarity that there is no going back to anything. And there was only one other way to go—across the mountains. He had started with the knowledge vaguely in the back of his mind that he must cross the mountains before the snow fell. He could not spend the winter in the high country. But he had started without a plan and now he had to make one.

Forty miles to the west, across bare alpine summits that rose twelve thousand feet above sea level, lay the Mexican settlements of the upper Rio Grande. Santa Fe was far to the south of them and Taos to the north. Between these two, the major settlements of the Spanish Southwest, were half a dozen little towns, each commanding a narrow mountain valley, where beans and chile grew and small herds of scrubby goats grazed on steep slopes above the fields. These were the most primitive and isolated communities in all the Southwest. The men who inhabited them were more than half Indian, of the same stock as the peons down in the main valley. But they were not peons. The ricos had taken all the good lands in the main valley and reduced all the common people there to peonage, but here in the mountains had grown up a small society of freeholders. They owned their houses and their tiny patches of farmland. They were poor but free and fiercely independent. Almost all of them belonged to the order of the Penitent Brothers, which was in fact a religious fraternity of the poor. Many of them were thieves as well, who went down into the valley to work now and then, picked up a stray ewe or a range horse when they had the chance, rating it a worthy enterprise to rob the rich, whom they hated.

Daniel knew all about these settlements by hearsay. He also knew the old Indian trail across the mountains, as far as the summit, and he knew he could find his way down the other side to one of the little mountain towns. He knew the Mexicans would take him in. A poor Mexican would take in any man who came to his door and asked for food and shelter and would accept the guest as a sacred trust.

That was just as far ahead as Daniel could plan. He felt as though his first and most urgent need was simply to regain a contact with his fellow beings. For the first time he understood how completely he had exiled himself. He had left the only life and the only society he knew. His destiny now was a thing to be discovered.

—7—

A change in the weather speeded his going. Next morning the sky was dark and a strong, cold wind ruffled the grass and rippled the water, tearing yellow leaves off the aspens. As he turned his back on the little valley and started up the spine of a long ridge leading to the crest of the range, he knew that it might be snowing up there even now. At sunset he camped just below timber line where the spruce grew thick and short and there was hardly any forage for his horse. It was very cold that night and he woke to see a light powdery snow falling.

Now he knew he ought to turn back. Snow would bury the trail which was faint enough at best, a blizzard might blind him to every landmark, drifts might pile up too deep to cross. He knew also it would be folly to try to take a horse across the mountains. A horse traveling on grass needs good forage and nearly eight hours a day to graze. Snow would bury the grass and once he had started he must keep going until he had crossed the divide and reached timber on the western slope.

He knew he ought to turn back but he also knew he was not going to do so. He took the bell and hobbles off the gray and turned him loose to find his way back to the valley. Then he rolled most of his outfit in the tarpaulin and boosted it into the lower limbs of a spruce which he marked with a large blaze. Maybe sometime he would come back and maybe not. He took nothing but ax and rifle and one blanket in which he rolled a small supply of bacon and flour, coffee and sugar. All of his preparations were made with dispatch, with an exact knowledge of what he had to face. Equally well he knew this was a fool expedition. It was not at all necessary for him to battle this storm. Snow would not hit the lower levels for weeks yet. The sensible move would be to go back to the little valley or even lower, and wait until the storm was over. Even if a foot of snow fell on the divide it would be far easier to cross the mountains in clear weather. But he knew he was not going back. He was in no mood to sit down and wait for anything. Moreover, he was lifted now by a spirit of elation, of relief, as though the struggle that lay before him was a needed thing. He slung his rifle across his back by a thong he carried for the purpose, with his rolled blanket over the other shoulder like a soldier's field kit, took his ax in his right hand and set his face toward the high country. After a hundred yards of slow ascent he stopped and looked back. The gray stood staring after him, with lifted head and ears cocked in an expression of equine amazement that struck him as funny. He laughed aloud, turned and went on.

"He thinks I'm crazy," he remarked to himself. "And maybe I am, but here I go."

When he emerged upon the open country above timber line the snow was still a skimpy windblown thing. He could see the Truchas peaks a few miles to his left and he laid his course by them. He knew he had to pass along the foot of them and then drop off to his right into the head of a canyon called Quemado. A plain trail led down the canyon to a little town of the same name. There was no clear trail across the bare uplands but in bright weather the country was like a great topographic map. As the snow thickened later in the day the peaks were blotted out and the range of his vision steadily narrowed. He knew now he could keep a course only by using the utmost care. A man who has no bearings always feels that he is traveling in a straight line but he always in fact bears slowly to the left, will finally travel in a circle. So Daniel now would fix his eye on a rock or a tuft of grass, march straight to it and then select another objective.

As snow thickened in the air and deepened on the ground he traveled in a growing isolation for every wild creature goes to cover in a storm and the earth seems lifeless. Only the silent windblown snow seemed alive. It seemed to be surrounding him, steadily shrinking the circle of his vision, creeping along the ground in windy drifts both before and behind him, as though it were trying to bar his path and also keep him from turning back. It seemed a malevolent living thing, incessantly working against him.

Soon he found himself growing weary and his feet were wet and cold. He was going more and more slowly, wondering about his chances of getting across the divide before dark. For he had counted on getting across and reaching timber on the other side before the day was over. Once he reached timber he could build a great fire and spend the night safely. A man in timber with a good ax can survive the coldest weather. But here on top no timber grew—nothing but rare patches of arctic willow and of a kind of ground pine, which made a matted growth a few feet high, crouching before the winds and under the snow that no tree could withstand. If he had to spend the night here in the high country a patch of brush would be his only hope and it would be a poor one. He would have to spend the night grubbing out wood to keep a flame alive. And there was no assurance he could find enough timber even to do that.

He knew now his situation might become desperate but it was a curious fact that as he went on, more and more slowly, his anxiety seemed to die within him. A great somnolent weariness came over him, so that he dragged his feet and plunged into each new drift with a growing reluctance. He became aware that he wanted to stop and rest, to lie down in the snow and sleep. And all the time he knew that if he lay down now he would never get up again. He knew that death was right under his feet and it did not terrify him at all. It was as though the whispering snow had hypnotized him, lulled him into a mood of easy surrender. For the first time in his life he felt the temptation of death, the love of death, which is always hidden somewhere in the spirit of man, beneath the fear of death by which he lives. Death as violence is always frightening but death as easy sleep is sweet to the weary. It would be easy now to lie down and sleep in the great feather bed of the snow, the blowing, billowy snow, the gently caressing snow, the cold quiet lover that carries the kiss of death.

He wanted to lie down but he fought against his own desire—for he also wanted greatly to live. He had never known before how deeply he believed in living. Merely to stay on top of the snow and keep going seemed now a great assertion of faith in life. It would be so much easier to die. And he also wanted to defeat the storm, to elude the circling, treacherous snow. He knew he could do it if only he could find wood. He gave up trying to hold a straight course. Instead he traveled an erratic one, investigating every bulge and hollow that might conceal a patch of brush. It was hard hunting because he could only see about forty yards now.

Suddenly snow exploded before him in a roar of wings and a little band of ptarmigan, still in their brown summer plumage, went whirring away and vanished into the storm. He knew the birds lived on the arctic willow and he went plunging frantically in the direction they had taken. They never flew far. He found himself floundering up a little draw with a rill of water in it, bucking the deep snow it had gathered, until he stumbled over a tangle of limbs and went sprawling in what he sought. On all fours he fumbled in the snow, breaking off dry willow twigs, scratching snow away with both hands, eager as a digging dog. He whittled shavings, struck a match with numb fingers, crouching over his tinder, saw red flame leap and glow. It was the very blossom of life to him. Man is a weak and naked creature but he owns the secret of fire and with fire he conquers the earth. For hours now he worked with his ax, chopping every bit of brush he could find, even grubbing up the roots. There was ground pine as well as willow and with that he built a windbreak to stop the drifting snow and reflect the heat of his fire. At last he could stop long enough to broil bacon on a twig and make coffee in the pint cup he carried.

With hot meat and drink inside him he knew he had triumphed. His belly now was a fortress of defiant vitality in a hostile world. Toward morning he even dared to sleep a little while on the ground his fire had warmed. He woke very cold to revive his fire and see the sun rise in a clear sky.

With the peaks standing white against the blue it was easy

to cross the summit and find the trail down the other side. Downhill going was easy too, and soon he was out of the snow, traveling through a pine forest where bluejays screamed at him and a few late flowers still bloomed. He walked with a long, swinging downhill stride feeling curiously light and free.

A little spike buck popped out of a patch of scrub oak and stopped to look when he whistled. He sat down, very slowly and carefully, resting both elbows on his knees, and shot the buck square between the forelegs. It went down like a pole-axed beef. He ran to it, drawing his knife, slit it open with one long clean stroke and spilled its guts on the ground in a steaming heap. Eagerly he fished out the liver, the only thing fit to eat with the body heat still in it. He washed it in a pool of rainwater, made a fire, heated a flat stone and cooked and ate it all. Then he lay flat and rested a long time, full as a tick and no more troubled. He had crossed the mountains, he had conquered the storm—he had crossed a barrier in his destiny.

IN EXILE

HE SAW the town first from a mile away and a thousand feet above. It was built on the tip of a long finger ridge, where the mountains broke and fell toward the Rio Grande—a tight little cluster of earthen houses about a plaza dominated by a small church. Perhaps three hundred Mexicans lived there and many of them, he knew, had never seen a man with a fair skin.

Now that he was about to face people again, he was suddenly overcome by a great self-consciousness. It was only two weeks since he had gone into the mountains, but he felt as though he had been alone for a long time, an indefinite time. The Dark River Valley, and everything that had happened there, seemed incredibly remote, as though in crossing the mountains he had left the past very far behind. He looked back upon the man he had been, the part he had played, with a detachment such as he had never known before, almost as though he were contemplating another person. And he felt curiously sure he would never become the same kind of man again—one who stood apart and addressed his fellows and commanded them. He did not know what he sought or what lay before him but he felt that it had to be something new, that he had left one self behind and was in search of another.

He knew it would not be wise to march into the town with arms in his hands. Ax and rifle he rolled in his blanket and carefully hid them under a shelving rock in a bed of dry oak leaves where he could easily find them again. Then he went down to the creek and bent over a smooth pool to wash. His image was faintly reflected in deep blue water and he saw it with a start. His face looked gaunt and long, his eyes large and bloodshot. His hair was a matted mass and a reddish beard fringed his chin. His clothes were ragged, and dirt and soot and ashes were all over him. But there was also something strange in his expression, something fierce and intent. He looked like a wild man, as though a feral spirit had gotten into him there in the wilderness, in his struggle with it, and confronted him now in his own mirrored face. . . . He washed himself as best he could, then rose and went down the canyon, finding his legs a little weak—a great shambling figure of a man, an empty-handed fugitive in search of reunion with his kind.

— 2 —

When he walked into the plaza dogs greeted him first as they almost always do in a Mexican village. The poorer Mexicans are the more dogs they have. Daniel found himself beset on all sides by gaunt yapping curs, with more coming in response to the racket. He stood stock-still, knowing dogs will seldom attack a man who stands his ground with empty hands. Behind the dogs came children, about a dozen of them, dirty little brown brats of all ages up to fourteen. They stood and stared at him in round-eyed, open-mouthed amazement. After the children a woman came running in pursuit of her offspring. When she saw him she stopped, as though she had hit the end of a tether, and gave a shrill scream. It brought three more women, all on the run, and they all formed a black-shawled, whispering, suspicious group a little way behind the dogs and children. Presently one of them, a very old woman, came slowly forward, knelt before him, bowed her head and crossed herself.

Daniel knew Mexicans well enough to understand this gesture. These people were always looking for a messiah who would work miracles in their lives. A certain number of professional messiahs, most of them Mexicans from farther south, were always going about among the villages, professing to cure illness by incantation and the laying on of hands. He knew his strange and sudden appearance was perfectly calculated to strike a superstitious imagination. But there was nothing he wanted less to be than a messiah.

It would be terrible if these people set him apart, treated him as a demigod, brought him all their sick and asked him to work cures by magic. He wanted to be accepted simply as a human being in need.

When the old woman lifted her face he smiled at her and spoke gently in Spanish.

"I commend you to God, Madam," he said. "I am very hungry."

While she still knelt there, staring up at him, he saw a man coming rapidly across the plaza. He was a short, muscular, bowlegged man, and his very gait seemed to express purpose and authority. As he drew near Daniel became aware of a dark, square aquiline face, small deep-set shrewd-looking eyes and heavy black hair shot with gray. The man might have been fifty or more but he seemed to be of no particular age. He scattered the crowd, dogs, children and all, with a quick gesture, a few emphatic words, then turned his attention to Daniel, holding out his hand, smiling broadly.

"You are welcome, friend," he said. "My name is Solomon Valdez. I am the Alcalde here."

Daniel gave his name and thanked the man.

"You must be tired and hungry," the Alcalde said. "Come with me. My house is yours."

A little later Daniel found himself in a situation which had long been familiar to him in the Dark River Valley. He was seated on the floor with a whole Mexican family, gathered about a great steaming pot of beans cooked with red chile and a little goat meat, dipping up his hot food in a tortilla rolled to make a cup. It took a certain grace and skill to eat this way, and also an accustomed palate to swallow the burning chile, but Daniel was wholly equal to the occasion. This and his good command of Spanish made him an easy guest.

The Alcalde's wife was a large dark woman, and there were only two children, a pretty girl of sixteen and a boy a few years younger. These three were shy and silent but evidently trained to accept with submissive grace whatever Papa brought home, however strange it might look. The Alcalde, on the other hand, was a man of facile and voluminous discourse. He talked about the weather and the crops, the news from Santa Fe, the good hunting in the mountains and many other things, all trivial and insignificant. Like most Mexicans he was a master of the art of chatting. In all their conversation he asked Daniel not a single question, and Daniel understood perfectly the courtesy and convention of this attitude. He knew that many of these mountain Mexicans were bandits. They were not criminals in their own eyes. They had lived here for generations partly by preying on the flocks and herds of the ricos in the valley. To them the rich were legitimate objects of plunder. But they were a community of outlaws and outlaws do not ask questions of the fugitive stranger in any country or any language. So the Alcalde acted as if it were the most usual thing in the world for a giant gringo to walk across the mountains in two feet of snow and land upon his doorstep.

At a proper interval after the meal, Daniel rose and bowed, thanking first the wife and then the master of the house.

"But you cannot go," the Alcalde protested. "My house is yours as long as you wish to stay."

Daniel could see at a glance there was no room for him here. "You are too kind," he protested. "Is there not an empty house or a room where I can make my bed?"

He knew that every Mexican village contains deserted houses, and he had expected to take up his abode in one of them, but the Alcalde could do better than that.

"There is a good room behind the church," he said. "The Padre stays there when he comes, but that is only a few times in a year. It is yours for as long as you want it."

So Daniel slept that night in the quarters reserved for priests—a little whitewashed room with a corner fireplace, a good pallet of sheep pelts with an old Navajo blanket spread over them, and a doll-like image of the Virgin of Guadelupe staring down at him from a niche in the wall.

— 3 —

Within a week Daniel had become as much a part of the town's life as though he had lived there a year. These people were just like children in that they contemplated him at first with suspicion and astonishment but when he had received the benison of the omnipotent Alcalde, and even more importantly, had proved himself a beneficent person, they accepted him without question as the gift of a just and provident God.

He was beneficent chiefly as a provider of good red meat. When he led the Alcalde up the canyon and showed him the Winchester he had hidden there, along with fifty cartridges, the man's eyes shone with delight and he fondled the weapon with reverent hands. Poor Mexicans were always meat-hungry. Their goats were primarily a milk herd. They made a good cheese and killed an occasional kid, but abundant meat they seldom had except when they stole it.

"We have not a single good gun in the village," the Alcalde explained. "Nothing but a few old trade muskets and hardly any powder for them. Now we can hunt!"

Hunt they did, in the laborious fashion of men to whom hunting is necessary business and meat is life. They drove four pack burros up into the heads of the canyons, where the deer always abounded and more had been driven down by the deep snow. It was easy to kill them and hard work to skin and butcher, cut up meat and pack it on the burros, standing blindfolded so that they would not run from the smell of blood. When they came back after three days in the mountains, meat was distributed to every house in town and many families sat up most of the night about bonfires, broiling bits of venison on sharp sticks, laughing and singing over their feast. Red meat seemed to put new life into the whole town and the bellies of children visibly bulged.

When men hunt and camp together, sharing action, work and hardship, matching their skills, they come to know each other well in a short time, and in the mountains Daniel and the Alcalde became good friends. At night they sat smoking and talking between their windbreak and a great red fire. The Alcalde did most of the talking. He still asked Daniel no questions but he was eager to talk about himself. Evidently he wanted Daniel to know that he was no mere villager but a traveled man, a man of the world—at least of all the world that was anywhere within his reach and ken. When young he had repeatedly gone south as a packer with the conductas, the annual trading trips, all the way to the city of Chihuahua, and he also had been east on buffalo hunts as far as the staked plains of Texas. More than that, he had gone down into the valley to work as a sheep shearer, a business at which he had great skill, not merely to Taos and Santa Fe but as far south as Albuquerque. He knew all about the ricos, their great houses and their luxurious lives, their feuds and scandals. He regarded them with a humorous cynicism, and although he did not say so in plain words, it was evident that he considered their movable property as something to be appropriated whenever it was possible to do so with safety and discretion. It gradually became apparent that he regarded Daniel as a fellow spirit in this respect, and this was not surprising. A man would not walk across the mountains in a snowstorm just for fun. Obviously he must have been in rather urgent need of both departure and refuge. Having been himself often just one jump ahead of the law, the Alcalde could sympathize and understand. After the subtle fashion of his kind, he made it clear that he accepted Daniel as a fellow outlaw, and Daniel did not see how he could explain himself in any terms the Alcalde would understand. After all, he was a refugee, if not exactly of the kind the Alcalde supposed.

After they had returned to the village, the Alcalde continued to call upon him almost every day, and he became increasingly candid about himself and his position in the village. He was not only the Alcalde but also the Hermano Mayor of the local chapter of the Penitent Brothers, which made him in effect both the temporal and the spiritual ruler of his own small domain. For the Penitentes were the organized religion of all these mountain communities. Every man was a member. The great whips they used upon their own backs every Good Friday hung openly in the vestry of the church, and there too was the cart of death they used in their processions with its crude figure of a dark angel holding a drawn bow and arrow in his hand. This church belonged to the Penitentes no less than did the windowless Morada on the hill above the town and the great wooden cross where one of their number was every year crucified with ropes. Their domination of the community was obvious and it was a familiar fact to Daniel, yet it was rare for a Penitente even to mention his membership in the fraternity. The impression grew upon Daniel that the

Alcalde must be telling him all this for a purpose—must be leading up to something important. His shrewd little eyes were full of friendliness but also of calculation. He still refrained from any direct questions but he was at pains to learn that Daniel was a literate man. The Alcalde could neither read nor write and neither could any of the others in the village, but he brought Daniel an old Santa Fe newspaper and asked him to translate an item in which he professed an interest. When he learned that Daniel could read and write both Spanish and English, it was plain to see that he was deeply impressed.

The impending revelation came during his next visit. After a little preliminary chat, he looked Daniel in the eye and spoke with great earnestness.

"My friend," he said, "I think God has sent you among us for a purpose. I have thought so ever since that day when you walked into the plaza. In a world ruled by a just God these things do not happen by chance."

Daniel nodded his head slowly several times. He knew this occasion called for the utmost in dignity and appreciation.

"You do me great honor," he said.

"I trust you," the Alcalde replied, "as I would trust my own brother. That is why I speak to you now. . . . You know that the Penitentes are many. Here in the upper river country we outnumber all others. Moreover, we act and think as one. In the town of Mora on the other side of the mountains we have our headquarters, and there lives the great brother who rules us all. There are no dissenters or traitors among us, for such cannot live."

He paused to let this revelation sink into his auditor's mind, but it was no revelation to Daniel. He had been dealing with Penitentes for years. He knew they had a tight and powerful organization, which was not merely a religious fraternity but also a league of poor men against the rich who had always oppressed them.

"I know that what you say is true," he replied.

"We are poor and ignorant," the Alcalde said. "Under the Mexican government all we could do was to care for our own, and also sometimes we could take care of our enemies. Those who are wise have always respected our power. But under the American government we might do much more. I am an ignorant man myself but I know that votes are power now and we have many votes. What we need is someone to speak for us in Santa Fe—someone who knows the written word and also the ways of the Americans. . . . My friend, I think God has appointed you to serve us!"

"You do me too much honor," Daniel protested. He was at a loss what else to say, for the Alcalde's proposal had stirred within him a conflict of feeling that surprised himself. He could not believe he was going to do this thing, and yet it made an appeal to his sympathies and his imagination that he could not deny. The Alcalde was vague about what could be done by this powerful advocate he wanted, but Daniel knew the man was not talking nonsense. He knew that anyone who had the Penitente vote in his pocket would be a man of power. He knew also just what it would mean to achieve that power. The Alcalde now was speaking his own thought.

"You would of course become one of us," he said. "You would take the vows of the Church as well as those of our Order. You would mingle your blood with ours. You would become our brother in the blood of Christ. . . ."

He would kneel in a little dark room and they would cut his bare back from neck to waist with a sharp flint. Perhaps they would lift him to a cross and bind him there. And when he came down he would be one of them and their power would be his.

"This is a grave matter, my friend," he said. "I must have time to think.'

The Alcalde was quick to see that he had won an advantage. He knew when to stop.

"Surely," he said, "you must meditate. And we could do nothing until spring when the snows melt and we can go to Mora. . . . But I am sure this is your destiny in the eyes of God. You cannot refuse."

It was true, Daniel had to admit to himself. He could not refuse. At least not now. He was glad that nothing could be done for a matter of months, for he saw that once more, as so often, he faced a battle with himself.

— 4 —

Snow had fallen again and winter winds had stripped the last leaves off the willows along the creek when the Alcalde came to Daniel's room one evening, breathing hard with excitement.

"The sheriff in Taos is looking for you!" he blurted. "Pablo Gonzales was there today and they asked him if we had seen you. He said no, of course, but that makes no difference. The sheriff is a Mexican but he has a gringo deputy and that man is much too busy. He will be here surely. You must let us hide you. Believe me, we Penitentes know how to hide men. They will never find you, and these things are always forgotten. But there is no time to waste. . . ."

He was stopped by Daniel's incredulous expression.

"But I have done nothing wrong," Daniel said, shaking his head in bewilderment.

The Alcalde gave him a long look, his eyes shrewd and narrow, unbelieving but kindly.

"My friend," he said, "why do you not trust me? We are as brothers. Perhaps you had a fight and killed a man. There is no reason why you should hide that from me. Any man may kill in the heat of his blood. I have never killed a man but I have tried. At a dance one night in Taos a fellow tried to take a girl out of my arms. I had a knife for him. It took four men to hold me. Believe me, friend, I know what it is to lust for the blood of an enemy!"

"But I have never killed anyone," Daniel protested.

The Alcalde smiled.

"I didn't think you had," he admitted. "I have no doubt you stole. Probably you stole cattle from those rich gringos in the Dark River Valley. You are not the only one. How is a poor man to live? The rich have everything except what you take away. I conceal nothing from you, my friend, and you should trust me. I have been stealing sheep for twenty years. When I worked for Don Augustin Romero in Taos I used to steal a few sheep from him every spring and sell them back to him in the fall. And why not? He had thousands and I had none. One old ewe I stole so often she used to bleat a greeting when she saw me coming."

"But I have not stolen anything," Daniel interrupted him to protest.

"Very well," the Alcalde said. "I believe you. If you have neither killed nor stolen, then it must be a woman!"

He paused, watching Daniel's expression with those acute and penetrating eyes. He saw a flicker of change there, for Daniel, badly puzzled, could think of but one human being who might be looking for him. It was hard to believe but it was possible.

The Alcalde threw back his head and laughed. He was evidently relieved.

"Why should you deny that, of all things?" he demanded. "'A sin of the flesh is no sin at all.' It is an old Spanish saying. But such sins can overtake a man and capture him. You must let me put you where she can never find you. This is no time for you to fall into the hands of a woman. If you want to marry later, I will take care of that. I will bring you a beautiful virgin with breasts like ripe melons. But we must let no one take you away from here now. We have work to do!"

Daniel sat shaking his head, smiling a little sadly. He knew it was going to be hard to make the Alcalde understand and he had a great regard for the man.

"If the sheriff is looking for me, I must go to Taos," he said. "I have done no wrong. It must be a mistake."

"It is no mistake," the Alcalde said firmly. "The deputy described you and there could be no other man like you."

He finally went away, shaking his head, evidently convinced that this strange man would not listen to sense.

When he returned next morning, Daniel was preparing to go. He refused the loan of a horse and handed the Alcalde his rifle and his ax.

"Keep these for me and use them," he said. "If I do not return they are yours. Let them remind you that we are friends."

The Alcalde was deeply moved by this gift but neither his gloom nor his disappointment was relieved.

"It is folly for you to go," he said sadly. "If the law does not get you, the woman will. But I see you cannot be dissuaded. Remember always that my house is yours."

They shook hands and Daniel set out on his thirty-mile walk, taking only the few dollars he owned and the small bundle of his belongings. He turned once and looked back and waved his hand to the Alcalde, who stood watching him out of sight, and then went on his way, feeling curiously guilty, knowing that he had begotten a dream and a hope and was deserting them.

EPITHALAMIUM

Weary from long walking, Daniel crossed the dusty plaza in Taos and presented himself at the sheriff's office. Its chief functionary was an old cowpuncher named Shinburn—a man of fifty, with a deeply lined, heavily weathered face and small deep-set blue eyes, lean in build and bowlegged from long years in the saddle. As the first American officer of the law in Taos County he had made a reputation by rounding up a great many cattle rustlers and horse thieves and by restoring much livestock to its legal owners. He looked Daniel up and down with a mild and weary curiosity.

"So you're Daniel Laird," he said at length. "Sit down."

Daniel sat.

"I heard you were looking for me," he said. "What do you want me for?"

"Don't you know?" Shinburn inquired.

Daniel shook his head.

Shinburn expressed his skepticism in a wry smile. He produced a plug of tobacco, offered it to Daniel, who refused, cut himself a chew with a pocket knife, stowed it in the corner of his face, and spoke judiciously.

"I reckon the best I can do is to take you across the plaza and turn you over to the plaintiff," he said. "I hope to God you and she can settle out of court. If you can take her off my hands,

I'll sure thank you. She's been more nuisance than forty horse thieves. Let's go."

He led Daniel across the plaza to the old Fonda, which had been housing visitors to Taos for many years—a low, rambling adobe, built around a courtyard, with iron-barred windows and weeds growing out of its earthen roof. They passed through the hall which pierced the front and into the courtyard.

"You wait here," Shinburn told Daniel. He knocked on a door, was admitted and disappeared for about three minutes. Then he came out, nodded to Daniel, gesturing over his shoulder with his thumb.

"Go to it," he said, "and God be with you."

Inside the low-ceilinged room, dimly lit by a single window, they stood staring at each other, as though neither could quite believe in the other's existence. Betty was the first to recover.

"Sit down, Daniel," she said. "You look all tuckered out."

Daniel sat awkward and tongue-tied. He knew at once and instinctively that he had come to the end of his wandering, had found his fate, but as always he was tangled in his own inner conflicts. For him there could never be the undivided moment, the complete acceptance, the single mind. But he was bewildered also by the impression that he looked at another woman, that she had undergone some great and unaccountable change. She wore a plain gingham dress, like the wife of a ranchman, her cheeks were innocent of rouge and powder, her hair was pulled straight back from her face and bunched upon her neck. Her face was thinner and looked older, dominated wholly by her eyes, which held a troubled look. A slender, weary woman he saw, with something almost austere about her, and something fearful.

"I had to find you, Daniel," she said, speaking rapidly, almost breathlessly. "I don't know why. When I walked out on you that night I thought I was all done, honest I did. And then when I heard you had gone I knew I had to find you. I never thought I would go trailing after a man like a lost dog, but I did. I sold out for what I could get and took the stage to Santa Fe. I thought of course you would have to go there first. I put on this kind of a dress and a sunbonnet and talked nice and ignorant and told them you had done me wrong. It was the only way I could get them to hunt for you. A young fellow there in Santa Fe offered to marry me, even if I was in trouble, honest he did. But nobody had seen you or heard anything about you and I knew there would be no mistaking your looks. . . . It was a funny thing but the longer I hunted for you the more I had to find you, no matter what. I seemed a little crazy to myself. . . . When I came up here it was the same story for a long time and I began to think maybe you were dead. I camped on that Shinburn's trail; I just practically sat on his doorstep. He was the only man around with enough gumption to do anything and he didn't want to be bothered. He ain't interested in anything but livestock. But I wouldn't let him rest. If I had been a man he would have kicked me out long ago but you can't kick a woman. . . . Then finally he got a story from a sheep herder about a big gringo that walked across the mountains in two foot of snow. I knew it must be you because nobody else could do it and nobody else would try. . . ."

She stopped, breathless, her cheeks flushed, her lips parted, watching his unrevealing face. A look of something like terror came into her eyes.

"O my God!" she cried. "Don't you want me?"

For the first time now Daniel felt a great warmth inside him. This was not the woman who had flung him an impudent challenge and captivated his flesh, nor yet the provocative vision that had followed him into the wilderness and driven him out of it. In this moment she was only a fellow human who had a great need, who had uttered a cry for help. He rose and went and sat beside her, put his arm about her shoulders, kissed her lifted lips.

"Yes," he said, "I want you. I was a fool ever to try to deny it. You have been with me somehow all the time."

The instant he touched her she was transformed, confident again, possessive, running her hands over his face and through his hair, as though contact with him gave her new life.

"I'll take good care of you, Daniel," she said tenderly. "Don't you worry about a thing. You don't know it yet but I'm just what you need."

EPILOGUE

By JAMES LANE MORGAN

WHEN I rode into the valley of Taos in the spring of 1906 I was going back to the past in a double sense. I was returning to the scenes of my own youth, and Taos at that time was perhaps as perfect a relic of a vanished world as could be found anywhere in America. As I rode across the little valley, green with its new-sprung crops and leafing cottonwoods, flashing with silver waters, perfumed by the great banks of blossoming wild plum along the ditches, I was aware this must be almost exactly what the mountain men had seen sixty years before when they returned each spring, eager for the arms of women, for bread and sugar and the white whisky of Turley's still after months in the wilderness. And there was the solid earthen town in the distance, squatting upon its low hill, just as it had been for a century. There are places so deeply imbued with the spirit of the past that change can touch them only lightly, and such a place, it seemed to me, was the valley of Taos.

It may surprise the reader that I had never seen this country since I left it the year after Ballard's death. There was no place for me on the grant after Blore's rise to power, but I had remained in the West for several years, leading a vagabond life as a hunter and prospector, simply because I could not bring myself to leave the mountains. I carried always a pan and rock hammer, I found a few pockets of gold-bearing quartz and bought a few claims and stock in others. I called myself a mining man and made a little money, but I knew I was evading my proper destiny. I knew what kept me in the West was a love of physical freedom, adventure and excitement. I knew I was hanging onto my youth because I had found it sweet. My adult business was back in New York, and there finally I returned, to assume the management of my father's property, to practice law and finally to become a judge, to marry and raise a family. I had been successful in a modest way, I had performed all the routines and obligations of a good citizen—and I had been haunted all those years by the memory of my life on the frontier, as some men are haunted by the memory of an early love which made life briefly more intense and vivid than it could ever become again. I had at once cultivated and assuaged my nostalgia for the mountains and the past by becoming an amateur historian, by collecting Western Americana, by writing monographs for the journals of historical societies. I had visited the West more than once, and I had always intended some time to return to Taos and the Dark River Valley, but I had postponed the day because I knew what a perilous thing it is for any man to go back to the places where he was young—to look upon the wrecks and relics of a vital period in his own life.

I was going back at last because my own researches made it necessary. I had long planned to write something about the Ballard grant and the Dark River Valley, and the significance of the story had grown upon me for years. I was impressed especially by the fact that the struggle to possess and dominate that little empire had produced men with a genuine capacity for leadership—men, it seemed to me, who might have played a part upon some much larger stage if the opportunity had been given them. Ballard was easily the greatest of them, but

EPILOGUE 301

Blore, an inscrutable figure to me and touched with evil, had certainly been a man of great ability, and so had Tighe. I had met him only once, but I knew well the story of how he had tamed the grant single-handed. Daniel Laird was the most enigmatic of the four who had exercised some kind of power in the Dark River Valley, and to me the most interesting of them all—a man with a touch of genius who had never found the means of his own development, but had nevertheless somehow evolved his own set of values and remained faithful to it.

Laird was the only one of the four who still lived, and he not only lived but flourished. I had called upon him the year before at his ranch in the San Luis Valley of southern Colorado and we had spent a long evening talking about Ballard and the old days on the grant—about everything, in fact, except Daniel himself. He was not the kind of man who would tell you his own story, and I soon found that his serene reticence on that subject was impenetrable. I knew that after Blore had taken over Laird had assembled the ranchmen and made a famous speech in which he told them how they had all been cheated. I knew that Blore finally had somehow forced him out. Like all idealists he had won only the moral victory of refusing to compromise.

I knew a woman had played a part in his story and that he had married her, homesteaded in the San Luis Valley, and become the moderately prosperous owner of several hundred acres of alfalfa and a fine herd of white-faced Hereford cattle. More than that, he had become also a political figure of local note, for he sat in the state legislature and was known as its most uncompromising radical. First as a member of the Populist party and later as a follower of William Jennings Bryan, he was always in the minority, often a minority of one, thundering in his mighty voice against the trusts and Wall Street, predicting the day when humble men who worked with their hands would rise in their organized power and smite the mighty. In a word, he was the same old Laird, the born champion of lost causes, the man with a vision of the future, the leader of the humble, the prophet of change. He had a good deal more intellectual sophistication now, but the same stubborn fidelity to his own lights, the same hatred of greed armed with authority, the same blind courage and bull-voiced eloquence. I think he never won a victory on the floor of the legislature, but he was unbeatable at the polls, partly because he could go into the Mexican precincts and completely charm the natives by addressing them in their own language and with a perfect inflection. He was said to be even more eloquent in Spanish than in English.

In appearance I found him little changed, except that his great shock of hair was nearly white. He was a good deal less shy than the man I remembered, but otherwise he seemed exactly the same fellow with whom I had gone fishing along the Dark River and eaten dinner in his cabin. Again he poured me a large jolt of whisky and took none himself and again he asked me so many questions that I found it hard to query him. Now as before he made the impression of a man at peace with himself, sustained by a love of life for its own sake.

No doubt Laird's public career was his own, but his worldly success was by common report ascribed almost wholly to his wife, whom I met at dinner the day I called upon him. She, like her husband, was a person with a legend, and I had heard a good deal about her. I was told that she had been a famous queen of the night life in Dodge City when it was the wildest track-end town in the West, that Blore had brought her to the Dark River Valley for reasons known only to himself, and that she had somewhat mysteriously emerged from that phase of her life as the wife of Daniel Laird. Apparently, she was about the only thing he had taken with him when he left the grant, and evidently she had proved to be an important asset, for her business ability was famous. It was said that Daniel never signed a paper or spent more than ten dollars without consulting her. His political career she regarded as a huge waste of time and energy, but with a certain good-humored indulgence. Her own life had been devoted largely to the raising of four sons, three of whom were already grown and the owners of ranches in the San Luis Valley, so that the Lairds were now the head of a veritable clan.

Betty Laird's story was a usual one, in that many of the dance-hall beauties of the Old West finally married ranchmen and became models of domestic propriety. Certainly there was nothing about her when I made her acquaintance to suggest a lurid past. I saw a small, quiet, gray-haired woman with careful manners, somewhat modified by an irreverent sense of humor. It was evident that she declined to take anyone seriously, including her famous husband. She had been heard to thank God that her children inherited his muscle and her own brains. Nevertheless, it was evident that these two were devoted to each other, and that they had a highly effective working partnership. Different as they were, both of them were rebels and individualists, so that perhaps they understood each other well enough.

— 2 —

I have been impressed all my life by the fact that no man can escape the inner drive of his destiny. Whatever kind of power is in him, that he must use, for better or worse, and even though it consume or destroy him. It was evident that Daniel Laird would be defying the mighty and defending the humble in his thunderous voice as long as breath was in him, and Clay Tighe had remained all his life a terror to the lawless, a man who imposed order by force and fear. The frontier needed such men and Tighe was no ordinary gunman. His whole career showed that he was a man with a genuine sense of justice, always ready to fight for his principles, and he had also some innate quality of power and authority that was hard to define. More than one man who had known him testified that he could stop trouble by his mere presence, without lifting either his hand or his voice, and that it was curiously hard to look him in the eye when he meant business. Moreover, he had no love of battle for its own sake, at least in his later years. When he retired to his Berenda ranch, north of the Dark River Valley, he let it be known that he was hanging up his gun—that from then on he was a cattleman and nothing more. He married a beautiful Mexican girl and raised a family, but he never found the peace he was seeking, never was able to go among his fellows unarmed without risking his life.

The late eighties were the period in which cattle rustling reached its height and was finally suppressed, partly by the law but largely by the action of organized vigilantes. Clay Tighe founded the first cattlemen's association in the Southwest, was its first president, and by reason of his talents and prestige, the leader in its struggle with the rustlers. A hard man but a just one, he would not countenance lynching, never shot a man unless he had to, dragged a great many rustlers into court and sent them to the penitentiary. Most of these were out again in a year or less so that his strict principles only multiplied his enemies. When he lit a candle one night to get a drink of water a rifle bullet smashed the window within an inch of his head. For years he did not dare to sit by a lighted window and in public he still followed his long-time custom of keeping his back to a wall.

There were no witnesses to his death except his murderers, but the story was recorded in tracks on sandy soil. He was driving alone in a buckboard across the open country east of the Dark River Valley when he slowed down to cross a narrow wash, fringed with sage and rabbit brush a few feet high. Rifles cracked at long range and Tighe fell backward into the bed of the vehicle. His spirited team ran away and brought his body home. Although he had been shot through the heart it was found that he had drawn his six-shooter and fired it once before he died.

— 3 —

Major Blore had died in Denver a few years before my visit to the West. If he had been alive I would have called upon him. I have no doubt he would have received me with impeccable politeness and told me nothing at all, for he was a man in whom a cold and deadly cunning hid behind an impenetrable surface. I knew of him only that he had returned to Denver after the second sale of the grant, a substantially richer man, and that he continued to grow richer to the day of his death. His cunning seemed unbeatable. He was one of those men of whom it is said that everything they touch turns to money.

He never married, but lived in a large house with a housekeeper whom he had brought from Virginia on one of his rare visits to the East. She was a very large girl, nearly a head taller than the Major, quite pretty in her buxom way, quite simple-minded and wholly devoted to her employer. In his later years Major Blore was afflicted by diabetes, which caused him to shrivel like a potato in the sun. He rarely appeared in public, but never missed a horse race or a horse show. One who saw him about 1900 described him as a tiny, frail-looking man, all of whose life seemed to be concentrated in his great blue eyes, which were as bright and hard and unrevealing as ever. For a long time before he died he was a house-bound invalid.

It is said that his housekeeper used to pick him up in her arms like a baby and carry him to bed.

— 4 —

There were men in the Dark River Valley and elsewhere in the West who remembered Ballard, and all of these I intended to see and question, for none of them would live much longer. But there was only one survivor of those days, other than Laird, with whom I could claim a personal acquaintance, and she was the occasion of my visit to Taos. For there, in the old family homestead, Consuelo Ballard still lived, and she was still, to all accounts, a great lady.

The building of the railroad and the invasion of the Southwest by men and money from the East had destroyed the feudal society of the Mexican regime in little more than a generation. Some able individuals of the old families had made a place for themselves, but as a society the ricos were almost extinct and the country was littered with the crumbling remnants of their great earthen houses. Here in Taos their way of life had survived with less change than anywhere else in the state. The Coronels had declined in wealth and importance, but they still owned some thousands of sheep and valuable lands in the valley, and they were still patrons to the poor Mexicans who worked for them. The male head of the house, a nephew of Consuelo, was an able man who so little trusted the new regime that he never entered a bank, but kept his cash in an iron strong box and guarded it with a rifle. By common report Consuelo was the matriarchal head of the clan, greatly respected by the whole community, ministering to the poor just as she had done in the days when Ballard ruled the grant.

She received me in the long sala, the very room in which

Ballard must have courted her, with the gracious dignity which I remembered as her distinguishing quality. She spoke perfect English in a voice which retained all of its richness and power, and she had nothing of the primitive provincialism of her male relatives. She would have been wholly equal to any society in the world.

Over thick chocolate and cigarettes we talked for hours, fumbling for common ground at first, but finally awakening a flood of memories that truly carried us both away and back through the years. "Do you remember?" We asked the question over and over, and the words were like a magic formula, for although we had known little of each other we had loved the same things. Between us we recreated the old house in the Dark River Valley, the roaring fires on the great hearths, the table that seated its hundred guests from all over the world, the dances and receptions, the daily arrival of the stagecoach with its various human cargo. Consuelo went further back than that and told me something of her early years in the valley, when the Arapahoe were a menace and grizzly bears raided their sheep herds. That, I am sure, had been the great epoch of her life and love. Her eyes shone and her voice was music when she spoke of it.

Of Jean Ballard she said little, and I had not expected that she would, but her last words, before she told me good-by, were about him.

"He was a great man," she said. "No one else could ever take his place. It was never the same after he died."

— 5 —

That, I knew from my own inquiries, was the exact truth. What Ballard had created died with him. Blore had sold the grant again within two years of Ballard's death and at an enormous profit. It was bought this time by a group of British capitalists and was one of the first large foreign investments in the American cattle business. Under this British regime the old house went through its last phase and had a last moment of glory before it fell into ruin. This was also the last time the dominion that Ballard had founded was ruled as a whole. A titled younger son came from England to take charge of the grant. He had the house done over in a style and with a magnificence never before seen in that part of the country. A grand piano was part of its furnishings and the wife of the baronet, a gifted musician, played Bach and Beethoven late at night, while Mexicans gathered outside to listen and coyotes answered in chorus from the hills. This lady also served tea under striped umbrellas on the lawn and her husband set up a cricket field. He astonished the natives by posting over the mountain trails on a flat saddle and scrutinizing them through a monocle. His operations in the livestock business did much to improve the local breed, for he imported registered bulls and the surrounding ranchers appropriated a large part of their offspring.

It came to be said the grant had a curse upon it, for nothing ever prospered there after Ballard's death, and the British regime soon came to an end in bankruptcy. The grant passed into the hands of another syndicate, a Dutch one this time, which formed a stock company and sold stock both in the United States and abroad. This concern employed a press agent who was an imaginative artist of no small power. I saw a brochure he prepared for the benefit of foreign investors. It showed the Dark River as a navigable stream, with steamboats tied up at a wharf and cultivated lands spreading to the horizon.

The Dutch company did build the dam that I had dreamed about and Blore had talked about, but it proved to be a shoddy job. In a spring of great freshets it washed away, sending a great wall of yellow water down the valley, with houses and wagons riding on its crest. Some irreverent spectators took ironic pleasure in the fact that for about twenty-four hours the Dark River looked as wide as it had in the company's advertising.

The future of the town was settled finally when the railroad passed it by, about twenty miles to the east, and did not even build a spur into the valley. The railroads then were the arbiters of destiny all over the West. Every town they touched was given new life and those they ignored were doomed.

— 6 —

When I left Taos I rode across the mountains to the Dark River Valley by the same trail Ballard must have followed more than half a century before, and I saw almost exactly what he must have seen. Since the building of railroads and highways the mountain trails were little used, so that the country was wild as ever, with not a human habitation visible to mar the beauty of the long forested ridges falling away to the prairie.

There in the mountains and there only did I briefly recover the illusion of a return to the past, for I was riding through the same country where I had spent so many days alone with a rifle or a fishing rod when I was twenty-six. It was so little changed that I could identify a great spruce in a canyon meadow where I had often stopped for lunch and a deep blue pool in which I had taken many a cooling plunge. I remember the thrill with which I watched a black-tail buck go bouncing through the down timber in twenty-foot leaps, and a flock of wild turkeys set their wings and sail across a canyon. I had always loved the mountains and I took pleasure in the fact that their massive resistance had saved something from the sweep of change, the corrosion of human greed.

So I came to Dark River, a sleepy little cowtown at the end of a bad dirt road. There I returned, with something of a jolt, to the dusty reality of the present, for the house Ballard built was now a ruin, the great cottonwood trees that had shaded it were dying of old age and neglect, the hollyhocks had run wild all over the dooryard. Nothing here was the same except the view when one looked eastward to mountains. Nor could I find anyone in the tiny town with whom I could claim an acquaintance, but I found half a dozen men who had been young when Ballard died and others who had heard about him from their parents. All of them loved to talk about the old days, had a curiously strong sense of the local past as a time somehow hallowed and significant. All of them knew about Major Blore, who had here achieved a posthumous fame as a figure almost diabolical, and Tighe and Laird were also remembered and had taken on somewhat legendary characters, as though Tighe's skill had grown with the years and Laird's voice was even louder in retrospect than it had been in fact. But the thing they all liked most to talk about was the open-handed magnificence of Ballard's establishment in its best years, when no man was ever turned away from his table and his wealth lay unguarded, as though all this had been a flowering of human life that deserved commemoration. "You'll never see anything like it again," was a phrase I heard several times, and it seemed a fitting epitaph for an epoch. Certainly the modern world, whatever its merits, seems a bit tight-fisted and calculating by comparison with that reckless and ample day.

To me the droning tales of these old-timers had the quality of elegy. I felt as though I were witnessing the process by which the past becomes a beloved myth, simplified in memory so that one may see the meanings that are always obscured by the noise and dust of the present. The sleepy inertia of the little town made its past seem truly heroic. In the days when I had known it and before, a great gust of passion and energy had struck this place and blown itself out and left in its wake the ruin of a proud house and a legend in the memories of aging men.

THE END